"You're not God, Roarke. You're only a man like any other man. You can be stopped from taking advantage of others."

"Perhaps not God, Brianna," Roarke said softly, bending close and looking her directly in the eyes. Indigo blue clashed with velvet brown. "But perhaps I'm the Devil you make me out to be. Have you considered that notion? And if you don't move that pretty little butt of yours soon, I'll show you just how much hell I can raise." His eyes flicked over her and his voice grew harsh.

Brianna paled. While on board the *Black Angel*, she'd learned that he didn't make empty threats.

"All right." she muttered defiantly. She swung her feet to the floor. "I'll go with you now, but you can't make me stay."

Another cruel little grin curled up Roarke's shapely lips. "I wouldn't place any bets on it, Brianna. . . ."

THE
BLACK
ANGEL

Cordia Byers

FAWCETT GOLD MEDAL • NEW YORK

A Fawcett Gold Medal Book
Published by Ballantine Books
Copyright © 1993 by Cordia Byers

Library of Congress Catalog Card Number: 93-90085

ISBN 0-449-14783-5

Manufactured in the United States of America

First Edition: June 1993

Chapter 1

The sky wept. Its tears drenched the bare-limbed trees and made rivulets through the mound of freshly turned earth beside the open grave. The black-robed minister, his wrinkled features pinched against the inclement weather that had already soaked him to the skin, read the final verse, "Ashes to ashes, dust to dust." He glanced uncertainly toward the man and girl who stood beside the coffin. There was no dry soil to symbolize the passage, only mud to toss upon the newly planed wooden lid. Giving a sniff and a swipe at his reddened nose, he nodded to Lord Montague, conveying his sympathy as well as the end of the funeral services. He turned away, anxious now to be back at the priory, where his housekeeper would have dry clothing and a nice pot of hot tea awaiting him.

The few mourners who had attended the funeral soon followed the minister's example, leaving Lord Montague and his stepdaughter alone while the gravediggers shoveled the clumps of mud into the gaping hole. The soggy earth landed with dull thumps against the coffin while tiny rivers seeped down the steep sides of the grave to form a muddy lake around the ugly wood island.

Brianna trembled and clamped a hand over her mouth to stifle the scream of anguish rising in her throat. Her mother lay entombed in the box now slowly filling with water. She would no longer be there to hold Brianna when she had a bad dream, she would no longer be there to buffer Lord Montague's temper, she would no longer be there to keep Lord Montague from coming into Brianna's room.

Brianna trembled and squeezed her eyes tightly together, chagrined by her selfish thoughts. But she couldn't stop wondering what would now become of her without her mother's protection.

"Come, child," Lord Montague urged, draping a comforting, fatherly arm about Brianna's shoulders and leading her away from the grave site. "You can do no more for her now. She's at peace. She wouldn't want you to stay out in this weather and make yourself sick."

Unable to follow her instincts without making a scene that could set off Lord Montague's mercurial temperament, Brianna shrank inwardly at his touch but made no visible withdrawal. She desperately wanted to scream at her stepfather. To take his hands off her shoulders. But everyone would think she had lost her mind to react in such a way to the man who had taken her and her mother into his home when they had lacked wealth and family name.

A peer of the realm and a rich member of the House of Lords, Montague was well respected by his acquaintances and neighbors for his generosity in the county of Berkshire. However, he was also a man few knew intimately enough to call friend. Only Brianna and her mother saw the true man behind the mask Lord Montague showed to the world. He was closer to being the devil than the saint people believed him to be.

Brianna drew in a shuddering breath and allowed her stepfather to lead her back to the expensive, well-appointed coach embellished with the Montague coat of arms on the glass-windowed doors. Inside she took her seat in the far corner and pretended to stare out into the gray day. She jerked with a start when Lord Montague covered her hand with his own and squeezed.

"It's going to be hard, Brianna. But time has a way of making all things easier. You know I'll do everything within my power to help you through the next few weeks. All you have to do is come to me and I'll try to make you forget your pain for a little while."

Brianna swallowed with difficulty, sensing the underlying message in his simple statement. She knew exactly the kind of comfort he wanted to give, and as in the past, she had no intention of accepting it. However, she no longer had her mother's protection. She was now alone; dependent upon the very man who sought to abuse her. Though educated far more than the normal young woman of her class, she had no means to support herself at the present time. And until she could make her own way in the world, she'd have to continue to accept Lord Montague's charity as well as to fend off his lascivious advances.

Brianna pulled her hand free and felt her stomach turn as she murmured, "Thank you, my lord. You have always been kind to my mother and me, and I'm grateful." The words nearly choked her. How many times had she prayed that her mother would finally gain the courage to take her away from Montvale so she'd not have to feel Lord Montague watching her every move. Like a hawk seeking his prey, he seemed to find her wherever she sought to hide. The expression in his dark eyes always had the power to make her feel unclean.

Lord Montague smiled smugly and leaned back against the soft velvet seat. He cast one last glance at the grave where his wife lay buried and felt like laughing aloud. Finally the bitch was gone and her whelp was left at his mercy. He'd waited and planned this for years. Now she was his. He'd watched Brianna grow since the age of twelve, when her young breasts had just begun budding into the luscious mounds that now pressed so enticingly against the thin bombazine of her mourning gown. He could imagine the soft swell of hips that had blossomed from the slender, boyish shape she'd possessed at twelve when she dressed in the stableboy's breeches to go fishing. Six years had changed her from the lanky-limbed tomboy who climbed trees and spent her days by the pond. She had become a beauty with hair like ebony silk and skin like the finest porcelain.

Her mother, Sabrina, had been a beauty in her own right. That was what had attracted him to her in the first place. In his desire to possess her beauty, he'd overlooked the fact that she had been a penniless widow with a coltish young daughter who showed no signs of ever rivaling her mother in looks. However, in the months that followed his hasty wedding to Sabrina, Brianna had begun to bloom. Even at the height of her beauty, Sabrina could never have held a candle to her daughter in appearance. The girl was magnificent in face and form. And had it not been for Sabrina's constant vigil over Brianna during the past years, the girl would have already shared his bed long before now.

Lord Montague folded his arms over his chest and allowed his pleasure to show with the curling of his lips into a triumphant smile. He'd waited, and soon he would receive the rewards for his patience. Brianna McClure would be in his bed before the fortnight ended.

Lord Montague's satisfaction deepened at the thought of how he'd planned this moment. Two years ago when Brianna had turned sixteen, he'd decided it was time to be rid of his wife. The urgency of the matter hadn't come home to him until he'd learned Brianna had told her mother that Squire Radford's son, Jeremy, had asked her to marry him and that she had fallen in love with the young gentleman.

The boy had been easily manipulated. Threats of foreclosing on Squire Radford's estates for the loans he'd taken against his crops had seen the young man on a stage headed for London without a fare-thee-well to the beautiful Brianna. He'd promised never to see her again, to protect his family and his own future inheritance.

Lord Montague closed his eyes and dreamily began to go over the plans he'd made for Brianna's future. He'd taken care of her past; now he would see her ensconced at Montvale in her mother's bed. However, he wouldn't make the same mistake he'd made with Sabrina. Though Brianna was far more beautiful, he'd not marry the girl. She would become his mistress. She'd lack for nothing as long as she pleased him, but he wouldn't give her the power of his name.

Possessing a man's name made it too simple for a woman to make demands. A husband was far different from a lover. A husband just couldn't toss his wife out on the street as a man could do his mistress if she didn't obey his every command. A mistress's livelihood depended upon her expertise in bed, not in the drawing room, like a wife's.

No. He'd never marry again. And Brianna would be grateful for what little crumbs of affection he tossed her way or she'd find herself on the streets selling her wares like all the other whores.

The coach dipped and swayed through the mudholes and then turned off the main thoroughfare onto the graveled drive leading up to Lord Montague's three-story manor. Built in the 1650s and possessing a hipped roof, balustrades, cupola, and dormer windows, it resembled Sir Roger Pratt's original design for the elegant Coleshill House, which was still considered one of the finest residences in Berkshire even after more than a hundred years. Eight tall chimney stacks rose from the slate roof. Wide double doors with an elaborate entablature opened to gray granite steps that fanned down to the cobbled drive, which circled around a gurgling fountain where dolphins and cherubs played amid the cascading waters. Visitors to Montvale thought the fountain a cheerful sight, but not Brianna. She saw the cherubs and dolphins frozen in time and space. Like herself, they were captives without bars or walls to confine them. They, too, were held prisoner by a wealthy man who possessed them only for his own enjoyment.

The coach swayed to a rocking halt. The driver jumped down and opened the door. He stepped back to allow Lord Montague to exit. Black cape swinging about his wide shoulders, Lord Montague glanced up at the drizzling sky and held out his hand to assist Brianna down the narrow steps. Brianna ignored it. Exiting the coach under her own power, she sped up the steps and into the house without a backward glance.

Lord Montague's face flushed a dull red with annoyance and his eyes narrowed as he followed Brianna into the house. His gaze never left her straight little back as he tossed his cape to the butler. Ignoring the man's greeting, he watched Brianna like a hunter after the stag. As fleet and agile as the beautiful wild beast, she ascended the stairs to the second floor.

Lord Montague's nostrils flared, scenting his quarry. Soon my dear, he thought. A muscle in his cheek twitched from his mounting irritation, and a cruel little smile tugged up the corners of his full-lipped mouth.

The chit might try to evade her fate by ignoring him, but it wouldn't work. She lived in his house, under his beneficence. She'd do as he demanded or suffer the consequences just as her mother had done. Foolishly Sabrina had failed to remember that he always made good on a promise or a threat. She had thought she could keep on defying his wishes concerning her daughter and not pay for her arrogance. She had learned differently.

Brianna's destiny had been foreordained the day she'd entered Montvale with her mother. It could not be denied any more than could her beauty. He'd ridded himself of his wife to possess her, and he'd claim her just as he'd claimed every object he'd desired throughout his life. And there would be no one to tell him nay.

Lord Montague turned toward his study. As he'd already proven, he was a patient man. He could wait a few days longer before making Brianna aware of her fate. He'd allow her time to grieve before beginning her new duties as his mistress.

Brianna locked the door behind her and breathed a sigh of relief. For the moment she was safe. Lord Montague wouldn't break down the door in broad daylight. There were too many servants about who would be eager to spread gossip across the countryside. No. He'd not risk ruining his reputation. He'd wait until night, when there would be no witnesses to his vile actions. Then he'd come clawing at her door like the rat he was, scratching and cajoling in an attempt to convince her to unlock it.

Brianna flipped back the concealing veil, revealing her lovely features as she untied the damp ribbons of her black bonnet and then tossed it into the Queen Anne chair that sat beside her dressing table. A mass of dark hair spilled down her back in a curtain of silk, rich and shimmering against the dull black of her mourning gown. She shook her head and ran her fingers through the heavy mane, relieved to be free of the pressure of the confining bonnet.

A frown etched a furrow across her smooth brow as she brought her fingers up and began to slowly massage her temples. The dull ache that had begun at the cemetery had now become a steady throb. The pain robbed her of the energy she needed to make plans for her future. All she knew was that she had to keep Lord Montague at bay for at least one more night. Hopefully after a good night's rest, she would be able to decide which course to take. Before her mother's accident, she'd considered moving to London and seeking employment as a governess. The only thing that had kept her from doing so had been her mother's pleas not to leave her at Montvale alone. Now with her mother dead, there was nothing standing in her way, with the exception of one more night under Lord Montague's roof.

Brianna crossed to the tall window and looked out across the wide expanse of land owned by her stepfather. She'd lived at Montvale for six years, yet she'd never considered it her home like the tiny cottage they'd lived in before her mother's marriage to Lord Montague. At Montvale she'd always felt like an intruder, never quite fitting in to her luxurious surroundings. Even the servants had managed in their own way to remind her that she was an outsider who could never actually become a true part of the Montague family, no matter how many times her mother married above her station.

Brianna couldn't claim the prestigious lineage of her stepfather's illustrious family. Her father had been only a knight, a title earned on the battlefield and one that carried little influence or wealth. But it had been given to a handsome man who had won her mother's heart the first time she'd seen him. The daughter of a minister, she'd thought Brian McClure wonderful and exciting, and she had not listened to anyone who had tried to make her realize that he was a man who loved soldiering more than anything else. It had been that love that had finally taken him from Sabrina, leaving her to rear her daughter alone. Her life had not been easy living on her widow's pension. When the rich and powerful Lord Montague came into her life, offering her the security of his name and wealth, he'd seemed God-sent. Sabrina McClure had not hesitated in accepting his proposal of marriage.

"But you soon learned that what had seemed sent from God was actually the devil in disguise," Brianna murmured quietly to herself.

It hadn't taken Sabrina long to realize Lord Montague was a chameleon, his moods varying with the atmosphere while he secretly harbored a temperament so violent that it was dangerous to rouse. Brianna had witnessed it firsthand on several occasions. He'd taken his strap to her the first time only a few months after he'd married her mother. He'd found her fishing in the pond and had been infuriated. He'd whipped her soundly before allowing her to change out of the stableboy's breeches. Without the protection of her skirts, her backside had been bruised for weeks by the leather strap. That had been the first time she'd also become aware of the fact that Lord Montague liked touching her. As the years passed and she matured, she had begun to understand why. The thought sickened her.

Face taut with suppressed emotions, Brianna balled her fists at her side as the memories came back to haunt her. She'd tried not to place any blame upon her mother, though she knew Sabrina had been aware of Lord Montague's feelings toward her for years. Brianna sought to understand her mother's reasoning as well as her fears of once more being impoverished should she leave her husband. Brianna knew they had nowhere to turn for help and that her mother had felt that as long as she managed to keep her husband away from Brianna, no harm would be done. Sabrina never knew of the terror Brianna had lived with each day, nor the dread she felt when night began to spread its shadowy cloak over Montvale. Each night Brianna lay in her bed, fearing to sleep and fearing not to. Her main occupation had become avoiding Lord Montague.

Brianna caught her lower lip between her teeth and absently nibbled it. She turned away from the window, her gaze sweeping the soft Persian carpet at her feet, the silk-covered walls, and the tall four-poster bed with its lace and satin counterpane. From there she looked to the armoire bulging with expensive gowns of every description. On the dressing table a pair of earrings and matching necklace lay glittering in the soft lantern light; another sign that she lacked for nothing. Lord Montague had always seen that she was provided with everything she needed. Brianna suppressed a shudder. The gowns and jewels as well as the luxuriously appointed bedchamber were only Lord Montague's ways of gaining his desires. They had not been given to her as gifts but as bribes. A chilling hand seemed to rest on the nape of Brianna's neck. She knew her stepfather would soon expect to collect on his investment of the past six years.

"Never," Brianna ground out between clenched teeth. As long as she had breath in her body, she'd never give in to Lord Montague. "Mother might have been afraid to leave Montvale, but I'm not. I'll beg on the streets before I'll degrade myself in such a manner."

A knock at the door jerked Brianna from her morose musings. She tensed visibly until she heard the feminine voice of her maid, Rachel. "Mistress Brianna? Lord Montague thought you might be hungry, so he had me bring up a tray for you. You didn't eat anything this morning or at luncheon."

Relieved, Brianna opened the door. She smiled at the girl who had been her childhood companion, joining her when she sneaked off to the pond to play or fish. Of the same age, they had enjoyed each other's company until Lord Montague decided it wasn't fitting for Brianna to associate with the servants and forbade her friendship with Rachel. "I've little appetite, but you may leave the tray on the table."

Concern etched Rachel's young face as she crossed to the tea table crafted in the Louis XIV design. She set the tray down and lifted the covers to reveal fresh-baked bread, cheese, and fruit, as well as a pot of hot tea. Wedgewood china and a silver knife and spoon completed the setting. "You should eat. Her ladyship wouldn't want you to make yourself sick grieving over her."

"I'll eat in a little while. I just need time."

"It's hard, I know. When I lost Ma I thought my heart would break. There's no other in a person's life that means as much as your mother. She gave you life, and it's hard to let go. A part of yourself seems to die."

Brianna nodded, unable to voice her grief so soon. She'd had little time to grieve for her mother. Every-thing had happened so fast. Yesterday morning her mother had been vibrantly alive, anxious for her morn-ing ride. Within the hour she'd been found with her neck broken and her horse grazing peacefully at her side. Lord Montague had ordered her funeral immediately since Sabrina had had no other living relatives. Today she had been buried in a muddy grave, leaving Brianna to face her loss.

When she saw the stricken look on Brianna's pale face, Rachel's heart went out to her longtime friend. Ignoring Lord Montague's orders to keep her place, she crossed to Brianna and hugged her close. Rachel crooned to her as if she were a child, giving Brianna the comfort and sympathy she'd been denied by her stepfather.

"Now, there. It's all right. Cry it out," Rachel murmured as Brianna broke down and wept. "Tears are God's way to heal the hurt."

Brianna drew in a shuddery breath. "Don't talk to me of God, Rachel. He's the cause of my hurt. He took Mother from me."

"Don't talk like that, Brianna," Rachel said, swiftly making the sign of the cross over the front of her white pinafore apron. "God in His wisdom knows what's He's doing. He has His reasons." Rachel reached up and wiped away the crystal droplets cascading down her friend's cheeks. "And He doesn't put anything on us that we can't stand."

"I'm sorry," Brianna whispered, wiping at her reddened nose. "It's just hard to accept Mother's death. She was all the family I had."

"Aye, I know," Rachel sympathized. Like most of the servants at Montvale, she well understood the situation that existed between Brianna and Lord Montague. She'd seen the way he watched Brianna and knew from the heated look in his eyes that he didn't possess any fatherly feelings toward his stepdaughter. Rachel's sympathy mounted and she swore under her breath at the predicament Brianna now faced. With Lady Montague gone, she would be at the evil man's mercy.

The look of compassion and understanding on her friend's face was nearly Brianna's undoing. Another wave of self-pity rose up within her, but she staunchly pushed it back. She desperately needed comfort, but she couldn't, wouldn't, accept it. Succumbing to her emotions might leave her vulnerable to Lord Montague as it had two years ago when Jeremy Radford had jilted her. She'd been so happy when Jeremy had asked her to marry him and then had promised to speak with Lord Montague the next day. Her happiness hadn't lasted long. Jeremy never returned to Montvale, and a week later she had learned he'd taken off for London without even a good-bye. She'd been heartbroken and had given in to her emotions in front of Lord Montague. He had laughed in her face and had added to her humiliation by forcing her to realize how foolish she'd been to believe in Jeremy's love. Lord Montague had heaped further humiliation upon her when he'd told her that Jeremy, like other young men, only wanted one thing from a young woman without wealth or a title, and that most certainly wasn't marriage.

Brianna clenched her teeth together and squared her shoulders at the memory. Her chin came up in the air. Never again would she let Lord Montague humiliate her. She knew he'd even use her grief for her mother to his advantage if he thought he could weaken her defenses against him.

"Thank you, Rachel. I want you to always remember I've treasured our friendship even in the times when we weren't allowed to openly admit it."

Rachel cocked a sandy brow at Brianna and then frowned. "You sound as if you're saying good-bye."

"I am. You know I can't remain at Montvale with Mother gone. I have nothing to hold me here now."

"Where will you go?"

"To London, I guess. Hopefully I will be able to obtain a position there as a governess or housekeeper. It's all I can expect, and I can't be picky since I have no title nor money."

"I'm going to miss you, but I understand why you have to go," Rachel said.

"And I shall miss you. I'll write when I get settled. Maybe someday you can come and visit me."

Rachel shook her head and sadly gave Brianna a rueful smile. "I doubt I'll ever be fortunate enough to leave Berkshire. It's where I was born and it's where I'll likely die. But I wish you well, Brianna. You deserve far more happiness than you've found here at Montvale."

The rain splattered against the leaded windows as the two friends fondly embraced. Both were unaware of the man who stood in the hallway eavesdropping upon their conversation through the door that Rachel had left ajar.

Lord Montague's eyes glittered with sparks of anger, and the muscle in his cheek began to twitch once more. He'd be damned and in hell before he let Brianna leave Montvale. He'd not have all his plans for her ruined. She was his, and he was going to prove it to her once and for all.

Lord Montague pushed the door open with such force, it slammed back against the wall. The two startled young women jumped apart and turned in unison to see Lord Montague's girth filling the doorway. His dark eyes latched on to Brianna, locking in place as he ordered Rachel from the room. The maid glanced uncertainly at Brianna before catching up her skirt and fleeing. Both girls knew the maid would be of no help against the master of Montvale. And to refuse to obey his commands would only get her a sound beating and then a dismissal.

"My lord, is there something wrong?" Brianna asked, unconsciously fidgeting with the somber material of her gown.

"I hadn't thought so until just a few moments ago when I overheard what you told the maid."

Brianna raised her chin in the air. Her gaze didn't waver under his accusing stare. She'd hoped she could leave without Lord Montague realizing her intentions, but now that he knew, she'd not deny her plans. "Then you know I intend to leave tomorrow."

Lord Montague's smile grew icy. "I think not. Your mother could not rest in peace should I allow you to leave your home and then some mishap befell you." He shook his dark head. "No, Brianna. In memory of your dear mother, I can't allow you to leave Montvale."

"As you well know, Montvale has never been my home. And my mind is made up, my lord," Brianna said, undeterred. Lord Montague's gall of using her mother's memory in an attempt to persuade her to remain at Montvale only added to her determination to leave.

"I'm sorry, my dear, but you will, as they say, just have to unmake it. You will stay at Montvale, where you belong," Lord Montague said, his eyes narrowing as his temper mounted with her defiance.

"No, my lord. I will not. I will not remain a moment longer than necessary under your roof. Had Mother not begged me to stay, I would have left Montvale long before this."

"Damn you, Brianna," Lord Montague swore, closing the space between them in less than two strides. He reached out with his blunt-fingered hand and clamped down on her upper arm, drawing her toward his powerful body. "You are mine, and it's time you realized the fact." Before Brianna could protest, he captured her chin within the palm of his other hand and lowered his mouth to hers, crushing her lips with his urgency.

Revolted, Brianna began to beat wildly at his chest, but his strong hands kept her prisoner until he had satisfied himself of the taste of her mouth. He raised his head and smiled smugly down at her. "We will do well together, Brianna. You will see."

"Like hell we will," Brianna swore, pushing herself out of his arms and frantically wiping at her mouth with the back of her hand. Her thick hair swung about her shoulders as she violently shook her head. Her words tumbled over trembling lips. "If you ever touch me again, I'll kill you, I swear."

"Come now, Brianna," Lord Montague said softly, cajolingly. "You enjoyed that kiss as much as I did. Why don't you admit it? You're a woman grown now, with a woman's desires. And I will fulfill all of your innermost fantasies. You know that I can."

"The only thing I know is that you are despicable. You sicken me. Now, get out of my room." Brianna's courage wilted as she watched her stepfather's expression alter to reveal his pent-up anger. A shiver of fear passed down her spine and she wisely began to retreat as Lord Montague moved toward her once more.

"Don't say I didn't give you a chance to accept my generosity. Now whatever happens is your own fault. You shouldn't bite the hand that feeds you, Brianna. However, you're still young and don't understand what you're turning down. But after I've had you, you'll be licking my hand in gratitude. I assure you of that."

"You are mad. I would rather die than surrender to

you," Brianna said, backing up against the tea table where Rachel had left the tray of food.

Lord Montague's expression hardened into icy fury. His cold eyes glittered with menace as he approached Brianna like a stalking hunter. "That could easily be arranged if you don't satisfy me like a good mistress should."

Brianna's eyes darted over Lord Montague's shoulder to the open doorway. His wide girth blocked her only avenue of escape, and there was nothing left for her but to try to defend herself against his assault. Her breasts rose and fell rapidly with her breathing as she frantically sought any weapon to ward him off. Her heart drummed violently in her ears as her fingers closed over the knife on the tray beside the beautiful Wedgewood china behind her. Instinctively she brought the knife around in front of her as Lord Montague's hands imprisoned her shoulders in their steely grip. Intent upon his quarry and too angry to note the glitter of metal, he jerked Brianna against his hard body. The long, sharp blade of the paring knife sank deep into his belly.

Lord Montague stiffened and Brianna froze. Her eyes widened as she stared up into her stepfather's shocked face. It seemed an eternity before the color slowly began to drain from his flushed features and he muttered, "Bitch, you have killed me." His eyes rolled to the back of his head as he fell to the carpet at Brianna's feet.

Numb with shock, Brianna slowly looked down at her blood-covered hand still firmly holding the knife. Her gaze slid from the dull red liquid congealing upon the shining silver to the man sprawled lifelessly at her feet.

"My God! What have I done?" Brianna whispered, horror-stricken, unable to look away from her stepfather.

A gasp from the doorway jerked Brianna from her trance. She looked up to see Rachel staring at her with eyes wide with fright. The knife tumbled slowly from her numb fingers as she shook her head. "I didn't mean to kill him. I didn't mean to kill him. I only wanted him to leave me alone."

Brianna's agonized words sent Rachel into action. She quickly closed the door and latched it securely behind her. She didn't want any of the other servants to stumble upon the same scene she'd witnessed. God, she thought, the man deserved to die, but Brianna doesn't deserve to hang for it. Taking no time to consider her own involvement, Rachel crossed to where Brianna still stood frozen in place. She took her by the arm and drew her away from the supine form on the floor.

"Brianna, you've got to get hold of yourself. There's no time for guilt. You have to get away from Montvale before anyone knows what has happened," Rachel said as she led Brianna across the room to the dressing table. She quickly dipped a towel into the water pitcher that sat nearby and began to cleanse Brianna's hands free of Montague's blood. Numb with shock and unable to comprehend the situation or the consequences that would follow when the authorities learned she'd killed Lord Montague, Brianna stared at Rachel, bewildered. "I didn't mean to kill him."

"That will make no never mind with the sheriff. They'll hang you just as if you'd meant to kill the devil."

"I don't understand," Brianna said. "It was an accident. He attacked me."

"Who's to believe you, Brianna? As you've already said, you've no title nor money. But look at the man you killed. He was powerful and rich. He was also a devil at Montvale but well liked by those who didn't really know him. They'll never believe he attacked you. To his neighbors he's always acted just like a father to you. They know nothing else."

Brianna's already pale features blanched a deathly white. Desperation filled her and she gasped out, "I have to get away."

Rachel nodded smugly. "That's what I've been trying to say. You can't stay here and remain alive."

"But where will I go?" Brianna asked, too frantic to remember her earlier plans.

"You could go to London, but that will be the first place they'll look for you. Your only hope is to reach the coast and take the first ship out."

"Oh, God, Rachel. I wanted to leave Montvale but not England. How will I survive?"

"You have your mother's jewels. And Lord Montvale keeps a strongbox in his office to pay our wages each month. You'll have to take what you need from there."

"I'm a murderer and now a thief."

Rachel shook her head. "You're not a thief. You're only taking what you need to survive. Had Lord Montague not been such a devil, you'd have no reason. The blame is at his door."

"Will you come with me, Rachel?"

Rachel glanced back at the still figure whose blood now tinted the light carpet, and nodded. "Looks like I have no choice, and I doubt you could make it safely away in your state of mind without me."

"Thank you," Brianna whispered as tears misted her eyes. For years she'd wanted, planned, to leave Montvale, but not as a murderous thief in the night. However, she knew Rachel was right. She had no other choice. It was either flee or hang, and she didn't prefer the latter. Brianna sniffed back her tears and looked at her friend. "As you've said, we can't go to London now. Do you have any suggestions where we should go?"

Not waiting for her friend's answer, Brianna turned to the dressing table and opened her jewelry box. The gems glittered brightly in the light. She wasted no time. She dumped the contents into a velvet traveling pouch and tucked them into her bodice.

"I know nothing of England beyond Berkshire," Rachel confessed.

"If we are to take a ship, I think Bristol would be our best choice," Brianna said, feeling her numbness begin to recede. She knew their lives were now her responsibility. "I'll go down to the study while you pack a few things for us. We must travel light and with as little notice as possible if we are to escape." Brianna looked once more at her friend. She staunchly kept her gaze away from Lord Montague's body.

"I understand," Rachel said, already turning to the armoire. She threw open the doors and drew out an old portmanteau and began to stuff it with Brianna's most subdued gowns. Traveling light would be no problem since Brianna had few dark-colored gowns. Her mother had encouraged Brianna to wear bright colors to enhance her dark hair and eyes. The girl possessed only the mourning gown she now wore and two silk gowns, one brown and one gray, that could be considered subdued enough to go without notice.

Chapter 2

Intimidated by her first exposure to the world beyond Montvale, Brianna stared at the flurry of activity surrounding herself and Rachel on the docks. She wondered where she'd ever conceived the idea that she would be the one to take care of them once they reached Bristol. The tall masts of the many ships anchored in the channel looked like a defoliated forest swaying in the autumn breeze while the seamen and stevedores worked on the wharf like ants gathering food. They lifted the heavy barrels and crates, lugging them on and off the vessels, up and down the gangplanks, trailing one another like the insects preparing for winter.

Bristol, Brianna thought, perturbed, was nothing like what she had envisioned when they had escaped Montvale. In her girlish fantasies she'd been so sure that when faced with having to make her own way in the world, she'd not find it difficult. She now knew otherwise. She'd quickly learned there was little room in the world for two women alone.

The thought roused Brianna's ire. It wasn't fair that men could move freely about while women who wanted to travel were required to have male companions for protection or be thought of as women with unsavory reputations. But Brianna had to admit, no one ever said life had to be fair. Lord Montague had proven that fact for her more than once. Life was what you made of it, and she'd be damned if she allowed herself to become so intimidated that she failed to get them safely away from England. She'd survived this long, and she was determined to keep on surviving.

Brianna stiffened her spine. She had no alternative. She faced the gibbet should she be caught. She had to book Rachel and herself passage on board one of the ships sailing to the West Indies. From what she'd read, she would have preferred the American colonies since it would be far easier to lose one's identity there. However, the war between England and the New World had put a stop to travel.

"Do you think we can book passage on that ship?" Rachel asked anxiously, pulling her tattered shawl closer about her shoulders to ward off the chill blowing in from the sea.

"I sold part of my jewelry this morning, so we have the money they require. Hopefully they will also have space available and will carry unescorted women. The last two ships refused us passage because we didn't have husbands. The last captain said single women and sailors don't mix on the high seas. After a week or so, he would have trouble on his hands if he allowed us to come along."

Rachel absently rubbed at her cold arms as she glanced nervously about. "I pray they'll take us, Brianna. By now the authorities are scouring the countryside, and if they find us, we'll hang for sure."

"Hush, Rachel. Everything that happened at Montvale is behind us. We've chosen our course and can't turn back now."

"I know. And I understand, but I can't stop worrying.

Lord Montague had powerful friends, and if we don't sail soon, they'll find us."

Brianna placed her hand on the rope that railed the gangplank of the trader. She smiled at her friend. "Wish me luck, Rachel. This is the last ship sailing to the West Indies this week."

"Maybe this captain will like the color of your coins," Rachel said, and gave Brianna a wavering smile.

"I pray he does," Brianna said as she turned and strode up the gangplank. She stepped down on the clean, sand-honed deck, pausing only long enough to ask one of the crew the direction to the captain. He pointed toward a tall, bearded man on the quarterdeck. "That be Captain Benjamin, my lady."

Brianna thanked the sailor and took the shortest route across the deck, sidestepping coils of hemp rope and piles of thick white canvas being readied to hoist up the masts. She took the steps that led up to where the captain stood with hands braced behind his back, watching his men hoist cargo aboard.

Brianna hesitated briefly, taking in the captain's well-groomed appearance, from the top of his graying head and gray, bushy beard to his polished leather boots. Satisfied with what she saw, she cleared her throat, drawing the man's attention away from the men on deck.

"Captain Benjamin," she said, forcing her voice to remain steady under the stern look he cast in her direction. "I was told I should see you if I wanted to book passage on the *Merry Widow*."

Captain Benjamin nodded as he in turn inspected Brianna from head to toe. He was apparently satisfied with what he saw; his craggy features relaxed. "Aye. If you're awanting to travel to the West Indies, you should."

"Then you will sell me passage?" Brianna asked excitedly.

Thick, bushy gray brows lowered over equally gray eyes. "You seem quite eager to be gone from England's shores, missy. Is there anything I should know about before I agree to accept you as a passenger on the *Merry Widow*? Your attitude makes me believe there is."

Brianna shook her head. "No. There's nothing. I'm just glad to find a ship that will take two female passengers without male escort."

Again bushy brows shadowed deep-set eyes. "You didn't ask for two passages, missy. I've not said that I have room for more than one on board this trip."

Brianna's hopes wilted, as did her smile. "Then I fear I'll have to seek elsewhere. I won't leave my friend behind. She is like family to me."

For the first time, a tiny smile touched Captain Benjamin's tightly held lips. "Nor did I say I didn't have room for more than one, missy. Don't jump to conclusions so easily. It makes life much harder on a person."

Again Brianna's face lit. "Then you will sell me passage for two to the West Indies?"

Captain Benjamin nodded. "The *Merry Widow* can take ten passengers, and I've only eight booked for this trip, so I've the room."

"Thank you, Captain," Brianna said. She opened her reticule and retrieved several pieces of the gold she'd received from the sale of her jewelry. She handed them to the *Merry Widow*'s captain.

Captain Benjamin grimaced and shook his gray head as if dealing with a wayward child. "Missy, you should also learn not to be throwing your money around. You've just given me enough gold to pay for the eight already on board as well as several more."

Chagrined, Brianna felt her cheeks burn. "I'm sorry. I should have asked how much the passage would be."

Captain Benjamin handed the gold coins back to Brianna, with the exception of the price of two passages. "Missy, I've never been a father that I know of and it's out of character for me to act like one, but in this instance I'm going to. You're much too young to be out in the world alone. Take back your money and go home until you're old enough to make your way in the world." He released a long breath. "Now, that's all the fatherly advice that's in me, and I hope you'll take it. I'd hate for it to go to waste."

"I'm grateful for your concern, Captain. But my friend and I have no home to return to. We're traveling to the West Indies in hope of finding a new life. I've heard it's easy for women to find husbands there." Brianna lied brilliantly and felt a moment of pride for how easily she'd invented a reason for two women traveling so far from England.

Captain Benjamin shrugged. "As I said, that was all the advice I had, and if you don't want to use it, it's up to you. I've nothing more to say on the subject except that we sail within the hour, so you'd best bring your luggage aboard. One of my men will see you to your cabin."

Anxious to let Rachel know of her success, Brianna turned away only to come to a halt at Captain Benjamin's last question.

"Missy, I'll need your name for me books."

She looked back to the burly sea captain and said, "Brianna," before realizing her mistake. Her voice faded to a whisper. She lowered her gaze away from his curious eyes and sought an answer that would appease Captain Benjamin without jeopardizing her escape from the authorities. Her cheeks flushed a dusty rose.

"Brianna what, missy?"

"Tarleton, Brianna Tarleton."

"And the name of your friend, Mistress Tarleton?"

Brianna frantically sought a name for Rachel. Her face brightened as she said, "Her name is Mistress Sabrina Berkshire."

Captain Benjamin nodded his satisfaction. His logbook would now be in order. "Best not tarry, now, Mistress Tarleton. As I said, we sail within the hour. The *Merry Widow* waits on no one, not even the escort the ministry has ordered us to use."

Brianna wasted no time collecting Rachel and the few pieces of luggage they had managed to bring along. As Captain Benjamin watched from the quarterdeck, a sailor who sported a patch over one eye showed them down the narrow flight of steps to the small cabin that they would occupy until they reached their destination. It possessed two narrow bunks and a washstand, which was little more than a shelf with a hole cut in it for the washbowl. A peg in the wall served to hold linens, had they brought linens along to use.

Captain Benjamin glanced toward the open sea. The ministry had ordered him to await an escort, but he didn't have the time for such nonsense. The *Merry Widow* carried passengers, but its main business was to transport cargo. Its hold now contained barrels of black powder that was being sent by way of the islands to the colonies for the British soldiers to use against the rebels. Captain Benjamin also carried a shipment of cloth and other goods needed in the islands. When he reached Jamaica, he'd sell the dry goods at a good profit and then buy sugar and fruit to take north. At present, the British army was paying premium prices for the supplies he brought them. Their own ships were being raided by a pirate who sailed the seas under any flag that suited his purpose at the time. No one knew him or where he'd come from, nor did he seem to hold any loyalty to a particular country. The villain seemed to consider any ship that met his fancy a prize to be taken. Captain Benjamin didn't worry about the pirate. In his years at sea he'd faced much worse and come out without a scratch.

Brianna lifted her face to the freshening breeze, savoring the warmth that had replaced the late autumn's chill as the *Merry Widow* sailed southwest. She felt gloriously alive, more so than she'd ever felt in her life. The farther south they sailed, the more vitality she seemed to gain. She eagerly awaited the day they would make port and she could start the new life she'd yearned to have for so long.

Guilt pricked Brianna's conscience as she glanced toward the dark clouds forming on the western horizon. She felt so vital, so content; she wished Rachel could feel the same. Her friend had been violently seasick since leaving Bristol. She could keep nothing in her stomach and lay now in her bunk, sleeping off the laudanum the ship's surgeon had prescribed to help ease her misery. He'd told Brianna that there was nothing to fear. Even the most stalwart sailor at one time or another came down with a bout of mal de mer. Brianna prayed the little man was right. She could never live with the knowledge that she had been responsible for Rachel's death after the sacrifice her friend had made for her.

The thought sent an icy foreboding chill tingling down Brianna's spine. She instinctively pulled her shawl closer before she squared her shoulders determinedly. She wouldn't allow herself to even think such things. Nothing was going to happen to Rachel. She would be well by the time they reached the islands.

"How is your friend today?" Captain Benjamin asked as he paused at Brianna's side and leaned against the rail. He clamped his lips about the stem of his clay pipe and puffed, drawing deeply to keep the tobacco lit in the brisk breeze that fluttered and snapped the sails overhead.

"I'm afraid she's no better. I managed to get her to eat a few bites of bread this morning, but she couldn't keep it down."

Captain Benjamin nodded his gray head sagely. "It's like that at times. Some people are born for the sea, while others have their feet firmly locked on solid ground. The two don't mix. A sailor gets land-sick if he's beached too long, while the landlubber gets ill when he gets water beneath his feet." He smiled sympathetically. "I'm told it's not an easy sickness."

"Sabrina swears she's dying," Brianna said, unable to stop her own lips from curling into a smile.

Captain Benjamin chuckled. "They all say that. I've seen grown men turn green and swear that they'd be meeting their maker within the hour. But that doesn't help your friend's plight now. Nor do I envy her the next few hours, Mistress Tarleton." He raised one long-fingered hand and pointed toward the clouds massing on the horizon. "We've a storm a-brewing, and at this time of year, it can get rough."

Brianna glanced once more at the dark clouds that had now turned an ominous greenish gray. "Is there any reason to be concerned?"

Captain Benjamin shook his head and took another draw on his long-stemmed pipe. His thick brows drew together over his nose. "From the looks of it now, there's nothing to fear. I've been through worse. I've already asked the other passengers to stay below. It'd be best if you and your friend did the same. It's the safest place for anyone not experienced with storms at sea. And as sick as your friend is now, she's going to need you once the *Merry Widow* sails into the maelstrom. No matter how easy the *Merry Widow* takes the fury, it's going to take its toll on Mistress Berkshire."

"How long will it be before the storm hits?" Brianna asked, watching the waves crest into whitecaps that rolled down the deepening valleys of water before banging against the side of the *Merry Widow* with increasing force.

"I'd say less than two hours. Now, if you will excuse me, I need to make sure the ship and her crew are ready to face the tempest awaiting them. You'd best go below and prepare your friend."

Brianna was forgotten immediately. Captain Benjamin turned on his heel and began giving orders. His crew, knowing all the lives on board the *Merry Widow* depended upon their obeying their captain's commands, scurried to do his bidding. Some, like monkeys, scampered up the tall masts, while others hurriedly tied down anything that might move. Ropes were stretched across the deck as safety rails.

Brianna glanced one last time at the sky turning a sinister black and hurried back to her cabin, where Rachel slept soundly, oblivious to the approaching danger.

As if ordained by the captain's timetable, the *Merry Widow* sailed into the storm one hour and forty-five minutes later. Though it was only three o'clock in the afternoon, the sky darkened like night. Thunder boomed and roiled, sounding like cannons exploding overhead, while lightning fingered through the air, searing the atmosphere with its power. The sea seemed to respond to the call of the elements, becoming a great gray-green monster frothing at the mouth as it tried to devour the tiny ship between its wet jaws.

The *Merry Widow* groaned her protest, dipping into each carnivorous valley and then fighting upward before she could be crushed between the sea's toothless jaws. Battered, the ship fought on, her crew and their prayers carrying them farther into the swirling maelstrom.

Brianna sat braced at Rachel's side in an attempt to keep her friend from being tossed from the bunk by the motion of the vessel. Rachel had awakened when the storm struck and now lay nearly paralyzed with fear. The greenish hue to her skin had faded to a ghostly ash white as she lay gripping the side of the bunk with one hand and clutching Brianna's hand with the other.

Neither girl spoke. There was nothing either could say to comfort the other. They shared the terror, each understanding in the gray gloom of the small cabin that together they were facing death once more.

The first indication that the *Merry Widow* was surrendering to defeat began as a high keening somewhere deep within the bowels of the ship. Sounding much like that of a woman grieving over the death of a loved one, it grew in volume until the entire vessel seemed to tremble with it. Boards and nails, tar and timbers, buckled under the strain, splitting beneath the force of wind and water, crumpling to the whim of the monster. Shouts came from overhead to abandon ship, but it took Brianna a few moments to realize the meaning of the words because of the agonized sounds emitted from the dying ship.

White-faced, she grabbed Rachel by the arm and forcibly dragged her from the bunk. She urged her toward the cabin door. With an effort, she forced the portal open. At the same moment she remembered the small bag of coins tucked beneath the mattress of her bunk. Unable to leave their resources behind, she quickly retrieved the money and tucked it safely into her bodice before urging Rachel out into the passageway. Water spewed in through the opening and ran down the stairs, making the passageway a slippery stream bed. The ship veered sharply to the starboard side, making Rachel lose her balance. She dragged Brianna down with her as she fell. The frightened passengers who were also trying to make their way above deliberately ignored the two women's plight as they struggled to regain their footing.

"Wait! Help us," Brianna cried, clutching one panic-stricken passenger's leg. He cast her a fleeting glance, shook free of her hold, and bolted up the steps. "In a time of crisis, look out for yourself and to hell with your fellow man," Brianna muttered sarcastically as she clambered to her feet.

"Go on and leave me," Rachel whispered weakly, floundering beneath the heavy weight of her wet skirts.

"I'll do no such thing. Now, get up, damn it. We don't have time to argue, nor do we have time for you to sacrifice yourself for my sake, because I'm not going anywhere without you. We got into this together and we're going to get out of it together. Now, come on. We have to get to the small boats before they are all launched."

Knowing Brianna would stubbornly stay at her side and go down with the ship, Rachel used the last of her faltering strength to undo the cords to her heavy skirt and strip off the wet material hampering her movements. Wearing only her bodice and petticoat, she forced herself to her feet. She leaned heavily upon Brianna for support as they made their way up the last few steps and out through the hatch to the deck.

The lion's roar of the wind met them, as did the brunt of its force. They staggered and nearly fell under this new assault, but Brianna held fast to Rachel. She kept her upright even as the ship shifted again, dipping dangerously toward the waves. A great burst of white spilled up into the air and crashed down over the *Merry Widow*'s deck, sending the two young women into the ropes that had been lashed between the masts to give the sailors a handhold. Brianna and Rachel clung to the thick hemp as the wind and water attempted to toss them overboard into the frothing, murky depths of the violent sea.

Through the blinding salt water that ran down her face, Brianna glimpsed the last small boat as it went over the side into the raging tempest. She opened her mouth to cry out, but another wave crashed over the deck, filling her face and mouth full of water even as the sound of cracking wood rose above the keening wind. A moment later the planks of the small boat burst back upon the deck as if the ocean displayed them as trophies of its triumph over man's attempt to escape. Along with the boards came the lifeless form of Captain Benjamin. For a moment his body lay illuminated by a streak of lightning before another wave crashed over the deck and took him into his watery grave.

Terrified, Brianna urged Rachel back toward the hatch. The small boats were gone and there was no place else for them to go. The distance back to the hatch seemed miles instead of only feet. The effort, combined with the knowledge that they had been left to die, drained Brianna and Rachel of their strength. Rachel, already depleted by her illness of any resources to keep fighting, collapsed at the foot of the steps and lay trembling in the streams of water gushing in beneath the hatch door. Brianna sank down beside her friend and hugged her close. She would not leave Rachel's side again. Rachel had fled England with her to keep Brianna from going to her death at Tyburn Hill. Her friend's generosity of spirit would now see her die alongside Brianna when the *Merry Widow* sank to the bottom of the sea.

Through the gloom, Brianna looked down at her friend's gaunt features and spoke what was in her heart. "I'm sorry I brought you to this pass, Rachel. You deserved much better. I didn't mean to bring you to your death. I only wanted us to have a better life."

Rachel blinked up at Brianna and gave her a weak smile. "Brianna, you take too much upon yourself. I came with you because it was what I wanted. I could have stayed at Montvale and denied that I knew anything about Lord Montague's murder or your whereabouts had the authorities ever thought to question me. Don't feel any guilt for what has come to pass. I chose the path I wanted to travel of my own free will. You didn't force me."

Brianna smiled down at her friend and hugged her closer. She rested her cheek against Rachel's wet hair. "I know what you're trying to do, and I'm grateful. You've always been a good friend to me."

The agonized cry from the bowels of the ship brought their conversation to an end. Tense and terrified, Brianna and Rachel sat huddled together, expecting the next moment to be their last. There were no more words to say as the minutes lengthened into anxious hours. The wind and sea battered the *Merry Widow* relentlessly, giving no ground to the floundering vessel. Eventually exhaustion overruled their fears and they succumbed to sleep. Exhaustion also claimed the furies, overcoming the tempest's violence, transforming the angry black sky into tranquil blue, calming the monster sea until its rippling waves reflected the golden light of the late afternoon sun. The *Merry Widow* rocked back and forth with the gentle motion of a cradle, soothing the tension left by the storm and making her two lone passengers continue to sleep until the sun rose again in the east to begin its westward journey.

Cramped and aching from head to toe from the battering she'd taken from the elements the previous night, Brianna awoke the next morning. She yawned and stretched before her body sharply reminded her of the abuse it had received from the storm. An "ouch" escaped before she could close her lips. The sound roused her equally sore companion.

Rachel rubbed her eyes and blinked up at Brianna. "Are we dead?"

"I don't think so," Brianna said, and grimaced as another pain shot through her behind when she attempted to get to her feet. "The minister always said there'd be no pain in death."

Rachel cocked her head to one side and listened. "Then the storm has passed?"

Brianna struggled to her feet with a groan and made her way up the steps to the hatch. She pushed open the portal and grimaced again as bright sunlight blinded her. "Rachel, we're alive; the storm has passed and it's a beautiful day."

Laughing softly, and feeling suddenly exuberantly alive, Brianna ignored her own painful muscles as she turned back to help Rachel up the steps. They staggered out onto the deck, which now only held the remnants of the masts and canvas sails. The lines lay tangled and twisted like snakes about the deck, splintered by the force of the elements and the heavy timbers that had once reminded Brianna of tall, bare-limbed trees. What remained of the mast and sails now floated along the starboard side, the tangled ropes clinging to the ship like roots of a tree seeking the earth.

A creaking sound drew Brianna's attention to the slanting quarterdeck, where the wheel swayed hypnotically back and forth as if a ghostly captain still tried to guide the broken vessel. "Why have we not sunk?" Rachel asked, struggling to maintain her balance on the lopsided deck as well as keep her knees from buckling beneath her.

"I don't know, but I won't question our good fortune. We have survived the storm, and as long as we're afloat, we have a chance to be rescued."

Bracing herself against the hatch, Rachel shaded her eyes with a hand and scanned the vacant horizons. There was nothing but water as far as she could see. She glanced back at her friend but kept silent. She'd not voice her doubts. Reality would descend far too quickly, for even now the sea was lapping up the deck as the *Merry Widow* slowly lost her battle to stay afloat.

"You don't have to say anything. I know exactly what you're thinking, and I realize that it's very unlikely that we will be spotted by a passing ship. But you also have to understand, we can't lose hope when it's all we have," Brianna said, repeating the very words she'd heard her mother speak before she married Lord Montague. When there had been little money for food, or for the rent or any of the necessities of life, Sabrina would always tell her not to lose hope. Brianna shook off the memory. She had far more pressing matters at hand than to dwell upon memories. The *Merry Widow* was sinking, and they would go down with her if they couldn't find some way to stay afloat.

Rachel glanced toward the water lapping at the deck. "Hope is a fine thing, but can we sail in it?"

"No, but we can try to find something to keep us from going down with the ship."

"The crew and the passengers took all the small boats. We've nothing left but a few planks."

Brianna's face brightened. "That's it, Rachel. We'll make a raft like the one Thomas made when we were children. We sailed across the pond on it, remember?"

Rachel's face lit with something akin to excitement. She well remembered how Thomas had built the raft. He'd strapped planks and logs together with rope. "This isn't a pond, Brianna, but it seems a raft is our only chance."

"You get the rope and I'll start salvaging the planks and whatever else I can find."

Brianna and Rachel set to work, feverishly constructing the raft that hopefully would save their lives. The day wore on, sapping what little strength Rachel still possessed, yet she refused to give in to the weakness that made her insides tremble like newly cooked pudding.

The sun rose higher in the sky, and the *Merry Widow* sank lower into the jade green waters. By late afternoon the two girls had managed to rig together a square of planks, timbers, and ropes that would stay afloat. They rescued a keg of water that had miraculously managed to rise through the flooded passageways to the surface. They also cut away a piece of the sail. They were standing in ankle-deep water when the last piece of hemp was tied securely together.

Neither said a word, but the look that passed between them spoke of their feelings far more eloquently than any words. Each knew that the moment of truth had finally arrived and their hastily crafted vessel would now save their lives or they would go down with the *Merry Widow*.

Water splashed up through the cracks and the raft shifted dangerously beneath their weight, oscillating awkwardly before finally steadying enough for Brianna to release the breath she'd been holding since boarding their haphazardly built vessel.

Brianna gave Rachel a feeble smile and swallowed uneasily as huge bubbles began to burst on the surface around them. The air escaping the sinking *Merry Widow* created a swirling current that sent their small vessel once more into a frenzy of dipping and swaying motion.

Rachel cried out and frantically reached for Brianna as a wave nearly sent her over the side. Brianna clung to her friend, giving and receiving support in turn. The barrel of water rolled over the edge and bobbed away in the current, but neither girl noted its absence. They were too intent on survival at the present time to worry about the future.

The *Merry Widow*'s last great belch of air swirled the raft away from the force of the whirlpool that began to form from her descent into the depths. Fear paled the sunburned cheeks of the two girls as they watched the water barrel get caught in the eddy and spin downward until it disappeared from sight.

"That could have been us," Rachel whispered, her throat too tight with terror to speak any louder.

Brianna nodded. Again they had escaped death. Brianna closed her eyes and thanked the God she'd called unmerciful for His mercy.

Chapter 3

Like great white clouds, the sails appeared on the horizon. Brianna, her lips swollen, her throat a desert from lack of water, squinted at the taut canvas billowing from the tall masts. For a moment she thought the sun was once again playing tricks upon her. During the past three long, torturous days, she had searched the empty horizon for any sign of rescue. On several occasions she had imagined she'd spotted a ship. She soon realized what she saw was only a cloud or a cresting wave. This time, however, the image did not fade. Beneath the sails appeared the dark hull of a ship.

Momentarily energized by a burst of renewed hope, she lifted the small piece of canvas she'd used to shade Rachel from the brutal sun and peered down at her still companion. Her voice was little more than a hoarse croak as she whispered, "Rachel, we're saved. Hold on just a little longer, then we'll have help."

There was no response from her companion. Brianna hadn't expected one. After the first few hours adrift on their makeshift raft, Rachel had lapsed into a stupor brought on by her exhaustion and illness. Using the canvas and bits and pieces of her own gown, Brianna had managed to construct a simple shelter to protect her friend from the sun. She herself had paid a heavy price for her unselfish act. Her own skin had burned and blistered under the scorching, relentless orange ball of fire.

Brianna carefully eased herself to her knees and pulled the white canvas away from Rachel to use as a flag. Her eyes burned, but her body was too dehydrated to shed any tears of relief as she lifted the canvas above her head and waved it frantically at the approaching vessel. Even from the distance she saw the bright flash of reflection from the spyglass as it turned in her direction, and knew her efforts to gain their attention had succeeded.

Brianna ran her fingers through the tangled mass of her dark hair and sat back on her heels. She drew in a shuddering breath. For the first time since the *Merry Widow* sank, she allowed her own exhaustion to creep over her. Her shoulders sagged as she stretched the canvas protectively back over Rachel. A numbness seemed to flow through her, making it impossible to comprehend anything beyond the fact that they were to be rescued. Her mind latched on to that thought and clung tightly as she calmly waited for the approaching ship.

"Damn me, Captain. But it looks like a woman floating on a raft," Nick Sebastain said, handing the spyglass to Roarke.

Roarke flashed Nick a dubious grin, revealing even white teeth, before he raised the spyglass and peered toward the speck adrift on the sea. His grin faded into a perplexed frown as he saw the woman watching the *Black Angel*'s approach. He lowered the glass and looked once more at his friend and second in command. "You've always an eye for the ladies, Nick. Even if it is in the middle of the ocean."

Nick shrugged and his own shapely lips curved into the rakish grin that he used to charm women. "Can I help it if I've been blessed with knowing how to make women swoon?"

"The only thing you've been blessed with, Nick Sebastain, is a heavy dose of the blarney. Did I not know that you were half-French and half-Portuguese, I'd think you came from Ireland with all the malarkey you spout."

"But it is my French blood that makes me so irresistible to the fairer sex, *mon ami*. I do not spout malarkey when I say the women can't get enough of me."

The wind caught a strand of black hair and webbed it over Roarke's finely chiseled profile as he turned his attention once more to the raft and its passenger. He shook his head and chuckled as he absently brushed the hair back from his face. "Next you'll want me to believe that your women even follow you to sea."

"Perhaps. We'll just have to wait until we reach her to see for sure. Won't we?" Nick said, and grinned again. Both men laughed, fully understanding each other. Their game of conquests had begun many years before when they were both young and untried.

At thirteen years of age and just discovering their own sexuality, Nick and Roarke had watched with envy as the older sailors enjoyed themselves with the dockside whores. Neither had wanted to admit his own inexperience at the time, and the game had begun when Nick had boasted that he could get one of the whores to take him upstairs with her before Roarke could. Roarke, already developing into the man who would one day be able to seduce any woman to his bed, had taken up the challenge. In the space of a few minutes, he'd won the bet.

Roarke never confessed to Nick that he'd had an advantage over his friend from the beginning. At thirteen he already knew exactly how to deal with women who sold their bodies to survive. He understood them well because he'd known them all of his life. Nick hadn't realized that whores didn't care who gave them the coin nor how much their customers knew about lovemaking. They didn't get emotionally involved with their clients. It was a business, a way to put bread in their bellies and nothing more.

Though Roarke understood them, he used them like any other man. However, his own life had given him a different perspective toward all women. Whores were whores, but they were also honest enough to admit what they were instead of pretending to love a man to get what they wanted. With a whore, a man knew what to expect. Roarke's grin turned cynical. In his opinion, all women were whores whether they occupied a fancy house and called themselves ladies or whether they rented a room above a tavern to service their customers for a half hour. Women were all alike. One was just as good as another. He'd only met one woman in his life whom he viewed differently from the rest: Elsbeth Whitman. She wasn't a whore because she was as close to being an angel as God made possible on this cruel earth.

Roarke shook his thoughts of women away. They were there when he needed them to ease his lust, and that was enough. He enjoyed his life as it was without the complications of involvement. He'd made two vows that he intended to keep: one, that he'd never tie himself down to any one woman, and the other, that he'd not make the mistake of leaving any offspring behind when he decided it was time to taste new fruit. He liked variety in food and scenery as well as in the women he took to his bed. It added the spice to his life. And he didn't need to add any more bastards to the world. No child deserved such a fate.

Roarke handed the spyglass back to Nick. "When we're close enough, send out one of the small boats to collect our sea nymph. Then bring her to my cabin."

Roarke turned and strode away, already putting the strange incident from his mind. He had been working on the plans for his new ship when he'd been summoned on deck and was anxious to get back to the detailed drawing he'd made for the shipbuilder in France.

Roarke opened his cabin door and crossed to the table where the plans lay. He unrolled the parchment and settled himself once more in the chair. He took the quill pen from the holder and dipped it into the inkwell. With an expert hand, he added another instruction for the shipbuilder. When he returned to France for the new shipment, he planned to order the vessel built.

Roarke smiled to himself. The next *Black Angel* would be the fastest ship at sea. When the wind filled her sails, no vessel would be able to outrun her. She'd make him an even wealthier man.

Roarke leaned back in the chair and let his hand relax as he thoughtfully peered out the stern portholes. When the war was over, everyone would soon learn that they could no longer spit upon Roarke O'Connor. On his return to Virginia, he'd be rich enough to make his dreams become a reality and even perhaps offer a loan to his high-handed cousin, Hunter Barclay. Since the redcoats burned Barclay Grove as well as Hunter's ships, his illustrious cousin knew what it was like to have nothing. It would feel good to have the upper hand for once in their long relationship.

Roarke absently ran a hand beneath his collar and with his fingertips traced the edge of the scars that marred the flesh of his back from the nape of his neck to his trim waist. His smile faded and his deep blue eyes darkened to nearly black as they narrowed with the resurrection of painful memories.

Hunter was just beginning to learn what Roarke had known all his life. Life wasn't easy when you didn't have the power of wealth and family behind you.

Roarke's expression hardened. Living on the waterfront while his mother whored for their living had taught him lessons that no child should have to learn. He'd gleaned his knowledge of whores firsthand from his own mother, and he'd run away to sea at the age of ten with a misplaced belief that he'd find a better life. His back now bore the evidence of how he'd paid for his knowledge of the sea.

Hunter as well as others called him a pirate, but Roarke didn't care. He had no qualms about the methods he used to secure his fortune. Unlike his cousin, he hadn't been blessed with being born on the right side of the blanket. When his mother had been ostracized from the Barclay family for giving her love to the wrong man and conceiving his child, she wasn't the only one who had suffered from her father's decision. Since the moment of his birth, Roarke had been punished. He'd had nothing given to him. He'd had to fight for everything he'd ever received.

What he had now, and whatever he gained in the future, was earned. And he'd be damned if he allowed anyone to take it away from him once this blasted war was over. His plans were made, and he'd not veer from the course he had set.

A knock at the door jarred Roarke back to the present. "Captain, the women have been brought on board," Nick Sebastain said.

"Women?" Roarke muttered in disbelief as he came to his feet and opened the door. "Did I hear you say 'women'?" he asked.

"Aye. 'Twas two women on board the raft," Nick said as he crossed the threshold with his limp burden. He gave his friend a wry grin as he laid the unconscious girl on Roarke's large double bed. "And so help me, I don't know either one of them."

Shamus O'Keefe followed upon Nick's heels with the girl Roarke had seen through the spyglass. Her dark hair fell over the seaman's arm in a mass of tangled curls that reached to his knees. Unlike the other girl, she was conscious but didn't seem aware of her surroundings. O'Keefe laid her beside the other girl.

Roarke looked from the two young women to Nick. "What in the hell you think you're doing?"

Nick's grin deepened. "Following orders, Captain. You said when they came aboard to bring them to your cabin."

"I didn't tell you to dump them into my bed." A look of repugnance crossed Roarke's face as he looked at the two sunburned and blistered women. "I'd never have one of them in my bed even if I couldn't have another woman for the rest of my life."

Nick chuckled and then shrugged. "Never say never, Captain. Sometimes we have to resort to desperate measures."

"I'd have to be more than desperate. Have you taken a good look at them?"

"*Oui.* I agree they are not much to look at, but they are women. And in the dark they all look alike."

"Get Fielding up here. From the looks of these two, they won't live long enough for you to get them into your bed."

"As you wish, *mon ami*," Nick said. "Hopefully the quack won't let them die before I get my chance. I need a few extras to my credit just to insure that you'll never break my record."

"I broke your record before we ever began to keep count. Now, get Fielding. I don't want these two dying in my bed."

Nick left Roarke standing at the side of the intricately carved bed he'd had made specifically for him. It was the size of a full double bed, occupying nearly the same space as Nick's entire cabin. Roarke watched the door close behind Nick before he looked once more toward the bed. Chagrined, he realized that the girl he'd first seen was staring up at him from her sunburned face. It took a moment for Roarke to realize that she was too dazed from her ordeal to understand his insult of a few moments earlier. She slowly ran her tongue over her blistered and peeling lips and made an attempt to speak. Her dry, swollen tongue slurred her words, but he managed to understand "Water."

Having held nearly every position on a ship before captaining his own vessel, Roarke didn't hesitate to act as nurse. He turned to the small table that held a canister of water alongside several bottles of brandy and rum. He poured a glass of water and then turned his attention to the girl on the bed. He raised her shoulders enough to allow her to swallow a few drops of the refreshing liquid.

Brianna gulped the water and nearly cried out in protest when Roarke drew the glass away before she could satisfy her thirst. "It's best to just take a little at a time. If you drink too much, your body will reject it. From the looks of you, you need to keep everything you can down."

"Thank you," was Brianna's hoarse whisper as Roarke settled her back against the pillows.

Roarke glanced across Brianna to the unconscious girl and asked what he'd been wondering since spying the girl's tiny craft. "Why were you two set adrift?"

"The storm sunk our ship," Brianna croaked, unable to keep her eyes open a moment longer. The exhaustion that had claimed her when she'd realized their rescue was at hand now settled over her like an oppressive blanket. It was too heavy to fight any longer. She needed to rest, to recuperate. In moments she slept.

Roarke set the glass aside as Nick and Fielding entered the cabin. He glanced at the physician. "Do what you can for them, but I doubt all your potions and hocus-pocus will be able to help them. They've been at sea for nearly a week."

Nick looked puzzled. "Did the girl speak?"

Roarke nodded as he crossed back to the table and his plans for the next *Black Angel*. "She said only a few words before she lost consciousness, but they were enough for me to surmise that the storm the *Black Angel* went through four days ago was the same one to sink their ship."

"Was it Benjamin's ship: the *Merry Widow*?"

"I don't know. We'll just have to wait and ask the girl. If she lives."

Fielding glanced at his captain and sniffed disdainfully. "You can ridicule my potions and my spells all you want, but they work, Captain."

"So much so that they nearly got you hanged in Martinique."

Fielding bent over Brianna and felt her burning forehead before he dignified Roarke's statement with an answer. "You know as well as I that my potions and spells had nothing to do with my sentence. The governor wanted my life for taking a few—" he raised his hand and left less than an inch of space between his forefinger and thumb "—and I mean a very few liberties with his young wife. And they were on her bequest. She needed my advice on the best way to please her husband in bed, and I felt it was only right to show her. The governor should thank me instead of trying to stretch my neck."

Roarke chuckled. He knew the story of George Fielding and the governor's wife, but he couldn't resist harrying him just a little for entertainment. He also knew the good physician practiced the type of medicine that only those familiar with the West Indies accepted. He'd taken his medical training in England but had traveled to Martinique to be with his young bride's family. After the death of his wife and child, he'd become involved with the native potions and religion.

Roarke wouldn't be surprised to learn that George also participated in the voodoo ceremonies that combined the Christian and African religious practices. However, George's beliefs were his own, as were any other man's who served on the *Black Angel*. If a man did his job, he could believe any damned thing he wanted.

"If it was the *Merry Widow*, that means we don't have to worry about Benjamin's shipment to the British troops. The muskets and powder that were meant for them are now at the bottom of the ocean."

"But if it wasn't?" Nick asked, arching a dark brow.

"Until one of Fielding's patients can tell us for sure, we'll continue on as before. We have no other alternative."

"If it was the *Merry Widow*, what are your plans?"

Roarke glanced down at the drawing on the table. "We head back to St. Eustatius to reprovision the *Black Angel* for her next voyage."

Nick's face lit with pleasure and he grinned. "Ah, then it is to France?"

"Yes, my friend. Then to France. We will take on cargo at Brest."

"The same as the last time?" Nick asked.

"Aye." Roarke didn't elaborate. There was no need. Every man on board the *Black Angel* knew Roarke smuggled guns and powder to the colonials.

"Captain," Fielding said. "This one is well enough, but the other, she may not live. I need a place large enough so I can stay with her. She'll need constant care if she's to survive."

"Nick will have to give up his cabin."

"Then where will I sleep?" Nick said, frowning at being put out of his own quarters.

"The forecastle," Roarke said without hesitation, flashing Nick a look that dared him to protest.

Nick shrugged good-naturedly and looked from Roarke to George Fielding. "Make them well, good doctor. I will have recompense for my inconvenience. And should they not have any money, I know the perfect way for them to work off the debt."

Fielding shook his head, the motion sending a stray blond curl onto his forehead. He brushed it back with a wide, blunt-fingered hand. "Captain, this man is the one who needs his neck stretched for dallying. Is there no woman safe from him? He's already making plans to bed them while they lie near death."

Nick chuckled. "Get them well, Doctor, and I will show them much about *la petite mort*."

Fielding released a resigned breath. Why did he even try to make the man feel a little guilt over his behavior? Nick Sebastain thought with his balls. He lived to bed women. "We'll take this one down to Nick's cabin, but this one—" Fielding pointed at Brianna "—will have to stay here. There's not enough room for both."

"I'll be damned," Roarke sputtered, his attention centering on the doctor. He had freely offered Nick's cabin, but he wasn't prepared to share his own, especially with a woman so ugly, it would turn your stomach to look at her.

"It would seem you don't have a choice," Nick said, enjoying himself at his friend's expense. He always liked it when the tables were turned on Roarke, because it happened so seldom. "It's either here or the forecastle with me." He chuckled. "Once she regains consciousness, she'll give the crew a few days diversion before we reach St. Eustatius."

Roarke flashed Nick a black look and ground out between clenched teeth, "Now I remember why I've never allowed women to sail with us."

Nick could hardly contain his mirth. His eyes crinkled at the edges and laughter tugged at his lips. "Look on the bright side, *mon ami*. You will have the pleasure of her company in your bed, and on the long nights ahead, you may come to appreciate what fate has tossed your way."

"I seriously doubt I'll ever do that. Now, get the blazes out of here. I have work to do," Roarke growled, jerking the chair about and settling himself once more at the table. Ignoring the other two men and the woman they lifted from the bed, he picked up the quill and began to write.

The sun sank below the horizon and the moon crept across the sky. The dinner the cabin boy had brought his captain several hours earlier sat forgotten and untouched on the table. Roarke worked on the plans, as had become his habit of late. He honed the drawing, polishing it as if he had been born a ship designer, making sure every last detail was to his specifications.

A moan from the bed broke Roarke's concentration. He frowned and glanced irritably toward the source of the sound before looking at the clock hanging over the desk. Damn! It was nearly midnight and too late to summon his cabin boy or Fielding to tend the girl. Roarke's expression reflected his annoyance as he slid back his chair and crossed to the bed. He'd given the girl water earlier, but he wasn't prepared to act as her nursemaid on a continual basis. The first thing tomorrow, he'd order her moved. But that was neither here nor there tonight. She mumbled something as Roarke touched her brow to test it for fever. Eyes still closed, she jerked away from his touch as if burned and began to toss and thrash about, knocking the sheet and blanket off. She shook her head from side to side as she muttered, "Stay away from me! Don't touch me! I'm warning you, stay away or I'll kill you!"

Roarke's expression mirrored his exasperation, but his words came soft and soothing as he tried to calm the delirious girl. "Hush now. No one is going to harm you."

She violently shook her head, further tangling the mass of dark hair about her like a silken web. She put her hands out in front of her as if to ward him off. "I didn't mean to. Don't, don't. I didn't mean to hurt him."

Roarke's frown deepened. He knew the girl was delirious, but the fear he heard in her voice was all too real. His brows knit over the bridge of his sculpted nose as he studied her weather-battered face. This girl, no matter how soft-spoken she'd been when she thanked him for the water, was hiding secrets that only escaped in her delirium.

A cynical little smile touched Roarke's firm lips. Like the *Black Angel*'s crew and even himself, the girl could keep her secrets. All he wanted from her was for her to get well and get out of his bed. Roarke bent and retrieved the blanket and sheet from the foot of the bed as he again attempted to soothe the girl without touching her. "You're safe now. I know you didn't mean to hurt him. Rest now. You'll feel better tomorrow. . . ." Roarke's words faded into oblivion as his gaze came to rest on the pair of shapely legs exposed by the girl's thrashing.

Against his will, his eyes locked to the small, slender feet and gradually moved upward past her trim ankles to the curves of her calves. Roarke's mouth suddenly went dry and he felt his sex stir. Unable to resist the temptation, he allowed his gaze to slide up over the dimpled knees to the downy thighs that ended in a graceful sweep beneath the edges of her gown's tattered hem. His hand itched to lift the worn fabric covering the softly curved hips and the girl's femininity, but with an effort, he managed to resist.

Swearing under his breath, he tossed the bedding over Brianna and left her mumbling fitfully to herself. She could fight her own ghosts without his help.

Roarke walked across the cabin to the table that held a decanter of brandy. He poured himself a liberal amount of the amber liquid and then tossed it down his throat. With glass still in hand, he turned his velvet blue gaze upon the girl in his bed and wondered at his own reaction to her. He shouldn't even have been tempted. He'd had Roselee to warm his bed at St. Eustatius, and she awaited him there at his house on the mountain. He had no need to become aroused at the mere sight of a girl's legs. Roselee had appeased all his appetites before he set sail, and he had been at sea for only two weeks.

Roarke's hand tightened about the glass and his eyes narrowed. If he couldn't control himself after a few weeks at sea, what would he be like by the time they returned to St. Eustatius and set the women ashore?

Roarke turned back to the brandy decanter and refilled his glass. Perhaps it was time to get rid of Roselee. Her prowess in bed was phenomenal, but he'd begun to grow bored with her as he had with so many other women in his past. Something was wrong if he could become aroused by a girl who looked like a shriveled old hag. He laid the blame at his mistress's door. Roarke smiled grimly, satisfied that it was Roselee and not himself at the root of his problem. He tossed the last of the brandy down his throat and blew out the lantern. He took off his boots and swung himself into the hammock he'd had strung in the corner of his cabin. He braced his hands behind his head, easily keeping his balance in his temporary bed. He'd slept in hammocks as well as on deck far longer than he'd slept in a captain's bed.

A tenuous little smile flickered across his lips at the thought of the last time he'd slept in the hammock. It had been less than a year ago when his young cousin, Cecilia, had occupied his bed, making the *Black Angel*'s captain sleep in the same spot as he was tonight. Fortunately the girl was now safe with Elsbeth. She had to remain in hiding until the war ended, but at least the British hadn't managed to find and arrest her for killing the man who had abused her.

Roarke closed his eyes and relaxed. He didn't regret helping the girl, though she was Hunter's sister. She had been far too young and beautiful to hang for defending herself. No woman, be she whore or lady, should have to countenance rape of her person.

A muscle twitched in Roarke's jaw and he shifted onto his side, cushioning his head with his arm. He didn't set many rules to live his life by, but there were certain ones he adhered to, and he saw that his men did likewise. He'd overlooked past indiscretions in his men's lives, but he'd not countenance rape from any member of his crew when they took a vessel. The passengers, especially the females, were treated with respect. Roarke's brow furrowed and he shifted again trying to shrug away the memories that came so often to haunt his nights.

He'd seen his mother raped by a sailor who refused to pay for her services once she'd brought him back to their little shack behind the tavern. Asleep behind the curtain that divided the lone room and accustomed to the constant comings and goings of his mother's clientele, Roarke had been jerked from his dreams of the sea by his mother's anguished cry and the sailor's angry curses.

Understanding that something was different about his mother's cry than from the other times when he'd heard her with men, he'd come to her aid, all four feet of him, with fists swinging. The tall, muscular sailor had brushed the boy off with a backward swipe of his meaty paw. Roarke had landed against the wall with a thud and sank, dazed, to the rough-hewn floor. From that vantage point, and cringing from his own inability to protect his mother, he'd watched the huge man grab her by the neck and throw her down on the corn-shuck mattress that lay in the corner of the room. He'd knelt over her, exposing his large sex as he ripped her clothes off like an animal in heat. He'd hit her in the face each time she made an effort to struggle. At last she lay limp and yielding as he pumped into her battered body.

An icy chill moved over Roarke and he shivered as if he were still that seven-year-old boy watching helplessly as his mother was violated. Even at seven he had understood what his mother did to earn a living for herself and him. She had whored, but she hadn't deserved what the sailor had done to her. And Roarke had made it a steadfast rule that should any man serving on the *Black Angel* be caught attempting to rape a woman, he'd be keelhauled and then, if he lived through that, he'd earn fifty lashes. To date, Roarke had never had to carry out the punishment.

The crew of the *Black Angel* was a rough bunch. They felt no qualms about raiding, plundering, and killing when they took a British merchant ship or any other quarry, but they didn't break the rules he set.

Moonlight spilled in through the stern portholes, illuminating the girl who now lay still and quiet on the bed. Roarke's features softened at the thought of the women he'd wooed to his own bed. All of them had been more than willing. He'd made seduction an art, giving as much pleasure as he took. He didn't need violence to slake his desires. He'd yet to find the woman who could resist him once he set his mind to have her. With that enjoyable thought in mind, Roarke surrendered himself to Morpheus.

Chapter 4

Brianna awoke to find herself staring up into the most devastatingly handsome face she'd ever seen. Eyes so blue they seemed black stared back at her before a chiseled mouth gave a slow, hesitant smile.

"Good morning," the man said in a deep, resonant voice that seemed a caress in itself. "I presume you are feeling much better than when you were brought on board?"

Puzzled by his question, it took a moment for Brianna to remember her rescue. Eyes widening in distress, she asked, her voice little more than a frog's croak, "How is Rachel—I mean—ah . . ." Brianna froze for a moment, helplessly searching her memory for the fake name she'd given Rachel before sailing from Bristol. At last she whispered, "I mean Sabrina."

Roarke cocked an ebony brow curiously at her. Perhaps the girl's illness prevented her from recalling the other girl's name, but her hesitation only roused his suspicions further.

"Your friend is doing better, but she's still very ill. The ship's surgeon has been caring for her night and day. You are lucky that you both didn't die."

Brianna nodded mutely, her throat too dry to speak. She glanced longingly at the decanter of water.

Noting the direction of her gaze, Roarke swore under

his breath for his own lack of thought and quickly brought her a glass of water. He allowed her to sip it slowly, taking only one swallow at a time to give her empty stomach time to adjust.

Her thirst momentarily satisfied, Brianna smiled up at Roarke and cautiously tested her voice again. "Thank you for everything that you've done. We would have died had you not found us."

"What ship did you sail upon?" Roarke asked, ignoring her thanks. He was far more interested in gaining the information he sought about the *Merry Widow* than the girl's gratitude. He didn't want to be out chasing a ghost ship when it was imperative for him to get to France as soon as possible. The money and arms awaiting at Brest were desperately needed by the Continental army.

"The *Merry Widow*," Brianna said, her voice fading at the thought of the fate of the vessel's crew and passengers. After seeing Captain Benjamin's body washed into the ocean's depths by the ferocity of the storm, she doubted there were any survivors beyond herself and Rachel.

Roarke smiled and released the breath he'd unconsciously been holding as he awaited her answer. "Good," he murmured, unaware that he'd spoken aloud.

Brianna's shocked velvet brown gaze locked upon Roarke's handsome face in horror. "How can you say such a thing? Everyone on board except myself and . . . Sabrina died."

Roarke's dark brows lowered and his voice reflected his irritation. The woman thought to censure him when she would now also be at the bottom of the ocean were it not for him. "I am the captain of the *Black Angel* and I shall say whatever I want," he answered arrogantly, his expression hardening. "I regret any man's death, but the cargo the *Merry Widow* carried would have caused far more deaths than the few men who went down during the storm. But I don't have to explain myself to you. You are here—" he gave a wave of his long-fingered hand, encompassing the entire cabin "—under my benevolence. And I would suggest you remember it in the future."

"I will most certainly try to do so, Captain," Brianna said sarcastically, displaying an unusual burst of spirit. Energy spilled through her, rekindling her defiance. She raised her chin into the air as she looked up at the scowling man. After everything she'd already endured, she'd be damned if she ever allowed another man to make her cower again. In less than two months she'd been forced to mature beyond her eighteen years. There was no little girl left within her now. Nor were there any little-girl dreams of a future where knights in shining armor waited to come to her rescue. She had faced the real world, where such fantasies were shattered by death and men like Lord Montague.

A sense of triumph and pride filled Brianna. She had taken her life into her own hands and had survived. No. She'd never cower again or allow anyone to run rough-shod over her or those she loved. She'd murdered to escape such a life, and she'd not return to it. She'd rather be dead than to know she had inherited her mother's weakness.

Brianna pushed aside her ungrateful, resentful thoughts, consciously chastising herself for blaming her dead mother for placing her in such an untenable situation. However, in the secret recesses of her heart, she couldn't stop herself from wondering why Sabrina had put her into a situation where she'd had to take a man's life to protect herself.

"I suggest you don't just try, mistress. Do it."

Brianna wiped her peeling brow with the back of her hand and leaned back against the pillows. She didn't feel completely up to arguing with the forceful captain in her present condition. Reluctantly she said, "I will most certainly do so, Captain. Now, if you will be so kind as to leave my cabin, I would like to rest."

A wry, cynical grin quirked up one corner of Roarke's chiseled lips. "Mistress, this is my cabin."

Brianna's eyes widened in surprise. She shot a quick glance about the room. Her blistered cheeks flushed a deeper red. When she awoke, the cabin's elegant furnishings as well as its size should have immediately made her aware that she was in no ordinary sailor's quarters. However, during the past days, she'd felt too unwell when she awoke from her fitful dreams to even inspect her surroundings. After the storm and the three days adrift, all her body had wanted was to recuperate.

"I'm sorry to have put you out of your own quarters, Captain," Brianna said, chagrined that she was apologizing to the man who felt no qualms about making her aware that she was only alive because of his charity.

Roarke shrugged and crossed to his desk, where the thick ship's log lay open. "You didn't put me out, mistress. I've slept here every night."

Brianna's pink cheeks turned crimson again and she swallowed uneasily before she managed to squeak, "You mean we have shared this cabin?"

Roarke settled his sinewy frame into the chair. He glanced back at the woman in his bed. He nodded and said, "Yes" before he turned his attention back to the work at hand. He dipped the quill into the inkwell and wrote, his penmanship as graceful as his drawings: *Mission complete. The* Merry Widow *sunk in storm: (date) 1779. Two women survivors. No trace of others.* Black

Angel *setting course for St. Eustatius to reprovision for journey to France.*

Brianna looked at the strong back turned to her and thought she would die of humiliation. This man had slept in the same cabin with her. She rolled her eyes toward the ceiling. He could have seen or done anything he liked to her while she lay unconscious. She cleared her throat.

"Captain . . ." She paused, uncertain how to proceed. Roarke's hand stilled and he glanced back at her, a muscle in his jaw ticking with annoyance at her interruption. She moistened her peeling lips and drew in a shaky breath to gain enough courage to proceed. "I—" she stuttered, "I would know what happened while I was unconscious."

His mind upon the mission to come and completely oblivious to her anxiety, Roarke said, "You slept a great deal. There were only a few times during the course of your fever that you talked. I could only understand a few words at a time."

Brianna's heart lurched to the pit of her stomach. Her nostrils flared as she drew in a deep, steadying breath and asked in a wavering voice, "What did I say?"

Roarke gave another nonchalant shrug, yet his dark, suspicious gaze never left Brianna's paling features. "You mumbled something about not meaning to hurt him and warned me to stay away or you'd kill me."

Brianna turned ashen as she drew her eyes away from Roarke and focused her attention on the hands she clasped tightly in her lap. Her knuckles grew white from tension. "I must have been delirious to say such a thing after everything you've done for me and . . . Sabrina."

Roarke's eyes narrowed thoughtfully. "It seems you

have a fair amount of trouble remembering your friend's name."

Brianna's head snapped up. She stared at Roarke, unaware that her eyes reflected her fear of discovery. "I—I'm still slightly confused after everything that's happened."

Roarke smiled knowingly. "That's understandable. There are members of my crew who have the same problem, though they've never been stranded in the middle of the ocean on a small raft. Their lack of memory stems from the fact that there are things in their past that they don't want others to know. Could such a reason have anything to do with yours, mistress?" Roarke cocked a brow. "By the way, what exactly is your given name? I can't keep calling you 'mistress' until we reach the islands."

"My name is Brianna Tarleton," Brianna lied, seizing upon the opportunity to change the subject. She had no intention of telling this man anything about herself. He had saved her life, but no matter how grateful she was, she couldn't trust him with the truth. It was too dangerous. He could turn her over to the authorities when they reached port, and she'd be sent back to England to hang. No. She'd keep up her ruse for the rest of her life if need be.

Again Roarke's shapely mouth curled into a wry grin. He'd expected no less. The girl had adroitly evaded his question. "So, Mistress Tarleton, what was your destination before the *Merry Widow* sank?"

"The islands," Brianna answered, smiling with relief. She was becoming an expert liar. She wasn't proud of her new accomplishment but knew it was necessary for her survival.

Roarke's smile deepened. "Which island?"

Brianna's smile faded and she shifted her gaze away

from his intriguing stare. "I . . ." She looked back at Roarke and asked, "What is your destination?"

"We sail to the Dutch West Indies to the leeward island of St. Eustatius." Roarke watched the girl's face brighten.

"How wonderful and how fortunate for us," she said with far too much enthusiasm. "That is exactly our destination."

I'm sure it was, was Roarke's cynical thought before he said, his voice mirroring his disgust at the lies, "Then it would seem fate has been especially kind to you, Mistress Tarleton. Now, if you will excuse me, I have duties on deck."

Roarke rose from the chair and walked toward the door. However, Brianna's next question stopped him before he turned the latch. "Captain, would it be too much trouble for you to arrange for me to have my own cabin or to share Sabrina's? I don't want to inconvenience you any further."

"It is kind of you to think of my convenience, but I fear there are no more cabins available. As for staying with your friend, that is impossible since Dr. Fielding is caring for her around the clock."

"But . . . but . . . I can't remain in your cabin now that I'm feeling better. It wouldn't be right."

"Mistress Tarleton, you have no other choice unless you want to sleep in the forecastle with the rest of my crew. I don't advise such a move. However, it is your decision."

"It's improper for an unmarried woman to share a man's bedchamber. What would your crew think?"

"I can assure you that my crew will think nothing of my having a woman in my cabin," Roarke said, grinning roguishly.

"But it's not right," Brianna spluttered, her stomach quivering oddly under Roarke's smile.

Roarke shrugged. "I've never been one to be governed by what others think, nor what society considers right or wrong. And while you're on the *Black Angel*, I suggest you do the same. I am the only person on board whom you must please, Mistress Tarleton. I am society and convention rolled into one. I set the standards and rules on the *Black Angel*, and as long as you abide by them, you have nothing to worry about. Now, if you will excuse me."

Brianna watched the door close behind the *Black Angel*'s captain before she allowed her gaze to sweep once more over the man's living quarters. Spying the hammock strung up in the corner, she breathed a sigh of relief. At least the man hadn't shared her bed while she lay delirious with fever.

Her cheeks caught fire again at the thought of the dark-eyed captain lying next to her in the large bed. She shook off the quivering, prickly sensation that traveled up her spine and made her shiver with something akin to pleasure. Brianna gave a snort of disgust and forced the feeling away. No matter how attractive the man might be, no matter how many strange new feelings his very presence aroused within her, she'd be damned if she'd let down her guard. The only two men who had ever meant anything in her life had both betrayed her. Jeremy had broken her heart when he'd abandoned her, and Lord Montague had defiled the only image she'd had of a father figure. Men, she'd come to believe, were not to be trusted under any circumstances.

Putting the thought aside, Brianna threw back the covers and sat up for the first time in a week. She was determined to see Rachel. The captain had said Rachel was still very ill, and she'd not leave her friend completely in the unknown Dr. Fielding's care. Rachel would be terrified should she awake to find herself with the stranger. Unaware of her own weakness, she slid her feet to the floor and stood. The muscles in her legs trembled from the exertion and she became lightheaded, but she refused to return to bed.

Brianna gripped the edge of the table and took a tentative step toward the stern porthole. The floorboards seemed to buckle beneath her. She staggered unsteadily toward the large desk and managed to catch the back of the captain's chair for support. Gratefully she sank into the well-worn leather seat that Roarke had abandoned earlier. Breathing heavily, she brushed her tangled hair out of her face and braced herself against the desk, trying to regain her strength. Her eyes came to rest on the large book lying in front of her.

Brianna couldn't stop herself from reading the captain's latest entry. She frowned. What kind of mission had the *Black Angel* been on when they'd come across their small craft? And why had the *Black Angel*'s captain been so callous about the *Merry Widow*'s plight?

Brianna had no idea, and in truth, in her present state of mind and body, she didn't really want to know. She suspected the less she knew about the captain and his missions, the better it would be for her. Even as she hardened herself to ignore the sensations she'd experienced earlier, she found her thoughts wandering back to the *Black Angel*'s handsome captain. The man intrigued her. There was a nearly piratical air about him. With his thickly fringed blue eyes, his black hair tied with a piece of ribbon at the nape of his tanned, corded neck, the rakish grin that she'd glimpsed several times during their conversation, and the flashing gold earring in his left ear, he looked like she'd always imagined a pirate:

boldly handsome with a roguish, dangerous air about him. Brianna shivered. She'd feel much safer when her feet were once more on solid ground.

Brianna pushed herself back to her feet and turned to the door, determined now to find Rachel's cabin. Again the floor seemed to ripple beneath her bare feet and the room began to whirl about her. She stumbled and blindly reached out for support just as the door opened.

"What in the devil are you doing up?" Roarke said, catching Brianna before she sank to the floor at his feet. He lifted her easily into his arms and strode back to the bed. He deposited her in the middle of the thick down mattress and propped several pillows behind her. "You're still too weak to be about."

Covering her eyes with her hand to shut out the image of the spinning room, Brianna answered shakily, "I wanted to see Sabrina."

"I told you she was doing better."

"I wanted to see for myself."

Roarke rolled his eyes in exasperation and turned toward the desk. "Women! Do you always have to make everything difficult? Don't you realize this is not a passenger ship, Mistress Tarleton? I can't have you roaming freely about, especially half-naked. I'll have a mutiny on my hands, because my men don't give a damn that you look like a piece of fried meat. All they want is to slake their lust."

Shock, insult, and fury mingled as one, boiling away Brianna's faintness. Her head snapped up and she stared at the arrogant man towering over her as if he thought himself a pagan sea god, and she his slave. Her cinnamon and gold eyes snapped with fiery glints as she spat, "How dare you say such a thing to me."

"I dare, mistress, because I have a ship to run. I can't

have half-dressed women making my crew foam at the mouth."

The words "half-naked" and "half-dressed" finally penetrated Brianna's fury. Slowly she looked down at herself and felt faint again. Her legs lay bare and exposed to the captain's perusal. After using pieces of her skirt to shield Rachel from the sun, only several inches of the material now remained to cover her femininity. The neckline, which had once held a lace fichu to cover her breasts, now revealed so much cleavage that if she took a deep breath, she'd pop over the edge and expose her nipples.

Burning with embarrassment, Brianna jerked the covers back over herself, pulling them all the way to her chin. Shamed, she covered her face with her hands, unable to look at the *Black Angel*'s captain. The man had seen her in this humiliating manner since the day she'd been brought on board.

Satisfied that he'd made his point, Roarke did nothing to ease her embarrassment. The girl needed to understand that there were no saints among the crew of the *Black Angel*. The crew understood his orders, but they were men, and it was best to take precautions. It took only one spark to set off a keg of powder, and a half-dressed woman could easily ignite a revolt. Men, like any other animal in heat, thought only of their needs when aroused. Especially ignorant men who lived by their emotions instead of their wits. They'd not think twice of mutiny if their lust overcame reason.

Roarke had no desire to put himself into such a situation. He knew he had Sebastain's and Fielding's support, but they were only three men. He didn't want to have to choose between saving his ship or the girl's life.

Roarke turned away and crossed to the armoire bolted to the wall. He turned the key in the lock and opened the door to reveal his wardrobe. Taking down a velvet dressing gown, he tossed it onto the foot of the bed at Brianna's feet. "Put that on when you get out of bed. It should do well enough until we reach St. Eustatius, where you can buy more gowns."

At the mention of purchasing new clothing, Brianna's hand automatically went to her bodice, where she'd hidden her treasure before abandoning the *Merry Widow*. The small bag of coins was gone. She looked up at Roarke. "My money is gone."

"You probably lost it when you were on the raft," Roarke said absently as he seated himself at the table. It was time to work on his ship's plans.

"No. I had it with me. I'm sure. Did you take it?"

Roarke's blue-black gaze locked upon Brianna, and his face hardened. "Mistress, I assure you I have no need to take paltry coins from unconscious women."

"Then someone else on board robbed me," Brianna accused. She was growing more frantic by the moment. How would she and Rachel survive without any money to buy food and lodgings?

Roarke's expression darkened. "Mistress, it's rude to accuse your rescuers of theft."

"But my money is gone. I have no way to pay for food or a place to stay when we reach the islands."

Roarke turned back to his drawings. "I suspect that, like most women, you'll manage."

Brianna frowned, bewildered. "What do you mean? How can we manage without money?"

Exasperated that the girl wouldn't let the subject drop so he could concentrate on his work, Roarke said, "You'll manage like women have been managing since the beginning of time. There are sailors and taverns aplenty on St. Eustatius. For a few of your favors, they'll willingly surrender their gold."

Roarke's statement hit Brianna like a lightning bolt, searing her to the core. Nostrils flaring, she threw back the covers and scrambled from the bed, too angry to remember her state of undress. This last insult had pushed her past reason. Incensed, fury roaring in her ears, she stalked toward Roarke, and before he understood her intentions, she drew her hand back and slapped him. "I am no whore."

A dark curl of blue-black hair tumbled over Roarke's brow as his head snapped back. His cheek burned like red coals, but he didn't acknowledge the pain. A wave of fury passed over him, sapping his reason. Before he knew what possessed him, he grabbed Brianna by the wrist and jerked her across his lap. He raised his hand to swat her behind in retaliation. It froze in midair as his gaze came to rest on the downy thighs and cleft of rounded bottom exposed beneath her short, ragged hemline.

Roarke heard a buzzing in his ears and felt his sex stir. Brianna tried to squirm free of his lap. The movements added embers to the fire already kindled in his loins. He swallowed against the dryness filling his mouth and closed his eyes to shut out the sight of temptation. Drawing in a long, steadying breath, he made an effort to ease the tension that caused every muscle in his hardened body to grow taut with desire.

Roarke forced himself to relax, releasing a slow, resigned breath. Resolutely keeping his eyes away from her firm, round buttocks, he put his hands about Brianna's small waist, lifting her off his lap and setting her back on her feet. He didn't release her as he stared up into her weather-battered face. The sight of her dry, peeling skin helped quench the heat in his blood. He cleared his throat. "You had best never do that again. I warn you now, Brianna Tarleton, I allow no man or woman to raise a hand against me. Do you understand?"

Sensing that she'd escaped far more than a beating at the pirate's hand, Brianna nodded mutely.

"Now, get yourself back to bed and stay there until Dr. Fielding tells you that you can get up." Resisting the temptation to look once more at her shapely legs, Roarke kept his eyes glued to her stiff little back as she made her way back to the bed. He ran a weary hand over his face and felt as if he'd just sailed through a storm.

Disgusted with his own display, Roarke turned back to his drawing. Twice now he'd allowed the girl's shapely limbs to stir his blood. Fortunately he'd also had the gumption to refrain from taking what he wanted. But the temptation still lurked in the back of his mind. The girl could easily be seduced if he set his mind to it.

Damn, he swore silently. He was going to have to get hold of himself. Roarke grinned sardonically at his phrasing. What he really needed was for someone else to get hold of him. He glanced toward the bed, where Brianna sat curled into a ball, warily watching him.

"Stop staring. I won't eat you, blast it!" he growled, and could have hit himself again for the lurid thought that passed through his mind as soon as the words left his lips.

Brianna's chin inched stubbornly into the air as she reaffirmed her earlier statement. "No matter what you think, I'm not a whore."

Roarke had nearly been pushed to the limit by the girl and his own wayward body and thoughts. "I don't give a damn what you are. Just be quiet and leave me alone. I need to work."

Brianna lay back against the pillows, surreptitiously

keeping an eye on the captain of the *Black Angel*. Female instinct told her that she'd stirred something beyond his anger, but he'd managed to control himself. Unlike Lord Montague, whose mercurial moods swung like a pendulum if he didn't get what he wanted, the captain hadn't forced himself on her, nor had he struck her when she'd angered him.

The captain of the *Black Angel* was a species of man she'd not encountered before. Thoughtfully Brianna turned on her side, no longer worried that he might pounce upon her as Lord Montague would have done. She closed her eyes, tired from her exertions and emotional upheaval. She suddenly felt safe. However, she wasn't a fool. She'd take the captain's warning to heart. A man whose self-discipline could hold his emotions under such strict restraint was not a man to put to the test. She didn't doubt he would follow through with his threats with equal intensity and equal control.

Brianna hoped this was one of the times she was being wise to use restraint of her own. She'd like to throttle the man for his presumptions about her, but she felt it was in her own best interest to let matters lie for the moment. She'd not instigate a tempest she was too inexperienced to handle. She knew in such a storm, there'd be no way to make a raft to float safely out of his reach. She'd have to face the consequences alone.

Hands braced behind her head, Brianna stared thoughtfully up at the ceiling, absently watching the lantern sway back and forth from its brass chain. During the past two weeks she had managed to live congenially in the sphere of Roarke's world. She'd kept to herself, speaking seldom to the man who in his spare time continually huddled over the table and paper, scribbling his heart out. Her days were monotonously the same. She'd rise, do her ablutions, eat the breakfast the cabin boy brought, and then go visit Rachel, whose recovery was progressing slowly.

Her friend was now well enough to stay by herself, but Dr. Fielding seemed to have taken an overt interest in Rachel. He kept a constant vigil at her side, leaving the cabin only for meals and when he was needed elsewhere. His presence hampered all but the most trivial of conversation between herself and Rachel, leaving Brianna frustrated that she couldn't voice her apprehensions about the *Black Angel*'s captain.

As much as she'd hated Lord Montague's watching her every move, she herself had become a voyeur at night when Roarke was engrossed with his inks and paper. She watched him, studying his movements, his chiseled profile, his hard, lean body. When she'd first begun the habit, she'd told herself that her actions stemmed only from instinct for self-preservation. She'd managed to convince herself that she needed to keep a wary eye on the man at all times. She ignored the fact that since their encounter the first week she'd been on board, he'd made no other attempt to touch her.

Now it had finally come to the point where she had to admit that her surreptitious scrutiny of the *Black Angel*'s captain each night stemmed from her own attraction to the man. Handsome in face and form, he possessed a physical allure that was undeniable. However, she realized his appeal to her senses ran far deeper than mere physical appearance. He intrigued her. He was nothing like any man she'd ever known before. He was as hard as granite, ruling his ship with an iron hand, yet he never raised his voice or lost his temper. His men respected him and scurried to obey his commands. On the one occasion she'd been allowed on deck for a few breaths of fresh air, she had seen

Roarke's method of command. Unlike Lord Montague, who took everything for granted, never giving a word or sign of appreciation for a job well done, Roarke had praised his crew for their work. Watching the scarred, weather-beaten faces light up from his praise, Brianna suspected that the *Black Angel*'s crew would follow their captain into hell with a smile if he ordered it.

Brianna wasn't comfortable with the feelings that Captain Roarke O'Connor aroused in her. She wanted nothing to do with men in general but found herself drawn to him in spite of all her resolves to do otherwise. Like an animal that found itself confronted by the cobra and could not run away, her fascination overrode all logic. Brianna glanced toward the hammock where the man of her thoughts slept. It was empty, as she had expected it to be at this time of morning. As had become his routine since she'd usurped his bed, Roarke had vacated the cabin soon after rising to give her a few hours of privacy while he was busy on deck.

Brianna threw back the sheet and slid her feet to the floor. She reached for the velvet robe that had become the staple of her wardrobe when she was in her cabin, and slipped it on. She stretched her arms over her head and looked into the oval mirror over Roarke's washstand. She frowned at the reflection. Though it had been two weeks since her rescue, her face had as yet to heal completely from the severe sunburn. The dry, dead skin had peeled off in patches, leaving the new skin pink and soft beneath. Unfortunately, her appearance was anything but appealing, and until she fully healed, she'd continue to look like a leper.

Brianna shrugged, the movement making Roarke's robe slip off one shoulder. There was nothing she could do about her appearance, and perhaps it was best that she remain looking like a shriveled old hag. In her present state of emotional confusion, she needed every weapon at her disposal to ensure that the uneasy truce that had developed between herself and Captain O'Connor remained intact. Brianna jerked the robe back into place.

"This is ridiculous," Brianna said aloud, feeling slightly foolish for her thoughts. She didn't need to worry about Captain O'Connor. He'd given no sign that he was even attracted to her. He'd treated her with respect since their encounter, making no attempt to bring her to his bed. And if she acknowledged the truth of that encounter, she would have to admit she had instigated the entire situation by striking him. Her ego suddenly piqued by the thought of his lack of interest, Brianna crossed to the stern glassed windows and stood staring out at the wide expanse of ocean.

What's wrong with me? she asked herself even as she raised a hand to her newly peeled cheek. She had her answer. Her eyes sparked with golden glints as her ire rose. The man considered her ugly. Her velvet brown eyes narrowed thoughtfully. When he'd taken her over his lap, she'd felt his response to her. It wasn't until he'd looked into her burned face that he'd set her free.

Brianna abruptly folded her arms over her breasts. Men were all beasts. Lord Montague had only wanted her because of her looks, and now this ... this pirate hadn't given her a second glance because he thought her ugly. The deep brown of her eyes heated to dark chocolate sparked with gold leaf. Let the man believe what he would! She'd make no attempt to show him otherwise. Maddened, she raised her hands and ruffled her hair into a mass of tangles. There! Perhaps that would completely convince the *Black Angel*'s captain that she was an ugly old hag.

"Good morning, Mistress Tarleton. I hope you slept

well last night," Roarke said as he entered the cabin. Noting her messy hair, he gave her a puzzled glance and then turned toward his desk. He caught the look of loathing Brianna flashed at him and nearly stopped in his tracks. He frowned, wondering at her mood. "Well, I see you must not have slept well."

"What does that mean?" Brianna asked, too angry to choose the wisest course for herself.

"Your disposition, for one thing," Roarke said, settling himself at his desk. He opened the logbook.

"Exactly what is wrong with my disposition, Captain O'Connor?" Brianna challenged, her temper soaring to new heights. She knew he would have reserved his criticism of her mood had he thought her appealing. Men overlooked many things of beautiful women. Suddenly feeling she had to defend every woman who had been abused or denied anything because of the stigma of her appearance, Brianna refused to back down when Roarke shot her a censuring look. She stuck her chin out in return, daring him to respond. He accepted the dare.

"For one thing, Mistress Tarleton, it leaves much to be desired."

"Exactly how would you have me act, Captain? Like a docile little church mouse? Should I bow obediently and tiptoe around while you're present? Tell me, Captain, how should I act?"

"I don't give a bloody damn how you act as long as you don't vent your ill humor upon me or my crew," Roarke swore, his own anger rising. This woman had invaded his life, taken his bed, and now thought to release her bad mood upon him and get away with it. Not likely. She wasn't dealing with any dandified Englishman now, and it was time that she knew it.

Face granite-hard, Roarke came to his feet. "Mistress, you should remember your place. You are here at my benevolence. Should I choose, I can have you and your friend tossed overboard, and there would be no one to say me nay. I command the *Black Angel*, and I would suggest you remember it in the future, because I'll tolerate no more of your outbursts."

Adrenaline pumping through her veins and ready to give the good captain a piece of her mind, Brianna took a step forward, unaware that she'd stepped on the excess length of robe lying about her feet. Her movement jerked the garment once more off her shoulders. Before she could stop it, the robe, seemingly taking on a life of its own, slithered down to expose the tops of her creamy breasts. She grabbed the wayward garment and frantically sought to cover herself. Embarrassed and humiliated, she flushed a deep scarlet and kept her eyes glued to the floor.

The scene brought a wry grin to Roarke's tightly held lips. His temper melted away. He could throttle the wench for irritating him, but he had to admire the chit. Here she was in the middle of the ocean, standing nearly naked in the only piece of clothing she possessed, his robe, and she still had the spirit to stand up for herself. He had to admire her courage.

Against his will, his eyes moved over the soft skin exposed by the runaway robe. He could also admire her in other ways, he admitted honestly as he raised his eyes to her bent head. The girl was far from beautiful, but oddly enough, he found himself attracted to her because of the vibrancy she possessed. Her spirit appealed to him, affecting him in the same ways as did other women's beauty. He'd seen her anger fire her golden brown eyes and couldn't stop himself from wondering what it would be like to fire them with passion.

Roarke took charge of his senses before he could make a fool of himself in front of Brianna. He cleared his throat and said, "Now that we have come to an understanding, I will leave you to repair your attire."

Heart in her throat and feeling a fool for her childish outburst, Brianna watched Roarke go. Tears brimmed in her eyes as a sense of defeat swept over her. She didn't understand her feelings any more than she understood what made her react so violently to Captain Roarke O'Connor. She was beginning to believe the sun had baked her brain during the three days she'd been adrift on the raft. It was the only reason she could find for her crazy behavior of late.

She prayed it was only a temporary affliction. Hopefully she'd regain her wits by the time they reached the islands, because without money or friends to help her and Rachel, it would take all of their wits to survive.

Chapter 5

The Black Angel *sailed into Gallows Bay, her sleek hull* black against the crystal blue waters. In the distance the rocky twin peaks of the extinct volcanoes rose like sentinels on each end of the island, their volcanic craters long since cooled and now green with the lush vegetation of a tropical rain forest.

Standing on the quarterdeck, Roarke looked at Statia, as most chose to call St. Eustatius. From the multinational flags fluttering high atop the masts of the ships that clogged the port, he could well understand how the island had become known as the Golden Rock. Roarke's indigo gaze swept over what was little more than a volcanic outcropping rising from the blue sea. Only seven miles square, Statia had made itself the richest port in the Caribbean with its interests centered on trade and neutrality.

Roarke smiled, glad to be back to the island he'd called home for the past two years. Statia's Dutch government could swear to Britain and other nations that it was neutral, but he knew otherwise. Even British merchants who wanted to avoid their king's and Parliament's proclamation against trading with the rebelling colonies brought their goods to Statia. The island had turned into one great depot for materials being shipped to and from America. As a free port, its commerce kept the warehouses stuffed with merchandise and the merchants' pockets filled with the profits.

Roarke's gaze rested on the large building toward the west end of Gallows Bay. His smile deepened. He might be considered a pirate by friend and foe, but few knew that behind the guise lay a shrewd businessman. He'd taken his profits from the *Black Angel*'s expeditions and invested them. The warehouse, now filled to capacity with tobacco and cotton meant for the European market, belonged to him, as did the house at the base of the volcanic rock of a mountain known as the Quill. Even now he could see its tiled red roof shimmering beneath the midday sun. It rose from the thick green blanket of vegetation surrounding it, like a beacon calling him to rest. From the distance, the cleared land beyond, where several farmers attempted to grow sugarcane, looked like a patchwork quilt draped over the side of the mountain as decoration.

Roarke's gaze traveled back to the pier where the *Black Angel* would dock. Roselee would be awaiting him there in all her flamboyant glory, eager for him to be done with business. Her flashing dark eyes would devour him as he came down the gangplank, leaving no part of his anatomy untouched. With a cry of joy, she'd launch herself at him when he reached the dock and then she'd wrap her voluptuous charms about him to ensure that her body reminded him of the times in the past that he'd enjoyed her erotic little games.

Roarke knew Roselee's habits well. They'd return to the house, where she'd have had the cook prepare his favorite food, and then after he'd finished his meal, she'd be awaiting him in his bedchamber, naked as the day she was born. There would be no need for seduction or even foreplay to arouse her; she'd already be wet and hot for him.

Roarke's smile faded. He wondered what it would be like to have the young Mistress Tarleton hot for him. Since their last encounter, she'd kept to herself, though he had caught her warily watching him on several occasions. At times he'd almost convinced himself that instead of wariness, he'd seen interest, even desire, in her expressive cinnamon eyes. However, logic always reinstated itself and told him otherwise. From the way the girl had avoided talking with him, he couldn't expect civility, much less any deeper emotion from the shrewish-tempered chit.

A frown edged a wayward path across Roarke's brow as he squinted against the sun. His fingers tightened against the smooth mahogany rail as he leaned forward and glanced down into the crystalline waters of the bay. Why he wanted to arouse any emotion in the girl was beyond him. He had to admit her appearance had improved since she'd come on board. Her skin had now begun to heal, leaving her complexion soft and smooth instead of red and peeling. However, she seemed not to care how she looked, doing little to control her wild mass of hair. At times she looked much as one would imagine a sea witch, with the tangled, frizzy mane hanging about her shoulders and down her back to her waist.

At the thought of her trim back and waist, Roarke's mind veered toward the memory of her shapely legs and the peek he'd had of her sweetly curved bottom. He shook the thought away. In less than an hour, he'd set Mistress Brianna Tarleton and her friend off the *Black Angel*, and that would be the end of their association. She'd go her way, and he'd go back up the hill to enjoy Roselee's experienced lovemaking until it was time to sail again.

An aching hollowness settled in the pit of Roarke's

belly as he raised his eyes once more to Statia's busy shoreline. He hated the feeling, but for as long as he could remember, he'd always felt the emptiness inside. The one thing he'd found to even partly fill it was adventure. Putting his life on the line, facing the enemy and coming away victorious, had been the only way to assuage the void. In the past years he'd been fortunate enough in his business dealings to become a wealthy man. At any time he could leave the sea and settle down like the other merchants on Statia, but he was driven by the hollowness within him. He feared he had to keep it filled or it would engulf him until he would no longer exist.

"Such a frown, Captain?" Nick Sebastain said as he paused at Roarke's side and looked toward the shoreline. "We are home, so you should be all smiles instead of wearing that mask of gloom."

"I was thinking of what we have to do before we set sail again."

"Are you certain your thoughts weren't on our passengers?"

Roarke flashed Nick a sharp look. "Whatever gave you that idea? I, for one, will be glad to be rid of them. I personally have never enjoyed sleeping in a hammock."

A roguish grin curled up one corner of Nick's mouth. "You mean that you haven't shared the wench's bed yet?"

Roarke rolled his eyes heavenward and shook his head. "Nick, I swear I'm beginning to believe Fielding is right about you. You'd bed a dead woman if she was the only female available."

"*Non, mon ami.* I wouldn't go so far. But, as for you, I don't understand. The girl, she is a real beauty. I'd think you would have sampled her sweets by now. She was only a few feet from you each night." Nick raised a curious brow. "Or are you getting so old, you're beginning to lose your touch with the fairer sex?"

Roarke gave Nick an incredulous look. "You can set your mind to rest on that score, old friend. My age has nothing to do with it. But I do want to know if you have really looked at the girl. She's far from the raving beauty of which you speak."

It was Nick's time to look incredulous. "You really haven't seen it, have you?"

"Seen what, blast it?"

"The girl. I know how she looked when she came on board, but even then you could see the beauty beneath the battered skin. Her cheekbones, her small nose, her thick lashes. *Mon Dieu.* That delectable mouth. You must be blind if you didn't notice."

"All I've seen during the past weeks that she's shared my cabin is an ill-tempered shrew."

Nick gave a nonchalant shrug. "Even shrews can be bedded. With their hot temperaments, they often make the best lovers when given the right incentive."

"I have Roselee to service my needs," Roarke said. "I don't need to give incentives to bring a woman to my bed."

"*Oui*, you have Roselee, but she's too full-blown to compare to the delicate nymph we fished from the sea."

"If you're so taken with the wench, then she's yours," Roarke snapped, irritated by his friend's conversation. It brought all his feelings to the fore where Mistress Brianna Tarleton was concerned, and he didn't like it. He wanted to get the girl out of his life and out of his system.

Nick smiled. "*Merci, mon ami.* Your gift will not go unappreciated. I give you my word."

Roarke caught Nick by the arm as he started to turn

away. "Nick, we've been friends for a long time, but you know I don't countenance taking a woman against her will. If the girl wants you as well, that is fine. But don't force her."

"As you well know, I've never had to force a woman before," Nick said, a flicker of annoyance brightening his dark Gallic eyes. "By the time I'm through with them, they are begging me to take them to my bed."

Nick's assurances did little to lighten Roarke's suddenly dark mood. He well knew that his friend had earned his reputation as a lover. The women loved him. He had the ability to make even the ugliest dockside whore feel special. He also had the knack of knowing exactly which strings to pull, what sweet words to say, to get the most reluctant woman to surrender to him.

Roarke didn't like the way the thought made him feel, yet he feigned indifference and lifted a dark brow dubiously. "I know how you handle women, Nick. But with this one you may be in for a surprise."

"There are very few surprises where women are concerned, *mon ami*. I know them all as well as I know the back of my own hand. Perhaps she'll play hard to get, but in the end, she'll warm my bed. I have no doubts."

"Well, it's time to put the thought of your women aside. You still have work to do before you set out to seduce Mistress Tarleton. It's time that you see the *Black Angel* secure in port," Roarke said, once more taking command of his emotions and his ship. He turned away and started giving orders to ready the vessel to drop anchor. Nick, knowing when to set friendship aside and return to his duties as second in command, did likewise.

Roarke entered the cabin and tossed a package wrapped in brown paper onto the foot of the bed. He turned to find his cabin-mate standing at the stern window watching the activity on the docks. From her strained expression, he suspected that the girl had been wondering how she would debark from the *Black Angel* with only her tattered gown. He smiled. He'd at least had the forethought to consider the same thing. The gowns in the package were his donation to her future on Statia.

"Mistress Tarleton, you'll soon be able to debark."

Brianna flashed Roarke an anxious glance and absently rubbed at her arms. She gave him a tremulous smile. "Thank you, Captain. I know you'll be glad to have your cabin to yourself again."

Roarke nodded. "I had the cabin boy go ashore to purchase you and your friend something to wear. I didn't think you'd want to make your first appearance on Statia wearing what you had on when you came on board the *Black Angel*."

Relief swept over Brianna like a wave of refreshing cool water. Her face lit with a smile. "Captain O'Connor, I don't know how I can ever repay you for all you've done. I know I've been an inconvenience to you, and I also know my temperament at times has not been the best. But I do want you to know how grateful I am. Sabrina and I owe you our lives."

Roarke crossed to the desk and seated himself. He turned his attention to the thick book in front of him. Unused to such sincerity or gratitude, he didn't like the sudden feeling it roused in him. He felt the void widening and sought to stem it. "I did what anyone else would have done. Now I suggest you and your friend dress yourselves and debark. I have work to do."

Against every instinct she possessed, Brianna surrendered to her need to touch Roarke O'Connor before she walked out of his life forever. She crossed to where he sat with his back to her and tentatively touched his dark, silky hair before placing her hand on his shoulder. He looked up at her in surprise and she swallowed uneasily, moistening her suddenly dry lips with the tip of her tongue before she ventured, "You have my gratitude forever whether you want it or not, Roarke."

His name slipped from her lips before she realized she'd said it. Embarrassed by her brazen behavior, her cheeks burning with color, she made to turn away. She had to get the gowns and get out of the cabin before she made a bigger fool of herself.

Before she could withdraw, Roarke's hand captured hers. Without a word he drew her back to him as he slowly came to his feet. His hands went to her waist, holding her prisoner as he slowly lowered his head to hers and murmured, "Mistress, for all we've shared, I think a good-bye kiss is in order."

Mesmerized by the intense light in Roarke's indigo eyes, Brianna didn't resist as he claimed her mouth for the first time. Her heart lurched and then seemed to take wings, beating like a wild thing within her breast. The blood roared in her ears and her pulse pounded as she slowly raised her arms about his neck and wound her fingers in the curls at his nape. Instinctively she opened her lips to Roarke's tongue, savoring the heady taste of him as he tasted of her.

She'd only been kissed once by Jeremy, a brief brushing of lips before they'd separated, embarrassed by their risqué behavior. At the time she'd thought Jeremy an experienced lover, a man of the world. Now, as Roarke's tongue and lips played havoc with her emotions, she knew exactly how young and callow Jeremy had been. Roarke kissed her as a man with desires, a man full of confidence, a man experienced with women. The thought chilled the heat flowing through Brianna.

She gasped as she jerked away from the temptation of his sensuous mouth. She raised a trembling hand to her own lips and looked up at Roarke, shaken to her very core. She drew in an unsteady breath and said in a voice that was little more than a whisper, "Good-bye Roarke."

Before he had time to grasp her more firmly in his arms, Brianna slipped free, grabbed the package from the bed, and fled. The door slammed behind her. The sound echoed eerily through the cabin, where Roarke stood staring at the closed panel. The void within him opened up again, darker and deeper than before.

Denying there was any connection between the feeling and Brianna's sudden departure from his life, Roarke released several oaths, damning everything under the sun, including himself, and stomped from the cabin. He had work to do. He didn't have time to stand around and mope over some unappealing little chit who had the sweetest lips he'd ever tasted. Unaware of the incongruity of his thoughts, he made his way on deck and threw himself into the work of seeing the *Black Angel*'s cargo readied to be shipped to his warehouse.

Brianna slammed the door behind her and leaned back against it. Breathing heavily, she clutched the package to her breasts and looked at her friend sitting up on the side of the bunk. Rachel's shocked expression relayed her question without her saying a word.

Confused and beset with a multitude of warring emotions, she looked at her friend and realized that she couldn't explain to Rachel what had just transpired. She didn't really understand it herself. Drawing in a deep breath, she gave Rachel a little, wobbly smile and held the package out in front of her in an effort to avoid her friend's question. "Captain O'Connor purchased us gowns."

Rachel returned the gesture with a smile equally feeble. She ignored the package and looked her friend directly in the eyes. "Brianna, I've something I've been meaning to tell you."

Rachel's tone made Brianna pause. All thoughts of Roarke faded under the chilling premonition that she didn't want to hear what her friend had to say. However, she couldn't stop herself from asking, "What is it?"

Rachel glanced nervously from Brianna to the hands she had folded in her lap. Her words came soft and low. "Dr. Fielding has asked me to marry him."

Astonished, Brianna stared at Rachel. She'd wondered at the doctor's constant vigil over her friend but had assumed it stemmed from a sense of dedication to his profession. "And what did you say?"

Rachel looked up at Brianna. A tentative smile touched her pallid lips. "I said yes."

Feeling suddenly abandoned, Brianna challenged, "But you don't know anything about the man."

"I know I love him," was Rachel's quiet reply.

"Love him! My God, Rachel. How can you love a man you've only known a few weeks?"

"I don't believe love has a time limit, Brianna. You can fall in love with a person on sight or it may take years to come to love someone. But when it happens, you'll know it."

Brianna gave a snort of disgust, dismissing Rachel's words and ignoring the very emotions that had sent her fleeing Roarke's cabin only moments ago. "Rachel, you can't do this. Dr. Fielding doesn't even know your real name. You can't go into a marriage with a lie."

"I know," Rachel answered, shifting her gaze once more to her hands.

Brianna's face slowly drained of color. The foreboding chill of a moment before now lay like an icy lump in the pit of her belly. She shook her head. "You didn't tell him the truth about us, did you?"

Rachel nodded and moistened her lips before she looked once more at Brianna. Her eyes pleaded for her friend's understanding. "I couldn't marry George without telling him the truth."

Brianna felt suddenly light-headed. She slowly moved to the side of the bunk and sat down. Shoulders sagging, she rubbed a shaky hand across her face in defeat. "Do you realize what you've done? He will tell Captain O'Connor, and he'll turn me over to the authorities."

"No. George gave me his word. Your secret is safe with him. He swore he'd leave it up to you to tell Captain O'Connor the truth," Rachel said, reaching out to take Brianna's hands within her own. "George loves me and he'd do nothing to hurt me."

Resigned that there was nothing she could do to stop Fielding should he choose to reveal the truth about her, Brianna nodded. She squeezed Rachel's hands reassuringly. Rachel had always been a friend to her, and she'd not begrudge her this bit of happiness, no matter what transpired later. It was good to know that her friend would have someone to take care of her, someone to love her. In a sense it was a relief that now Brianna only had to care for herself when she left the *Black Angel*.

"I'm happy for you, Rachel. I pray your Dr. Fielding is the kind of man you deserve, because you only deserve the best."

A smile lit Rachel's pale features, making her look once more like the woman who had left Montvale, healthy and eager for adventure. "Brianna, George and I want you to come back to England with us."

"England? You're going back to England?" Brianna asked, unable to hide the anxiety she felt. She'd thought Rachel would remain on St. Eustatius. At least then she'd have had one friend in this new land.

Rachel nodded. "Yes. George wants me to meet his family. He said he's tired of roaming. He wants to return to Lancaster and do what he was trained to do: be a doctor."

"But he's a pirate. How can he go back to England?"

Rachel smiled, feeling an even deeper bond with the man she loved. "He's a privateer, Brianna, and that's entirely different from a pirate. But it doesn't really matter what he's done in the past. I love him and he loves me, and it's all that counts. We're going to make a new life for ourselves, and the past will remain as it should, in the past for both of us."

A chasm seemed to open in front of Brianna, and all she could see was emptiness. She was faced now with making a life of her own in this new land with a new identity. Nearly overwhelmed by the prospect, she swallowed back the plea that rose to her lips for Rachel not to abandon her, and smiled. "When do you leave?"

"George said there'd probably be a ship ready to sail tomorrow. There are ships sailing nearly every day from Statia."

"So soon?" Brianna asked, stunned to lose her friend before she even had time to adjust to the idea.

"George sees no reason to wait. There's nothing here for us. He's going to speak with Captain O'Connor when we dock." Rachel squeezed Brianna's hand. "There's nothing here for you either. Come back to England with us. In Lancaster no one will ever know that you're not Brianna Tarleton."

Brianna shook her head. "I can't go back to England, Rachel. The day we sailed I knew I would never see

Britain again. All it holds for me are bad memories. No.
I'll stay here. At least I don't have to always be looking
over my shoulder for someone who might recognize
me. With hard work, I have a chance to make a future
for myself."

Rachel nodded her understanding. When she returned
to England, she would be free. Should the authorities by
chance ever find her, she would be innocent of any
crime beyond helping her friend. However, Brianna
wasn't. Her life was at risk. "You will be in my
prayers."

"Thank you, Rachel. I may need all the prayers I can
get."

Relieved she'd finally told Brianna of her plans, Rachel cocked her head to one side. "That doesn't sound
like the Brianna McClure I know."

Brianna's smile wavered. "I'm afraid that girl you
knew is gone, Rachel. She'd had to grow up in the last
months."

"The girl may be gone, but I suspect the woman still
possesses the same spirit that didn't let Lord Montague
intimidate her into surrendering to him. She's still a
fighter even after a few small setbacks like a ship-
wreck." She paused and hugged Brianna close. "I have
no doubt you'll be all right. You're like me, you're a
survivor."

Brianna returned her friend's hug. She'd not tell Rachel that she seriously doubted she'd be all right without any money to buy food and lodging. She'd already
burdened her friend enough without allowing her to
carry another worry into her marriage. Let her believe
everything would be fine. When Rachel sailed away
with her Dr. Fielding, Brianna wanted her friend to look
toward the future, not the past. She deserved to be
happy.

* * *

The last rays of the sun splashed the horizon in red, gold, and mauve as Brianna stood waving toward the merchantman bound for England. Everything had happened so fast—too fast. She'd still been in Rachel's cabin when George Fielding had come to tell Rachel that he'd managed to book them passage on a ship sailing for England on the evening tide. He'd also managed to arrange for them to be married before they set sail, and if they didn't hurry, they'd miss their own wedding. He'd dumped an armload of packages onto the bunk and told Rachel to get ready while he resigned from his position on the *Black Angel*. A short while later he'd returned to the cabin, smiling from ear to ear. It seemed Captain O'Connor had offered his home for the ceremony since his mistress, Roselee, would already have a feast prepared for his return.

Brianna let her arm fall and turned away from the dock. She glanced up at the darkening sky and wondered what she would do now. In less than six hours, her world had once more turned upside down. She was completely alone and without friends on St. Eustatius. And all her worldly possessions were upon her back.

With the thought of her gown came the memory of the man who had given it to her. She frowned. She didn't like the odd sense of disquiet that claimed her each time she thought of Roarke and the woman named Roselee.

She knew it was none of her business what the man did or with whom, but she couldn't stop the memory of Roselee flaunting her charms in Roarke's face after Rachel's wedding. He'd not rejected her pursuit. He'd laughed and danced, enjoying himself and the woman's obvious ardor. He had also completely ignored the fact that Brianna was a guest in his home.

Paying no heed to the direction or her surroundings, Brianna started down the street paved with broken shells and crushed coral. It didn't really matter which way she traveled. She glanced toward the dark-hulled ship swaying at anchor near the docks. Why Roarke's disregard hurt, she didn't know. He'd paid her no heed during the time she'd spent on the *Black Angel*, so why had today been different? Roselee's image cut across Brianna's thoughts. She felt her stomach lurch but ignored the fact that the very thought of the woman sickened her to her soul. Instead she placed the blame on her lack of food. She'd not eaten since early that morning despite the fact that there had been plenty of food at the wedding reception Roarke had given his friend. She'd never admit that her own lack of appetite had anything to do with Roarke or Roselee. She'd convinced herself that she hadn't been able to enjoy the food because she'd been too upset over her friend's departure.

"Mademoiselle Tarleton?" Nick Sebastain said, taking Brianna by the arm to halt her progress. After George and his new bride had boarded the merchantman, he'd stayed at the docks, hoping to get an opportunity to speak with Brianna. He had watched her wave until the ship sailed from sight. He'd started to approach her then, but had hesitated again when she'd turned and begun to wander aimlessly along the docks. His curiosity as well as other more potent emotions roused, he'd followed to see what she planned. It wasn't until he realized she was heading into the worst section of town that he decided it was time to stop her. "I fear you mustn't wander about the wharf without protection. It can be a very dangerous place for any woman, much less a beautiful one like you."

Startled from her reveries, she stared up at Nick, her

expression puzzled. She glanced uncertainly at her surroundings and realized she'd foolishly put herself in
jeopardy by allowing her thoughts to consume her. She
breathed a sigh of relief that it was the *Black Angel*'s
second in command who had stopped her. Again she
flashed a quick, nervous glance about. Several disrepu-
table-looking characters watched them from a shadowy
alley next to a tavern. Others, too drunk to stand, lay
sprawled unconscious against the walls and in the
refuse-strewn gutters. A loud giggle and a throaty male
chuckle in the darkness beyond the waiting line of men
told her far more than she wanted to know about what
was taking place between the two buildings. Brianna
swallowed uneasily and gave Nick a weak smile. "I fear
I am lost, sir."

Nick grinned, revealing even white teeth. "Then you
must permit me to escort you back to your inn."

"I don't have a place to stay," Brianna said, and then
realized her mistake. "I mean . . . I haven't had time to
find an inn because of the wedding. Everything has
happened so fast."

Nick's smile deepened as he placed Brianna's hand
through his arm and turned her in the opposite direction. He patted her hand reassuringly. "Then you must
allow me to assist you in finding proper accommoda-
tions. I know of one near the beach that is famous for
its clean rooms and good food."

Brianna hesitated, unable to decide what she should
do. She couldn't allow him to take her to an inn. She
didn't have any money. But she feared that to admit her
destitute position would only put her in a worse situation. She withdrew her hand from his arm. "Sir, I'm
afraid I must decline your offer."

Nick's smile faded. Looking at her taut features, the
worry lines edging her eyes and mouth, he wondered

what he'd done to upset the girl. He didn't want anything to jeopardize the plans he'd made for the young mademoiselle. It had taken him all afternoon to come up with a feasible scheme to get the girl into his bed, and he didn't want it to go to waste. "Mademoiselle, I meant no disrespect. I only want to give assistance. Nothing more."

Brianna released a long sigh. "Forgive me. I know you only want to help, but I fear at the present time I can't accept it. Now, if you will excuse me. I must be on my way."

Brianna turned to leave, but Nick's hand once more brought her to a halt. "Mademoiselle, is there something wrong? Have I offended you in some manner?"

Brianna shook her head, unable to answer.

"Then may I ask what is troubling you?"

The tender note of sympathy in Nick's voice broke Brianna's resolves to allow no one to know of her plight. She looked up at Nick, eyes growing misty with uncertainty, and finally answered honestly. "I don't have any place to go."

A man who thought he always knew exactly how to handle any situation with a woman, Nick placed a comforting arm about Brianna's shoulders. "There, now," he said, misconstruing her situation. "Don't cry. I told you. I'll help you find an inn."

"You don't understand. I have no money to pay for a room."

Nick's breathing stilled as he envisioned the avenue opening up before him. He could see all the glorious moments with Brianna naked in his arms, eager for his lovemaking because he had rescued her from her penniless plight. He smiled to himself. He alone would be her protector, and in return, she would willingly share his bed. Roarke could find no fault with him in that situation.

Nick smiled down at Brianna. Using the tip of one long finger, he caught a crystal tear that spilled over her thick lashes. He gently smoothed it away. "That is no problem, mademoiselle. We are friends, are we not?"

"I don't know." Brianna again answered truthfully. She was too tired to wonder at the man's sudden beneficence or the motive behind it. Since the *Black Angel* entered Gallows Bay, she'd been in an emotional upheaval, and it had drained her physically as well as mentally.

"Let me assure you that we are. And friends help each other when they're in trouble." His smile deepened. "Is that not right?"

Brianna nodded, remembering the only friend she'd ever had. A new wave of tears surfaced at the thought of never seeing Rachel again. She already sorely missed her.

"Mademoiselle, there is no need for tears. I am here to help you. Now, come. We will find a nice, quiet little inn and then have dinner."

Too tired to argue when he was offering her help, Brianna allowed Nick to lead her away. Neither was aware of the pair of indigo eyes that watched their departure. Nor of the angry glint that entered the midnight blue depths as he followed them toward the Statia Inn, a small tavern located near the waterfront. It was well known for the activities of its patrons. The owner, an ex-pirate who practiced voodoo, turned a blind eye to lovers meeting behind their spouses' backs or to sailors bringing prostitutes to their rooms. As long as they had the money to pay and didn't disturb the other patrons, they could do as they liked. For the right price, the owner himself would even help ensure his clientele's wishes were fulfilled by dosing the rum with one of the herbal concoctions he'd learned while traveling through the islands. It was supposed to induce the reluctant partner to relinquish her inhibitions.

The Statia Inn was no place for a decent woman, Roarke thought as he watched Nick open the door for Brianna. He waited only a few minutes before he followed them inside. He chose a table in the shadows to observe Nick and Brianna. He'd give Nick a little time before he called his game.

Chapter 6

Seated at the table, Brianna sipped the warm, sweet drink of fruit juice and rum. She found it delicious and fortifying after the day she'd just spent. Nick watched her from across the table, a satisfied smile curving up his shapely lips. His gaze roved over her, hungrily taking in the warm hue the rum had brought to her pale cheeks as well as the sparkle in her gold-flecked eyes. He watched as she visibly relaxed, the effects of the rum and herbs draining the day's tension from her. Nick savored her loveliness. He'd thought from the moment he'd first seen her that a true beauty lay beneath all the frightful blistered skin. Now he realized how right he'd been. He had to admit her appearance did leave something to be desired. Her hair could do with a good washing and brushing. However, her lack of toilet couldn't hide her exquisite looks from a man who considered himself a connoisseur of beautiful women.

Nick gave a mental shake of his head, wondering at Roarke's inability to see the girl as she truly was. All she needed to rival the greatest beauties in Europe were a proper gown and coiffure.

His smile deepened at the thought of Roarke. Fortunately his friend's blindness to the girl's beauty was his gain. Roarke would never question him when he learned he'd brought her to the Statia Inn, nor would he wonder about how he managed to seduce her into his bed. Roarke's attitude toward women would make him assume the girl had been so grateful to Nick for his attention that she'd willingly given herself to him.

Nick's gaze came to rest on the pewter mug in Brianna's hand, and his smile dimmed. He'd have liked to have the time to get the girl into his bed without the benefits of Ole Harry's herbal concoction, but he didn't. The *Black Angel* would be reprovisioned and set sail within the week, leaving him little time to properly seduce Mistress Tarleton.

Nick's conscience pricked him, but he shrugged the feeling aside. He'd never been a stickler for the rules Roarke set such store in. It might not be completely right to hurry the inevitable, but he really couldn't see the harm. He had no doubt about his charms, nor their effect on Brianna. Sooner or later she'd have ended up where he planned. As it was, he would have her tonight, and by the time he sailed out again, he'd have her ensconced in a small house, eagerly awaiting his return.

"Are you feeling better now that you've eaten?" Nick asked, watching Brianna's reaction to her drink.

She smiled easily at him before she took another long swallow and set the mug down on the rough-hewn table. "I feel wonderful. I don't believe I've been this relaxed since before we sailed from England."

"What made two lovely ladies decide to seek new lives in the islands?" Nick asked, curious about the young woman who would share his bed that night.

Brianna settled back in her chair and shook her head. The warm glow she felt from the drink made her unmindful of the way her explanation would sound to Nick. "R—Sabrina and I heard we could easily find husbands here since there are few English ladies of marriageable age."

Nick smiled to himself. He'd not been far wrong about the girl any more than he'd been wrong about the rest of the women in his past. All were after marriage; to have someone to take care of them. He hated to disappoint the lovely Brianna about their future relationship, but he wasn't the marrying type. She'd adjust to that notion soon enough. He'd see that she had everything else, with the exception of the words spoken in front of a priest. And as long as she made him happy, he'd see she lacked for nothing. He'd treat her as well as Roarke treated Roselee.

"I for one am grateful for your decision," Nick said, giving Brianna his most charming smile. "And Sabrina's marriage to George also proves you made the right decision. She found her husband before she even set foot on the island."

A wave of loneliness swept over Brianna, dulling the sparkle in her velvet brown eyes. She reached for the mug and finished the last of the rum drink with the hope that it would ease the abandoned feeling that again claimed her. Her shoulders sagged as she nodded and looked down at the pewter mug she clasped between both hands. "I hope they will be happy."

"I'm sure old George will do his best to ensure that they are. No matter how I've harried him in the past, he's a good man at heart."

Brianna looked once more at Nick and smiled gratefully. "Thank you. I needed to hear that. It reassures me to know that Sabrina has made the right decision for herself. Now all I need is to get my own life in order."

Nick reached across the table and placed his warm, strong hand over Brianna's. He squeezed it lightly. "I'm sure you'll have no problem in doing so. You're far too beautiful to have any worries."

Brianna self-consciously raised a hand to her wild

mane of hair and brushed it back from her shoulders. Embarrassment heated her cheeks for allowing herself to be seen in public looking like something that had been washed up on the beach after a storm. "It is kind of you to say, but I know how horrid I look. I've done little to make myself look presentable since you found us. I need a long, hot bath and a bar of soap to rid myself of the weeks at sea."

"Then you shall have it," Nick said, coming to his feet, his face lit with excitement. His night with Brianna would be far more pleasant with her sweet-smelling and looking the beauty he knew her to be. "I shall order it right away. And when you're finished you must promise me that you'll allow me to come and view the new you."

Bemused by the rum-and-herb drink, Brianna nodded her agreement. She saw nothing improper about his simple request after all he'd done for her. The drugs had left her too relaxed to have even a niggling suspicion about Nick's motives.

"Then it's settled. You will have your bath, and when you're done, I'll bring up a nice warm rum to celebrate the return of the beauty who sailed from England."

True to his word, a few minutes later Nick escorted her upstairs to the room he'd rented. Sitting in front of the small, cold fireplace was a large, round tub bound with brass strips. A thick towel and a bar of scented soap lay on a chair beside it. Through the open French doors that led out onto the balcony overlooking the beach, the light of the full moon spilled into the room. A long shadow cast by the tall palm growing toward the ebony sky moved to the mysterious rhythm of the warm breeze wafting in from the sea. The music of the surf caressing the beach drowned out the noise from the taproom and turned the rented chamber into a peaceful haven.

Suddenly feeling like a fairy princess over merely a bath in hot water, Brianna laughed aloud. She turned to Nick, her face lit with pleasure. "Oh, Nick, thank you," she said before exuberantly throwing her arms about his neck. "Thank you, thank you."

Nick tipped up her chin and lightly brushed his lips against her brow before he dislodged her arms from about his neck and set her away from him. "As I say, *mon chère*, that is what friends are for. Now enjoy your bath while I go downstairs and enjoy a smoke."

Brianna didn't question his benevolence. As soon as the door closed behind the handsome Frenchman, she quickly disrobed and stepped into the steaming water. She sank into the luxurious moisture, savoring every wet, warm drop that touched her skin. Closing her eyes, she relaxed against the age-smoothed wood and allowed the rum and warm water to soothe her weary muscles and ease the tension from her body.

She soaked until the water began to cool and then languidly lathered her limbs with the sweet-smelling soap, scrubbing until her skin glowed pink.

At last came her hair, and with something akin to excitement, she joyously ducked her head before lathering the tangled mass into a white froth. She scrubbed her scalp until it tingled and then rinsed her hair free of soap. The clean, wet strands of dark hair fell about her shoulders like gleaming silk.

She rose from the water like Aphrodite, her slender young body glistening in the golden lantern light. She reached for the towel and dried herself briskly, removing the last residue of dried skin and bringing back the soft, creamy tone to her flawless complexion.

Naked, Brianna stepped from the tub and crossed to

the open French door. Lazily she settled herself on the rug in the pool of moonlight and toweled her long hair. She stretched her arms over her head, arching her back like a satisfied feline, savoring the moment, enjoying the sense of freedom the moonlight and her own nakedness gave her.

Totally unaware that her uninhibited behavior was a result of the drink she'd consumed, she made a moue of disgust when at last she forced herself back to reality and got to her feet. She crossed to the small dressing table and found a brush and comb. She plucked the tangles from the dark strands until they fell in soft, curling waves about her shoulders and down her back to her waist. Satisfied she could do no more to improve her appearance, she slipped on her gown once more and settled herself down to await Nick's return. She didn't have long to wait. She'd just curled her bare feet beneath her in the chair when the knock sounded.

After hearing Brianna bid him to enter, Nick walked into the room carrying a tray with two more tankards of rum and fruit juice. Halfway across the room, he came to an abrupt halt at the sight of Brianna. His dark Gallic gaze swept over her appreciatively, taking in every inch from the tips of her tiny toes to the shining mass of silk curling softly about her shoulders. He smiled his pleasure. "Mistress, I had thought you couldn't grow lovelier, but you have proven me wrong. You make the moon and the stars envious."

Again Brianna's cheeks grew warm under Nick's praise. "Sir, I have you to credit for my transformation. You'll never know how grateful I am. Until tonight, I hadn't truly realized how much I missed baths and scented soap. I feel like a new person. I don't know how I'll ever repay you for all that you've done for me."

I know exactly how you can show your gratitude tonight, Brianna, Nick thought, but said aloud, "Then let us celebrate the new you." He set the tray down on the dressing table and handed a tankard to Brianna. He raised his own in a toast. "To the new Brianna Tarleton. May her beauty always shine as brightly as it does tonight. And may I always be the beneficiary."

Slightly puzzled by his last words, Brianna raised her tankard to accept his toast. The rich, spicy brew inside flowed smoothly down her throat and into her belly, warming her as it went down. The heat of it seemed to spread through her bloodstream, making her feel curiously displaced. She set the empty tankard aside and smiled up at the handsome man before her. Her skin grew flushed as wayward thoughts crept into her mind. Nick's dark good looks reminded her of Roarke. Roarke with the incredible eyes and the devastating kisses, Brianna thought, recalling the kiss that had shaken her to her very core.

Brianna moistened her dry lips and wondered why she suddenly felt so strange. Her heart suddenly began to pump against her ribs, and her skin tingled. She came to her feet. Her voice grew husky from the tension coiling in her belly as she said, "Nick, I fear the rum has gone to my head after all the excitement today. I want to thank you for what you've done and for the friendship you've given me. However, I fear I must ask you to leave. I need to rest." Again Brianna ran the tip of her tongue over her lips.

Nick closed the space between them. His dark eyes gleamed with a feral light as his arms came about Brianna, drawing her against his hard, unyielding body. He brushed the top of her head with his lips as he murmured, "Surely you don't want to send me away?"

Confused but unable to deny the warmth his embrace

roused in her, Brianna lay her cheek against his chest. "I don't want to send you away, but I must go to bed. The rum seems to have taken its toll upon me, and I'm afraid I'll not be good company."

"You'll always be good company for me, Brianna," Nick said, the tenor of his own voice growing deeper from the desire that coursed through his aroused body.

Completely unaware of her actions, Brianna rubbed her cheek against the rough material covering Nick's chest. She released a sigh of pleasure at the sensation it created within her. Her fingers curled against Nick's back as a new, far more intense heat began to blossom. "Nick, I . . . I need . . ." she murmured in nearly a moan.

Nick smile. "Yes, *petite*. I know exactly what you need."

As if a magnet drawn by a lodestone, Brianna molded her body to the length of Nick's steel frame even as she shook her head in an effort to clear the lethargy from her mind. "I don't know what's happening to me," she whispered, unconsciously pressing herself closer to Nick.

He caressed her slender back, his wide hand moving enticingly up and down, soothing away any resistance that might remain. "Don't worry, *petite*. I'm here to appease your needs. All you have to do is ask and I will fulfill any request." Nick's words came low and cajoling. "Just tell me what you want, Brianna."

Brianna felt on fire. Her heart pounded, her breath came in rapid little pants. She could feel a heat centering between her legs that made her want to move against the hard form of the man who held her. Reason tried to reassert itself over the rum drink. She pulled away from Nick only to feel that she'd left part of herself behind. She looked up at him, her eyes wide with fright. "What's happening to me, Nick? Am I ill?"

"You have nothing that I can't cure, Brianna. Now, come here, sweet, and let me care for you."

As if from a distance Brianna watched herself go back into Nick's arms. She obediently raised her mouth for his kiss and clung to him. Logic told her that what she was doing was wrong, but her mind couldn't make her body respond. It yielded to the need to feel his hands and lips upon her. And she trembled with desire as Nick lifted her into his arms and carried her to the bed. His white teeth gleamed as he smiled triumphantly and laid her down. He hovered over her for a long moment, watching her arousal mount, before he slowly began to unlace his britches.

Brianna watched him helplessly, knowing she needed to stop what was going to take place yet feeling as if she would die if she did. Torn between the two opposing emotional forces, she shook her head even as she lifted her arms to him. Her hips moved of their own accord, beckoning. Her breasts felt swollen and tender.

"Ah, sweet Brianna. Roarke will never know what he missed."

The image of Roarke rose again in Brianna's mind to torture her. She closed her eyes, longing for the captain of the *Black Angel* with such an intensity, she ached. "Roarke, oh, Roarke," she murmured as Nick bent over her and she wrapped her arms about his strong neck. "I need you."

"Damn," Nick muttered in disgust. She believed he was Roarke. The thought had the effect of a bucket of ice water dumped over him. He felt his sex wilt. He pulled away from Brianna just as the door came crashing open from the large shoulder levered against it.

His face a mask of fury, Roarke looked from Nick to

the girl on the bed and then leveled his gaze once more upon his friend. "What in hell is going on here?"

Nick smiled at the irony. The girl thought she was with Roarke, and Roarke thought she was with Nick, and Nick wished to hell he were with anyone else at that moment. "What does it look like, *mon ami?*"

Roarke's angry glance raked over Brianna once more, noting the glassy look in her eyes as she sat up and stared at him. Her thick lashes fluttered slowly downward before she jerked her eyes open and tried focusing on him at the foot of the bed. "What have you given her?"

Nick shrugged. "We had dinner and a few drinks. That is all."

"I saw how many drinks you had downstairs. That still doesn't account for the drugged look in her eyes."

Again Nick gave a nonchalant shrug and came to his feet. "Is it my fault if the girl can't handle her rum?"

"Blast it, Nick! You know how I feel about things like this. George told me about Ole Harry's brews. How far has it gone?"

Nick's expression darkened with anger, his pride already bruised by Brianna's cry for Roarke. "Not far enough, as far as I'm concerned. It seems the girl is in heat for you, dear friend. And I for one won't make love to a woman who thinks I'm someone else." Nick grinned, though there was little humor in the gesture. "I think it is the only reason that would stop me from making love to a woman."

"Nick, you're lucky. I love you like a brother, but had you taken this girl, I would have had to kill you."

"Damn it, Roarke!" Nick swore, his frustration mounting. "What I do off the *Black Angel* is none of your affair."

"When you drug a girl to get her to your bed, it is,"

Roarke said, his voice low and ominous. "You know my feelings on that."

"I know your feelings and I don't understand them. You'd kill a man over some little slut who came here just to find a man to take care of her?"

"If necessary. You can bed any woman you like if she's willing. But—" Roarke looked pointedly to the girl on the bed "—I seriously doubt Brianna would be in your bed had you not drugged her drink."

"But you'd like to think she'd be in yours, right, friend?" Nick snapped as he jerked the laces on his britches closed.

"I have Roselee."

"And I can have any whore on the docks, but that doesn't change anything. You want the girl as much as I do, but you won't admit it."

"What I want and don't want has nothing to do with this."

"Then why in the hell did you follow us and break down the door to rescue her?"

"I didn't want to have to keelhaul you, old friend. That would do little to improve your ugly looks or your appeal to the ladies."

Nick shook his head. "Go ahead and deny it all you want. You're as hot after the girl as she is after you. And damn it," he exploded, "you two are welcome to each other. I'm going to find a woman who will welcome my attention without calling me by your name."

Nick stormed from the room, leaving Brianna confused by the tempest that had swelled between the two men. She inched back against the headboard and stared at Roarke.

He closed the door, and it swung open again haphazardly. Disgusted, he slammed it shut and grabbed a straight-backed chair from the corner to brace beneath the broken latch. He turned back to the bed, where Brianna still sat. "Mistress Tarleton, it seems you have a knack for getting yourself in trouble. Now, once more, I've got you on my hands and don't know what to do with you. I've heard of how bad pennies always keep turning up, and now I'm beginning to believe it."

Unable to comprehend the entire situation in her befuddled state, Brianna looked up at Roarke. She saw only the man she wanted to touch her. Everything else had transpired so quickly that in her bemused mind, Nick's presence already seemed like a distant dream. She ran her tongue over her lower lip and smiled tentatively up at Roarke. "I don't understand." And she didn't. The drugged rum made places, faces, and things all tumble together in a blur. At the moment only the heat in her veins was real.

Roarke nodded and ran his fingers through his hair in disgust. He honestly didn't know what he would do with Brianna without creating more trouble for himself. He could take her back to his house, but that would only set Roselee off in another jealous rage. Since learning of the girl sharing his cabin, the woman had done little but rant and rave, and it was beginning to wear thin on his nerves. He didn't really care what Roselee thought, but he was in no mood to deal with her again tonight. Since docking the *Black Angel*, he hadn't had a moment to rest, and he was weary to the bone.

Roarke's gaze swept over Brianna. He couldn't take her with him, nor could he just leave her here alone. In her present state, she'd end up servicing all of the inn's customers before the drugs wore off.

"Damn," he muttered, vexed to find himself in such a predicament. He turned toward the balcony. He needed a breath of cool air to clear his mind.

Brianna slid her bare feet to the floor and crossed to where Roarke stood with his back to her. Ruled by the unfettered desire the herbs had roused to life, she wrapped her arms about his waist and pressed her cheek against his wide back. She felt him stiffen at her touch but paid no heed. The feel of him was like a balm to an open wound. It healed her even as it created a current of molten lava that streaked through her veins. What she'd experienced earlier was like a winter's day under this new wave of searing sensation. Her fingers clutched his hard middle and she quivered as she moved against Roarke.

Roarke clamped his hands down on Brianna's, dragging them away from him. In the same motion he turned to face her. Holding her at arm's length, he looked down into her passion-softened face and realized for the first time that he'd been too upset earlier to note the metamorphosis that had taken place since he'd seen her that afternoon. Roarke's indigo eyes turned as sooty as the night sky. His gaze swept over Brianna's features one by one. Every muscle in his body tensed and he swallowed with difficulty as he saw for the first time what Nick had tried to tell him. The girl was a true beauty. He cleared his throat. "Damn it, Brianna. Get hold of yourself. Will any man do just as long as you appease your lust?"

With an effort Brianna wriggled one hand free of Roarke's imprisoning grasp. Before he had time to recapture it, she reached up and caressed his craggy cheek. She looked up into his midnight-dark eyes. "I don't truly understand what's happening to me. All I know is that I need you to hold me." She paused and drew in a breath before she added in a sultry whisper, "Please."

Roarke released a long, slow breath and shook his

head even as he opened his arms to Brianna. He knew she didn't know why she was reacting to him in such a way. She didn't realize that Nick's heathen potion had stimulated her sexually, making her crave any man's embrace. And at the moment he was handy.

Fortunately for the girl, he understood what was going on inside her, and he would see that she didn't allow anyone to take advantage of the situation Nick had created.

Roarke frowned. Damn Nick. He knew better. The sad thing about it was that the man had no need to use such devious methods to get a woman into his bed. He could have any woman he wanted—well, almost any woman.

Unconsciously Roarke tightened his arms about the girl cuddling against him. Nick had said Brianna had called his name. That alone had been what had saved her from Nick's attention. Unaware of the caress, Roarke raised a hand and stroked Brianna's long hair. A tiny smile tugged up the corners of his sensuous lips at the thought of Nick's reaction at having a woman already beneath him on the bed and then hearing her call Roarke's name. Roarke chuckled and brushed his lips against Brianna's dark hair. It would be slightly disheartening. Again Roarke chuckled. If nothing else had been gained from this episode, he'd managed to find the humor in the situation.

Brianna moved against Roarke, rousing once again all the feelings he'd experienced twice before on board the *Black Angel*. His smile faded as he felt his sex harden and throb against his tight nankeen britches. He drew in a long breath and sought to quell his mounting desire.

"Damn it," Roarke muttered under his breath. He wasn't an animal. The girl didn't know what she was doing, and it would be little more than rape to have her in her current condition.

"Brianna," he said aloud. "Look at me."

Brianna obeyed his command, willing to do anything for the man who held her.

"You need to go to bed and sleep. You have to realize you're not acting like yourself because of the potion Nick gave you."

Ignoring his words, she molded her body to his as she said, "I don't want to sleep. I want . . ." She paused, her brow furrowing as she sought to find an answer to what she truly wanted from Roarke. She knew she wanted his touch, but somewhere deep inside, she burned for more, much, much more.

"You don't really know what you want. So you'll do as I say. Now, get into that bed and go to sleep." Roarke set her away from him and turned her in the direction of the bed. With a small shove, he set her on the course he'd ordered.

All her inhibitions vanquished, Brianna paused at the bed and looked back over her shoulder at the man bathed in the moonlight. A curious light entered her gold-flecked eyes and a small, seductive smile curled up the corners of her mouth as she slowly unbuttoned the bodice of her gown. With a sensual movement of her hips, she shed the garment. It pooled about her small feet. Slowly and with feline grace, she crawled onto the bed, making no attempt to cover her nakedness from Roarke's view.

Roarke groaned under his breath and knew the next time he saw Nick Sebastain, he would kill the man for putting him through such torture. Brianna's body called to him, beckoning every male instinct he possessed to go to her and slake his desire. He clenched his teeth together, fighting against the demands of his own body.

However, he couldn't stop his wayward gaze from moving over Brianna's delectable body. Against his will he savored the sweetness of her form. Her beauty mesmerized Roarke and sent fiery heat spiraling through his gut. He sucked in a deep breath of air, unable to turn away yet fighting to keep from taking the first, unalterable step that would propel him across the few feet to the woman who lay watching him with slumberous eyes. Her thick lashes hid the expression in their velvet depths, but her lips, slightly parted and moist, made Roarke crave the taste of their luscious sweetness. Roarke released a shuddering breath. His heart pounded in his ears as his heated blood surged through every muscle and tendon, making his work-hardened body throb with need.

"Brianna, cover yourself," Roarke ordered, his voice strangled from the emotions careening through him.

Instead of obeying, she turned on her side, giving him a full view of the soft globes of her young breasts. Roarke's eyes locked on to the small coral peaks. They seemed to harden under the caress of his heated gaze. His mouth went dry and he unconsciously ran his tongue over his lips.

He strove to pull his gaze away only to find it traveling on a different course down the delectable plateau that curved at her small waist and then rose in the soft swell of her hips. From there it moved along the length of her shapely legs and then back up to the dark forest of silk that shadowed the glen where he wanted to bury his own hardened sex.

It took every ounce of willpower left within Roarke to pull his gaze away from her tempting display and focus once more upon her face. He swallowed and cleared his throat again. His words came as a plea, a surrender, as he forgot the reason behind her response to him.

"Brianna, please don't do this. A man can stand only so much."

Brianna's lips spread into an enchanting little smile, so seductive, so provocative, that only a man made of iron would not break under its spell. She raised one hand, palm upward, with her own surrender to him and curled one finger, beckoning him to her.

His blood roared. Fireworks exploded, searing him until he could stand the torture no longer. Roarke took one step and then inexorably took another toward the bed. He paused and looked down at the woman smiling up at him. "I'm going to despise myself in the morning."

Her face soft with desire, her heart in her eyes, Brianna lifted both arms to him. "Roarke, I need you."

Roarke bent over Brianna, his strength to resist gone, his body's demands the victor in the battle of mind over matter. His words were muffled as he buried his face in the curve of her neck and surrendered to the desire coursing through his veins. His voice reflected the strain of his battle as he whispered, "And I need you."

His capitulation complete, Roarke breathed in her fresh, clean fragrance and shuddered from the impact of the sensation the mere smell of her created within him. He tasted the warm, soft flesh at the curve of her shoulder, savoring the sweetness before he began to work his way up the slender column of her throat to the lips he'd kissed only once before but had not been able to put from his mind.

Brianna clung to Roarke's wide shoulders, pressing her breasts against his chest, enjoying the sensation of the soft cloth of his shirt against her tender nipples. She opened her mouth to allow the invasion of his tongue. She tasted and teased him with hers, waging an erotic battle with the invader as it thrust in and out, temptingly

imitating the more intimate motions of love. She drew
in a sharp breath as Roarke's hand covered her sensitive
breast, his fingers massaging the soft globe, working
their way up to the hardened summit. He teased the
peak with the pad of his thumb, brushing back and forth
until he felt her quiver and press closer into his hand.
Tearing himself away from her luscious lips, he slowly
made his way down the curve of her throat before dipping his head to capture her nipple between his lips. He
suckled, laving the hardened peak with his tongue while
his hand prepared its mate for the same caress.

Brianna moaned and shifted restlessly against Roarke.
She craved the feel of his skin against her own hot
flesh. Thinking only of her own needs, she tore at the
laces of his white lawn shirt, revealing the muscles of
his chest. She pressed her palm against the hard plain,
feeling his rapid heartbeat, before curling her fingers
into the crisp mat of hair that covered the tanned expanse. Frustrated that the mere feel of him gave her no
relief from the fever in her blood, she moaned her vexation as she began to tug at the fabric that covered him
to his waist.

Roarke chuckled as he raised himself on his elbows
and looked down into Brianna's intense little face. His
smile deepened. "Ah love, so eager?"

Ignoring the reason behind Brianna's actions, Roarke
sat up and jerked the shirt over his head. He tossed it to
the floor. Next came his shoes, stockings, and britches.
He turned back to find Brianna smiling with pleasure at
her first sight of a naked man. She savored his beauty,
taking in his perfectly molded body and wondering at
the irony of hiding such a miracle of beauty beneath
layers of clothing. Boldly she reached out and laid her
hand on his shoulder, enjoying the feel of pure animal

strength that rested just beneath the surface of his supple skin.

Emboldened by his acceptance of her touch, and intrigued by his male body, she slowly ran her hand down his chest, feeling the hard sinew banding his rib cage and belly. His strong body looked sculpted of bronze. The lantern light gleamed against his skin, shadowing and highlighting the wide shoulders and chest that narrowed to slim hips. Dark hair covered his long, muscular legs. His thighs and calves, shaped by years of hard work, bulged with power.

Brianna's eyes brazenly roved over Roarke until her gaze came to rest at the juncture of his thighs. Soft, dark hair curled about the base of his swollen sex. Her eyes widened and her blood momentarily lost some of its heat from shock at her first sight of an aroused male. She swallowed nervously and looked back at Roarke to find him smiling at her.

Roarke arched one dark brow as he reached out and cupped her breast in the palm of his hand. He stroked the nipple with the pad of his thumb and he queried, "I hope you see nothing to displease you."

The mere touch of Roarke's hand dispelled any doubts Brianna might have felt. She shook her head and smiled as she leaned toward Roarke, her blood on fire. Her words were soft and husky. "I am well pleased."

Roarke chuckled with satisfaction as he bent to reclaim the mouth offered for his kiss. He pressed Brianna back against the mattress. The time for games had come to an end.

Sensation engulfed Brianna as her hands roved down Roarke's back to his firm buttocks. A sigh of pleasure escaped her at the feel of his skin. His flesh had the texture of washed silk. Brianna opened her legs to Roarke's questing hand and fingers, allowing him to touch her intimately as no other man had done. The muscles in her belly quivered and she felt a wet heat spread through her to dampen the soft flesh he stroked. His fingers moved back and forth, tantalizing her. Instinctively her hips moved to the rhythm he set with his hand. When he took his hand away to move between her thighs, she experienced a sudden sense of loss that she knew only Roarke could ease.

An experienced lover, Roarke gave pleasure even as he took his own. He stroked, he caressed, he aroused, until his own blood ran hot and fast. Pausing to savor the moment before he completely consummated their union, Roarke propped on his elbows over Brianna, his passion-swollen body molded against her slender frame, her hot flesh caressing his. He looked down at her as the muscles across his chest worked with his labored breathing. His eyes sought hers, seeking the answer to his silent question. He smiled. In the velvet brown depths he saw a need equal to his own. Lowering his mouth, he captured her lips as he began to fulfill their quest. He moved his hips, his sex hot and satiny, touching, tantalizing, the small bud that already stood taut with arousal. The key that would unlock the gateway of her passion, he stroked it temptingly.

The soft feel of him sent lightning through every inch of Brianna's body. She gasped and instinctively raised her hips, offering her innocence to Roarke.

Unable to deny his own pleasure any longer, Roarke drove into her softness, tearing away the thin membrane, sinking deeply into the virginal warmth of her young body. Brianna arched beneath him at the rending of her maidenhead. A whimper of pain escaped her lips as she tore them free of Roarke's mouth. Her hurt-filled eyes misted with tears as she looked up at Roarke, shocked by her first hurtful experience with love.

Roarke froze, unable to believe what had just transpired. He looked down at the woman beneath him and felt himself begin to wither. The girl had been a virgin! Roarke closed his eyes and drew in a deep, steadying breath as his mind sought to expel the truth of what he'd just done. How could he have been so foolish as not to suspect the girl's innocence? She'd staunchly defended her virtue on the *Black Angel*, telling him in no uncertain terms that she wasn't a whore. However, there were great distances between being a whore and a virgin. There were many women in the world who were not whores but who had shared a man's bed.

Roarke's breath whistled through his teeth as he released it and looked once more at Brianna. He had taken her innocence, and at that moment wanted nothing more than to put as much distance between them as possible. However, the light of passion still glimmered behind the tears brimming in her gold-flecked eyes, and Roarke knew if he left her now, her needs unsatisfied, she'd never overcome her fear of the sexual act.

"It won't hurt anymore, Brianna. I promise," he whispered as he felt himself swell again within the hot, moist warmth of her tight body.

The drug still raging in her veins, her mind confused by the sudden pain and the intense heat that curled in her belly from the hard maleness united with her body, and her heart aching with the need to believe this man, to trust him as she'd trusted no other, Brianna drew in a shuddering breath before her softly spoken words trembled uncertainly over her lips. "I know."

The trusting look in Brianna's eyes shot a thrill through Roarke. The sensation was entirely new to him. Never in all his years of bedding women had one made him suddenly feel like a king of all he surveyed. He swelled with pride as his body swelled with the need to make love to Brianna until he wiped the horror of the last minutes completely from her mind and she cried out in rapture.

Roarke reclaimed Brianna's mouth, tenderly at first, tasting, preparing, enticing, until he felt the last of the tension ease from her body. Her hips moved against him and her arms tightened about his neck as her tongue challenged his to a duel. The kiss deepened as Roarke began to move—slowly thrusting in and out. A moan deep in Brianna's throat told him her pain was forgotten and it was time to take her with him into the land where mystical fires burned the flesh until it exploded in a burst of ecstasy, making mortal man feel indomitable, a god of his own domain.

Guided by the fire burning through her body, Brianna gave herself up to her need to be one with the man driving into her body. She wrapped her legs around him, taking him in deeply, feeling him touch the core of her femininity. She gloried in the feeling and acknowledged that Nick Sebastain's aphrodisiac now had little to do with her response to Roarke. She had vowed never to trust or allow her heart to become involved with any man ever again after Jeremy's betrayal. Yet now those resolves seemed irrational under Roarke's gentle assault upon her senses. Her heart pounded against her breasts as she rode the current of electricity that spiraled from the very core of her being and exploded like a lightning bolt, shattering all thought beyond the feel of the man within her. She moved with him, giving of her body and her heart. There was no longer a future or a past for her. Only Roarke and herself existed in this new world created by his lovemaking.

Brianna could feel the sensation as it began to build. It started out as a tiny spark that grew to consume her completely in its fiery embrace. She arched against

Roarke and gasped his name as her fingers dug into the scarred flesh of his back. Wave upon wave of sensation rocked her as Roarke's back arched and he thrust deeply into her. His white teeth gleamed in the lantern light as his expression grew taut and he spilled his seed into the warm haven that sheltered life.

Roarke collapsed over Brianna and lay within her arms until his heartbeat returned to normal. Unable to find any words for what had transpired between them, he slid to her side and then pulled her into his arms. In moments they both slept the sleep of those sated, physically and emotionally.

Chapter 7

The cool breeze came in from the sea, chilling the early morning hours and making Brianna snuggle closer to the warmth at her side. Her movement didn't rouse Roarke completely. Accustomed to Roselee sleeping in his bed, he wrapped his arms about her and drew her against him without opening his eyes. A moment later a gasp of surprise jerked him fully awake. His midnight blue eyes widened at the sight of a pair of shocked, thickly fringed eyes staring back at him from across the same pillow. He blinked several times, but Brianna's image didn't fade. At last the memory of the previous night fought its way through the lethargy left by his exhausted slumber.

Before Roarke could form a "good morning," Brianna shot upright, dragging the sheet with her. She eyed him as if he'd suddenly turned into a snake. Panic-stricken, she asked, "What are you doing here?"

Roarke yawned lazily, and with the sinewy grace of a relaxed panther, he stretched his arms over his head, flexing his powerful muscles, before pushing himself upright. He looked at the startled woman beside him and answered calmly, "Sleeping, it would seem."

Inadvertently Brianna's gaze swept down Roarke's body. Her cheeks flushed and began to burn with embarrassment when she realized the man sitting next to her was completely naked beneath the swatch of sheet draping his lean hips. She jerked her gaze back to his face, resolutely forcing her eyes to remain above his wide shoulders. Swallowing hard, she tried to ask what exactly had transpired between them. However, as her gaze met his, the memories began to resurface: Nick, the potion, her desire for Roarke. Her questions dried up. Again she swallowed with difficulty and her breathing grew shallow, trembling across her lips as she raised shaky fingers to touch them. Her eyes widened into incredulous pools of brown velvet sprinkled with flakes of gold as she recalled exactly what she'd done. Once more Brianna made an attempt to speak, but no words would pass her ashen lips. She blinked back the rush of tears that burned her eyes and hung her head in shame, unable to face Roarke.

Roarke gazed down at her bowed head and suddenly felt like a son of a bitch. The look on her face had been one of a beaten cur. And he was partly responsible for it. He had no excuse for his behavior last night. He'd taken advantage of the girl's innocence when he knew she was under the influence of Ole Harry's potion. The unaccustomed pang of guilt that stabbed at Roarke didn't sit well with him. He shifted uneasily before sliding his feet to the floor. He grabbed up his britches from the pile of clothing and jerked them on.

"Damn," he muttered, disgusted with himself for allowing the girl to make him lose control. Roarke turned away, unable to look at Brianna any longer. He crossed to the balcony but found no peace in the quiet darkness of the early morning. Raising haggard eyes toward the sky, he silently condemned himself for the thing he despised: a rapist.

Roarke ran a long-fingered hand through his tousled, shoulder-length hair and absently tugged at the golden circle that pierced his ear. He'd been called many things in life, but until last night, no one could have ever accused him of being a rapist of virgins or any other woman, be she whore or lady. Roarke's stomach churned at the thought and he swallowed back the bile that rose in his throat. His memory re-created the rape he'd witnessed as a child; the perpetrator's face became his own, and Brianna was the victim who struggled and fought to defend herself.

Drawing in a deep breath, Roarke forced the past from his mind and rubbed the back of his neck, frustrated with himself.

Roarke ground his teeth together. He'd always prided himself on the fact that he'd never taken a virgin. There were enough eager women to share a man's bed without having to seduce innocents. The women he'd bedded knew what to expect and had been willing to accept his terms, fully understanding that their actions were their own and they were not his responsibility.

Roarke's eyes narrowed as he pushed his remorse aside and stubbornly set his jaw to ward off more unwanted, unneeded, and unaccustomed feelings. He'd managed to keep his personal life free of obligation or commitment to anyone except himself, and he intended to keep it that way, no matter what Mistress Tarleton might assume. For years his plans had been set, and he'd not change them for virgin or whore. Beyond his bedchamber, there was no place in his life for any woman. He had made that clear to Roselee when she'd moved into his house. She knew she was there as long as she pleased him. She also knew not to expect love, because he was incapable of feeling anything for any woman beyond a few minutes lust.

Roarke ran his hand over his face and froze as he inhaled the fragrance that clung to his skin. He could still smell Brianna's sweetness on his flesh. A sinking feeling settled in the pit of his belly as a new wave of heat mustered in his blood. This had to stop. He'd feel no guilt for what had transpired. She'd been the one at fault for inviting him into her bed. Nor would he allow himself to be lured back into her web again. He'd always prided himself on his self-discipline and he truly didn't understand what had made him lose control. However, it wouldn't happen again. This morning, with the sky lighting in the east, he could view everything logically. He'd set Mistress Tarleton straight if she thought she had a claim upon him because of the one night they had shared.

Suddenly angry at himself and Brianna, Roarke swore under his breath. His expression hardened as a sound from the bed drew his attention. He looked over his shoulder at the woman sitting curled against the headboard, the sheet stained with her virgin's blood pulled up to cover her nakedness. Her lower lip, still slightly swollen from his kisses, trembled before she caught it between her teeth to stay its involuntary movement. His temper exploded. He lashed out, heedless of the hurt his words would create. "Don't look at me as if I'm the one responsible for this. You're the one who wanted me in your bed last night. You're also the one who didn't see fit to mention that you were a virgin."

Confused by his sudden attack, Brianna frowned at the angry man glaring at her from across the room. She knew she was at fault. The memory of her abasement with Roarke made her sick to her stomach. She couldn't deny his accusations, but it didn't stop the hurt. Brianna's self-esteem plummeted into the quagmire of mortification. The tears that had misted her eyes now brimmed and ran down her cheeks as she whispered her apology. "I'm sorry."

Another attack of guilt stabbed at Roarke's conscience, but he staunchly ignored it. "You should be, damn it. You've now ruined your chances of finding that husband you so desperately wanted here in the islands. No man wants damaged goods."

Misconstruing Brianna's puzzled look, Roarke continued. "Don't act as if you don't know what I'm talking about. Nick told me the reason you and your friend left England."

Again Roarke misread Brianna's sudden ashen expression. "And don't think that because you gave me your virginity, I'll marry you. I already have a mistress who serves me well in bed, and I don't intend to ever have a wife."

Brianna relaxed. For a fraction of a second she'd feared Roarke had learned the truth of her flight from England. Her relief lasted only a moment before Roarke's tirade spurred a stronger, more volatile emotion to life. She inched her chin up in the air and glared back at Roarke, wanting nothing more than to slap his handsome face for his arrogant assumption that she'd even consider marrying him. She admitted she'd made a mistake, but she'd be damned if she'd allow him to continue to rub her nose in it. She'd not given herself the drugged rum. It had been his friend, his second in command. "For your information, I'd not marry you if you were the last man on earth. And it's none of your concern whether I've ruined myself and my chances to find a husband. What I do with my life is my own business."

Roarke strode purposely back toward the bed. Hands on hips, he stared down at Brianna. "You made it my business when you invited me into your bed."

"The hell I did," Brianna snapped, fury burning away any timidity or fear of the *Black Angel*'s darkly handsome captain. She clasped the sheet to her breasts and came to her knees in front of Roarke. Eyes sparkling, she ground out, "You didn't have to accept my invitation, Captain O'Connor. I'm sure any one of the men downstairs last night would gladly have helped me overcome the effects of the drugs your friend gave me had you found it within yourself to resist my invitation."

Roarke found his palm itching to smack the girl's haughty backside until she agreed that he wasn't at fault. The notion vanished as quickly as it had entered his mind. Roarke could never strike a woman. It would emasculate him in his own eyes. A muscle worked in his cheek. "Damn it, Brianna. I wanted to protect you from yourself. I knew Nick had given you one of Ole Harry's potions, and I knew what would happen if I left you on your own."

Brianna's lower lip began to quiver and new tears filled her gold-flecked eyes. "From the way it looks this morning, you didn't manage to protect me from you, much less myself. Did you, Roarke?"

The fight drained out of Roarke. He shook his head sadly and wearily ran a hand over his face. "No. I didn't." He reached down and picked up Brianna's gown. He turned it over in his hand for a moment, feeling the cheap fabric between his fingers. Brianna had nothing to her name beyond this gown, and he'd known her circumstances when she'd walked down the gangplank to the docks. He'd remained behind after the ship carrying George and his bride sailed away just to see what the girl would do. Already feeling magnanimous for buying the gown she wore, he'd felt no other responsibility for her. Again guilt pricked at Roarke's conscience for not giving her the aid she needed to get a good start on Statia. In the past he'd doled out money to dockside whores to help them better their circumstances without a second thought.

Roarke handed the gown to Brianna and ordered, "Get dressed. It's time we leave."

"I'm not going anywhere," Brianna said, clutching the gown and sheet against her as if it would ward Roarke off.

"Yes, you are. You're going back to my house. Maybe after a day or two of rest, I'll be able to decide what's to be done with you."

"You're not going to do anything with me. I'm not your property, nor am I your responsibility," Brianna said, easing away from Roarke.

"After what transpired between us last night, you are. Now, get dressed. At the present moment I'm in no mood to cater to your shrewish temperament."

"Shrewish temperament be damned. I'm not going anywhere with you. And as for what happened last night, I wasn't alone in this bed. If you will recall, no one forced you to make love to me, nor were you drugged," Brianna shot back, too angry now to care how furious she made Roarke. She had nothing else to lose. Her mother, her friend, her money, her jewels, and now her innocence had all been taken from her. All she had left was her pride, and it was sorely battered by her own actions of the previous night.

Roarke's face darkened. "Damn it, Brianna. You know exactly who's responsible for what happened here last night. The drugs only released you to do what you've been wanting to do since the day you boarded the *Black Angel*. I've seen the way you watched me like a hungry cat. Now, damn it. Get dressed. You're going with me whether you like it or not."

Roarke's words struck Brianna like physical blows, but she wouldn't allow him to see her hurt. Stubbornly she shook her head. "The hell if I will. No man will ever rule me again. And you can't force me to go with you. If you try, I'll scream for help."

Roarke's mind seized upon her second statement like a hound on the scent of the fox. His eyes narrowed suspiciously. "What man have you been with before, Brianna?"

Brianna felt her blood chill at the slip of her tongue but held her ground. She jerked the sheet up in front of her to reveal the red stain of her lost virginity. "As you found out last night, I've never been with another man. Now, get out of here, Roarke O'Connor, before I start screaming. I never want to see you again."

One side of Roarke's shapely mouth curved up into a wry, humorless grin. He arched a dark brow sardonically at her. "You think I care if you scream your bloody little head off. I've told you once before, Brianna, I do as I please, and there's no one here to say me nay any more than there was on the *Black Angel*."

"You're not God, Roarke. You're only a man like any other man. You can be stopped from taking advantage of others."

"Perhaps not God, Brianna," Roarke said softly, bending close and looking her directly in the eyes. Indigo blue clashed with velvet brown. "But perhaps I'm the Devil you make me out to be. Have you considered that notion? And if you don't move that pretty little butt of yours soon, I'll show you just how much hell I can raise." His eyes flicked over her and his voice grew harsh. His words grated out between clenched teeth. "Now, get dressed before I call up some of the men to help you. I'm sure they would enjoy helping you dress after inspecting your bountiful charms."

Brianna paled. From Roarke's cold, hard expression, she didn't doubt he'd follow through. While on board the *Black Angel*, she'd learned that he didn't make empty threats. "All right," she muttered defiantly. She swung her feet to the floor. "I'll go with you now, but you can't make me stay."

Another cruel little grin curled up Roarke's shapely lips. "I wouldn't place any bets on it, Brianna."

"I despise you, Roarke O'Connor," Brianna said, frustrated to have to give in to any man's demands, much less the man who stood towering over her like an ancient, avenging deity.

Roarke's grin never wavered, though her words pricked him far deeper than he'd ever admit. "That's nothing unusual, my dear. You've just joined the ranks of thousands. Now, get dressed. I don't have any more time to waste on you. The sun's already coming up, and I have to check on the progress of provisioning the *Black Angel*."

Roselee, her large breasts nearly spilling from the low neckline of her thin cotton blouse, stood with hands on her hips, eyeing Roarke and his new houseguest. The mutinous light in her dark eyes should have warned Roarke of the storm brewing within. But he hadn't noticed his mistress's expression since they'd arrived at the house. Nor had he considered how Roselee would react to his staying away all night and then returning with a female houseguest. He'd been concentrating on dealing with Brianna's irascibility since leaving the Statia Inn. He'd given no thought to Roselee's reaction to Brianna's presence.

"Why is she here?" Roselee asked, her jealous gaze never leaving Brianna. She'd thought after the doctor's wedding she'd seen the last of the woman Roarke had rescued. Roarke had denied that the girl meant anything to him, but Roselee had her suspicions. She'd seen the way Roarke had blatantly avoided the girl at the wedding, yet she'd also caught him furtively watching her. There was more between the two than Roarke wanted to admit.

Hostility prickled along Roselee's spine, making the hair at the nape of her neck rise like that of a canine sensing a rival for her territory. She'd be damned if she let the little chit worm her way into Roarke's life.

"She's my guest," Roarke said, heedless of how his words sounded to his mistress.

The air seemed to crackle about Roselee. "This house is not big enough for two women, Roarke."

Roarke's midnight gaze came to rest on Roselee, challenging her. "My house is as big as I choose it to be, Roselee."

"I will not have another woman here."

"In my house you will do as I bid of you. Now, I suggest you call Rhama and have her take Brianna to the west bedchamber," Roarke said, crossing to the table where the servants had left a pitcher of fruit juice. He poured himself a glass and turned to find that neither woman had made a move. "Didn't you hear me, Roselee? I said have Rhama take Brianna to the west bedchamber."

Hearing the hidden steel in Roarke's words, Roselee flashed him a venomous glance and then huffily stamped away, her sandaled feet smacking loudly against the cool marble floor.

"She doesn't want me here any more than I want to be here. Why don't you just let me leave now without causing further trouble?" Brianna said.

Roarke shrugged. "Roselee will get used to your presence."

"I seriously doubt it. Can't you see that the woman loves you? I saw it the day of R— I mean Sabrina's wedding. She doesn't want another woman under the same roof with you, much less the woman who shared your cabin on the *Black Angel*. And I would hate to think what she would do should she learn of last night."

"Roselee knows her place here. She also knows that what is between her and me has nothing to do with love."

"How can you be so cruel? Don't you have a heart? The woman gives herself to you, and you use her like you'd use a fork or knife or even the glass in your hand. She's only a vessel for your lust," Brianna said, her words laced with rancor.

Roarke's eyes narrowed. "Mistress, it is none of your affair how I live my life. Roselee is well satisfied with how I treat her. Her life here is far better than she had before."

"I can't imagine how anyone could be satisfied living under the same roof with you."

Roarke's lips curled up at the corners and his eyes lit with something akin to deviltry. "Last night you had a different opinion, Brianna."

"Last night I was drugged. Now I'm stone cold sober and I can see you as you really are, a heartless, arrogant beast who only uses women to satisfy his own lust."

Roarke's smile faded and he shrugged. "That is your opinion, not Roselee's. She appreciates the fact that I took her off the streets. She accepts me as I am because it's far better than having to spread her legs to every sailor who has the price for a fifteen-minute tumble. You would be wise to keep that in mind. You could easily end up on the docks like she did after her parents died. Like yourself, she had no money, nor friends to help her."

"I won't end up on the docks. I can work for a living."

Roarke's grin turned sardonic. "Perhaps you think making a living on your back is easy, but I doubt Roselee would agree with you. She would say she worked for her living far harder than any servant. I found her in the gutter after one of her clients had smashed in her face, blacking both eyes and breaking her nose. No, Brianna. A whore's life isn't easy by any stretch of the imagination."

Brianna shivered at the thought of what could have happened to her last night had Roarke not seen fit to intervene. Nick would have used her like one of the dockside whores and then have left her to survive on her own. Though she raged at Roarke, calling him every name under the sun, she had to admit things could have been far worse. He had been a gentle lover, bringing her to the height of ecstasy. He'd made the act of love beautiful when he could have degraded her and selfishly fulfilled his own needs, with no thought to hers. And he hadn't left her.

The memory of her moments in Roarke's arms made her shiver again; however, this time it was with pleasure. Realizing the train of her thought, Brianna forced her mind back to the present and the man who stood before her. She glanced away from Roarke's scrutiny, afraid her face revealed her wayward thoughts. She looked down at the hands she held tightly clasped in front of her. "I admit I shouldn't have been so hasty in my judgment. However, I wouldn't turn to prostitution, no matter what happened."

"There has been many a good woman who made the same statement until her belly began to chew at her ribs, or her children's stomachs swelled like melons from lack of food. There are things in all of our lives we say we won't do, but when it comes down to survival or death, we'll do anything."

As she'd done at Montvale, Brianna thought. She would never have believed herself capable of murder until Lord Montague attacked her. Brianna swallowed and her cheeks flushed with contrition. She had no right to judge anyone after what she herself had already done. Roarke might be a pirate who roved the seas, raiding and sinking ships for profit, but she knew he wasn't heartless. The man's own words revealed that he understood people and their actions far too well not to have suffered himself. They also mirrored the compassionate man who existed beneath the guise he presented to the world.

Brianna raised curious eyes to Roarke's handsome face, studying each feature, searching out the true man behind the cold, dominant captain of the *Black Angel*. Oddly, her examination of Roarke led her to look inside herself. She realized that, inch by inch, she was in truth finally becoming a woman. She'd thought after the sinking of the *Merry Widow* that she'd matured, but now she knew that it didn't happen overnight. It took time to grow from being a child to an adult.

A curious sense of well-being rippled over Brianna. Her future had looked dark when she'd opened her eyes at dawn. Now she felt that somehow everything would be all right. Roarke didn't know it, nor, she suspected, would he ever admit it if he did, but he'd brought her to his house just as he'd brought Roselee, out of the goodness of his heart.

Brianna allowed her gaze to pass over Roarke, moving over the elegantly furbished room to the balcony that overlooked Fort Oranji and Gallows Bay. For now she would accept his hospitality without her earlier trepidations. In truth she had no other recourse without taking up Roselee's previous profession. But she vowed that before the *Black Angel* set sail again, she'd have found work and would not have to depend upon Roarke's generosity. What little pride she still possessed would not allow her to become a Roselee who didn't pay her way.

Roselee blocked Brianna's path to the balcony. Her painted scarlet lips curled in distaste as she eyed her up and down, taking her rival's measure. "You cannot have him."

Brianna released a long breath. She'd been expecting this moment for the past few days. Only in Roarke's presence had Roselee seen fit to hide her animosity toward Brianna. "Roselee, I don't know why you think I'm here, but you're mistaken if you believe I'm trying to take Roarke away from you."

Roselee gave an audible "humph," ignoring Brianna's denial. She knew exactly what was going on. Roarke would have already come to her bed if he'd not been so interested in seducing the little English bitch. He could deny it until hell froze over, but Roselee knew Roarke's passionate nature too well. He didn't do without a woman in his bed when he was in port. "You don't have to lie to me. I am not blind. I have seen the way you look at him. You could eat him alive, but it will do you no good. Roarke is mine."

"I'm not lying to you. I'm only here because Roarke forced me to come. Now, if you will excuse me," Brianna said, and made to step around Roselee. A hand on her arm stopped her.

Roselee eyed Brianna with disbelief and dug her painted nails into the soft skin of Brianna's upper arm. "What do you mean Roarke forced you? Roarke doesn't have to force women to do as he bids."

"Well, with this woman he does. I didn't come all this way to depend upon any man. I came here to be free. And it's all I've wanted since the day I set foot on Statia. But because of Roarke and Nick Sebastain, I've not had the opportunity. Now, if you will excuse me," Brianna said firmly. A grimace of pain flickered over her face as she jerked her arm free of Roselee's hand and turned once more to the balcony. Roselee followed close upon her heels.

"What has Nick to do with Roarke bringing you here?"

Brianna focused her attention on the azure waters of the bay in the distance. It looked like a huge, smooth mirror reflecting the sun's golden rays.

Brianna's silence didn't deter Roselee. "I asked you what Nick has to do with Roarke bringing you here."

Brianna set her jaw and squared her shoulders obstinately. She had no intention of taking Roselee into her confidence. She'd humiliated herself enough without broadcasting it to the world, especially to a woman who already despised her for something she had not done. "Roselee, just forget what I said. You'll soon be rid of me, I promise."

Roselee lifted a dubious brow, unable to understand any woman wanting to leave a man such as Roarke or the luxury he provided in his home. "Are you really telling me the truth? You really want to leave here?"

Brianna let out a long breath and looked back at the woman who stood anxiously awaiting her answer. She couldn't stop her smile of sympathy. Roselee wore her emotions on her sleeve for everyone to see. "Yes, Roselee. I want to leave. When I came to St. Eustatius I had no intention of coming to live in Roarke's home. However, until I find some means to support myself, I have no other choice but to accept his hospitality."

Roselee shook her head, still unable to believe what

she was hearing. "You mean you would leave here if I were to help you find work?"

Brianna's face lit with surprise. She nodded. "Yes, immediately."

"Then I will help you," Roselee said, smiling smugly.

"If you can help me find work, then why have you not helped yourself?" Brianna asked, suddenly doubting the woman's ability to help her.

Roselee eyed Brianna as if she'd suddenly lost her mind. "Help myself?" She gave a wave of her hand, encompassing Roarke's home. "I have helped myself. I have a beautiful house, a handsome lover. What more could a woman ask out of life?"

"Independence so you won't have to be at any man's beck and call," Brianna answered.

Again Roselee gave Brianna an incredulous look that plainly bespoke her opinion of Brianna's sanity. "I have tasted what you call independence, and I don't like it. It's far better to be at the beck and call of only one man than to have many men use you so you can buy a few bites of food." A knowing smile spread across her red lips. "And when your man loves you as Roarke does me, then it is all pleasure to be at a man's beck and call." She gave Brianna a condescending look laced with something akin to sympathy. "Someday perhaps you will understand. Someday you will find a man to love you as Roarke loves me."

An unexpected flash of jealousy pierced Brianna at Roselee's pronouncement that she held Roarke's love. She shifted her gaze back to the sparkling waters that surrounded the island and bit down on her lower lip to stay the denial that threatened to burst from her. Perhaps Roarke did love Roselee and all of the women he had in different ports. It didn't matter to her. He meant nothing to her, Brianna staunchly avowed. Just because she'd made one mistake with Roarke, she'd not add to it by imagining she cared for the man.

Brianna gave a mental shake of her head. No. Roarke O'Connor meant nothing to her. She had owed him her life when they reached Statia, but after their night together, Brianna felt the debt paid in full. As soon as she could leave his home, she would put Roarke O'Connor and everything that had transpired between them behind her. But even as the avowals formed in her mind, a dull ache also formed in her heart. She couldn't stop the thought that overshadowed her vows. What if Roarke did love Roselee?

Brianna shook the thought away and looked back to Roarke's mistress. "Roselee, I will always be in your debt if you help me."

A cunning light entering the flashing dark eyes that reflected her Spanish heritage, Roselee smiled at Brianna. She raised two fingers and crossed her heart solemnly. "I will help you, Brianna. I will see that you never have to worry about Roarke interfering in your life again. I promise, you will never have to set eyes on him again once you leave here."

The waves lapped against the sand, rolling shells, crabs, and bits of coral from the depths onto the beach. The breeze coming in from the sea chilled the night. Roselee shivered and wrapped her shawl closer about her bare shoulders. The moon had as yet to rise, though the stars overhead seemed to brighten the night, making it possible to see the whitecaps of the tumbling waters.

Roselee ignored the ocean, scanning the beach for any sign of the man she'd come to meet. Walker Ford, her brother, had said he'd be near the water at nine o'clock.

Roselee again searched the darkness for any sign of

her brother. Her foot tapping against the moist, hard-packed sand reflected her vexation. If Walker didn't want to be skinned alive, he'd better not be in some tavern too drunk to remember their meeting.

"Hallo, Rosie," a voice said, making Roselee start with surprise.

"Where have you been? I've been waiting here for nearly an hour. Roarke will soon be home, wondering where I am this late at night," Roselee said, hands on her full hips.

Walker gave her a broken-toothed grin. "Just tell him ye've been visiting yer relatives. That'll ease his mind."

"Roarke doesn't know I have any relatives. He believes that when Ma and Pa died, I was left an orphan."

Walker chuckled and rubbed a callused hand across his scraggly, beard-stubbled chin. "And ye didn't see fit to tell him otherwise?"

"Why should I? Had he known about you and Zeb, he'd never have taken me in, and I'd still be selling my ass on the docks."

"Living up in that fine house of his ain't helped to refine yer language none, sis. I would have thought that by now ye'd be putting on the airs of a real hoity-toity lady."

"I do what I have to do to keep Roarke happy. But that's not the reason I asked you to meet me. I need your help."

"I figured as much. I ain't heard from ye in nearly a year, but when ye need help, ye come running to old Walker. Nothing ain't much changed since ye were thirteen and conceived yer first bastard under the wharf with that sailor."

"I don't want to talk about my past. I need you to help me or I may lose Roarke."

Walker Ford eyed his sister curiously. A thin streak of

moonlight crept over the horizon, illuminating her worried face. "Yer really in trouble, huh?"

"I don't really know, but I don't want to take the chance of finding out."

Again Walker rubbed his bristled chin. "Exactly what is it ye want me to do?"

"I want you to get rid of someone."

Walker shook his oily head. A greasy strand fell across his blackhead-pitted brow and he absently swiped it back. "I've done many a thing in the past, but I ain't no assassin, as ye well know."

"I'm not asking you to murder anyone," Roselee said, exasperated.

"Then exactly what do ye want me to do to get rid of 'em?"

"I thought you might know of a ship that would sail before the end of the week and whose captain wouldn't object to an extra, unscheduled passenger."

Walker nodded and smiled. "I might just do that, but it's going to cost ye, sis. Me friends nor meself work for nothing. How much are ye offering?"

"I have what I've saved from the gowns Roarke bought me."

Walker eyed his sister skeptically. "How can ye have money from gowns yer man bought ye?"

Roselee raised her chin proudly in the air. "I'm my mother's daughter. After I wore the gowns once, I took them back and demanded a refund because they didn't fit properly. During the last months I've accumulated a nice little nest egg of my own."

"And yer man knows what yer doing?"

"I didn't say that. Roarke never questions me about what I wear. He's away most of the time anyway, so when he comes home, he really only notices what I don't have on."

Walker chuckled his admiration. "Damn me, sis. Yer a card. Ma would be proud of ye. Ye take yer business sense after her."

"I learned early on how to handle men. And Roarke's no different from any other man when it comes to what's between his legs. Give him a roll and he'll give you what you want. He's only different when it comes to whores and kids. Everyone believes he's a heartless pirate, but the man has an obsession about helping whores and brats. I've seen him dole out coin until he emptied his pockets to the little beggars that follow him about when he goes down to the docks."

"I've heard the man makes a relentless enemy, sis. I just hope ye know what yer doing when yer playing him false. I'd hate to see ye with yer throat cut."

"Roarke won't hurt me, because he's never going to find out what I do with the gifts he gives me. I make him happy in bed, and that's all that he thinks about."

"I thought you loved the bastard."

"I do," Roselee said. "That's why I want you to help me get rid of the bitch who's come to try to take him away from me. I can't allow that to happen. Mistress Brianna Tarleton has to go, one way or the other."

"Well, if ye've got the coin, me and me friends will take care of the rest. Being yer brother and all, I can't stand around and see ye made unhappy."

"Your brotherly concern warms my poor heart," was Roselee's sarcastic answer. "It's just like the concern you had when I started whoring for a living. You kept bringing me clients so I wouldn't go hungry." Roselee laughed at the look that passed over her brother's face. He could pretend regret all day long, but she knew he'd pimp for her again if Roarke replaced her with another woman.

Walker grimaced. "Ain't no call to act that way, sis.

If I hadn't done it fer ye, Ma and Pa would have. At least with me, we only had to split yer coin two ways instead of three."

Roselee nodded. She couldn't deny what Walker said about her parents. Every child Pearl and Sam Ford had brought into the world had been taught to make a living by any means available. Two of her sisters had died from the French pox, and one brother had been hanged for piracy. That left her, Zeb, and Walker out of six children. And their lives were little different. She whored for a living, while Zeb and Walker hired out their services for anything that brought in a few coins. Walker could swear that he'd not stoop to murdering for a price, but she knew differently. Life meant little to her brothers, and both would kill anyone, even her, if they needed the coin.

Chapter 8

Nick braced one shoulder against the doorframe and peered down at the woman examining a large scarlet hibiscus bloom. She bent, smelled, and then, with a wry grimace, brushed the golden, powdery pollen from the tip of her nose. Nick smiled at the girl's innocent gesture and felt like kicking himself for the thousandth time for letting her slip through his fingers. He glanced back at the man seated behind the desk, with his booted feet propped upon its shiny surface. Crossed at the ankles, his leather boots gleamed like the polished wood beneath them. Nick shook his head and turned away from the view in the garden below.

"Damn it, Roarke, you're the damned luckiest man I've ever met."

Roarke glanced up at Nick and tossed the papers he'd been reading aside. He arched a curious brow at his friend and swung his feet to the floor. "What makes you say that?"

Nick cocked his head in the direction of the garden. At Roarke's puzzled look, he finally said, "You know exactly what makes me say you're lucky. How many men do you know who have two beautiful women at their disposal and under the same roof at the same time? I would have thought by now they would have been clawing each other's eyes out to see who gets you."

Nick shook his head in amazement. "But no. Not Roarke O'Connor's doxies. They live happily together." Nick raised a brow and smiled roguishly. "Do they both come to your bed at the same time?"

Roarke's congenial expression faded as he came to his feet and crossed to the French doors. He spied one of the subjects of Nick's scurrility as she settled herself on the small bench beneath a tall palm. She slowly fanned herself with her wide-brimmed straw bonnet as she stared off into the distance, completely unaware that she was once again the subject of conversation between the two friends.

Spurred to defend Brianna against Nick's slander, Roarke glanced at the man who had come to stand at his side. "Nick, Roselee is the only woman in this house who shares my bed."

Nick frowned. "You don't have to lie to protect Brianna's reputation, Roarke. We both know what happened at the inn."

Roarke cocked a brow at Nick and folded his arms over his wide chest. "Oh? I must be getting old and forgetful, because I could swear you left the inn soon after my arrival."

"Hell, you know what I mean. You stayed with her. And I know she was hot for you. I heard it with my own ears. I also know you and women, so I have no doubts about what transpired after I left."

"You're mistaken, Nick. Nothing happened after you left. I only stayed to assure Brianna didn't fill your place in her bed with an even more disreputable character," Roarke said, the lie slipping easily from his lips as he glanced once more at the young woman in the shade.

Nick gave Roarke a dubious grin, his dark eyes narrowing suspiciously. "I don't believe a word you're saying, friend. But I'll accept your explanation."

Thick black lashes shielded Roarke's midnight eyes as he pinned Nick with his hard gaze. "You have no other choice. And I had best never hear anything other than what I have just told you."

Nick's grin faded. "Roarke, what in hell has gotten into you of late? You've turned into a real son of a bitch. You know you don't have to threaten me to keep your confidences. From the way you've been acting, if I didn't know better, I'd think you've let yourself fall in love with our Mistress Tarleton. You act as if she's made of glass."

Roarke chuckled and slapped his friend on the shoulder. "You know better than to even consider such a ridiculous notion, Nick. And I'm sorry if I've acted like an ass of late. I've had things on my mind. According to the missive I received yesterday from our colonial friends, it's growing more imperative by the day for us to get to France and meet with Beaumarchais to receive the munitions. As before, the rendezvous will take place in Brest. Beaumarchais will be there as a representative of the private trading house of Roderigue Hortalez and Company."

Nick smiled good-naturedly and added his own tardy apology. "I'm also sorry for the things I've done, Roarke. It wasn't right to drug the girl to get her into my bed. I know my actions have put a wall between us." He glanced toward Brianna and gave a rueful shake of his dark head. "But damn me, looking at her now, I believe she just might have been worth a keelhauling."

"You'll never change," Roarke laughed, and turned back to the desk. He opened the top drawer and withdrew a small casket bound in leather. He handed Nick a pouch that bulged from the golden contents. "Here's your cut from the last voyage. The way you work, it should keep you in wine and women for at least a week."

"Well, I'm not as lucky as you are," Nick said, tucking the pouch away in the inside pocket of his coat.

"Luck has nothing to do with it," Roarke shot back, a roguish grin curling his lips. "It's charm, pure and simple. Now, I've work to do if we intend to be ready to sail by tomorrow."

Nick smiled, accepting his dismissal graciously. "Since you no longer want my company, I believe I'll go down to Fort Oranje and see how many women are willing to share my bed when they see my coin."

"Nick, if you're wise, you'll not spend everything you make on whores. Right now we have letters of marque from the Continental Congress, but when the war is over, we'll be branded pirates if we keep roving the seas."

Nick shrugged, unperturbed by his friend's predictions for the future. "I'm not like you, old friend. I can't stuff my money away in warehouses and ships. I need to enjoy the profits of my work. I'll let the future take care of itself."

"It's your life, Nick," Roarke said. They'd had the same discussion in the past. He kept trying to convince Nick that things didn't remain the same. The world was changing by leaps and bounds. The colonies were a prime example of how fast.

No. Things didn't stay the same, and Roarke intended to change with them. He'd still enjoy life, living every minute to its fullest, but he'd use his brain and not squander everything he made on women and rum. He'd lived too long in poverty, while those more fortunate scorned him, to go back to such a life for only a few moments immediate pleasure.

Nick settled his sailor's cap on his dark head and

gave Roarke a salute. "Should you by chance get bored up here with your beauties, come down to Statia Inn and I'll buy you a few drinks."

Nick didn't wait for Roarke's answer. He turned and sauntered out of the office, a rakish grin curling his lips as he envisioned the evening ahead. He paused briefly on the walkway near the garden, tempted to pay the lovely Brianna a visit. The thought evaporated as quickly as it had come. He'd not face Roarke's temper again today. Though his friend refused to admit it, Nick suspected the girl had found some tiny nook or cranny in the heart Roarke swore he didn't possess.

Smiling smugly with the knowledge that he knew Roarke far better than Roarke knew himself, Nick turned and strode back to the two-wheeled donkey cart he'd rented. He wasn't comfortable on horses. He knew the sea, but when it came to animals, the female of his own species was the only one he wanted to ride. Others, he just used when it was absolutely necessary. Climbing onto the small, narrow seat, he clicked the reins against the donkey's back. The beast turned his head, gave Nick a condescending look, flicked one long ear, and gave a wag of his tail before he decided to start moving at his own pace. Nick swore under his breath and settled back to endure the tedious journey down the winding mountain road.

His thoughts still on his conversation with Nick, Roarke absently locked the casket and returned it to the drawer before he strolled out onto the balcony. His gaze traveled once more across the spacious lawn to the woman sitting in the shade of the tall palm. She looked so lovely resting there in the soft muslin gown he'd purchased for her the day after she'd come to live in his house. He'd managed to appease his conscience by buying her clothes, but little else had changed between the two of them.

Roarke's eyes narrowed thoughtfully. Before he left, he wanted to settle things between himself and Brianna, and as a peace offering, he'd let her have the use of his home while he was away. Hopefully in some small way his offer would make amends for the past. It wouldn't wipe out the mistakes, but at least she'd have a place to live during the coming months.

Satisfied with his decision, Roarke turned to the stairs that led to the garden below. He made his way across the green lawn toward his houseguest as a servant brought out refreshments. A moment later all thoughts of his invitation vanished as he watched Brianna lift the glass of fruit juice to her lips. Roarke paused, savoring the sight, his hungry gaze locking on to Brianna's coral-tinted mouth as she sipped the sweet, cool drink.

Roarke's body heated in response before his mind fully registered the innate sensuality in her graceful gesture. His gaze lingered on her mouth for a long moment before moving slowly over Brianna, taking in the warm flush of her sun-tinted skin, the feathery lashes shadowing her soft eyes as she stared toward Gallows Bay, the elegant line of her throat, and the enticing flesh that swelled above the neckline of her gown.

Roarke swallowed and drew in a deep breath in an effort to control the burst of desire that made his blood pound in his temples. His reason for coming to the garden now completely forgotten, he crossed to where Brianna sat.

The crunch of his boots against the crushed-shell path drew Brianna's attention to him. He smiled down at her, his indigo eyes holding her prisoner. "It's such a lovely day, I thought you might enjoy a tour of the island since you plan to make your home here."

Brianna's first impulse was to accept Roarke's invitation, but she hesitated, uncertain of exactly how she should react to the man who had made her a woman but who had also shown no interest in her since the day she'd entered his home. If anything, Roarke had gone out of his way to avoid her.

Seeing her uncertainty, Roarke cajoled, holding out a strong hand. "Be a good girl and don't argue with me this time, Brianna. This will be the last opportunity for me to show you Statia before I sail tomorrow evening."

A sudden, inexplicable sense of loss wiped away Brianna's uncertainty. Tomorrow Roarke would be gone from her life, and she would never see him again. Brianna stood and took Roarke's hand. She smiled. "I would love a tour of the island. I've wondered what the rest of Statia is like. It looks beautiful from up here."

"I'll have Thomas bring round the carriage," Roarke said, his spirits suddenly soaring with Brianna's acceptance. Until that moment he hadn't realized that he'd dreaded her rejection. He was relieved, his steps much lighter as he returned to the house to order the carriage prepared for their ride.

Brianna watched Roarke go. She couldn't stop herself from admiring the dashing figure he made in his nankeen britches and loose-flowing white lawn shirt. The tight fabric of his britches emphasized the muscles in his firm buttocks and his thick, corded thighs. Brianna jerked her gaze away, embarrassed by her own perversity.

She didn't understand the strange power Roarke O'Connor had over her. One minute she could despise him with every fiber of her being, and in the next she would have attempted to give him the world had he asked it of her.

Brianna frowned, wondering at her mercurial moods

where Roarke was concerned. She wanted to be free of him as soon as possible, yet when the opportunity neared, she found the prospect depressing. Brianna gave a mental shrug and lifted her skirts away from the white crushed shells that paved the path. After today she wouldn't have to worry about Roarke. He would sail out of her life on the *Black Angel* as he had sailed into it.

Brianna's depression deepened as she ascended the stairs. Blinded by the bright sunlight, her thoughts on Roarke, she didn't see the woman awaiting her as she stepped through the doorway. Sharp fingernails digging into her arm jerked her to an abrupt and painful halt.

Roselee's dark glance swiftly ascertained that they would not be overheard. She bent close to Brianna and said, her voice low, "I've done as you asked. I spoke with my friend, and he says that he'll help you. He knows a man who needs a governess. We're supposed to meet him tonight at eight o'clock."

"Thank you, Roselee, I'll be ready," Brianna said absently, her mind still on the man she was to meet in a few minutes. Easing her arm out of Roselee's tight grasp, she didn't note the hostile light in the woman's flashing eyes. "Now, if you will excuse me. I need to change."

Roselee let Brianna go, but her narrowed gaze stayed riveted to her rival's back until Brianna closed her bedchamber door. She pressed her painted lips tightly together and fought to constrain the urge to go after the girl and tear every strand of her dark hair out of her beautiful, treacherous head. She'd seen the bitch in the garden with Roarke. The girl could lie until her face turned blue, but Roselee knew from the expression on Brianna's face as she talked with Roarke that she had come here for one purpose alone: to try and take Roarke away from her.

Roselee smiled to herself. She'd known the truth all along. Since first laying eyes on the girl, Roselee had known she meant nothing but trouble. Roselee turned and strode down the hallway in the opposite direction of temptation. She'd let the little bitch have her afternoon with Roarke. It would be her last. Tonight Roselee would have the final laugh when Walker fulfilled his end of their bargain.

Roarke wouldn't have time to wonder what happened to the girl before he sailed. And when he returned to Statia, Brianna Tarleton would only be a distant, unpleasant memory for both of them.

The verdant landscape gave way to beaches made of fine volcanic sand. Brianna breathed in the fresh sea air, savoring the moment to the fullest. The drive down the winding mountain road with Roarke relaying the history of the island had been like an English outing between old friends. Several times he'd drawn the carriage to a halt where the tall trees gave way to the view of the ocean surrounding the outcropping birthed by the extinct volcanos. He patiently explained how the Dutch island of St. Eustatius had become known as the Golden Rock. And by the time they reached the beach, Brianna was marveling at the man sitting at her side. Hearing Roarke proudly speak about the island and its commerce made him seem more like a merchant banker than a rogue pirate.

Enjoying the afternoon with no thought to the past nor the future, Brianna allowed Roarke to lift her down from the carriage. For a frozen moment in time he held her aloft, his penetrating midnight blue eyes locked with hers, a gentle smile curving his sensuous lips. At last, with something akin to a sigh of regret, he slowly allowed her feet to touch the sand.

The spell broken, Roarke took her by the hand and led her down to the water's edge. The beach, secluded from the rest of the island's population by a steep formation of rock that seemed to divide the island, was quiet. The only sounds to disturb the solitude were the calls of the gulls overhead and the gentle lapping of the waves against the shore.

Brianna laughed with pleasure as a tiny crab spilled out of the surf and raised his claws fiercely into the air to ward them off. Valiantly he backed slowly toward the waters that had pushed him ashore. She bent to inspect the little warrior from the sea, intrigued by its courage against such large enemies. Gently she helped the tiny crustacean on his way and promptly received a pinched finger as a reward. Sucking her injured appendage, she looked up at Roarke, who stood smiling down at her.

"It would seem he didn't appreciate your help," Roarke said, bemused by his own reaction to Brianna's sweet naïveté. He had never met a woman like her before. She was no innocent, yet the very air surrounding her seemed to proclaim her purity of spirit. She had known man's deepest inherent desires to their fullest, yet they had not ruined her sweetness of heart or she would not now be looking at him from her gold-flecked eyes as if he were her friend. Wanting nothing more than to lay her back against the moist, sandy beach and make love to her, Roarke forced his hand to remain steady as he extended it to help Brianna stand.

"No. It would seem he didn't," Brianna said, holding her injured finger out for Roarke's inspection.

Her guileless gesture broke the restraint Roarke had fought to maintain over himself since watching Brianna sip the drink in the garden. His eyes locked on to the mouth he'd craved to taste all afternoon. He moistened his suddenly dry lips as his imagination conjured up the memory of their last kiss. His desire to taste her luscious lips magnified tenfold. Before he could stop himself, he took her hand and brought her finger to his lips. His gaze never left her face as he kissed her finger and then touched it tenderly, erotically, with his tongue.

At his caress, sensation careened through Brianna, taunting every fiber of her being, making her completely aware of Roarke as a man as well as her own sensuality. She drew in a sharp breath as her gaze locked with his, but she didn't withdraw her hand, couldn't withdraw her hand. Her heart beat rapidly, her pulse pounding at the base of her throat, fluttering there like a butterfly captured within a silken net. In an unconsciously seductive gesture, she ran the tip of her tongue over her lower lip and fought against the sudden impulse to throw herself into Roarke's arms.

Roarke let out an audible moan as he surrendered to his own needs. He swept her into his arms, crushing her against his hard body as he captured her mouth in a soul-searing kiss.

Brianna didn't resist. Possessing a will of their own, her arms crept up the front of his white lawn shirt and wrapped themselves about his corded neck. Her fingers laced in the dark, curling hair at the nape of his neck. Her body, like a ship at sea seeking its home port, molded itself against Roarke. They stood together, a current of electricity flowing between them like the elements of a fermenting thunderstorm. Lightning sensations spiraled through Brianna, making her tremble from the shock. Her knees grew weak and she clung to Roarke for support.

Tenderly Roarke released her mouth. He cupped her small, oval chin in his hand as he gazed down into her velvet-soft eyes. A small smile curved his sensuous lips, and his words came softly. "Brianna, what am I going to do with you? You make me act like an untried boy eager for his first taste of love. When you're near I can only hear the heated message in my blood that tells me to make love to you. I've tried to resist it, but I don't have the strength when I look into your lovely face."

Brianna thought her heart would burst with the pleasure Roarke's words created. She understood his efforts to resist as well as his lacking the willpower to control his own wayward emotions. She felt the same way. She knew she shouldn't now be standing in Roarke's arms, enjoying his kisses, but she couldn't deny herself the pleasure. Tomorrow he would be gone from her life, but today she would savor her time with him. In the eyes of the world she would be judged a wanton, unfit for a decent man or marriage, but at the present moment, with Roarke's warmth pressed against her, she didn't care. That was in the future, and for now there was no future or past.

They stood alone on the beach in a world of their own, the hands on the clock frozen, the sun standing still, allowing no time to pass.

The message in her blood mirrored Roarke's. This time she couldn't vindicate her actions by using drugs as an excuse, and she accepted it. During the past days she'd tried to keep her thoughts away from Roarke and their time together at the Statia Inn. But now the memories burst to the surface like an explosion of fireworks, making Brianna tremble as she faced the truth. She wanted this man to make her his once more, to give her the ecstasy she had known in his arms on the night he'd made her a woman. Right or wrong, she wanted Roarke to make love to her.

"Love me, Roarke," Brianna whispered, her voice

soft with the emotion welling within her heart as she looked up into Roarke's eyes and realized that her feelings for him went far deeper than merely physical attraction. Somehow and somewhere along the rocky path of their relationship she had allowed this man to capture her heart.

A relieved sigh passed over Roarke's lips as he lowered his head and took Brianna's mouth once more. His tongue was welcomed as it delved enticingly into the sweetness beyond her lips. The erotic duel that transpired left both Roarke and Brianna breathing heavily.

Unable to wait a moment longer, Roarke scooped Brianna up in his arms, grabbed the lap blanket from the carriage as he passed, and carried her to the shade beneath several tall palms. There he released her only long enough to make a bed for them upon the sand. Kneeling on the blanket, he held out his hand to Brianna. She accepted it with uncharacteristic timidity, her cheeks flushing with color at her own eagerness.

Roarke's soft laughter was caught on the breeze and carried away as he pulled her down to him. They tumbled back onto their freshly made bed.

"Ah, my sweet innocent. How charming you are," Roarke said before he claimed her mouth once more.

Again the world stilled about them. The song of the brightly colored birds became the music of love, the roiling waves quieted to a placid lake that reflected the gentle beauty of the moment, and the wind held its breath on a sigh as the two lovers undressed each other and came together.

Brianna gasped her pleasure as Roarke entered her. She curled her arms about his neck and wound her legs about his waist to receive all of him. Eagerly she sought out his mouth, gently sucking on his tongue as their hips moved together, each thrust igniting more fire until it consumed them in a torrid inferno of sensation.

Unable to contain her cry of pleasure, Brianna tore her mouth free of Roarke's as she arched her throat back to release a rapturous moan. Roarke claimed the slender column, nibbling greedily, tasting her sweet flesh until he could no longer contain his own release. He sucked on her skin, wanting to consume her totally in his need to possess her as he spilled his seed deep within her warm body.

Roarke collapsed over Brianna, breathing heavily, his face buried in the curve of her shoulder. He thrilled at the gentle hand that slowly caressed his dark hair and then moved down to his neck and shoulders, tenderly wiping away the beads of sweat that dewed his scarred, sun-bronzed skin. The aching void within him began to slowly fill under Brianna's loving ministrations.

"Roarke, sweet Roarke," Brianna murmured lovingly against his sweat-dampened hair. Words of love rose to her lips, but the past reared its ugly head, freezing them like dew on a winter's morn. Once before she had made the mistake of giving her heart to a man who didn't love her in return, and had suffered the pain of his betrayal. She'd not make the same mistake twice. No matter how she felt about Roarke, he'd never know of her feelings until she knew he loved her in return. Roarke had made no vows of love or even a commitment to further their relationship. He would leave tomorrow without a backward glance at the woman he left behind.

Brianna's eyes misted with tears as she stared up at the blue sky overhead. The clouds scurried across the heavens as the waves crashed violently onto shore. The birds squawked angrily, annoyed by the lovers who had disturbed their afternoon rest. Brianna tightened her arms about Roarke's shoulders, wondering what had changed in the last few moments. But she knew. She had allowed herself to fall in love with a pirate who cared nothing for her beyond the moment. Her heart ached as she clutched Roarke to her in a last desperate attempt to hold on to the fantasy she had subconsciously woven about herself while in Roarke's arms.

Sensing the tension in the soft, warm body beneath him, Roarke knew something wasn't right. He raised himself on his elbows above Brianna. A frown creased his brow at the sight of the crystal drops of moisture cascading from the corners of her eyes. Tenderly he wiped the tears away with the tip of one finger. His husky voice mirrored his concern as he asked, "Did I hurt you?"

Brianna shook her head and attempted a wobbly smile. "No. I was only thinking of tomorrow."

Roarke shifted his weight off Brianna and reached for his britches. He pulled them up over his lean hips before he looked back at her. "That's what I've been meaning to speak to you about."

Embarrassed now by her own nakedness, Brianna quickly retrieved her gown and slipped it over her head. She kept her attention focused on buttoning the bodice as she asked, "What did you want to tell me?"

"I want you to feel free to remain at the house for as long as you need. There's no reason for you to leave," Roarke said as he pushed his arms into the sleeves of his shirt and then pulled it on over his head. The white lawn fabric kept him from seeing the flicker of pain that passed over Brianna's face.

She turned to look out across the blue waters. "I thank you for your invitation, Roarke. But I don't know if I should accept it. It might be best if I left as soon as I find work."

Roarke couldn't see Brianna's expression, but he

sensed from her tone that he'd said something to displease her. Frowning, Roarke ran a hand through his hair in exasperation and rubbed the back of his neck as his muscles tensed with dread. He wanted to avoid any more dissension between them. When he sailed away tomorrow he wanted to remember Brianna as she'd been that afternoon instead of the angry termagant he'd dueled with in the past. Not knowing what else to say, he said, "You know what is best for you."

His answer didn't have the desired effect. Brianna shot to her feet and walked away from him. Puzzled, Roarke stared after her. He honestly didn't know what he'd said, but he'd be damned if he'd go running after her to apologize when he'd only been trying to help. Annoyed now himself, he pushed himself to his feet and jerked up the lap blanket and gave it a good shake to rid it of sand before he turned and stamped back to the carriage, where Brianna awaited.

Neither spoke as they made their way back up the winding hill road to Roarke's house. As he drew the carriage to a halt in the circular drive, Brianna quietly said, "Thank you for the lovely afternoon, Roarke. I will remember it forever." Without waiting for his answer or his assistance, she jumped down from the carriage and hurried up the walk.

"Brianna," Roarke called after her, but she didn't act as if she'd heard him. She opened the door and disappeared inside.

"Damn," Roarke swore, once more disheveling his dark hair with his long fingers in a show of exasperation. Everything had been so perfect until he'd offered her the use of his house in his absence. He shook his head as he snapped the reins against the horse's back and urged him in the direction of Fort Oranje. Perhaps a few drinks with Nick would improve his mood and his outlook on women in general.

From the shadows of her room, Brianna watched the carriage until it rolled out of sight. The tears she'd fought to suppress on the beach now ran freely down her cheeks and fell heedlessly onto the soft cotton of her bodice. Roarke had offered her the use of his home but had said nothing about wanting her here when he returned. The omission spoke plainly of his feelings for her and any future relationship between them. He'd made no effort to try and talk her out of leaving, only telling her the decision was hers to make.

Brianna turned away from the window and crossed to the dressing table. A haggard-faced creature stared back at her, the misery in her eyes evident to the world. Brianna raised her hand to the purplish bruise on her throat and drew in a shaky breath. Roarke O'Connor had left his mark on her, branding her his whether he wanted her or not. He had laid claim to her heart as well as her body, leaving her powerless to the emotions he evoked within her.

Pain lashed through Brianna and she squeezed her eyes closed to shut out the image of the woman she had become. Her breath came in ragged pants as she realized that she now understood her mother. Sabrina had also been powerless where Lord Montague was concerned. She had feared the consequences of losing him more than she had loved her own daughter.

The thought jerked Brianna's head up and her eyes widened as she stared at her reflection and saw her mother. Brianna shook her head, denying that she had inherited her mother's weakness. She inched her chin up in the air and glared at her image. She'd not allow herself to be controlled by any man. She couldn't allow herself to disintegrate into a woman who lived only for the man she loved, no matter how much it hurt and no matter what her heart urged her to do. She didn't want to end up like Sabrina, who had become only a shadow of a woman because of her weakness for a man and his possessions.

Brianna turned toward the door, her disturbing thoughts setting her into action. The sun was sinking low in the west, and the clock ticked toward the hour of seven. She needed to find Roselee so they could be on their way to meet her friend. Hopefully after tonight she'd not have to depend upon Roarke's hospitality much longer.

Smugly Roselee assessed Brianna as they made their way down the road to Fort Oranje. The girl didn't seem happy after her afternoon excursion with Roarke. Roselee smiled, satisfied that she knew the reason behind Brianna's somber mood. The girl had gotten her hands on too much of a man and didn't know how to handle him. As young and stupid as she was, Brianna had probably made the mistake after they'd had sex of telling him that she loved him. Knowing Roarke as she did, Roselee didn't doubt he had quickly set Brianna straight about his feelings.

Roselee nearly burst into laughter at the thought. The bitch deserved what she got. Brianna had trespassed on her territory, and she could feel no sympathy for her. The only feeling the girl inspired in Roselee was hatred. But after tonight, Roselee's problem would be solved.

Roselee chuckled aloud, drawing Brianna's attention away from the view between the donkey's large ears where she'd been blindly staring since leaving Roarke's home. "It won't be much longer, Brianna. My friend said to meet him near the warehouse where he works.

From there he'll take you to the man who needs a governess for his little girl."

Brianna glanced up at the darkening sky. "Isn't it a little odd to interview a governess this late in the evening? Instead of coming to the docks, I would think the gentleman would want me to come to his home and meet the child."

Roselee hesitated, frantically trying to invent answers to pacify Brianna. "Normally he would invite you to his house, but he's been too busy of late. Since the war started between the colonies and England, it's kept him busy sending out supplies," Roselee said, drawing upon conversations she'd overheard between Roarke and his second in command. She paused, drawing in a steadying breath. "My friend's employer is a widower, so he has to be mother and father to his little girl. And at times like these when he's so busy, it's really hard on the poor man. You can see why he has to do things sometimes in unusual ways."

"I guess you're right," Brianna said, still wondering at the lateness of the hour. She'd been so bemused by Roarke's invitation to show her the island earlier in the day that she hadn't considered the oddity of the hour for the interview. But perhaps on Statia they did things differently than they did in England. She couldn't imagine an English gentleman doing business after five o'clock in the afternoon. They would consider it highly improper and in very poor taste after high tea.

The donkey cart jolted over the cobbled street, jarring Brianna's teeth together until she clamped her jaw tightly shut. She clung to the narrow seat, warily keeping an eye on the shadows. She remembered well her last time on the wharf. Two women would only be twice the enticement to the slugs who inhabited the taverns along the quay.

Roselee maneuvered the cart down a narrow lane at the end of the wharf. She drew the donkey to a halt and jumped down. She glanced up at Brianna. "Come on. I don't have all night. Roarke will be home soon and expect to find me there as well."

Roarke's name propelled Brianna to her feet and down to the sandy lane. In the distance she could hear the sound of the waves as the tide came in to eat away at the beaches. She looked about nervously. "Are you sure this is where your friend wanted to meet us, Roselee?"

"Of course," Roselee snapped, her hand itching to slap the girl's face. "Walker will be here in a few minutes."

Brianna hugged her waist and looked anxiously into the darkness surrounding them. The hair at the nape of her neck rose in warning. Something wasn't right about this meeting. She looked back to the woman who had promised to help her find work. "You didn't bring me here to be interviewed for a governess's position, did you, Roselee?"

Roselee let the guise crumble. Her lips spread into a cruel little smile of triumph as she looked at Brianna through narrowed, hate-filled eyes. "So the bitch has finally figured it out? I wondered how long it would take you to realize how stupid you were to believe I'd help you do anything."

A foreboding chill tingled down Brianna's spine, but she suppressed a visible shudder. She'd not allow Roselee to see her fright. It would only make things worse. "Roselee, I don't know why you're doing this, but it's time for this game to end."

Roselee chuckled and shook her head. "I'm playing no game, Brianna. My life is at stake here, and until you're gone, I won't be safe."

Brianna frowned. "I don't know what you're talking about. You have nothing to fear from me."

"So you've said before, but I've seen you with Roarke and I can't allow you to come between us. Roarke loves me."

Sensing her own life was now in jeopardy if she couldn't convince Roselee that she wasn't her rival, Brianna lied, "I know he does. He told me so this afternoon. Why do you think I want to leave Roarke's home? There is no place for me in Roarke's life because he loves you, Roselee."

"You're right. Roarke does love me, but I won't test his love by allowing you to stay on Statia."

Brianna held her hands out in front of her, palms upward in supplication, as she began to slowly back away from Roselee. "I will leave Statia if that's what you want, Roselee."

"That's what I want, bitch. But I intend to see that you leave whether you want to or not. Walker has already made the arrangements. And by the time Roarke returns from his next voyage, you'll only be a bad memory."

Comprehending Roselee's plans for her, Brianna knew she had to escape before it was too late. She turned to flee at the same moment a meaty arm clamped around her middle like a steel vise. A callused, blunt-fingered hand came down over her mouth and nose at the same time, stifling her scream for help. Her captor chuckled and jerked her off her feet.

"I reckon I got here just in the nick of time, sis. This un's a feisty wench."

"Damn you, Walker. You were late being born and you've been late ever since. Had she escaped me before you arrived, I'd have slit your throat myself."

"Ain't no call for getting yerself all riled, sis. I arrived in time, didn't I? And yer the one who had to brag about what was to happen to her before I got here to help. So don't lay all the fault upon me."

Brianna twisted and squirmed against the man holding her but couldn't escape. The hand clamped over her nose and mouth was suffocating her. She fought for air but couldn't draw in enough to fill her aching lungs. Her ears began to ring and a buzzing sound whirled through her brain as he stood arguing with Roselee. Brianna moaned her protest as the dark shadows of unconsciousness floated down over her eyes and she slumped against Walker Ford.

Walker released Brianna's mouth as she went limp in his arms. He stared down at her, momentarily dumbfounded by her faint. He looked back to his sister. "Now look what you've made me go and do. I've killed the wench. Zeb ain't going to be none too happy about this little episode. He had it all arranged so we could make a pretty penny off her from Captain VanNess. He trades with them Eastern heatherns that pay a high price for white women for their brothels."

"I don't give a bloody damn what Zeb thinks. I paid you to get rid of her, and I don't care how you do it. If she's dead, give her to the crabs. If she's still breathing, do what you will with her as long as she's gone from Statia by daylight," Roselee said, closing the space between them. She touched Brianna's throat and felt a pulse. The girl wasn't dead, only unconscious. She eyed her brother with disgust. He was just like their pa. Too simple-minded to survive without someone telling him what to do. "The girl's not dead, but I suggest you get her on board Captain VanNess's ship before she recovers and begins to scream for help."

Roselee turned to the donkey cart once more. Seating herself with great aplomb, she took her time straightening her skirts about her before she looked once more toward her brother. Her face hardened as she threatened Walker, "I warn you, now. Don't make any mistakes with this one. Should anything happen, I will personally see you and Zeb hang for murder if I don't kill you first myself. I'm fighting for my life here, and I'll do anything to protect what I have worked so hard to gain. So make no mistake or it'll be your own life in jeopardy."

Walker lifted the limp girl into his arms. He didn't argue with Roselee. He knew her well enough to know she'd keep her threats. She had enough evidence on him and Zeb to get them hanged three times over. "I won't make any mistakes, Rosie. The girl will be sailing on the next tide."

Roselee smiled smugly, tossed Walker a bag of coins, and then clicked the reins against the donkey's back, urging him back in the direction they'd come earlier. She didn't see the dark-eyed man lounging in the shadows of the tavern doorway, well into his cups.

Nick noted Roselee's passing but thought little of it. Roarke had only left him a few minutes earlier after several hours of imbibing rum and whiskey, so he figured the woman had come in search of her lover. He glanced in the direction of the dark, sandy lane that led to the end of the wharf and noted a man carrying what looked like a heavy seaman's sack over his shoulder. The man passed through a pale beam of lantern light spilling through the doorway of the tavern across from the docks. Nick smiled as he realized the seaman's bag was in fact one of the dock whores who'd had too much rum and had passed out on her client. That sight, too, was nothing unusual. The whores who worked the docks often drank themselves oblivious.

With a hiccup and a glance toward the heavy-breasted tavern maid who sauntered provocatively into view, Nick put the matter from his mind. Let Roarke handle his mistress when she found him, and he'd handle the barmaid. Nick grinned. He'd handle all of her bountiful charms before the night was through.

Chapter 9

*"Where in hell is everybody?" Roarke called out drunk-*enly before giving a loud hiccup. He slammed the door behind him and staggered down the hallway to his study, where he promptly slouched into a leather wing-backed chair. Grimacing at not receiving a response from a soul living under his roof, he tugged off his boots and tossed them into the center of the floor. They thumped loudly against the ceramic tile. Roarke wiped a hand over his face to clear his vision and then shook his head before letting out another bellow. "I said, where in hell is everybody? Can't a man get a drink in his own house? Or am I not good enough to serve?"

His expression darkening as his subconscious re-leased his long-hidden insecurities, Roarke pushed him-self to his feet. He'd be damned if he had two women in his house and have to serve himself when he wanted a drink. That's why he provided them with a place to live and the food that they put in their bellies, especially Brianna. Roarke's frown deepened. He'd nearly drunk himself into a stupor tonight, but he still hadn't been able to get Brianna out of his mind. Their time together seemed embedded in his memory, and he couldn't let go of it no matter how he tried to turn his thoughts to more important matters. His temper rising as his determina-tion mounted to have it out with her once and for all,

Roarke staggered down the hallway toward Brianna's bedchamber.

"Brianna Tarleton, it's time you started earning your keep," he roared, pushing open the bedchamber door with such force that it slammed back against the wall. He held on to the doorframe, wavering back and forth as he squinted inside, trying to see through the darkness that hid the woman he'd come to see. "Brianna, damn it. Didn't you hear what I said? It's time you started earning your keep. Get your pretty little bottom out of that bed and pour me a drink."

Silence greeted Roarke's order. His rummed temper snapped. "Damn it, woman. Do I have to come and force you to obey me? I am master in my own home, and you'd best remember it if you want to stay here much longer."

Again silence. Fuming, his head foggy from the effects of the alcohol he'd consumed, Roarke made his way haphazardly through the obstacle course of furnishings toward the outline of the large four-poster bed. He stumbled over a small footstool, but a kick sent it spiraling across the tiled floor to land against the wall. Next came the chair. Too large to kick out of his path, he moved around it, cursing the recalcitrant piece of furniture beneath his breath. Finally he reached the bed. He felt for the object of his quest but found only smooth coverlet beneath his searching fingers.

"Brianna, where in hell are you? There's no use in hiding. You know I'll find you one way or the other. Come out now before you make me lose my temper."

Roarke received no answer. Puzzled, he fumbled about on the bedside table for flint and tinder to light the candles. After several attempts, nearly oversetting the crystal candle holder, he managed to light the wick. Golden light spilled about him, drenching his bemused features in warmth and revealing Brianna's empty bed. His gaze flicked over the room; he quickly determined that Brianna had not slept in her bed, nor did she occupy the chamber.

"Damn," Roarke muttered, his dark eyes narrowing suspiciously. "Where could she be?"

Roarke blew out the candle and turned toward the door. Roselee would know of Brianna's whereabouts. The woman had kept her under surveillance since he'd brought Brianna into his home. His steps still unsteady, Roarke made his way to the east wing, which he shared with his mistress. He slammed open his bedchamber door, expecting to see the heavy-bosomed woman lying in wait for him upon the satin counterpane, her many sexual charms exposed to his view.

Roarke shook his head to clear it as a glimmer of understanding began to surface through the fog of alcohol wreathing his mind. In all the months Roselee had been under his roof, he'd never looked upon their relationship as making love. They had had sex; good sex, he couldn't deny, but only sex. It was nothing like what he had experienced with Brianna on the beach that afternoon or even the first time at the inn. With Roselee he'd never known the well-being that had come over him as Brianna held him in her arms. Her touch had soothed and helped ease the dark void within him.

Roarke gave a snort of disgust at his maudlin thoughts. "Damn, I must be drunker than I thought if I'm beginning to believe Brianna has something to do with the way I feel. We had sex." He paused and grinned roguishly to himself. "Superior sex, but that's all it was, nothing more." He ignored the hollow sensation widening again with his declaration.

"Roselee," he called as he ventured into his bedchamber.

"What is it, Roarke?" Roselee gasped from behind him. Out of breath after rushing from the stables, where she'd left the donkey cart only moments before, she smiled enticingly at Roarke.

Roarke's eyes narrowed upon his mistress; he wondered at her flushed cheeks and heaving breasts. "Where have you been? I've been calling for you for hours."

"I took a walk. The night was far too beautiful to stay indoors."

"You know I want you here when I need you," Roarke grumbled. In his bemused state he didn't question Roselee's sudden interest in the beauty of the night when in the past she'd shown no particular concern for anything to do with nature beyond the bedchamber.

Roselee smiled. "I'm here now, Roarke." She slowly began to unlace her blouse as she seductively crossed the bedchamber toward him. Pausing in front of Roarke, she let the garment fall from her shoulders. She gave him ample time to view her breasts before raising her arms and looping them about his neck. She ran the tip of her tongue erotically over her full lips as she pressed her large breasts into his chest and moved against him, her hips fitting with his, her breasts rubbing against the material of his white shirt. Her voice held the heat of a tropical night as she murmured, "I'm here now Roarke. Let me taste you, let me feel you all over me, let me take you deep into my mouth and body."

An overwhelming sense of revulsion passed over Roarke as he looked down into her painted face. It took every ounce of strength he possessed not to shudder. Roselee's coarsely blatant seduction had once excited him. Now he found it repulsive after tasting Brianna's sweet innocence. Roarke pulled Roselee's arms from about his neck.

"I need a drink," he grumbled, moving past her toward the door. "Isn't there one damned servant in this house at this time of night?"

"I'll get you a drink," Roselee said sweetly, fighting to suppress the urge to stamp her feet in rage at his rejection. Before the little English slut entered Roarke's life, he would have immediately tumbled her onto the bed to have his way with her. He'd have given her no chance to disrobe further but would have tossed up her skirts and opened his britches, taking her violently with his feet still on the floor for leverage and his hands filled with the soft mounds of her breasts. His dark blue eyes would never leave her face as he watched her surrender to his need and her own passion.

"Then get it," Roarke demanded, his voice low with irritation. "I'm damned tired of having a house full of women and no one to greet me when I arrive or to offer me the comforts of my own home."

"I tried, but you refused," Roselee said before she could stop her wayward tongue. She readjusted her blouse and tied the ribbons at the neckline as she moved ahead of him and turned down the hallway to his study.

Roarke flashed her a heated look. "I'm in no mood for any female harangue tonight. This is my last night home, and I intend to spend it peacefully even if I have to throttle someone."

Roselee entered the study and crossed to the table that held the crystal decanters full of rum, brandy, and Scotch whiskey. She poured Roarke a drink and then moved back to where he'd once more slouched into the chair. She sank down on her knees at his side and handed him the drink. "I'm sorry, Roarke. I didn't mean to upset you. I want your last night at home to be happy, and I promise I'll do everything within my power to see that it is."

Roarke raised the drink to his lips and sipped the sweet brew of the islands. It slid smoothly down his throat, further warming his blood. He looked down at the woman seated at his feet. "Where is Brianna?"

Roselee shrugged without looking at him. "I don't know. She should be in her bed this late."

"She's not in her bed, nor has she been in it this night," Roarke said.

Roselee's heart began to race. "Perhaps she decided to take a walk as I did. The night is lovely."

Roarke glanced away from the dark head at his knee to the moon-drenched balcony beyond the slatted doors. The moon had finally crept over the horizon, spreading its silver light across the countryside and bathing the night in splendor. Nature's perfume of hibiscus, oleander, jasmine, and rose scented the evening air with a sweetness that stirred the blood.

Roarke released a long breath and downed the last of the rum. How he'd like to make love to Brianna in the moonlit garden before he sailed away on the *Black Angel*. The thought of the magnificent night combined with Brianna's exquisite beauty rocked his senses to the core. His sex hardened even as a curse left his lips, and he came abruptly to his feet. He turned on the woman looking up at him, wanting to vent his passion upon her but knowing his body would not allow him to couple with anyone but the woman it craved with every fiber of his being.

Roarke turned abruptly and crossed to the table. He refilled his glass and tossed the rum down his throat as if it were water. Again he poured himself a sizable drink. He looked back to Roselee. "Sleep in your own chamber tonight. I need a full night's sleep to rest me before I set sail tomorrow evening."

Hiding her fury well, Roselee came to her feet and

stood on tiptoes to place a warm kiss on Roarke. She tasted his closed lips with the tip of her tongue before she smiled up at him. "I know you need your rest. Sleep well, my darling Roarke. I want you to return to Statia healthy and ready to see me again."

"Good night, Roselee," Roarke said, suppressing the grimace her touch created. "We'll speak in the morning about my return."

Blowing him a kiss off the tips of her fingers, Roselee made her way back to her own bedchamber. Once the door closed behind her, her fury broke loose in a blind rage. She crossed to the sewing box sitting by the chair and grabbed a pair of scissors. Eyes narrowed, she moved toward the bed. She lashed out at the pillows, stabbing viciously, mentally killing her rival time and again, mutilating her as she wished she had done before allowing Walker to have her. When she finished, the room looked like a chicken market with piles of downy feathers on the slashed counterpane and floor.

At last tears came to relieve the pressure building behind her eyes. They ran down her cheeks as she stared at the mess she'd made of her bedchamber. When no more moisture would come, she wiped her eyes, crossed to the dressing table, and viewed her disheveled, red- and swollen-eyed image.

"You may not want me, Roarke. But I've seen to it that you will never have her either," Roselee said triumphantly to her reflection, and then smiled coldly. Emotion spent, she could again think reasonably. When Roarke returned, he'd need her body, and she'd be waiting. However, she might just punish him a tiny bit for putting her through the hell of the past few days and the trouble to get rid of Brianna Tarleton. Roselee's smile deepened. Yes, dear Roarke would pay. She'd come away with more gowns to add to her nest egg. She could see him now. He'd be very apologetic and very generous when he returned to Statia ready to satisfy himself upon her body.

The morning sun spilled into the study, rousing Roarke from his inebriated slumber. He squinted against the blinding light and grimaced at the pain that shot through his skull. He raised a hand to shield his eyes from the torturous sunlight. Lips curling downward at the corners, he made a moue of disgust. His dry mouth tasted like a week-old fish smelled. His stomach rebelled at the thought, rumbling and churning threateningly beneath his ribs.

"Damn!" Roarke swore, pushing himself out of the chair where he'd spent the night. His muscles screamed in protest from the hours of being sprawled at odd angles. Roarke winced as he staggered toward the table and poured himself a glass of fresh fruit juice a servant had brought without disturbing his sleep.

Downing the tangy drink, Roarke didn't move until his stomach accepted the offering and quieted. Feeling somewhat better, he drew in a deep breath and turned his attention to the study, puzzled. Why had he spent the night in his chair instead of his own bed? It took a few moments to dredge up his last conscious minutes and his drunken thoughts before he passed out in the chair.

Roarke frowned. He'd waited for Brianna, but she had not returned before he had either passed out or fallen asleep. She had not returned! The words slammed into Roarke's brain, setting him into motion as an apprehensive chill careened down his spine. His bare feet made no sound on the tiled floor as he hurried toward Brianna's bedchamber in the west wing. His heart nearly stopped when he saw the empty bed.

Roarke braced an arm against the doorframe and leaned his brow against it, trying to organize his thoughts over the throbbing ache in his temples. It was obvious Brianna hadn't returned from her walk, but where was she? What had happened to her? Had she decided after their time together on the beach that she could no longer stay under the same roof with him? The questions boiled in Roarke's brain, each one more unanswerable than the last.

"But I'll find out if it's the last thing I ever do," Roarke swore, pushing himself erect. He cast one last glance around the bedchamber before he turned and started bellowing orders to the servants at the top of his lungs. He'd search every inch of Statia to find Brianna. But he'd start with the grounds of his own home in the event that an accident had befallen her.

In less than an hour the search had ended. Sitting behind his large desk, his face pale and haggard from his indulgence the previous night, his expression reflecting his exasperation, Roarke listened to the last servant's report and dismissed the man before he slammed a fist down on the polished wood to vent his frustration. No clue had been found to indicate that Brianna had taken a walk last night. She'd vanished from the face of the earth.

"That's impossible," Roarke growled, coming to his feet as the study door swung open to reveal his second in command.

"What's impossible?" Nick asked as he sauntered into the room, looking immaculate in his clean shirt and tight nankeen britches. He didn't appear to have had any ill effects from his night spent carousing on the waterfront.

"Brianna's disappeared," Roarke said.

"What happened? Did you two have a lovers' spat?"

Nick asked, a shrewd little smile curling up the corners of his shapely lips.

Roarke's mood blackened. "Nick, I warn you. Don't test our friendship today. I'm in no mood for your jabs. My head feels as if it's ready to leave my shoulders at any moment, and Brianna has disappeared. Now, if you've come to help me find her, you can stay. If not, you'd best leave before I say or do something that an apology can't amend."

Nick's smiled faded. "You're serious? The girl is gone?"

"She wasn't here when I returned home last night, but Roselee said she'd gone for a walk. I waited for her, but she didn't return," Roarke said, mentally flagellating himself for falling asleep before he could assure himself that she was safe in her own bed. He crossed to the balcony doors and stared out at the bay in the distance. Though the day was clear, gray clouds tinted the horizon, forecasting turbulent weather. Roarke paid no heed, his thoughts centered upon Brianna instead of the conditions that might affect his setting sail with the evening's tide.

"I don't see why you're so upset. Didn't she tell you she intended to leave here as soon as possible?" Nick asked.

The frown creasing Roarke's handsome brow deepened.

"Aye. She said she wanted to leave, but Brianna is not the type to abscond in the middle of the night. She'd hold her head up, square her shoulders, and walk away in broad daylight, daring anyone to say her nay," Roarke said, his voice reflecting his respect for the woman who had given herself to him with such passion. In all of his dealings with Brianna, she had as yet to show any weakness. She didn't simper or whine. She stood her ground, giving as good as she got, whether in anger or passion.

Roarke looked back over his shoulder at his friend. "I have to find her, Nick. I need to assure myself that she's safe before we sail tonight."

"Even if she doesn't want you to find her?" Nick asked, suddenly realizing by Roarke's tone that he'd been right about his friend's feelings for the girl.

Roarke nodded, though the thought edged the void within him wider.

"Then we'll find her," Nick said reassuringly, and smiled with confidence.

"Aye. We'll find her. And when we do, I'm going to wring that pretty, ungrateful little neck of hers," Roarke answered resolutely.

Roarke sank down in the chair and lifted the tankard of ale to his lips. He took a deep swallow as his gaze once more swept over the docks. From his vantage point in front of the tavern window, he could view most of the wharf.

"Well, it looks as if your lady has vanished from Statia as if she'd never set foot upon it," Nick said after taking a refreshing drink to quench his thirst. The heat of the afternoon had settled oppressively across the island, and anyone with any sense stayed inside, out of the sun. He looked at his friend. They had been searching Statia from one end to the other since that morning. As had most of the *Black Angel*'s crew. Roarke had set them to work looking for Brianna soon after their arrival at the docks.

"No one can just up and disappear. There has to be some clue to where she's gone. Someone has seen her or knows of her whereabouts," Roarke said, setting his own tankard back upon the scarred tabletop. He absently traced one of the deep knife grooves that marked the wood as he scanned the docks once more.

"So it would seem, but we've asked nearly everyone who lives on the island if they've seen the girl, and no one has."

Roarke's indigo eyes narrowed. "Someone knows something, but they're not telling."

"It's hard to keep a secret on an island as small as Statia. Sailors are much like old women. They love to gossip. A woman with Brianna's looks wouldn't go unnoticed, *mon ami*."

"Aye, we'd hear it if she'd come openly to the waterfront. But if she didn't want to be seen, she could easily have disguised herself or left the island."

"She's not left the island by ship. There's only been one that sailed since yesterday, and that was Captain VanNess's *Sea Dragon*."

A furrow of worry plowed a crease across Roarke's brow. "VanNess?"

"Aye. The *Sea Dragon* sailed with last night's tide."

Roarke's frown deepened and a chill streaked down his spine. "Surely Brianna wouldn't have been foolish enough to board VanNess's vessel. A woman like her would be worth a fortune to a bastard like him."

Nick lifted his shoulders in a non-committal gesture. "Don't ask me, Roarke. You know the girl far better than I do. If you will recall, I spent only an hour or so with her."

Roarke couldn't shake off the foreboding sensation making the hair prickle at his nape. He shook his head in denial. "She had no reason to flee. We had begun to settle things between us. I had even offered her the use of my home while we were away."

"I bet your offer really set well with Roselee. No wonder she came to the docks last night looking for you. She thought you were with Brianna," Nick said before taking a deep draft of ale.

Roarke's gaze locked on Nick's face. "What are you talking about? Roselee was waiting for me when I got home."

"Then she must have wings," Nick said, one side of his mouth curving into a sarcastic grin. "Because I saw her down here last night after you'd left me to enjoy myself with sweet Flora's charms."

"You have to be mistaken, Nick. Roselee was at the house when I returned."

"I admit we drank pretty heavily last eve, but I know your mistress when I see her. She was driving the donkey cart."

The suspicion his rum-fogged mind had refused to acknowledge the previous night again reared its head and struck out at Roarke. His face darkened. "Was anyone else with her?"

"No. She came out of the lane at the end of the wharf." Nick paused, recalling the man he'd seen with the woman tossed over his shoulder. His own expression grew grim. "But there was a seaman who followed her a few minutes later. He was carrying one of the dockside whores over his shoulder."

A chill of premonition careened down Roarke's spine. Somehow Roselee was involved in Brianna's disappearance. Roarke came to his feet, tossed a few coins on the table, and turned toward the door without waiting for Nick.

Nick followed quickly upon Roarke's heels. "What are you thinking?"

Roarke flashed his friend an ominous look. "I think my sweet little whore knows far more about Brianna's disappearance than she told me this morning when I questioned her."

"Surely the woman's jealousy wouldn't force her to have Brianna shipped out on VanNess's ship. Knowing the fate of the cargo VanNess takes to the East, no woman could do that to another."

"Roselee could. The woman thinks only of herself."

"Bloody Jesus, Roarke. The woman shares your bed."

"Aye. She shares my bed, but she also doesn't give a rip-roaring damn about me beyond what she can get. She sells every gown I buy for her."

Nick gaped at his friend. "You know what she does and you haven't said anything about it?"

Roarke shook his head. "Why should I? The gowns cost me no more than I'd have given her for her services if she'd only asked to be recompensed. It's a game between us that she thinks she's winning." Roarke's face grew grim. "But I'm afraid she's played this hand too far if she's behind Brianna's disappearance. I won't countenance such treachery from anyone."

Roarke towered over the woman seated in the high-backed chair with head bowed and hands clasped tightly in her lap. Nick silently watched and listened as his friend interrogated her relentlessly.

"It would be best for all concerned if you'd tell me the truth, Roselee," Roarke said, his tone giving the woman no leeway.

"I've told you the truth, Roarke. I know nothing of the girl's whereabouts. The last time I saw her was when I went for a walk last night."

Roarke's face darkened with anger. His fingers itched to jerk Roselee from the chair and shake the truth out of her. He flexed them, opening and closing the fist at his side as he stared down at the bright head before him. Roarke abruptly crossed to the brandy table and poured himself a drink before he could succumb to the urge.

Violence would do no good on a woman like Roselee. She'd grown up on the docks and was used to such methods from men.

Roarke tossed the amber liquid down his throat, flashed Nick a grim look that said he'd have the truth before he was done, and then crossed back to where his mistress sat. "Roselee, there's no use lying. You didn't go for a walk last night, you went to the waterfront. You were seen by a very reliable source, and so was your cohort. All I want to know from you is why you'd have Brianna taken to VanNess. You know exactly what type of man he is and the cargo he trades in."

Roselee's composure broke. Her head snapped up and her black eyes glittered with all the malice she felt. Her scarlet-painted lips curled in a sneer. "I had her sent with VanNess because I know what's been going on between the two of you. I'm not blind. I know you want that little slut, because all you do is sniff after her like a dog after a bitch in heat. You won't even look at me anymore. You haven't slept with me since you brought that bitch into this house."

The fury Roarke had been restraining erupted with the force of an exploding volcano. His eyes flashed with blue fire as he turned to Nick and ground out between clenched teeth, "Get her out of here, Nick, before I lose what little control I have left." He looked once more at Roselee. "Take what money you've hoarded from the gowns you've sold and get out. I never want to lay eyes on you again."

Roselee's bravado vanished. She paled with the realization that she'd allowed herself to tell Roarke the truth. She slid from the chair and grabbed Roarke about the knees. Tears spilled down her cheeks as she looked up at him and pleaded, "Please, Roarke. Don't send me away. I love you."

Roarke looked contemptuously at the woman wrapped about his legs like a succulent vine that drains the lifeblood of its host. All the revulsion he felt was reflected in his face as he ground out, "You love like all whores, Roselee. The emotion lasts only until the next man comes along. Now, get out."

Roselee shook her head violently. "I did it for us, Roarke. She couldn't have made you happy. With her simpering ways, Brianna was not woman enough for you. Didn't you realize that after making love to her yesterday afternoon?"

Memories flooded Roarke's mind, spurring a swift, unusual ache in his chest. "Roselee, Brianna is far more a woman than you'll ever be. She knows how to give of herself without expecting to be paid for her passion." Roarke bent and pried Roselee's arms from about his legs. "Nick, get her out of here. When she's off the property, come back. I'll have new orders for you and the crew."

The smug, knowing expression that Roselee's words had brought to Nick's face faded into a puzzled frown. His brows drew together across the bridge of his narrow nose. "Are you going after the *Sea Dragon*?"

"Aye. Brianna's in jeopardy." Roarke moved behind his desk and seated himself in the large, well-worn leather chair. He didn't look at his ex-mistress again as Nick led her from the room, crying out his name and begging his forgiveness. He was too engrossed in charting the *Black Angel*'s new course. Fortunately, his ship was already provisioned for the journey to France.

Roarke rubbed the back of his neck as he stared down at the paper in front of him. VanNess was less than twenty-four hours ahead of him. If all went well, he'd manage to catch the *Sea Dragon* and rescue Brianna once more without putting his mission to France in jeopardy.

Roarke rubbed at the dull ache in his temples. It seemed his real mission in life had become one of rescuing the beautiful vixen from one disaster after another. He couldn't stop himself from wondering what it was about this one woman that made him react so protectively. In the past he'd helped women down on their luck, starving children who reminded him of himself on the docks in Yorktown, as well as old salts who had nothing to show for the years of abuse at sea. After doing his good deeds, he'd left them behind without a second thought. However, he was finding Brianna Tarleton was an entirely different story. She brought out all his protective instincts whether he liked them or not. He couldn't just put her out of his thoughts and walk away.

Chapter 10

Becalmed, the ocean looked like glass. No whisper of a breeze stirred its still surface or filled the *Black Angel*'s canvas as she sat like a great black heron, perched for flight but needing assistance from the wind to lift her great wings and fly across the waters. The liquid mirror reflected the brilliant sunset, making the world surrounding the black-hulled ship into spun gold. Heaven and earth blended, wrapping the *Black Angel* and her crew in an eerie, unearthly atmosphere as they waited beneath the improvised awnings for the elements to set them once more free from the invisible bonds that held them imprisoned.

The golden loop in Roarke's ear gleamed even brighter as he stared intently out across the smooth surface surrounding his ship. His knuckles whitened as he gripped the mahogany rail and swore, "Damn, if I had used my head, I'd have kept the *Black Angel* in Gallows Bay until after the storm passed. But no; I thought we could easily sail through it."

"And we did, *mon ami*. We just took a small detour when we were blown off course," Nick said, a wry grin curling his sensuous lips.

Roarke ran his hand over his beard-shadowed cheek and shook his head in exasperation. "I don't know what I thought to accomplish with such a decision." He flashed his friend a disgruntled look. "I don't know what's gotten into me."

Nick chuckled knowingly. "I do. And she's named Brianna."

Roarke frowned. "Don't be ridiculous. Brianna has nothing to do with the way I've been acting. I've just had too much on my mind of late. That's all."

Again Nick chuckled. "*Mon ami*, you may refuse to recognize the truth, but I don't. You've allowed the girl to worm her way into your heart." Nick shook his head at the indignant look that crossed Roarke's swarthy features. He raised a hand. "No. Don't deny it. Because I won't believe a word you say. A man does not go chasing halfway across the world for a woman he doesn't love."

"This man does," Roarke snapped, shifting his troubled indigo gaze back to the quiet ocean surrounding them. "And this predicament now proves how big a fool I am for making that decision. If the wind doesn't pick up soon, everything will have been for naught. VanNess will have reached port, and it will be too late to save Brianna. She'll be sent to the interior to become the concubine of some Arab sheik or she'll be sold to a brothel that peddles white flesh. Either way, we'll never find her."

A look of disgust crossed Roarke's features as he turned his face up toward the cloudless sky. "And if the wind doesn't pick up soon, we'll also miss our rendezvous with Beaumarchais."

"Perhaps the *Sea Dragon* is also becalmed," Nick said, offering his friend a glimmer of hope as he gave Roarke a brotherly, though less than gentle, pat on the shoulder.

Roarke glanced sideways at his friend and smiled. "I

can only hope we'll find Brianna and then make it to France in time to secure the arms that are awaiting us."

"*Mon ami*, the fates have as yet to desert you. You've always had the luck of the devil with anything you've set your mind on. This time will be no different. You'll get your Brianna back as well as meet with Beaumarchais."

"She's not my Brianna. I have no claim upon her," Roarke said, though somewhere deep inside, Nick's words felt all too right to him.

"No? You certainly could have fooled me. I've never seen you so set on protecting any woman's virtue like you have the beautiful Brianna's. If you will recall, you denied even to me, a man who is like a brother to you, that there was anything between the two of you. However, I was there when you didn't even attempt to deny Roselee's accusations about sleeping with the girl."

"What I do or don't do is my business and no one else's."

"True, friend. But you have to admit that with this girl, you've not acted like the man I've always known. In the past I would have been the first to know you'd had sex with her."

Irritation flushing his features a deeper hue, Roarke looked Nick squarely in the eye. He didn't like the comparison of what he and Brianna had shared to what he had had with other women. A muscle worked in his cheek as he ground out between clenched teeth, "I made love to Brianna."

Nick could no longer suppress his smile. He clapped Roarke on the shoulder good-naturedly. "That's exactly what I've been saying. In the past you had sex with whores, but with Brianna, you made love. You're the one who's made the difference between the women in your past and the woman who has found a place in your heart. Deny it all you like, *mon ami*, but you've fallen in love."

"And you've finally lost what few wits you possessed," Roarke said, lifting his face to the first, minuscule breeze to ruffle his dark hair in three days. He smiled. "It would seem the fates heard you boast that they'd not desert us. The wind is rising."

Roarke turned away from Nick and started giving orders to the men who had been lounging on deck. The heat and humidity within the *Black Angel* was debilitating, with no breeze to ease it. In an attempt to find some relief, the men had constructed makeshift awnings for shade against the blinding orange ball overhead.

Nick paused momentarily to watch his friend stride across the deck to the wheel. As he'd said, the fates had as yet to desert Roarke O'Connor. Though he knew of Roarke's heritage and life before going to sea, Nick still envied the man. Roarke had God or the Devil on his side at all times. Nick suspected the latter but would eagerly have exchanged places with his friend and captain. Roarke had charm, ability, and a mind so agile that there were few men or women who could outwit him.

Nick's smile deepened as he turned to the duties at hand. He wasn't so certain that Roarke hadn't finally run up against a woman who was his equal. Brianna Tarleton had managed what hundreds of other women had tried to do but failed. She had captured the heart of a man who swore he had none.

Nick's smile dimmed as he made his way down to the deck below. He prayed they'd not be too late to rescue the girl. He didn't know what Roarke's reaction would be should they fail. He didn't want to even consider it. Knowing his friend as he did, Roarke would probably declare war upon the heathens in an attempt to save her.

At the present time, Roarke had enough wars to fight without adding the Barbary states to his list.

Brianna swiped the beads of sweat from her brow and moistened her dry lips with the tip of her tongue as she stared out at the still water. The *Sea Dragon* was locked in an eerie realm in the middle of the ocean. Held by the invisible hands of nature, she was unable to do more than drift with the current that flowed beneath the quiet surface.

Brianna glanced toward the golden horizon and once more wondered how many days she'd been at sea. She truly didn't know how long she'd remained insensible after the captain ordered her drugged soon after she'd regained consciousness and realized she was being held captive. Under the influence of the opiate that had numbed her senses until she was little more than a biddable lump, she'd been unaware of the passage of time as well as her surroundings. When she had finally been allowed to regain her senses, she'd found the *Sea Dragon* imprisoned by the sea.

Brianna absently scratched at her itching skin before she realized her own actions and jerked her offending hand away. The stinging burn that followed as a result of her scratching quickly reminded her of the price she was paying for her incarceration in the tiny, hot, fetid cabin. The humid atmosphere made it hard to even draw in a deep breath. It had also prickled her skin with a red heat rash.

Brianna clamped her teeth together and fought to suppress the urge to claw at the irritation that speckled her skin. It itched unbearably. It took every ounce of willpower she possessed to keep from succumbing. She balled her fists at her side and drew in a determined breath as she battled the impulse that she knew would only add to her misery.

Brianna turned away from the porthole and purposely crossed to the locked door. As she'd done often in the past miserable days, she began to beat her fists against the panel. She'd found that venting her frustration and anger also helped ease her need to claw at her abused skin.

"Let me out of here!" she demanded for what seemed like the thousandth time. No answer came to her cry, nor had she truly expected one. Since she'd regained consciousness, she'd seen only the cabin boy twice a day when he brought her the unpalatable mess that the *Sea Dragon*'s cook called food. She'd begged to be allowed to speak with the captain, but her pleas had gone unheeded. She'd remained locked in the little oven to bake alive.

Brianna hit the door and added a kick for good measure before she once more began to pace the five-by-five-foot space that was her prison. She now understood why wild animals constantly roamed their tiny cages after their capture. Like herself, they knew it was a futile gesture; there was no escape. But also like herself, they couldn't stop or allow themselves to give up hope, or they knew they would die.

Agitation furrowing her brow, Brianna paused to look out the porthole once more. She smiled grimly. It was ironic that she had once dreamed of adventure, had even been eager for it only a few short months ago. Then within a few moments one tragic event had thrust her out into a world where adventure was only another name for the very deadly game of survival of the strongest.

Brianna squeezed her eyes closed against the golden brightness that cloaked the world in its eerie glow. Had she known what lay in her future, she would have told Roarke of her love for him on the fateful day when she'd realized her feelings. Now she would never have the chance. Her fate had already been decided by the man who ruled the *Sea Dragon*.

Brianna still trembled at the thought of what she'd overheard yesterday. Two of the *Sea Dragon*'s crew had been working in the passageway beyond her cabin door. As they worked, they discussed their destination and the fate awaiting her. They'd laughed and boasted to each other about what they would do with the extra wages they'd receive when the *Sea Dragon* reached the Barbary coast and she was sold to the highest bidder.

Brianna's shoulders sagged at the thought. She had no hope of rescue. Roarke would think nothing of her disappearance. She had vowed to do everything within her power to leave him when he'd forced her to go to his home. That promise combined with Roselee's lies would effectively assure that Roarke wouldn't follow. In fact, he was probably relieved to be finally rid of her.

Brianna released a long, desolate breath. She had sought to avoid punishment for murdering Lord Montague, but fate had decreed that she wouldn't escape. She would still pay for her crimes, though she would not be fortunate enough to hang. She would still breathe; her heart would still beat, but once she was sold into slavery, her life in truth would be over just as surely as if she'd died. Unfortunately death would not come fast enough to free her of the horrors awaiting her in the East. And she feared that before God saw fit to release her from this life, she would be forced to endure hell on earth.

Brianna felt the ship abruptly lurch beneath her feet, and her heart froze at the sudden motion. The wind had finally come to fill the *Sea Dragon*'s limp sails. With it also came the realization that with each league the vessel crossed, the nearer she came to her fate.

Brianna clung to the porthole and gasped in the refreshing air but felt no sense of relief from the cool breeze that stole into the hot cabin. She wished she had the courage to kill herself before being sold into slavery. However, she knew she didn't. The same force that had made her flee Montvale after defending herself against Lord Montague's attack wouldn't surrender to defeat even now. Nor would it allow her to extinguish the hope that still glimmered just beyond the edge of the dark clouds of despair that overshadowed her. Though dulled by reality and the nearly insurmountable odds against succeeding, the irrepressible light of hope still glowed and refused to allow her to give up.

The breeze grew stronger and the sails crackled and snapped as they caught the wind. Captain VanNess's brittle voice could be heard over the flapping canvas as he shouted orders to the crew. A flurry of activity followed his commands as the men scurried to obey.

"God, please let Roarke see the truth and come for me," Brianna whispered, her tortured thoughts making her voice hoarse. Logic told her it was ridiculous to believe he would come, but her heart wouldn't let go of the dream as she stared intently at the horizon as if to forcibly will the *Black Angel* into existence.

The golden sky grew muted and soon faded into mauve as evening approached. Brianna remained at the porthole like a sentinel on guard. Something she couldn't name held her there. She knew it was unreasonable, but she felt closer to Roarke.

The last light of the day had already begun its stealthful journey toward the horizon when Brianna first saw the full sails appear. She couldn't see the entire vessel, but every fiber of her being told her that the sails belonged to the *Black Angel*. Her heart lodged in her throat. Afraid to believe what she saw, she blinked several times and then rubbed her eyes to clear her vision. When she looked again, the image had not disappeared and grew larger as the minutes passed.

"Roarke," was Brianna's breathless cry. Her heart thumped wildly within her breast as a wave of joy surged upward, buoying her spirits. Her velvet eyes glistened with tears.

"Roarke, you've come for me," she whispered, her words sending her heart on another wild race about her rib cage.

Overhead Captain VanNess began hurling orders at his crew to man the battle stations. Fear jerked Brianna out of her joyful stupor. The dangerous reality that Roarke and his men faced hit her like a wet rag, wiping out her excitement. Brianna's heart froze with apprehension a few moments later when she watched the *Black Angel* come around, her gunports open, ready to broadside the *Sea Dragon* if necessary.

A flag of parley inched its way up the *Black Angel*'s mainmast. Though she couldn't see the response, she suspected Captain VanNess had answered in kind to the request for a meeting, because a few minutes later a small boat was lowered from the *Black Angel*.

Brianna paid no heed to the six burly sailors who clambered down the rope ladder to man the oars. She had eyes only for the tall, dark-haired captain who gracefully descended and took his place in the prow of the small boat. At the sight of the man she loved, her heart took wings, soaring toward the heavens. God had answered her prayers.

Intent upon the negotiations ahead of him, his eyes on the quarterdeck where Captain VanNess awaited, Roarke didn't see the pale little face staring at him from the porthole as he neared the *Sea Dragon*. He gripped the thick hemp with strong, long-fingered hands. The powerful muscles in his arms and chest bulged against the fine lawn of his shirt as he agilely climbed the rope ladder to the deck above. Looking every inch the rogue pirate, Roarke came face-to-face with the master of the *Sea Dragon*. Earring flashing in the evening light, a rakish grin curling his sensuous mouth to reveal the even white teeth that contrasted with the swarthy hue of his sun-bronzed skin, he doffed his hat with a graceful sweep.

"Captain VanNess, it has been a long time since our paths have crossed."

VanNess, his hostility evident by the hard expression that had frozen his pockmarked features into a grimace, eyed Roarke with loathing. "Not long enough, O'Connor. Now, get on with it. I know you didn't stop my ship just to pay a friendly visit, especially since we are not friends."

Roarke's cool smile faded and his tone reflected his icy contempt. "You're right, VanNess. We're not friends."

"Now that that's settled," VanNess snapped, "why are you here?"

"You have something which belongs to me," Roarke answered, comfortably repeating Nick's words.

"You must be mad," VanNess growled, wondering at Roarke's scheme. If he thought he could come on board the *Sea Dragon* and walk away with the cargo without a fight, the pirate was in for a surprise. He wouldn't leave the *Sea Dragon* alive. VanNess had already made certain of that arrangement. At his signal, the pirate would die from the pistol trained on his back.

"I'm not mad, Captain. I'm just determined to take back what is mine. You can either surrender it willingly or have it taken from you." Roarke's smile returned, yet there was no warmth in the gesture for the Dutch captain.

"And you can tell your men that they don't have a chance even if they're lucky enough to kill me. I've left instructions that the *Sea Dragon* is to be sunk with all on board if I should not return with my goods. As you and your men already know, you are outgunned and outmanned." Roarke paused to give his threat time to take root in the crew's minds. He flashed a warning look over the men assembled about their captain. "I make no empty threats. My second in command has fifteen guns now trained on the *Sea Dragon*."

"I'm telling you, O'Connor. I don't have anything that belongs to you," VanNess said, unable to hold his ground under Roarke's icy stare. He knew O'Connor's reputation and didn't doubt the man would do exactly as he had said.

"If I'm not mistaken, you have a young woman on board," Roarke said, his words laced with steely intent that brooked no argument.

"I . . . yes, but she's a passenger. She's not cargo," VanNess said, desperately trying to hold on to the most valuable thing on board the *Sea Dragon*. The girl was worth a fortune in gold.

"Then you're very fortunate. You'll earn her passage without being troubled by her company," Roarke said, and grinned sarcastically. He flashed the man standing at VanNess's side a withering look that sent a chill down the man's spine. "Go get the girl."

The man flashed his captain a helpless, uneasy look before he turned and hurried away.

"You have no right to order my men about," VanNess seethed.

Roarke shrugged. "Perhaps. But I don't have all day to await your order, Captain."

"You're going to regret this, O'Connor."

Roarke arched a dark brow. "Should I take that as a threat, Captain?"

"No. It's a promise," VanNess swore, his face flushing a dull red.

Unconcerned, his eyes locked to the hatch where Brianna would exit, Roarke shrugged again. "So be it."

A few moments later Brianna followed the sailor onto the deck. Her eyes went to the man who had come for her. In all his glory Roarke stood like a bronzed god. He exuded power and confidence over the poor, weak mortals surrounding him.

Brianna's heart surged with pride and love. She wanted to throw herself into his arms and weep with joy, but the warning look he flashed her stayed the impulse before it was completely born. Slowly she followed the sailor to where Roarke stood.

Never letting down his guard, Roarke took Brianna by the hand and drew her to his side. He eyed the captain of the *Sea Dragon* grimly. "VanNess, I seriously doubt you'll ever know just how truly lucky you are. However, I would suggest that in the future you refrain from dealing in human flesh."

"Damn you to hell, you bloody pirate. You have no say on what I do," VanNess growled, his fury overcoming his fear.

"So very true. But I can make you live to regret going against my wishes." Roarke gave VanNess a look that chilled even the heartiest of the *Sea Dragon*'s crew before he smiled again to reveal the gleam of white teeth. "Now, gentlemen, I will bid you good day. If you will excuse me and my lady, we will leave you to be on your merry way."

No man on the *Sea Dragon* made a move to stop Roarke as he lifted Brianna into his arms and easily made his way down the ladder where the small boat awaited to take them back to the *Black Angel*.

Roarke didn't release Brianna when they reached his ship. He gave orders to set the *Black Angel* on its original course to France before he carried her down to the cabin that they had shared weeks ago. He kicked the door closed behind them and leaned back against the wooden panel as he stood holding Brianna, savoring the feel of her once more in his arms.

Brianna clung to Roarke, burying her face in the curve of his throat. She had thought she could feel no deeper emotions for this man, but she had been mistaken. Now in the safety of his arms, she never wanted to leave them again. This man had risked his life for her, and her love for him knew no bounds.

Gently Roarke set her from him and stood looking down into her lovely face for what seemed an eternity. Even through the evening shadows he sought to absorb the loveliness that he had been denied during the month that they had been separated by the storm and the calm.

Tenderly he raised a hand to cup her cheek. Gently he brushed her skin with the pad of his thumb, enchanted by the feel of her warm flesh. His eyes sought out the sweet curves of her mouth. Unable to deny himself a moment longer, he slowly lowered his head, eager to taste the sweetness of her lips again as well as to reclaim the sense of well-being her touch always created within him.

Brianna wrapped her arms about his neck and returned his kiss with equal ardor. She molded her soft form to his hard frame and felt secure. She had come home.

With a moan of desire, Roarke crushed her to his

throbbing body. He devoured the mouth that could so easily make him lose all reason. His hands possessively captured Brianna's buttocks, pressing her against his hardened sex; instinctively he rubbed his hips against hers in the age-old expression of need.

Fiery currents of electricity shot through Brianna as she felt Roarke's arousal. She gasped as his lips left hers and he buried his face against her breasts. The feel of his hot breath through the material of her gown made her press closer to the heat. Her nipples hardened into firm buds that ached for the touch of his lips.

"God, Brianna. How I want you," Roarke said, lifting her into his arms and laying her down on the large bed in one swift movement. His gaze never left hers as he slowly unlaced her gown and opened it to expose the swollen mounds of her breasts. He swallowed with difficulty as his eyes drifted downward and came to rest upon her dimly lit flesh. Tenderly he cupped one breast, once more savoring her satiny skin before surrendering to his need to taste her. He came onto the bed beside her and lowered his mouth to the tempting peak. As he suckled her sweetness, his hands worked her gown downward. Divesting her of the garment, he tossed it away. His hands wandered at will over her flat belly and the swell of her hips as he began a slow, enjoyable descent with his lips and tongue.

Brianna stiffened under his caress and bit back the cry of pain that careened to her lips as Roarke's hand roused the demon in her skin. Feeling her withdrawal, Roarke looked up, puzzled. Seeing the expression that mirrored her pain, he instinctively sought out the reason for her reaction. Roarke swore under his breath at the sight of the red rash covering her skin. The soft expression in his eyes dimmed as his face turned grim. His words were filled with all the fury he felt as he growled, "I'll blow the bastard out of the water for this."

Roarke made to rise to carry out his threat, but Brianna stayed him. She shook her head as she pushed herself upright and looked down at her fingers. Again she envisioned Lord Montague's blood staining her hands. Her voice shook as she whispered, "Please, Roarke. I don't want any man to die because of me . . ." She choked back her final words before she could voice them: *ever again*. She looked up at Roarke with haunted eyes. "Let it be. I am safe now, thanks to you. And my skin will heal with time."

Tenderly Roarke captured Brianna's chin and lightly brushed his lips against hers. "You forgive far too easily, my sweet. But I will do as you ask."

"Thank you, Roarke," Brianna said, her heart in her eyes.

Roarke's own smile deepened. "Caution, sweet. If you look at me like that too much, I may forget that you're in no condition for my lovemaking."

Brianna thought her heart would burst from the surge of pleasure that washed over her at Roarke's words. Her lips twitched. "I'll do my best to heed your warning, Captain O'Connor."

Roarke rolled his eyes heavenward. Her expression was nearly his undoing. He cleared his throat and pushed himself off the bed. "It's time to see to your skin. You need a soda bath. It will soothe the rash and hopefully help heal your skin." He grinned and raised one dark brow roguishly. "The sooner the better, in my opinion."

Brianna caught herself before she scratched at the ridge of red pimples that circled her waist. She grimaced at the effort it took to control the urge. "That is also my opinion, sir."

Seeing the torment in her eyes, Roarke quickly gave orders for a bath and a meal to be prepared. He ordered the water left at the door, possessively guarding Brianna's privacy by allowing no one into the cabin while she was undressed. He expertly handled the preparations for her bath alone, dumping the buckets of water into the large, brass-bound tub before adding the soft white healing powder that cook used to make the biscuits rise.

When he finished, he lifted Brianna carefully into his arms and, as if caring for an injured child, lowered her into the soothing water. Scrupulous with his ministrations, he washed her limbs. At last he lathered her dark mane of hair and rinsed it free of soap before he made her stand.

Roarke's breath caught in his throat at the vision before him. She was naked as the day God had seen fit to bless the earth with her beauty, her body shimmering with beads of moisture, her expression soft and relaxed from his ministrations, her dark hair clinging to her curves like threads of gleaming silk. Roarke realized he'd never seen anything as beautiful as Brianna Tarleton. His body responded instantly to the sight of her, throbbing with each strong beat of his heart to know the soft warmth of hers. Roarke quickly wrapped Brianna in a large towel and lifted her from the tub before he could succumb to the heat cascading through his veins like rivers of molten lava.

Relaxed, Roarke's soothing touch having washed away all tension, Brianna halfheartedly hid a yawn behind her hand as Roarke set her back on the bed. He smiled at her gesture and lifted one shoulder in a shrug of defeat. "Perhaps it's for the best. I have work to do, and you need to recuperate."

Roarke pressed a light kiss on Brianna's brow. "Rest now. There will be time for us later." He turned to the door, but before he could open it, Brianna's words stopped him.

"Roarke, thank you for all you've done for me. I know you didn't have to come after me, and I'm grateful. I shudder to think what would have happened had you not."

A chill passed down Roarke's spine at the thought of the fate that had awaited Brianna at the end of the *Sea Dragon*'s voyage. It perturbed him to realize that the very thought of something so terrible happening to Brianna had the power to shake him so thoroughly. Since the day his mother died, he'd allowed no one nor anything to affect him in such a manner. Disturbed, Roarke opened the cabin door. He glanced back at Brianna sitting in the middle of his large bed, her luscious body shielded from him by the damp towel. He didn't know what to say or what to feel at the moment. He cleared his throat of the lump of uneasiness that clogged it and said, "Sleep now, Brianna. We can talk later."

Brianna smiled and smoothed out the rumpled covers at her side. Yes, they would talk later. And then she would tell him how much she loved him.

The evening breeze flapped the sails overhead and ruffled Roarke's dark hair as he stood quietly looking up at the starlit sky. He gripped the mahogany rail firmly with both hands as he sought to come to terms with the new and frightening emotions the woman in his cabin had inspired within him. He wouldn't call what he felt for Brianna love, because he couldn't force himself to admit such an emotion existed between men and women. He'd seen too much pain, too much abuse, and far too much deception to misconstrue what he felt as anything more than a powerful sexual attraction.

Granted, Brianna had claimed a small niche of her own in his life, but he'd not be foolish enough to call it love. He was physically attracted to her beauty and passion. Her innocence also made him want to protect her, but that was as far as it went. Roarke breathed a sigh of relief, suddenly satisfied with his assessment. He smiled to himself, confident that he had his emotions once more under control.

"What brings you on deck at this time of night, *mon ami*? I would think you would be with your lovely Brianna after everything you've gone through to reclaim her," Nick said, pausing at Roarke's side. He, too, raised his eyes toward the heavens.

Roarke glanced sideways at his friend. "Brianna is in no condition to accept my attentions. VanNess had her locked belowdecks, and her skin is ridden with heat rash."

"I would expect nothing less from our good Captain VanNess. The whoreson has no human feelings. All he cares about is gold."

Nick's derogatory comment about VanNess made Roarke shift uneasily. His friend's words pricked at all the insecurities he sought to ignore but found himself confronting far too often in recent weeks.

The night hid Roarke's expression from Nick and he continued, completely unaware of his friend's unrest. Nick grinned and clapped Roarke on the back. "Take heart, *mon ami*. You have your Brianna back now, and in time her skin will clear. Sometimes it makes the prize seem far more valuable if you have to wait to claim it."

Roarke shook off Nick's hand and turned away. "As I've told you before. She's not my Brianna, nor is she a prize to be claimed."

Nick's frown wiped away his smile. "Surely you're not still trying to convince me that you don't love the girl? Not after all we've gone through to rescue her from VanNess?"

Roarke ran his fingers through his windblown hair and shook his head. "I'm not trying to convince you of anything, Nick. I admit I feel things for Brianna that I've never felt for any woman before, but I have far more important matters to attend."

Nick gave a harsh, dubious laugh. "*Mon ami*, there isn't anything more important than a man's heart. I know you nearly as well as I know myself. There is something here that you're not telling me." Nick searched Roarke's shadowed features. "Has the girl rejected you?"

"No, she hasn't rejected me. There is nothing to reject. I intend to meet with Beaumarchais, and once our business is settled, I intend to take Brianna back to Statia and sail away without looking back, as always."

Nick saw the flicker of agony pass over Roarke's features and knew the torment his friend had suffered to come to such a decision. He shook his head sadly. "Surely you can't mean what you say?"

"I mean every word. There is no place for Brianna in my life, as you well know."

"I don't understand," Nick said, a puzzled frown puckering his brow.

Now it was Roarke's turn to cast a perplexed look at Nick. "You and I both know that men's lives depend upon us. I have no time to dally with a young woman who expects marriage and family from the man she beds. Brianna is a lady."

"A lady! How can you say that? You know nothing of her. If you'll recall, you found her stranded in the middle of the ocean."

Roarke smiled ruefully at his friend. "I know what you're trying to do, but it won't work, Nick. I don't have to know anything about Brianna to know I was the one who took her virginity. She was no waterfront doxy selling her wares but an innocent under the influence of the drugs you gave her. And I was too randy to withstand the temptation. I ruined her and I owe her, but I can't expect her to live as my mistress. She deserves far more."

"Then marry her," Nick said, watching Roarke's expression.

"You know I can't ask her to marry me. I'm little more than a pirate."

Nick exploded. "Damn it, Roarke. You and I both know we are not pirates, nor have we ever been. We've kept up that ruse in order to serve the cause we both believe in. Surely you've not come to believe our own ruse."

Roarke's hands tightened on the railing. His head dropped and he stared down into the black, murky waters lapping against the equally black hull of the ship he'd named after death. He released a long, weary breath before he glanced toward the man at his side. Suddenly all the old pain resurfaced. "Perhaps we're not truly pirates, but I *am* a dockside whore's bastard."

Nick rolled his eyes in exasperation. "*Mon ami*, what has that to do with anything? Surely you don't believe Brianna would view you differently if she knew of your heritage?"

Roarke's lips curled into a cynical smile. "Few women would want to associate with a man of my reputation, and even fewer would look favorably toward a whore's by-blow. Brianna would be no different from the rest." Roarke glanced out across the dark waters that met the indigo horizon. "There's only been one woman who didn't see my birth as a fault: Elsbeth Whitman."

Roarke's expression softened at the thought of his friend.

"You've always been a fair man with your men, Roarke. Be so with the girl in your cabin. Tell her the truth of your past and let her decide if she wants to stay with you or go, as you believe."

Nick's advice startled Roarke. He glanced sharply at him, puzzled by the man's sudden concern for honesty. This was Nick, the man he'd known and loved all his life, but also the man who believed in saying and doing whatever was necessary to get a woman into his bed. He had cajoled and charmed his conquests until he got what he wanted, and then he left with a smile of triumph. Nick had never been honest with a woman in his life, yet now he was urging Roarke to open up his soul to Brianna, to lay himself open to her ridicule and rejection. Roarke pushed the thought away.

"I can't tell Brianna the truth about my past any more than I can about our mission."

"Then, *mon ami*, you are a fool," Nick said, and turned away. He'd said his piece, and what conscience he possessed was free. He'd not badger Roarke further. His friend had a stubborn streak in him a mile wide, and it wouldn't be broached by arguing the point.

Thoughtfully Roarke looked toward the sparkling heavens. Perhaps Nick was right for once. Everyone, including Brianna, had secrets, but perhaps it would be best to tell her the truth about his past and give her the choice of staying with him as his mistress. If she chose to go, he would help her.

The very thought of Brianna leaving him seemed to prize the dark chasm within him wider, but Roarke's expression didn't alter. He'd lived with the void for so long, it was now only a dull ache instead of the acute pain he'd endured when he was a younger man.

Decision made, Roarke braced himself for the inevitable rejection that he knew lay in his future. He'd not make his offer until after they left Brest. That would give him a few more weeks to enjoy Brianna, a few more weeks to pretend that they were just normal young lovers instead of two people cast together by a chance of fate.

Chapter 11

A gust of wind, rain, and laughter entered the inn with the young couple. The patrons who were sitting at tables close to the door received the full blast from the open doorway. They cast annoyed glances at the newcomers and muttered a few disgruntled remarks before turning their attention back to their food and drink. George, ignoring the black looks cast in his direction, gazed down at his wife as she stood wiping away the moisture that had beaded on her face from the dash they'd made from their coach. "You look good enough to eat."

A blush of pleasure and embarrassment brightening her cheeks, Rachel flashed a quick look about to see if anyone had overheard her husband's remark. "Hush and behave. We haven't traveled all the way back here just to dally."

George Fielding arched a roguish brow. "Who said? We can pick up the furniture tomorrow but also 'dally,' as you call it, tonight. In fact, there's little else for us to do after we rent a room and eat dinner. Fortunately for me, the shops have closed for the day, and this weather will keep you at my side all night."

Unable to restrain her mirth a moment longer, Rachel shook her head and laughed. "You are a rogue, Dr. Fielding."

George shrugged and grinned. "And you love me for it, Mrs. Fielding. Don't deny it."

"Never," Rachel said. Taking the hand George extended, she followed him to the narrow little cubbyhole where the proprietor sat enjoying his own dinner. George registered them for a room and then escorted his wife to the inn's dining room for dinner.

The commotion near the door was of little interest to the man seated at the table in the shadowy corner near the rear of the tavern room. A shiver crept up his spine from the dampness that clung to his clothing after the afternoon gale. His pale features grew even more grim a moment later when the man he'd been awaiting finally arrived for their meeting. Suppressing another shudder, he downed the last of the warm brandy and set his blue glass aside. His sneering expression mirrored his distaste. He liked having the best of everything around him at all times and had no use for cheap imitation. Though Bristol was famous for its blue glassware, the tavern served their customers in glass made to resemble the works created by the well-known glassmaker on Temple street, Lazarus Jacobs. Lord Montague turned his attention away from the brandy and looked once more at the tall, ugly man who approached his table. Lord Montague didn't offer the man the courtesy of a seat, but after an uncomfortable moment, the man took the initiative himself. He folded his lean frame in the chair opposite his employer.

"What have you learned?" Lord Montague asked, extending the man no greeting of welcome. The man was an employee, paid well for his services, and he deserved nothing more.

Branson Tanner swiped away the last of the rain that had blasted him in the face just before entering the inn. The gale-force winds lashed and whipped through the streets, sending all sane men to their homes. "I've learned nothing more than I knew at our last meeting. I'm beginning to believe the girl just up and vanished from the face of the earth."

Lord Montague absently rubbed the still tender scar through the material of his embroidered waistcoat. He had been fortunate that Brianna's aim had not been more accurate. Had the knife pierced his abdomen a few inches lower, he'd not be here now searching for her.

"Tanner, I've paid you to find the girl, and I mean for you to do it. I don't want to hear any such nonsense about her disappearance. No one can do that. Someone, somewhere, knows where she is, and I intend to find them if it takes me the rest of my life. Brianna McClure will not escape punishment. The law may not be able to do anything about her attempt to kill me, but I can and will once I find her."

"I don't know where else to look. I've had my men scouring London and all the major ports. But if she's holed up somewhere in the country, it's doubtful we'll ever find her."

Lord Montague's expression turned deadly. He leaned forward and growled. "If you know what's good for you and your men, you'll find the girl. She's not holed up in the country, any more than we are at this moment. She has only the money she stole and what few jewels I've given her through the years. She and her little maid have to eat. They won't have enough money to live on for very long."

Branson Tanner's face flushed a dull red under Lord Montague's threat. He wished he'd never gotten involved with the snake of a man. He could well understand why the girl had stabbed him. From what little

Branson had learned from his dealings with Lord Montague, he deserved what she'd given him and more.

Branson gave a mental shrug at the futility of hindsight. It was now too late to back out on their deal. He'd taken Lord Montague's money and had already spent it on gambling and whores. And he didn't doubt that Lord Montague would have him killed if he didn't finish what he'd been hired to do.

The sound of laughter came from the table near the door. Lord Montague's annoyance mounted. He didn't like the thought of anyone finding pleasure when he himself was so miserable. Lord Montague looked toward the offending sound.

The shadows that shielded his and Tanner's presence in the corner were broken by the lantern on the wall above the table where the couple sat. Warm golden light spilled down upon the man and woman enjoying their dinner.

Lord Montague's eyes narrowed upon the young woman, and he sucked in a sharp breath. He'd never forget that face. She'd served in his household for too many years. There was no denying it; he'd found the servant Rachel.

Lord Montague caught himself before he came fully to his feet. He settled himself back in his chair and looked back at Branson Tanner. His gaze snapped with fury. "You lump. I hired you to find Brianna and her maid."

"Lord Montague, I've done my best, but I'm beginning to believe it's an impossible mission."

"Not so impossible when the maid is sitting across the room from us."

Tanner jerked about. His eyes widened in surprise at the sight of Rachel sitting calmly across the room, enjoying her dinner. He looked back to Lord Montague, and his face brightened with color again. "What shall we do?"

Lord Montague let out a long breath in disgust. "I would think you would know what to do since I'm paying for your services."

Tanner's flush deepened. "My lord, if you're not satisfied with my services, then perhaps I should resign from your employ."

Lord Montague felt his head would leave his shoulders from the force of the anger that shot through him. His own pale features flushed pink and he eyed Tanner with loathing. "You stupid bastard, you'll not leave my employ until I'm ready to release you. Now, you big lummox, you will find a way to get the information we need from that girl or you'll be sorry you ever laid eyes on me."

Tanner eyed Lord Montague sullenly but made no comment.

"Do you understand me, Tanner?" Lord Montague continued to harangue. "I've friends in powerful places, and I'm sure you wouldn't want them to take a closer look at the way you spend your time when you're not pretending to be a detective."

Tanner's heart stilled. An icy hand seemed to settle at the nape of his neck. The color drained from his face. "My lord, I've tried to do my best for you."

"Then you'd better try harder if you don't want me to tell of the little tavern where your cohorts smuggle out their goods. And I suspect your friends in London know a great deal about the warehouse robberies. I'm sure you receive more than the market price from your buyers since it's illegal to sell navy stores to the colonies. You and your friends could be charged and hanged for treason for less than I know about your activities."

Pale and shaken, Tanner stared at Lord Montague.

The man was the Devil incarnate, because only the Devil would have been able to learn so much about his involvement with the smugglers. "What do you want me to do?"

Lord Montague smiled confidently. As he had planned when he'd investigated Tanner and his activities, he had the man exactly where he wanted him. Tanner would do anything to save his own neck. "Exactly as I said. The maid will have the information we need, and I expect you to get it by whatever means it takes."

"I'm guilty of many things, but I'm not a murderer."

Lord Montague shrugged and lowered his voice as he leaned forward so that only Tanner could hear. "You are if that's what it takes to learn Brianna's whereabouts. Do you understand me?"

Tanner nodded.

"Now, I would suggest you go and get some men to help you. The gent with the maid looks too much for you to handle alone."

Tanner rose from the table. "I know my business, my lord."

"Good," Lord Montague said, also coming to his feet. "I'll await word from you in my room." He turned and left the tavern room by the door that led to the back stairs. He didn't want Rachel to see him and perhaps warn Brianna that she had not succeeded in her attempt at murder.

Lord Montague paused in the shadows at the stair landing and glanced back at the couple sitting at the table. His lips curled into a sneer. The bitch was so engrossed with the man that he could have walked by their table and she'd not have noticed. The sneer became a cruel little smile as he turned toward the stairs. She'd be aware of his presence soon enough. And she'd regret it to her dying breath if she didn't tell him exactly what he wanted to know.

Rachel finished the last bit of tender beef brisket and leaned back, replete on food and love. In all of her dreams, she'd never imagined that she could be so happy. It was sad to realize that the tragedy of Brianna's life had been her good fortune.

Rachel pushed the thought away as well as the prick of guilt that accompanied it. It was always the same. Every time she thought of Brianna alone on that island without friends, she couldn't stop the guilt.

"You're thinking again," George said, reaching across the table and capturing her hand within his own. He squeezed it gently, understanding the root to the faraway expression in his wife's eyes.

"Aye. It's at times like these, when I realize how fortunate I am to have you, that I think about Brianna."

"I've told you that you don't have anything to worry about. Roarke will see to the girl."

Rachel flashed her husband a skeptical look. "As you'd have seen to me if I hadn't insisted on marriage before we bedded."

"Even so, he'll not let any harm come to her."

"No harm? George, you're a physician and should understand women better than other men."

A grin crinkled George's lips. "I can't seem to remember you having any complaints about my understanding what a woman wants."

Rachel couldn't resist his devilry, though she was concerned about her friend. She smiled and shook her head. "Men! You're all alike. You don't understand that when an innocent young woman like Brianna goes to bed with a man, it's not just physical but mental. Her heart is involved, and Brianna's heart has already suffered enough without adding Roarke O'Connor's charm and good looks to confuse her further."

"Love, we've discussed this before and we can't ever agree. If you're so concerned about Brianna, we could go back to Statia."

Rachel paused. She searched her husband's face for any sign of a jest but found none. "You would go back?"

"Aye, if it would ease your mind so we could finally settle down and start a family of our own."

Rachel's expression softened. She'd wanted to wait until they were settled in their new house and he'd begun his practice, but after such a loving gesture, she couldn't hold her secret any longer. "You don't have to wait for us to start a family, George."

George's eyes widened and dropped to the edge of the table at his wife's waist. Stunned, he gasped, "You don't mean . . . ?"

Rachel nodded. "Aye. You're to be a father, George Fielding."

George threw back his head and gave a shout of joy. All eyes turned to the madman who jumped to his feet and grabbed the woman out of her seat and swung her into the air. "I'm to be a father!"

"Set me down, George. Everyone is looking at us," Rachel ordered between giggles.

"Let them look all they want. My wife is going to have my baby. Let them all have a drink in honor of my wonderful woman." George set Rachel back on her feet and ordered a round of drinks for the tavern customers. His generosity gained him a cheer as he swept Rachel up into his arms again and headed for the stairs. Taking them two at a time, he carried his wife to their chamber, where he tenderly disrobed her and laid her on the bed. He made love to her as if she were a piece of fragile porcelain. He worshiped her with his body, giving of himself as he'd given to only one other woman in his life, the fair Josette. However, that time was in the past, as was the hurt. Rachel and their child were now his future, his life.

Snuggled down beneath the comforter, their limbs entwined, their breaths mingling as they slept, George and Rachel lay replete from their lovemaking. The click of the door latch as the thin blade of the knife slipped in between metal and lock didn't disturb their rest. Nor did they hear the fugitive footsteps of the four men who stealthily surrounded their bed, ready and armed should George and Rachel attempt an escape.

Branson Tanner's rough shake roused George from his peaceful sleep. Groggily he opened his eyes and stared up into the thin, vicious face glaring down at him. He blinked several times to rid himself of the weird dream that had claimed him and absently wondered if the meat he'd eaten at dinner had been tainted. It had to be responsible for his mind conjuring up the image of the Devil and his henchmen. George shook his head to clear it and rubbed at his eyes. When he lowered his hand, his eyes widened in alarm. The vision hadn't dissipated into the night as he'd expected. An icy, foreboding chill careened down George's spine as reality set in. He instinctively bolted upright and reached for the pistol he kept on the bedside table. His life at sea and sleeping in strange ports had taught him to always be on guard. An enemy could come from anywhere, even from among the men you lived with day in and day out, men whom you considered your friends.

George's fingers groped empty air. He flashed a frightened look toward his sleeping wife before his gaze settled once more on the man smiling down at him. The flash of metal revealed the pistol he held trained on Rachel. Cautiously George relaxed back against the pillows and asked quietly, "What do you want?"

Tanner's smile deepened. "You're a wise man. I was afraid you'd want to fight, but I see you realize that you're at the disadvantage with the odds such as they are against you."

George glanced at the men surrounding his bed and felt cold dread settle in the pit of his belly. There were too many to even hope to defend himself and Rachel. "I asked what you wanted, not an assessment of my wisdom."

Tanner chuckled and tucked George's pistol into the waistband of his britches. "All I want is a little information."

George frowned as Tanner's voice disturbed Rachel's sleep. She shifted and then slowly opened her eyes. George took her hand and clutched it tightly, silently warning her to be still and quiet. He didn't want her to do anything that might set the four men off.

Rachel paled as she raised her eyes to the intruders, but she remained silent.

"What kind of information?"

"I want to know exactly where Brianna McClure is hiding."

Rachel shot George a frightened look and clung to his hand, silently pleading with him not to divulge her friend's whereabouts.

"I don't know any Brianna McClure."

Tanner's expression didn't give any warning of his next move. He backhanded George across the face. George's head snapped back, cracking loudly against the plaster wall. The impact momentarily staggered George's senses. Rachel whimpered and clung even tighter to her husband.

"I'm not here to play guessing games. The woman in your bed knows exactly why I'm here, and I want answers, or that's only a taste of what you're both going to get."

"My wife doesn't know anything," George said in an effort to protect Brianna. He dabbed at the tiny trickle of blood at the corner of his mouth.

A sneer curled Tanner's lips as he glanced toward his three cohorts. "It looks as if the good doctor wants a beating." Tanner's gaze swept back to Rachel. "Or perhaps he'd rather have us interrogate his wife. She's the one who has the answers anyway."

George shook his head. "Leave my wife alone. She's with child."

Tanner shrugged. "It makes no difference to me if she's breeding. I came here to get the information I need to find Brianna McClure, and I intend to get it one way or the other. It's up to you and your wife. If you want to give us the information freely, ye won't be hurt. But I'm warning you now, I ain't going away without it. I intend to bring Brianna McClure back to face her punishment for the crimes she's committed."

George looked at his wife, acceding to defeat. No matter how much he wanted to protect Brianna, there was no choice to be made when it came to the safety of his wife and child. "Tell him what he wants to know, Rachel."

"I can't do that to Brianna," Rachel whispered, shaking her head.

"Rachel, you have to think of the baby. Brianna is far away, and I seriously doubt they'll ever find her. And even if they should, Roarke won't allow them to have her. We can't risk our future and our baby's life for loyalty to a friend."

Tears welled in Rachel's eyes as she looked helplessly up at Tanner. Her lower lip quivered as she whispered, "Brianna is on St. Eustatius. That's all I know."

Tanner's expression didn't lighten as he leaned forward. His gaze narrowed upon Rachel's pale face. "You'd better not be lying or you'll regret it. That child you carry will never live to his first birthday if you've lied." He flashed George a warning look and then ordered George and Rachel to get dressed.

"We've told you what you want to know. What else do you intend to do?" George asked, cradling a trembling Rachel against his chest.

"I intend to see that the two of you take a long ocean voyage with me. You didn't expect me to trust you'd not lie to me, did you, Fielding? I'm no fool. If you haven't told me the truth, I intend to put an end to your miserable lives personally for all the trouble you caused me."

"Damn it," George said, his worry over Rachel's well-being overriding his wisdom. "We aren't going any damn place with you. We told you everything we know. Now, get out and let us be."

Tanner jerked the pistol from the waist of his britches and aimed it at George's chest. "I can leave you here with a piece of lead through your heart or you can come peacefully with your woman."

Having often seen the same mad-dog look in the eyes of men so callous and cold that they'd slit their own mothers' throats for a pence or a dram of rum, George knew it would do no good to argue. The man would think nothing of killing him and abducting Rachel until she served his purpose. Then he would rid himself of her with equal ease. George threw back the covers and slid his feet to the floor. He had lost one wife and one child, and he'd not do so again. He'd fight to his dying breath to protect Rachel and his unborn babe, even if he had to sacrifice his own life.

Rachel looked up at her husband with questioning, tear-filled eyes, but there was no answer he could give to comfort her. For the present they were being held hostage. And from what their captor had said, their only hope of survival was for him to find Brianna.

George held out his hand to his wife and gave her what he hoped was a reassuring smile. "It would seem, Mistress Fielding, that we haven't any choice in the matter of our travels."

Tanner chuckled and tucked the pistol back into the waist of his britches. "Now, if you know what's good for you, you'll get dressed and go downstairs without making any untoward moves. I'd hate to leave your guts splattered all over our good proprietor's inn, but I will if that's what it takes. Now, move. The night ain't getting any longer, and I have plans to make before we can sail."

The day dawned bright and chilly as the *Black Angel* sailed past the French naval squadron that had been positioned to discourage any close scrutiny of the ships that arrived and departed from the French channel ports. The crisp white sails overhead crackled in the wind, standing taut and proud as a new flag was raised over the mast. Brianna watched the yellow standard slowly inch upward and unfurl in the breeze to reveal a coiled snake. Puzzled by the change, she glanced toward the man who captained the *Black Angel* and saw him smile as the new flag snapped and fluttered.

Brianna felt her heart swell with emotion even as new questions rose in her mind about the man she loved. Roarke O'Connor remained as much a mystery to her now as he had been when she'd first come on board the

Black Angel. The past weeks at sea had been the happiest moments of her life, though at times she sensed that the close bond she felt between herself and Roarke was such a fragile, tenuous thing that a wisp of air could rend it asunder at any moment. She sensed that Roarke himself also felt the gossamer-fine line they trod with each other. They shared the most intimate of moments, reveling in the passion and ecstasy of their lovemaking, yet never crossing the delicate ground to delve within each other's hearts.

Brianna turned her gaze toward the coastline of France. By late afternoon they would make port at Rade de Brest for Roarke's rendezvous with a man he called Beaumarchais. He'd told her that Beaumarchais was a merchant who worked for Hortalez and Company, a shipping firm that acted as his agent in France. The meeting in itself also puzzled and surprised Brianna. It was so unexpected to find that Roarke, a man whom she'd suspected of being a pirate, dealt with merchants, trading and taking on cargo like any other merchant captain. His meeting with Hortalez and Company only heightened the air of mystery about him.

"Will you be glad to have your feet back on solid ground?" Nick Sebastain asked, pausing at Brianna's side. Since their short encounter on Statia, he'd managed to avoid Brianna. However, he now felt it was best for his friendship with Roarke to settle things between them once and for all. He didn't want to lose Roarke's friendship, nor did he want to put his friend in a position where he had to choose between himself and Brianna. If his suspicions about Roarke's feelings were right, Nick knew there would be no choice to make. Roarke's mind might staunchly deny his love for the girl, but his heart wouldn't allow him to let her go.

Brianna stiffened at the sound of the voice of the

Black Angel's second in command. Until this moment she'd been fortunate enough not to have to confront the man who had drugged her. She drew in a resigned breath as she braced herself to face Nick. She had known this moment would eventually come and had dreaded it, because she truly didn't know what to say or do. The man had tricked her, had abused her trust; however, had he not, she'd have never known the love of his friend, Roarke O'Connor. Torn by the two opposing thoughts, she looked Nick squarely in the eyes. "I had hoped this moment would never come."

Nick nodded, his expression chagrined. "I know. I, too, would wish our meeting could be more pleasant, but because of my foolish behavior, it cannot be."

"Then I would thank you to leave me be. I have no wish to speak with you ever again," Brianna said, turning her back to Nick.

"I understand your feelings, but I would ask that you allow me to apologize for my errant ways."

Brianna looked sharply at Nick. The feeble smile he gave her didn't quell the anger that surged through every sinew of her body as the memory of their time together reasserted itself. It was still unnerving to realize how close she had come to becoming one of Nick's many conquests. "You expect me to forgive you after what you did to me? You are reprehensible."

Nick's cheeks flushed a dull red and he nodded. "I know. I should never have tried to take advantage of your situation, but at the time I did not know that Roarke was interested in you."

Brianna's anger exploded. "So the only reason you now regret your abominable behavior is because of Roarke, not because you violated my trust and nearly my person?"

Mortified that he couldn't deny Brianna's charges, he

nodded again. "Roarke is my friend, and I would not have any animosity between us. I regret what I did and ask your forgiveness for the sake of the man we both care about."

Fury searing her, Brianna glanced toward the quarter-deck, where Roarke still worked. Her anger urged her to toss Nick's apology back into his face, but her heart warned her not to be so rash. She loved Roarke and knew he loved Nick like a brother. Should she ever gain Roarke's love, she'd not want her feelings for Nick Sebastain to come between them. Nor could she ever ask Roarke to choose between two people he loved. It wasn't right to put stipulations on any relationship. It was too heavy a burden for a relationship to bear without crumpling beneath the weight.

Brianna looked back to the man standing quietly at her side. The expression in his dark Gallic eyes bespoke his remorse and his sincerity. Brianna nodded briskly. She'd accept his apology as well as his love for Roarke. "For Roarke I will accept your apology, but I will not forgive you, because you have no regret for what you did."

Nick's lips curled in a roguish grin. His mood changed visibly. His eyes twinkled with devilment. "I ask no more, because the only thing I truly regret is not taking you to my bed before Roarke claimed you."

Brianna opened her mouth to give him a good set-down, but Nick raised one long-fingered hand to stay her censure. "Don't be upset with me, sweet Brianna. I only speak the truth. I envy my friend his good fortune because you are the most beautiful woman I've ever seen." Nick glanced toward the quarterdeck. "But Roarke has always had the devil's luck with women. They flock to him like bees to honey." Nick's gaze swung back to rest on Brianna's face. His expression softened. "But you, sweet Brianna, are the only woman whom he has not managed to elude. You've wormed your way into his life, but I warn you here and now, don't play the fickle female with my friend. Be true and honest with Roarke and don't hurt him. He's seen enough of pain in his life already without you tearing him apart with your female wiles."

Before Brianna could respond or question Nick's statement, he turned and strode away. She watched him go. She didn't understand the unspoken threat. She'd never do anything to hurt Roarke. *Be true and honest.* The words slammed into Brianna like a fist in the gut. She swallowed uneasily and turned her troubled gaze once more to the coast of France. How could she tell Roarke the truth about herself? How could she explain that she'd killed a man, though it was in self-defense? Brianna closed her eyes and gripped the mahogany railing as if it were suddenly a lifeline. She couldn't. She didn't have the courage to destroy the fragile bond between herself and Roarke. It was too precious to her.

Her decision made, Brianna drew in a resolute breath and inched her chin up. Lord Montague and her life at Montvale was in the past. She'd not allow it to destroy what future she might have with the man she loved.

Chapter 12

"I've recently received word that Admiral Count d'Estaing invaded Savannah on September sixteenth," Pierre Caron said before taking a sip of the fine burgundy that he'd ordered served in Roarke's honor. It wasn't anything unusual for the man known to many as Beaumarchais to use wine and food to enhance his business dealings. A jewelry maker, composer, and poet, as well as adventurer, Pierre Augustin Caron also had an astute business and political acumen. He knew well it was far cheaper for the French government to supply money and desperately needed military equipment to the Americans than to undertake their own war with Britain. With France's aid, the Americans could drain England of its soldiers, sailors, and money, giving France an opportunity to regain its holdings on the American continent.

Roarke smiled his pleasure. "Then things are going well. D'Estaing has the manpower to hold Savannah this winter."

"That should have been the outcome. Between d'Estaing's men and General Lincoln's continentals, the English General Provost faced a force of nearly seven thousand."

Roarke stiffened and uncoiled from his relaxed position in the comfortable Louis XIV chair. He set his glass on the side table inlaid with intricately designed wood. "What do you mean, 'should have been the outcome'? What's gone wrong?"

Caron drew in a long breath. He'd dreaded this moment. He enjoyed bragging about triumphs, not defeat. Even from the distance of three thousand miles of ocean, a mission's failure tasted very bad, especially when it was one of France's finest admirals who had suffered the embarrassment. "Unfortunately it seems our good admiral allowed the English general to outfox him. D'Estaing had Savannah in the palm of his hand, but he allowed Provost time to call for reinforcements. It also gave the English time to strengthen their fortifications. Instead of an easy conquest, Savannah has now turned into a siege."

"Damn," Roarke said, disgusted by the turn of events. "What of the Carolinas?"

Caron shrugged. "I fear after Savannah, Charleston will be next to fall. The British now believe it's even more imperative to thwart the rebellion since we signed the agreement with your Congress."

"It also makes it imperative for me to sail. Our men will be in desperate need of the munitions," Roarke said, coming to his feet. He ran a hand through his dark hair and frowned as a new problem arose. He had hoped to have time to take Brianna back to Statia, where she'd be out of harm's way. Now it looked like he'd have to take her with him to America or leave her here in France. He didn't like the thought of either solution, but he had no other choice.

Caron nodded as he, too, came to his feet. "When will you sail?"

Roarke picked up his hat and set it on his dark head, unconsciously adjusting the tricorn to an angle that gave him the rakish, devil-may-care look that was so appealing to the opposite sex. His gold earring flashed in the candlelight as he looked at Caron. His expression mirrored his grim decision of a moment before. "We sail just as soon as the cargo is on board and the *Black Angel* is provisioned. I had planned to visit the shipyards while in Brest, but it would seem my plans must now wait to a future date. There are far more pressing matters at hand. Every minute during the next week must now be spent preparing the *Black Angel* for her voyage."

"Monsieur O'Connor, should you need my further assistance, please feel free to contact me. We serve the same cause," Caron said, giving Roarke a gracious half bow in tribute to their cooperative effort.

"Your help is deeply appreciated, monsieur. The Continental Congress is greatly in your debt for the assistance you have given us in the past as well as the present," Roarke stated diplomatically. He knew well that Caron's help had come at a price that had not at first been explained to the fledging colonial government, who had believed in the beginning that France's generosity had come as a gift. When they learned of the debt they were incurring to the French government, they didn't like it, but they'd had no other recourse but to continue their transactions. The army would starve in the next few months of winter should they be denied the money and armaments that France could provide.

"Monsieur, we do what we must," Caron said with a gracious nod.

"Yes, we do," Roarke said, his thoughts already turning to the woman awaiting him on board the *Black Angel*.

Brianna recognized the sound of Roarke's footsteps coming down the passageway, and held her breath expectantly. No matter how many times a day he entered the cabin, her reaction was always the same at the sight of him. Her heart began a wild dance within her breast, and her blood began a slow simmer that wasn't cooled until Roarke took her into his arms and made love to her.

Brianna's cheeks heated at the thought of her own wanton behavior. She had tried to stop herself from behaving in such an embarrassing manner to Roarke's presence, but she had failed miserably. Her emotions were too raw where he was concerned. She loved every inch of the man. She loved to run her fingers through the thick silk of his raven hair, she loved to feel the slight roughness of his morning beard against her own flesh, she loved the smell of him after he'd been on deck, whipped by sea spray and wind. She even loved the hard, scarred planes of his back, though each time she touched the ridges, she felt like weeping from the pain she knew he had endured to become so marked.

Brianna realized in the society from which she'd come, she'd be an outcast for her feelings toward a man who had never offered her any hope that their relationship would go beyond their moments together on board the *Black Angel.*

The thought of the future dimmed Brianna's excitement. Old doubts and insecurities rose up to shadow her earlier mood. Before her rescue from VanNess, she'd vowed to tell Roarke of her love for him, and had even attempted to do so on several occasions during the past weeks. However, each time something stopped her. Perhaps it was her fear of his rejection or perhaps she instinctively sensed he didn't want to hear her vows of undying love. But whatever it was that had hindered her telling Roarke, the words still remained unspoken, though her feelings for him grew stronger by the day.

Brianna glanced at her surroundings and wondered at the changes that had been wrought since the day she'd awakened here in this cabin to find the *Black Angel*'s handsome captain staring down at her. She'd been so concerned about how the world would view her for sharing Roarke's quarters. Now she no longer feared what the world would think of her behavior. Let them judge her a wanton or anything else. Roarke was all that mattered to her.

A prickle of déjà vu suddenly raised the hair at the nape of Brianna's neck and made her shiver. Sabrina's image flashed into her mind to taunt her. Brianna sought to push the image away, but it wouldn't go. At that moment she and her mother could have been the same person. She had vowed never to allow herself to become like Sabrina, but here she now sat, ensconced in Roarke's cabin, dependent completely upon him, emotionally as well as physically, just as Sabrina had been with Lord Montague. Brianna sought to exonerate herself by telling herself that what she and Roarke shared was completely different from her mother's relationship with Lord Montague. However, she couldn't reconcile the fact in her own mind. Unable to endure the similarities a moment longer, Brianna came to her feet just as the door opened.

She looked at Roarke and wanted to cry. She loved this man with every fiber of her being, yet she now knew that without Roarke returning her love, their time together could only be a brief interlude. A chill of dread inched its way along Brianna's spine. She saw the barren landscape of her future stretching out before her. No matter how she felt, she couldn't remain with Roarke and allow herself to make the same mistakes as her mother. It would break her heart to leave him, but it was her only choice if she wanted to retain any self-esteem. Otherwise she'd become a slave to her own weakness as Sabrina had done.

Brianna hugged herself and turned to stare out at the bay's moon-silvered waters. She swallowed back her tears and sought to get control over her emotions. She couldn't allow them to show when she told Roarke of her decision. Brianna drew in a fortifying breath. At least she had her memories. She had them stored away like little treasures that she could pull out and enjoy in the future. She'd never regret her time with Roarke. It had been too precious. He had been the sun that had come into her life to brighten a world that had been dark and oppressive. Roarke had taught her how to love as a woman.

Brianna sensed Roarke's warmth behind her before he rested his hands on her shoulders and drew her back against his lean body. She inhaled the masculine scent that came with him, savoring the light fragrance of brandy, tobacco, and sea that clung to his clothing. Against all her resolves her skin tingled expectantly and her heart once more began its rapid tattoo against her breastbone. Brianna squeezed her eyes closed against the onset of sensation. God! How she loved Roarke.

"What's wrong, little one?" Roarke asked, feeling her body tense. Brianna drew in a steadying breath. She knew it was now or never. She had to tell Roarke of her decision before her resolves completely evaporated under his magnetism. Her voice reflected her disquiet as she said softly, "Roarke, we need to talk."

"Aye. I know we do. That is why I've returned early."

Roarke's serious tone made Brianna turn to look up at him. Her heart seemed to still at the look in his eyes. He wore a grim, determined expression that made another chill pass down her spine. Shaken, her concern for

Roarke overshadowing her own decision of moments before, she rested her hand against his chest and asked, "What is it? Has something happened?"

Roarke captured her hand within his own and held it against the hard planes of his chest as he looked down into Brianna's soft velvet eyes. They mirrored her concern for him. A leaden feeling settled in the pit of his stomach and he felt the chasm rip wider.

"I have something I need to tell you. I had meant to speak with you after you'd recovered from your ordeal with VanNess, but the time never seemed right."

Brianna's heartbeat roared in her ears and she swallowed hard in an effort to force her words past the lump of dread still lodged in her throat. "What did you want to tell me?"

Roarke allowed his eyes to sweep over Brianna's flawless features before he took her gaze once more. "I had wanted to tell you that I intended to take you back to Statia after we left Brest."

Brianna's heart did a somersault as old dreams reared their weary heads. "You wanted to take me back to Statia with you?"

"Aye. I'd know you'd be safe there while I was away."

Brianna held her breath and savored the warmth his words created. Roarke did care for her.

"But I'm afraid I've now had to change my plans."

"Oh," Brianna said dejectedly as her dreams gave a long, resigned sigh and then laid their battered heads back into the depressive gloom.

"I'll not be able to take you back to Statia," Roarke continued. He had to tell Brianna that she had to remain in France until he returned from America. *If* he returned. He had to make her aware of the danger. He couldn't—he wouldn't—have it otherwise. She had her own life to live.

Brianna felt the urge to burst into tears. Roarke meant to leave her here in France and sail away without a backward glance.

"I have to sail to America as soon as the cargo is loaded and the *Black Angel* is ready."

"Take me with you," Brianna beseeched. Her impulsive outburst expressed her heart's plea before her mind could fully realize the implications of her words.

Roarke looked deeply into Brianna's fathomless eyes as he tenderly caressed her cheek. "Brianna, you know not what you ask. The voyage to America will be dangerous. The *Black Angel* will carry a cargo that the British can't afford to have reach the colonies. They will do everything within their power to stop us, and that means we could well end up at the bottom of the ocean."

Suddenly afraid for Roarke's safety, Brianna said, "I don't care. I want to go with you."

Roarke released a long breath and stepped away from Brianna. Her request was too tempting when she was near, when he could breathe in her sweet fragrance, when he could look into her eyes and see her soul. He turned his back to her and braced himself to say the words that would send his soul into the black chasm. "It's best for you to remain here in France. I can't allow you to risk your life when you are not involved."

Brianna closed the space between them. Her love for Roarke overrode all of her concerns that she was making the same mistakes as her mother had made with the men in her life. The thought of losing Roarke forever made her realize that she no longer cared if she was like her mother. The important thing was that she be with Roarke.

Brianna wrapped her arms about Roarke's waist and

laid her cheek against his back. She could hear the strong, steady rhythm of his heart through the fine material of his dark coat and white lawn shirt. The words she'd tried to say so many times in the past now came easily to her lips. She'd not allow Roarke to leave her without knowing of her feeling for him. "It's too late, Roarke. I'm already involved."

Roarke pried her hands free of his waist and turned to face Brianna. "Brianna, you don't understand. The *Black Angel* will be carrying munitions for the rebellion in the colonies. You're not involved in this war, so I can't allow you to go with us."

"No, it's you who don't understand. I am involved, Roarke, because of you."

Roarke misconstrued Brianna's words, his face reflecting his exasperation as he looked down at Brianna and said, "Damn it. I'm in this war because I believe all men are born equal, no matter the circumstances of their birth. I want to see a land where men are judged by their own merits and not on their name. Don't you understand, I'm fighting for the freedom of all those like us."

"And I'm fighting for us," Brianna said softly, undeterred.

Her words took Roarke by surprise. His heart seemed to still within his chest and his indigo gaze locked with Brianna's. He frowned, bemused by the streak of excitement that suddenly shot through him as the full impact of her words registered. However, he still asked, "What?"

"I said I am fighting for us. I want to be with you, Roarke. I want to be at your side, no matter what I must face. It is where I belong."

"But why?" Roarke asked, needing, praying, to hear

the words that his heart desperately yearned to have her say.

"I'll tell you if you don't know by now. I love you, Roarke."

Roarke's blood roared in his ears as a sense of euphoria careened through him. He sucked in a deep breath in an effort to hold on to the brief moment before reason reasserted itself over emotion. He pulled Brianna into his arms and held her close, defying reality to try to stop the pleasure her words had wrought in his barren soul.

God! How he wished he could unequivocally accept Brianna's love without telling her about his past. The moment faded and he gave a mental shrug, resigning himself to the inevitable. He couldn't. He had to take Nick's advice and be honest with her.

"Thank you, Brianna. You'll never know how much those words mean to me," Roarke said against Brianna's dark hair. He stroked the silken mane, winding the curls about his fingers, savoring the rich feel of them even as he sought the words that might send her away from him. "But you may change your feelings about me once you know the truth."

Brianna leaned away from Roarke and looked up into his solemn face. She shook her head. "Nothing can ever change how I feel about you. No matter what everyone else believes of you, I know you as you truly are."

A cynical little smile tugged up the corners of Roarke's shapely mouth. "Are you saying that I may be a pirate but you love me anyway?"

Brianna nodded.

Roarke's spirits lifted. Perhaps Nick was right. Perhaps this woman also possessed a heart as true and pure as Elsbeth Whitman's. "But I'm not truly a pirate, Brianna. I am but a businessman whose mission is to try to help those who are giving their lives to gain their freedom."

It was Brianna's turn to smile. "At least I have now managed to solve one piece of the puzzle about you."

Roarke's brow furrowed as he asked, "Puzzle?"

"Yes, puzzle. I did think it odd for a pirate to live as you lived on Statia. I even found it more baffling when you were to meet with the representative of the trading company here in Brest."

Unable to stop himself, Roarke chuckled. He could understand Brianna's bemusement. The pirates he had encountered over the years had been a vicious pack of sea wolves who cared for neither life nor death, only their own ends. However, Brianna had yet to solve all the mysteries about him. Roarke's smile faded. "There are a few more things you need to know about me before you make up your mind, Brianna."

Before Roarke could stop her, Brianna wrapped her arms about his middle and hugged him close. Her words were soft and full of emotion as she said, "Don't you understand, Roarke? I don't care. I love you, and that is all that matters to me."

Roarke's arms came about Brianna and he held her close. He closed his eyes and tried to find the resolve to continue. He could not. The soft body pressed to his beckoned him with a warmth that could be denied no longer. He wanted to lose himself in Brianna's sweetness. He wanted the taste of her to make him forget all the torment that had shadowed his life since he could remember. He wanted to push all the darkness from his past into the chasm and seal it closed forever. His need to alleviate the bitterness, the resentment, the pain, was like a powerful force driving him into Brianna's arms. Until that moment he hadn't consciously realized it, but she had become his haven, a safe sanctuary against the demons that always hovered in the shadowy recesses of his mind.

"Love me, Brianna," Roarke pleaded as he tipped up her chin with his thumb and forefinger. The look in her eyes answered his plea. He lowered his mouth to hers.

Brianna held tightly to Roarke as he lifted her into his arms and carried her to the bed. She eagerly helped him disrobe her and himself. She needed no foreplay to make her body moistened to receive him. She opened her thighs and welcomed him into her warmth with all the love she possessed.

Mouth to mouth, tongue tasting tongue, breast molded to firm, hard chest, and hips joined as one by their intimate union, their bodies danced a graceful ballet to the sensual music flowing through their veins. They surrendered to their passion, tasting, touching, caressing, until they stood poised on the pinnacle of rapture.

Brianna clung to Roarke's scarred back, her fingers clutching him to her as she wrapped her legs about his waist and drew him into the very depths of her. She arched against him as wave upon wave of heady sensation washed over her and made the muscles in her belly quiver with release. She cried out his name as she felt his hot essence spill deep inside her at the same moment she reached her climax.

Sated and breathing heavily, his heart slamming against his ribs, Roarke collapsed over Brianna. He buried his face in the curve of her neck and braced his weight on his arms to keep from crushing her fragile beauty. In that moment all that existed in his world was the woman who wrapped her arms about his neck and held him close.

Roarke felt the sudden need to weep. Tears stung his eyes as he fought against the overwhelming urge. He'd never cried in his life, not even when he'd stood over his mother's grave. Now, resting in the arms of the woman who had given herself to him, heart and soul, he wanted to cry. It didn't make sense to Roarke, this tumble of emotions careening through him as wildly as his heartbeat. He swallowed and sought to regain control over himself. Only virgins cried after making love.

Roarke tensed and drew in a shuddering breath. In truth he had been a virgin only a few minutes earlier. Physically he'd had sex with more women than he could remember. However, until tonight with Brianna, he'd never experienced what he now knew was love.

The force of the thought made Roarke jerk upright. He looked down at Brianna as if he didn't recognize her. He swore and grabbed his britches. He jerked them on and stood before she could wonder at the sudden change that had come over him.

Roarke crossed to the table that held the decanter of brandy. He poured himself a dram and then tossed it down his throat. Again he ran his fingers through his hair. This couldn't be happening. He couldn't accept it. He wouldn't accept it. He needed Brianna's love, but he wouldn't allow himself to return the emotion. It wasn't in him to love. Had the ability to love ever existed within him, the past had obliterated it many years ago.

Roarke refilled his glass and crossed to the stern windows. The moonlight drenched him in silver, highlighting the planes of his wide chest and shoulders as well as his haunted expression.

"Roarke, what is it?" Brianna asked timidly from the bed. She sat clutching the sheet to her breasts as if the thin material might protect her from Roarke's answer. Her heart thumped with apprehension. The look on Roarke's face chilled her to her soul.

Roarke's nostrils flared as he drew in a deep breath

and closed his eyes. He couldn't answer her question when he himself had as yet to find an explanation for the strange new feelings he was experiencing. He took a long sip of the brandy before he turned to look at the woman on the bed. Her expression tore at him. He clenched his jaw against the urge to go to her and try to make her understand. He gave a mental shake of his head. That was another impossibility.

"Brianna, I've come to a decision, and nothing you can say will alter it."

Brianna began to shake her head from side to side. "Don't, Roarke. Please. Let me stay."

"Tomorrow I'll make the arrangements. I'll see that you have money and a place to live. You'll have everything you need."

"Except you," Brianna muttered, and then said with determination, "Roarke, you can't do this to us." She couldn't believe the change that had so suddenly come over the tender lover of only moments ago.

"I can and I will. I won't have your life in danger. You deserve better than what I can offer."

Brianna felt her world reel. She knew it would do her no good to continue to plead to stay with Roarke. She knew from watching him command his men that once he had made up his mind, he'd not change his decision. She swallowed back the tears tightening her throat and used every bit of willpower she possessed to force her voice to reveal none of her emotions. She calmly said, "I love you, Roarke, but I won't beg for your love."

Her words made Roarke feel as if a whip had once again been laid against his back. He stiffened from the unexpected sting of the blow. "Then it's decided."

He gulped down the last of the brandy and gritted his teeth against the urge to smash the glass against the wall. He abruptly set the glass down and strode from the cabin.

Brianna gave way to her tears when the door closed behind Roarke. She had told him of her love, and for a few brief, glorious minutes, had thought Roarke loved her in return. Brianna buried her face in the pillows and wept even harder as she smelled the scent of the man she loved upon the case.

"*Mon Dieu!* You can't mean what you say," Nick said, unable to hide his astonishment.

"I mean every word. Brianna is staying here in France."

"*Mon ami,* I don't understand you anymore. You care for the girl, but now you're going to leave her behind."

"It's in her best interest," Roarke said, and drained his tankard.

"Is that her opinion or yours?"

Roarke shrugged and tossed several coins on the table as he stood. "What does it matter? My decision is made."

"Then you are a fool, Roarke O'Connor. You've allowed your past to destroy your future," Nick said.

Roarke looked down at Nick and grinned, though Nick's words cut him to the quick. "And you've allowed yourself to become a maudlin old matchmaker." Roarke shook his head in bemusement and chuckled. "If someone had told me that an old lech like you could have a sentimental streak, I'd have laughed in his face."

Nick didn't fall for Roarke's bantering tone. He had known the man far too long not to sense his unrest. He could see the tension lines about his mouth and eyes, though he smiled to put up a brave front. Roarke didn't want to leave Brianna in France any more than he wanted the British to win the war. "Jest all you like, but your glib tongue doesn't hide your true feelings."

"I don't know what you're talking about, and I don't have the time to unravel all your innuendos about my behavior. I have a ship to run and a cargo to see loaded." Roarke cocked his head at Nick. "And I suspect you have duties that demand your attention as well."

Nick came to his feet and gave Roarke a snappy, impudent salute. "Aye, sir. I have duties to attend as usual when you want to get off a touchy subject. Isn't it strange that when we start to discuss your feelings for Brianna, I always find myself very busy indeed?"

Roarke clenched his jaw and his expression darkened. "Then I will see you back at the ship." He turned and strode away from the table before he could say or do something that he couldn't amend.

A cold wind whipped across the bay, blasting Roarke in the face as he stepped out of the tavern. Damn! He'd about had enough of everyone telling him how to feel. No one knew what it had taken for him to make the decision to leave Brianna in France. No one knew that the black void had all but consumed him in its cold, hollow depths.

Roarke jerked up his collar and hunched his shoulders against the cold that seemed several degrees warmer than the emptiness that filled his soul. He rubbed his chilled hands together and then jammed them into his pockets as he watched the last large crate being lowered into the *Black Angel*'s hold. Tomorrow they would sail.

Roarke crossed the cobbled street to the docks and made his way around the stevedores and up the gangplank. Tonight would be his last night with Brianna, and he intended to store up enough memories of their hours together to treasure for the rest of his life.

Brianna sat huddled near the tiny potbellied stove that warmed the captain's cabin. The day was cold, but the temperature had nothing to do with the chill that had settled about her since Roarke had told her she would remain in France when he sailed.

Twilight muted the sky overhead as the sounds of the men working began to dwindle with the ending of the day. The last of the crates bound for the colonies had been secured in the *Black Angel*'s hold, and now the crew was ready for a few hours rest ashore before the voyage began. They laughed and bantered back and forth as they passed the captain's cabin on their way to their quarters to collect enough coin to buy the wine and women they'd enjoy for the night.

Listening to the men's jocundity did little to improve Brianna's own gloomy state of mind. She knew from what she'd overheard of their conversations how they planned to celebrate their last night ashore.

Brianna came to her feet and began to pace the cabin. Her time with Roarke was coming to an end, and there was nothing she could do about it. She cast a worried glance toward the stern porthole. Tonight would be her only opportunity to convince Roarke that he was making a mistake by sending her away. Brianna rubbed at her chilled arms, her actions unconsciously mirroring the anxiety eating away at her composure.

A knock on the door a few moments later barely roused Brianna enough from her morose musings to bid the visitor to enter. Weighed down with a debilitating sense of futility, she glanced over her shoulder as the door swung open and the young cabin boy called John entered, bearing a heavy tray. He set it down on the table and uncovered the delicious meal Roarke had ordered the cook to prepare for their last night together. Brianna bit down hard on her lower lip to keep from bursting into tears at the sight of the fine burgundy wine, delicately browned partridges glazed in honey, rice from the Orient flavored with truffles, and baby carrots, as well as fresh fruit and pastries brimming with creamy fillings. It was a meal fit for a king, or the condemned.

Brianna knew she was the latter. Like one condemned for a crime, she'd been granted a sumptuous last meal before her sentence was to be carried out. Brianna blinked against the new rush of tears that burned her eyes. Perhaps she had not been sentenced to death, yet when Roarke sailed out of her life, a part of her would die.

"Enjoy yer meal, mistress," John said, but received no answer. He glanced toward the table, then back to Brianna, before he shrugged and shook his head. He was only thirteen, but he was already wise enough to know he'd never be able to figure out women. However, he'd like to be given the chance. He grinned at the thought of joining the other crew members ashore. Hopefully tonight he'd be lucky enough to find a woman willing to show him how to do what his body urged. John closed the door behind him, his thoughts entirely on the part of his anatomy that needed the experience.

Brianna turned away from the table, unable to bear the sight of the food and its meaning. She couldn't allow herself to accept the inevitable. She would continue to harbor the hope that Roarke might change his mind until she watched the *Black Angel* sail out of sight.

Consumed with her thoughts, Brianna failed for the first time to hear Roarke enter the cabin. She wasn't aware of his presence until he wrapped his arms about her waist and drew her back against him. He brushed her dark hair aside to give his lips access to her slender throat. "Um, you smell as good as the food looks."

His kiss sent lightning tingles down Brianna's spine, and she drew in a shuddery breath as gooseflesh rose on her arms. All Roarke had to do was look at her and she became like malleable clay in his hands. His very presence befuddled her senses until she forgot everything else.

Brianna stiffened, the thought pricking her like a needle. If she ever hoped to convince Roarke that he was making a mistake by sending her away, she had to keep her wits about her.

Brianna stepped out of Roarke's arms and turned to face him. She searched his dark blue eyes for any sign that he might have changed his mind but saw nothing there except the warm glow that always entered them when he was aroused. Brianna's insides trembled in response, but she refused to give way to the urge to throw herself into Roarke's arms. "Good evening, Captain O'Connor."

" 'Tis is a very fine evening, mistress," Roarke said, eyeing Brianna curiously. He glanced toward the table. "I see the meal I ordered has been prepared."

"I find nothing fine about the evening nor the meal," Brianna said, refusing to allow Roarke's charming manner to touch her.

Roarke released a long breath. "Brianna, this is our last night together. Let us spend it amicably."

"Amicably, Captain O'Connor? Like old friends?" Brianna shook her head. "I'm afraid it's impossible. You've made yourself very clear about how you feel about me."

"Brianna, the decision I made was for your safety, nothing more."

"Oh? Then you decided to leave me in France because of our friendship?" Brianna badgered, suddenly needing to hear the words from Roarke's own lips. He'd left too much unsaid between them when he told her of his decision. For her own peace of mind she wanted to hear him say that he wanted to be rid of her. She didn't want to hear any more of his concern for her safety. His decision stemmed from far more.

"Damn it, Brianna. I told you it's far too dangerous for you on this voyage."

Brianna's temper snapped. She squared her shoulders and braced her hands on her hips. "And I told you I didn't give a damn about the danger."

Roarke's golden earring flashed in the lantern light as he wearily shook his head. "I had hoped to make tonight memorable for both of us. Now I see the gesture was in vain."

Eyes sparkling with golden fire, Brianna gestured toward the table. "Your feast only confirms that I am to be exiled from your life."

Roarke frowned. "Woman, your exile might save your life."

"Roarke, why can't you be honest with me for once? Why can't you just tell me that you want to be rid of me? Tell me that I mean nothing more to you than Roselee. Then I'll not hold out any hope that you might someday come to care for me as I care for you."

Roarke closed the space between them in less than a stride. His arms came about Brianna and his mouth found hers in a fiery, debilitating kiss before she could open her lips to voice a protest. When at last he released her mouth, they were both breathing heavily. "Damn it, Brianna. Does that kiss answer your question?"

Brianna raised her fingers to her tingling lips and slowly shook her head. "No, Roarke. It only tells me that you and I share a passion for each other, and nothing more. You and Roselee also once shared the same passion."

Roarke rolled his eyes toward the ceiling, silently beseeching the Almighty to give him the strength and patience it would take to understand the woman in his arms. When he looked back at Brianna, his expression was tender, but his words were not what she longed to hear. "I want you safe, Brianna. That is all I can say now. When I return to France, we will then see what the future may hold for us."

"I'm afraid there is no future for us," Brianna said as she extricated herself from Roarke's arms. Tears stung the backs of her lids, but she blinked them back as she crossed to the small pile of clothing lying on the footlocker. It was all she possessed. She picked it up and held it against her breasts as if to create a shield against Roarke. "Will you have someone escort me to my new lodgings?"

"Brianna, don't do this. You don't have to leave until tomorrow," Roarke said.

"But I do have to leave, Roarke. As you have to leave tomorrow. We must do what we have to do, no matter how much it hurts."

Roarke glanced one last time at the table. "At least stay and eat your dinner."

Brianna shook her head. "No, Roarke. It's time that I go now. There's nothing else I can gain here but more misery."

Roarke drew in a resigned breath. Perhaps it was for the best. He turned toward the door. "I'll have Nick act as your escort and see that you have everything you need."

"Thank you, Roarke. I will never forget your generosity."

Chapter 13

Nick glanced down at the young woman huddled in the depths of a large woolen seaman's coat. The tall collar hid most of her face, leaving only her tiny red nose and large, misery-filled eyes visible above the coarse fabric. She clutched her few belongings to her like a lifeline as she silently followed him to the small cottage Roarke had found for her at the edge of town.

Nick swore under his breath and jammed his own cold hands down into his pockets as he looked up at the clear sky overhead. For the life of him, he didn't know how he'd suddenly gotten himself so involved in Roarke's love life. Tonight was his last night ashore, and here he was escorting Brianna instead of enjoying himself with one of the tavern wenches. Nick's breath fogged about him as he released a long, disgusted breath and then glanced once more at Brianna. He'd never been a man to give a rip-roaring damn about anyone or anything for more than a few moments of pleasure. Now here he was playing protector to a woman who thoroughly disliked him. Nick gave a mental shrug. He'd apologized for his behavior at the Statia Inn, and he could do no more to make amends.

Damn! That was exactly why he'd gotten involved. Nick's eyes widened with the realization. Subconsciously he'd felt responsible for Roarke's predicament because of his own behavior that night. Had he not drugged the girl with Ole Harry's potion, his friend would not have ended up in her bed.

Nick shook his head. He honestly couldn't believe that had been the motive behind his actions. That would mean he felt guilty for what he'd done. But to feel guilty, you had to have a conscience. And he didn't, Nick resolved as he swung open the gate to the neat little picket fence that enclosed the garden of the cottage.

"Well, we're here," Nick said, stepping aside to allow Brianna to pass.

Brianna paused and looked at her new home. It was beautiful with its thatched roof and white plastered walls. The window shutters and sturdy oak door had been made by a craftsman whose delicate workmanship reminded her of creamy icing on gingerbread. White-washed stones edged the flower beds and flagstone walkway. In all, the cottage looked like something from a fairy tale.

Tears of regret misted her eyes at what might have been. The tiny cottage could have become the lovers' bower that it resembled. However, it was now to be the home of an exile who would spend her days here, mourning the loss of a love she'd never won.

Nick unlatched the door and lit the lamp that sat on the table in the small foyer. Golden light spilled over the room beyond.

Glumly Brianna entered her new home. She looked over the main room and swallowed back a new rush of tears. Roarke had seen to everything, even the furnishings. The pieces he'd chosen were not extravagant but simple and comfortable, reminding Brianna of the small cottage she had considered home until her mother married Lord Montague. In her most trying times at Montvale she had often longed to return to that cottage, where she and her mother had shared a closeness that had seemed to evaporate as the years passed in the luxury of Montvale.

The thought was like a physical pain. She gasped and sagged down into the nearest chair, unable to hold back her tears any longer. She wept for her present loss as well as the past. Until that moment she hadn't truly realized she had lost her mother years before her death. Brianna's tears came faster and harder.

Nick shifted uneasily as he stood silently watching Brianna weep. He didn't know what to do. He was a lover, not a comforter of women's megrims. His unrest mounted with Brianna's tears. He fidgeted with the lamp and then resigned himself to the fact that he had only one option. He crossed to where Brianna sat, and knelt beside her chair. Tenderly he laid his hand against her dark hair, unsure as to how to proceed but knowing he had to do something to stop the flood of tears before she made herself sick. Roarke would have his hide if Brianna became ill when he could have stopped it.

"There now," Nick began tentatively. "This place may not be a palace, but you'll be comfortable here. Roarke wouldn't leave you unless he was sure of that."

Brianna sobbed even louder at the mention of Roarke's name. The only two people she'd ever loved were lost to her.

Nick flinched as he realized his mistake. He awkwardly stroked Brianna's hair in an attempt to soothe her and murmured, "I'm sorry, *chérie*. I know it must be hard on you."

Brianna raised her head and looked at Nick through tear-swollen eyes. She swiped at her nose with the back of her hand, and her lower lip trembled as she said, "I pray you'll never know how hard it is to love someone who doesn't love you in return, Nick. I wouldn't wish that pain upon my worst enemy." She wiped at her nose again as a new wave of tears spilled over her lashes and followed the crystal path left on her cheeks by its predecessors.

Nick's rueful smile was little more than a grimace as he acknowledged that Brianna still didn't consider him a friend. He seriously doubted she ever would, but they both loved Roarke. At least they had that in common. On that thin thread, he would do everything he could to try to make her understand that Roarke, too, was suffering from his decision to leave her behind. "Roarke sent you here for your own protection and for no other reason. We sail into war when we leave France, Brianna."

"Don't try to make it easier on me, Nick. I know why Roarke is leaving me in France. He wants to be rid of me," Brianna said, fighting to suppress another sob.

"You're wrong, *petite*. Getting rid of you is the furthest thing from Roarke's mind. He is leaving you here out of fear for your safety."

Brianna came to her feet and looked at the man who unfolded from his crouched position by her chair. "Nick, I appreciate what you're trying to do, but you can't protect me from the truth. I know how Roarke feels. He's made it clear to me from the very beginning that he has no room in his life for me. But I foolishly allowed myself to fall in love with him."

"*Mon Dieu!*" Nick exploded. "Did he tell you this?"

Brianna nodded, her cheeks heating from the memory of her first night with Roarke. She looked down at her hands, unable to look Nick in the eyes as she confessed, "He told me how he felt while we were still at the Statia Inn."

Nick rolled his eyes, and his Gallic features expressed his exasperation with Brianna as well as

Roarke. "The man only said that to protect himself. He loves you, but he's afraid."

"Afraid? Don't be ridiculous. Roarke O'Connor is not afraid of the Devil himself."

"No. He is not afraid of the Devil, but he is afraid of how you will feel about him once you learn about his background."

Brianna stilled, remembering Roarke's own words. He had thought she would reject him when she knew of his past, but she had refused to listen when he'd tried to tell her. She looked at Nick. "What does he fear for me to learn?"

Nick jammed his hands back into the pockets of his coat and strode across the room to the fireplace. He stared down into the empty fire pit, undecided as to what to say. He bent and tossed several pieces of kindling onto the grates to start a fire. It wasn't his place to tell Brianna of Roarke's past. He didn't look at her as he struck the flint to the tinder and set it to the kindling. "That's not for me to reveal. It's up to Roarke to tell you what he wants you to know."

In less than two strides Brianna closed the space separating them. She grabbed the sleeve of his coat and made him stand to look at her. "Nick, if you know something, then please tell me before it is too late."

Sadly Nick shook his head. His expression reflected his sympathy and understanding as he looked down into Brianna's anxious little face. Yet he said, "I can't break Roarke's trust. He is like a brother to me, and he'd never forgive such betrayal."

"But I love him, too, Nick. And until I know what it is, I can't help him overcome it."

"Leave it be, Brianna. I won't tell you anything of Roarke's past. However, I will tell you that I truly believe Roarke loves you, no matter what he has said or done." Nick paused and his lips curled into a semblance of a smile at the look of pure hope his words created. "But that is merely my assessment, because Roarke has not told me how he feels about you."

Brianna bit her lower lip, undecided as to what to do. Should Nick be right, Roarke was leaving her behind because he cared for her. However, he might not return if what he'd said about the British came to pass. An icy hand seemed to clutch Brianna's heart. She couldn't let the *Black Angel* sail without her. She had to be with Roarke, no matter what lay in their future. It was far better to die with him than to wilt away here, always waiting for him to return.

"Nick I can't stay here."

Nick frowned down at Brianna. "I don't see that you have any other choice. Roarke has made his decision, and once he sets his mind, it's made up."

"You have to help me," Brianna said, a glimmer of a plan beginning to form at the edges of her mind.

"That's what I've been trying to do all night," Nick answered as he turned and laid a log on the flaming sticks of kindling.

"No. You don't understand. I must be on the *Black Angel* when it sails tomorrow, and you're my only chance."

Nick stilled, waiting apprehensively for Brianna to continue.

"I can't remain here while Roarke sails into danger. I have to be with him. You must help me get back on the *Black Angel* without him knowing I'm there until it's too late for him to do anything about it."

Slowly Nick looked at Brianna. "*Mon Dieu!* Do you think me a half-wit? Roarke would have me keelhauled just to hear my screams." Nick shook his head. "Nay, *petite*. I've tried to make amends for what I did to you at the inn, but I have to think of my own hide."

"Don't do it for me. Do it for Roarke. If what you believe is true, we should be together, no matter what we must face."

Nick released a long breath and shook his head. "You ask too much, Brianna."

Brianna inched her chin up and eyed Nick obstinately. "Then I'll get on board without your help. But one way or the other, I'll be on the *Black Angel* when it sails tomorrow, Nick Sebastain."

"*Mon Dieu!* You're determined to get us both killed."

"No, Nick. I'm just determined to be with the man I love."

"Foolish woman," Nick growled, glowering at Brianna. "You could die. We aren't going on a pleasure cruise. The *Black Angel* carries munitions and supplies to the men fighting in the colonies."

"Roarke has already told me about his mission, but that doesn't alter my determination to be with him. He needs me and I need him."

Something akin to envy rose up in Nick. He had heard all the ballads of true love, listened to the old men sitting with their tankards of rum as they told of the days gone by and the many loves of their lives. He had even once thought himself in love with a little wench from the islands. However, after his lust was expended and a cool head once more ruled, he realized he'd been thinking with a portion of his anatomy that certainly wasn't his heart. And until Roarke had found himself involved with Brianna, Nick had believed love was an excuse people used to bed each other. Now he realized it went far deeper than the physical side of a relationship. Love was not merely the simple act of two bodies coming together in the heat of passion. It was sacrifice, it was sharing, it was two people willing even to risk their lives for each other. No man should be denied such love.

The thought conquered Nick's earlier resolves. He couldn't and wouldn't stop Brianna from being with the man she loved. "All right. I will help you get on board. You may stay in my cabin until the time you choose to make your presence known, but know it now, Mistress Tartleton. This is the last favor I do for you. I risk everything to help you: my place on the *Black Angel* as well as Roarke's friendship. And I'll do it no more. We are quits. My debt is paid."

Brianna threw her arms about Nick's neck and hugged him. New tears brightened her eyes as she looked up into his astonished dark gaze. She smiled tremulously. "Thank you, Nick. You are a good friend."

Nick couldn't stop his own smile, as he wondered if he'd survive having a friendship such as Brianna's. One could easily get oneself killed for it.

Less than an hour later, Nick paused at the bottom of the gangplank and scanned the deck for the night watch. Seeing the man on the quarterdeck talking with one of his cohorts, he whispered to Brianna, "Stay close to me. And keep quiet as if your life depends upon it. Because it may, if Roarke realizes what we are doing before we leave port."

Brianna nodded and hunched farther down into the woolen coat. She'd be quieter than a mouse if it meant she'd be on board the *Black Angel* when it sailed at dawn.

Nick grimaced at the sudden urge he felt to ruffle the dark hair exposed above the turned-up collar that nearly engulfed Brianna. She looked so little and helpless, much like an impish child set to do mischief. Nick gave himself a mental shake, firmly reminding himself that helping her with this escapade could easily cost him the friendship of a man who meant more to him than anyone else in the world. Nick bit his lip indecisively. He'd agreed to Brianna's badgering, but now he was having second thoughts. Roarke would never forgive him if something untoward happened to her while she was aboard the *Black Angel*.

Nick paused with his hand on the thick hemp that railed the gangplank and looked back at the girl close on his heels. He'd make one last attempt to convince her to abide by Roarke's wishes. "Brianna, won't you reconsider this scheme of yours?"

Brianna firmly shook her head. "No, Nick. If this is the only way I can be with Roarke, then nothing you can say or do will make me change my mind."

"I could expose your scheme to Roarke."

"But you won't, because you know we belong together, no matter what Roarke says to the contrary."

Nick nodded. She was right. Roarke might not agree. Hell! Nick knew he wouldn't agree. It went too much against everything his friend had schooled himself to believe through the years. But Nick knew Roarke deserved some happiness out of life, though he might have to force his friend to admit it.

"All right. We've come this far. It's now or never," Nick said, and quietly made his way up the gangplank. Brianna followed close upon his heels, her small form blending in with his much larger shadow. She held her breath as they crossed the deck to the hatch that led down to the cabins, and didn't release it as they quietly made their way along the passage to Nick's quarters.

A board squeaked underfoot, and Brianna froze until Nick growled. "Come on or we'll both find ourselves keelhauled."

The thought of Roarke catching them before she was

safely hidden in Nick's cabin spurred her forward. She grasped Nick's sleeve and held on for dear life until he closed the cabin door behind them.

Brianna felt her lungs would burst. Her heart slammed against her ribs as she gasped in a breath of life-giving air and said, "We made it."

Nick looked at her grimly. "So far so good. But we still have to face Roarke when he learns you're on board. That's not going to be a pleasant encounter, I can assure you."

"Roarke will understand," Brianna said, and prayed she was right.

"I hope so," Nick said as he gathered up a blanket and turned toward the door. He paused with his hand on the latch. "Keep this door locked. I'll bring you food and water when I have the chance."

"Thank you, Nick. You'll never know what this means to me."

"I hope Roarke doesn't make both of us regret this, *petite*."

"Roarke will never know who helped me, Nick," Brianna said, reassuringly.

"I suspect he will once he learns you've been staying in my cabin." Nick smiled and shrugged. "But that's neither here nor there at the moment, *mon ami*. We will face the tiger when the time comes to brave his fury."

"Good night, Nick," Brianna said.

"Sleep well, *petite*. You have managed to come this far with my help. Now the rest is up to you."

The pleasant sound of the crew's sea chantey filling the afternoon air, John crept down the passageway and paused outside the first mate's cabin. He bent close to the cabin door and pressed his ear to the wood. He smiled his admiration of the first mate when he heard the soft, feminine voice. Nick Sebastain was insatiable. He always had women when he went ashore, and now he had one all to himself on board the *Black Angel*.

John chuckled. Someday he'd be just like Nick, a man of the world, with women throwing themselves at his feet in every port. A firm hand at the nape of his collar made John's smile fade. He stiffened with apprehension as he straightened and turned to look up at the man who had him firmly under rein. He swallowed nervously and smiled weakly up at his stony-faced captain.

"What's this, John? Eavesdropping?"

John moistened his lips and glanced worriedly toward the cabin door. He couldn't tell Captain O'Connor what he'd been doing without getting Nick into trouble. He swallowed again but remained mute.

Roarke's frown deepened. "I asked you a question, John, and I expect an answer. Why are you snooping around outside the first mate's cabin?"

A grimace marred John's young, freckled face as he sought a plausible lie. Unlike the older men of his acquaintance, he had as yet to learn to be glib-tongued and ready with a yarn when the moment required. He shifted uneasily and bit his lower lip in confusion.

Roarke's annoyance mounted. John had been the best cabin boy he'd ever had aboard the *Black Angel*. He'd always been honest and willing to obey any command given him in the past. Roarke's thick-lashed eyes narrowed thoughtfully as he glanced toward the cabin door. There was something going on here that John didn't want to tell him. Suspicion mounting rapidly, he held John firmly by the collar as he raised his fist to knock on Nick's door. He received no answer.

John paled and went taut before shifting nervously from foot to foot. Roarke flashed him another questioning look and released his hold upon the cabin boy before giving the door another firm rap with his fist. He heard movement beyond the portal and then Nick opened the door mere inches, allowing his large frame to block out the cabin behind him. He looked from Roarke to John and then back at his captain, and then yawned widely.

"Something wrong, *mon ami*?" Nick asked. He made no move to open the door further.

"Yes, something is most definitely wrong when my first mate is spending his afternoons sleeping when he should be at his duties."

"I had watch last night, Captain," Nick said, flinching under Roarke's censure.

"Aye, as did several other members of the crew, but they are not sleeping the day away. Nick, we are friends, but you and I both know our friendship can't interfere with the *Black Angel*."

"Aye, Captain. I know my place aboard ship."

"Then I suggest you get to your duties."

Nick saluted. "Aye, Captain. Right away."

Momentarily forgetting the cabin boy, who looked up at him with eyes wide with trepidation, Roarke started to turn away. He caught a glimpse of John from the corner of his eye and came to a halt. He looked down at the young boy, and his face reflected his agitation. "The same thing goes for you. Get back to your duties before I decide you need to learn a lesson for dallying."

Nick closed the door and looked back at the young woman sitting on his bunk. He released a long breath. "That was a close one."

Brianna came to her feet. "Nick, I'm sorry I got you into trouble. Soon this will all be over."

Nick ran his long fingers over his chin and grinned. "I certainly hope so. I have little taste for sleeping in the forecastle. And I certainly have no penchant for thievery. This morning the cook nearly caught me slipping into the galley to get your breakfast."

"I know it has been hard on you the last two weeks," Brianna said.

"Aye. The men are beginning to wonder about me and my sudden interest in sleeping in the forecastle. A few have even hinted that perhaps I've taken a fancy to a member of the crew and want to stay near my heart's desire."

Brianna frowned. "But why would they say such a thing? There are no women in the crew."

"Just forget I said anything," Nick said. He shook his head in disbelief. After everything the girl had endured, she was still an innocent to the vices in the wicked world surrounding her. He could well understand Roarke's attraction. Her very innocence would be like a heady aphrodisiac for a man who had witnessed the lascivious side of life since his birth.

Nick turned to the door. He needed to get back to his duties before Roarke came looking for him. He opened the door and looked back at Brianna. "I will see you tonight."

He turned and came face-to-face with Roarke. Roarke's gaze traveled from Nick's paling features to the young woman standing in the center of the tiny cabin. Like lightning, Roarke's angry blue eyes snapped back to Nick's face. "What in the devil is going on here?"

"I can explain, *mon ami*," Nick said nervously, but wondered if any explanation he could give would be sufficient to keep him from getting keelhauled.

"I seriously doubt that you can explain yourself out of this, Nick," Roarke ground out.

"It's not his fault," Brianna said, coming to Nick's defense.

Roarke ignored her. "Nick, I'll have you in chains for this insubordination."

Brianna pushed herself between the two men. "You can't do this, Roarke. He did it for us. He was only helping me."

Again Roarke ignored Brianna. He took Nick by the arm and passed her by as if she didn't exist. He escorted the first mate down the passageway and out onto the deck. In front of the entire crew he ordered him chained and thrown into the hold.

Nearly sobbing with despair, Brianna followed. Again she tried to intervene on Nick's behalf. Roarke turned to her, his face set with fury. "Just feel fortunate, mistress, that you are not also thrown into the hold as a stowaway."

"But you don't understand. I made Nick bring me aboard. He didn't want to help me, but I forced him."

Roarke's smile was thin and cruel. "Forgive me if I doubt your word, Mistress Tarleton. But my first mate could not have been forced to bring you aboard against his will. As any fool can see, he's much larger and stronger than you. Knowing Nick as I do, I'm sure his actions were not motivated by his benevolence. After what you've already experienced with him, I would think you would not be so naive as to believe otherwise."

"No, Roarke. You're wrong. Nick meant only to help me, nothing more. You can't punish him for something that is my fault."

Roarke's expression didn't soften. "As I once told you, mistress, I can do whatever I damn well please. I rule the *Black Angel*, and everyone on board has to answer to me. That includes all stowaways."

He turned to John, who stood nervously watching the scene taking place between his captain and the beautiful young woman. The cabin boy didn't fully understand exactly what was transpiring, because for a while she had been the captain's woman, and then Nick's, and now he didn't know where she belonged. "Take Mistress Tarleton back to the first mate's cabin. It should be far more comfortable now that she won't have to share it."

The sun seemed to come from behind stormy clouds as it dawned on Brianna that part of Roarke's fury stemmed from jealousy. He had thought she had shared Nick's cabin with the first mate. Her heart swelled with emotion. Roarke's jealousy was just another sign that Nick had been right. Roarke cared for her. Brianna smiled up at Roarke as John stepped forward to escort her below. "Roarke, I haven't shared any man's cabin but yours."

Roarke's expression didn't alter. "That is your problem, madam, not mine. Now, go below before I change my mind and have you put in chains with your friend."

Roarke's harsh words caught Brianna off guard, and she flinched visibly as if he'd struck her. She looked at the man who held her heart and experienced her first doubts about the wisdom of stowing away on the *Black Angel*. Roarke was not acting like a man in love at the moment. Since the minute he'd seen her in Nick's cabin, she'd seen no inkling of the tender lover she'd known before reaching France. Before her stood the hard-bitten pirate who ruled his ship with an iron hand. He didn't give an inch when someone disobeyed his orders.

Chapter 14

A mutinous expression thinning her lips into a pouty line, Brianna turned to pace back across the small cabin. Nothing had gone as she'd first planned. Nick was still confined to the hold, and she remained quarantined away from the rest of the ship's crew and captain.

Brianna felt like screaming her vexation but knew it would do her no good. Roarke didn't seem to care if she was going stir-crazy locked away in the first mate's cabin. For the past two months he'd not even seen fit to visit her. She'd had no contact with anyone on board the *Black Angel* except the cabin boy when he brought her meals and water to bathe.

Brianna turned on her heel and crossed to the porthole. She stared out at the great expanse of blue water shimmering in the afternoon sun. Soon, from what little information she could pry out of John, the *Black Angel* would reach her destination.

"And it won't be soon enough for me," Brianna ground out between clenched teeth. At that moment she'd give anything to tell Roarke exactly what she thought of his treatment of her when everything she'd done had been to be with him. How dare the man be so arrogant as to lock her away without even giving her a chance to explain.

During the weeks of her confinement, she'd mulled

over their last conversation a dozen times, and each time she'd thought of it, she grew angrier. After everything they had shared before reaching France, Roarke had immediately assumed she'd allowed Nick to take his place in her bed as if she were a dockside whore. She'd been too stunned at the time to get angry over the insult, but the weeks of confinement had resolved that dilemma for her. In her present state of mind, she could easily tear Roarke's head off for even thinking such a thing about her. At first she'd allowed herself to foolishly believe Roarke's actions had stemmed from jealousy, but now she accepted the fact he'd only been outraged to find her a stowaway, and his first mate her ally.

Brianna pushed away the dull ache her thoughts created about her heart. She'd been over and over the scene between Roarke, Nick, and herself, but she still didn't understand how Roarke could be so unreasonable. His attitude had changed so swiftly toward her that she couldn't help but wonder if she'd been mistaken about everything she'd sensed between them during their time together before Brest. Brianna shook her head. She couldn't be that wrong about the man. She knew Roarke had cared; nothing could make her believe otherwise.

The sound of the key grating in the latch drew Brianna's thoughts away from the *Black Angel*'s enigmatic captain. She glanced once more to the bright sunlight flashing on the great expanse of water, and frowned. It was too early for her evening meal, and she had not asked John to bring her water to bathe.

The door swung open, and the cabin boy smiled widely at Brianna. John's gesture reflected his growing admiration for the young woman his captain kept confined under lock and key in the first mate's cabin. During the past weeks he'd come to like her, and in his thirteen-year-old heart, she'd found a niche with her gentleness, a very rare commodity in the world in which he lived.

John couldn't stop himself from marveling at Mistress Brianna's attitude. She'd never had a bad word for him, even when her vexation at being incarcerated was plainly visible in the tension lines about her lovely mouth and eyes. Most would have been so fractious that they'd have taken out their spleen on him. But not the captain's woman, as he once again had begun to think of her. She was a true gem of a lady. She'd not blamed him, nor had she caused him any undue trouble by making outrageous demands upon his time.

"Afternoon, mistress," John said, tipping his sailor's cap before courteously sliding it off his head. His smile broadened. He was pleased that the captain had allowed him to bring the news to her that she was going to be allowed on deck to take the air for a short while.

Brianna's frown didn't lift as she took in the young man's smiling countenance. "What is it, John? Has something happened?"

John shook his head. "No, ma'am. The captain sent me down to bring you on deck. He said you'd be allowed out for a while to take the air."

Brianna's expression didn't alter. "How very kind of your captain to think of me after so many weeks."

John shifted uncomfortably and his smile dimmed. Then he reaffirmed it bravely and said, "It's a lovely day, mistress. I'm sure you'll enjoy a few minutes out of this place."

"I would have enjoyed a few minutes out of this place several weeks ago, John. However, your captain didn't see fit to show any inclination of thinking of my feelings at that time. Why is he doing so now?"

John's smile faded and then vanished completely as he realized there were undercurrents here that he wasn't capable of crossing. He shrugged. "I know not, mistress. I just do as I'm ordered. Now, if you'll come with me, I'll escort you up on deck." Another glimmer of a smile tugged at his mouth. "I think ye'll like it. It's far warmer than we've been used to these last weeks."

The woeful look that crossed John's young, freckled face pricked Brianna's conscience. She had no right to inflict her angst upon the boy. It wasn't his fault how things had turned out between herself and Roarke. There was only one person to blame for that, and that was the captain of the *Black Angel* himself. Roarke's lofty, self-important, unfeeling, and distrustful nature had kept them separated when all she'd tried to do was to show her love for him. The thought again stirred the caldron of her annoyance until it simmered anew.

Brianna's chin came up and fire flickered in the golden brown depths of her eyes, making them look like shards of pure amber. Yes, she'd enjoy her time on deck in a manner that she seriously doubted Roarke expected after all these weeks. She smiled at John. "I'm sure you're right, John. I do need a few minutes on deck. Perhaps it will serve to help make my temperament more amicable afterwards."

John suddenly felt he was standing dangerously close to the edge of some precipice that could easily mean disaster for anyone close enough to it. However, he shrugged the feeling aside and smiled again at Brianna. "If ye'll allow me, mistress." He stepped aside for Brianna to pass in front of him and then followed close upon her heels as she emerged out on the sun-drenched deck.

Brianna paused, nearly blinded by the brightness of water and sun. She raised her face toward the white

canvas overhead and drew in several breaths of the refreshing sea breeze, bracing herself for her first encounter with Roarke in nearly two months. Her resolve
hardened as she took one last, fortifying breath and then
looked across the deck. She had to shield her eyes
against the glare of blue-white sea and sky as she
searched for the man who had taken her heart and then
tossed it back in her face without a thought to the hurt
his actions would inflict.

Spying Roarke on the quarterdeck, Brianna squared
her shoulders, lifted her skirts, and strode purposely up
the steps to where her dark-haired nemesis lover stood
leaning negligently against the mahogany rail.

Arms folded casually over his wide chest, Roarke
eyed her curiously as she approached but made no other
sign that there was anything out of the ordinary about
her determined stride and resolute expression.

"So I see you decided to accept my invitation above
decks," Roarke said as Brianna paused in front of him,
hands on hip, her face a mask of fury from the weeks
of brooding solitude in her cabin.

"Invitation?" Brianna almost hissed, her ire flaming
to new heights at his casual attitude.

Roarke shrugged. "Perhaps it wasn't exactly an invitation, but even a prisoner should be allowed on deck
for a few breaths of air when time permits."

"Have you allowed Nick out of the hold to enjoy the
air?" Brianna asked.

Roarke's face darkened. "I'll amend that statement to
a degree. I allow only prisoners on deck who I feel are
of no threat to the safety of my vessel."

"You know good and well that Nick is no threat to
the *Black Angel*. He is your second in command. He
would never do anything to jeopardize your ship or his
friendship with you."

Roarke arched a brow dubiously. "If you will recall, he has already done exactly that when he helped you stow away in Brest."

Her exasperation reaching an all-time new high from her incarceration as well as Roarke's continued obstinacy about Nick and herself, Brianna nearly exploded. "Roarke O'Connor, you are a blind, arrogant fool. You're like the man who can't see the forest because of the trees. For some ungodly reason you don't want to accept the fact that Nick did what he did because of his friendship and love for you."

"And you don't seem to understand that when I give an order, it must be carried out. Too many lives depend upon me to condone Nick's disobedience. A captain must rule his ship fairly, and punish even his friends if they think they are above his laws. Otherwise it would be anarchy."

"Blast your anarchy! You and I both know the reason behind Nick's imprisonment, and it has nothing to do with Nick. It's me you want to hurt. So punish me all you like, but allow Nick his freedom. He doesn't deserve to suffer because of his love for you."

Roarke's eyes glittered and his mouth firmed into a thin, obstinate line. "Mistress Tarleton, you seem to believe that what I've done is because of you. However, I fear you're disillusioned. The *Black Angel* is my first responsibility. I have lives who depend upon the cargo this vessel carries, and I can't allow my personal feelings to interfere with it."

"Roarke," Brianna said, suddenly feeling deflated. It was the same as the day he'd sentenced Nick to the hold. Roarke refused to listen to her. "I don't understand you anymore, nor do I especially like the man I now see. At one time I thought the arrogant captain I first came to know was just a guise you wore; now I know differently. I fear I fell in love with a man that truly doesn't exist if you can treat someone who loves you like Nick does in such an uncaring manner."

Brianna began to turn away, but Roarke's hand stilled her. She looked back into the face that she loved more than life itself and felt tears burn her eyes. She blinked rapidly and looked down at the hand on her arm to hide the tide of emotion washing over her. Roarke's only true love was the *Black Angel*.

"Mistress, you've not been dismissed. I've listened to what you have had to say; now it's my turn."

A new surge of anger surfaced at his haughty, unfeeling attitude. "Be damned with your orders, Captain O'Connor. I've had enough. I am not one of your crew to be ordered about. Nor will I listen to any more of your ship's laws. You've done nothing but bully me and order me about since we met. But no more." Brianna jerked her arm free and started to turn away again. Roarke's hand again stopped her.

"Mistress, when I give an order, you will obey," Roarke began, but before he could finish, Brianna turned on him; jerking her arm free, she gave him a swift push with both hands against his chest.

"Leave me be," she said, and turned to flee the quarterdeck. Blinded by tears of rage and pain, she ran back to her tiny prison and slammed the door behind her, welcoming the thin portal that kept her away from Roarke.

The force of Brianna's push sent Roarke backwards. His face mirrored a moment of dismay and then wide-eyed shock as he landed back against the rail with such force that it caught him off balance. He tipped backward. He sought a handhold as his large body hung momentarily in the air before his weight sent him over the side of the *Black Angel* and into the clear, sparkling wa-

ters of the Atlantic. His splash foamed with the waves
breaking against the black hull of ship. His cry for help
went unheard as the hands working on deck continued
to sing a sea chantey to keep time with their labors.

The man in the crow's nest spied Roarke's dark head
and frantically waving arms as the *Black Angel* sailed
past its captain. Unable to believe what he saw, he
rubbed his eyes to clear his vision. In the past he'd mis-
takenly thought manatees to be mermaids after looking
at the empty horizon for hours on end, and now he believed he saw his captain swimming behind the ship.
The lookout shook his head and peered again at the image in the ship's wake. It didn't disappear or change
into one of the playful porpoises that often accompanied
the vessel. Still unable to believe his eyes, the lookout
glanced toward the quarterdeck, where he'd last seen
his captain only minutes before. Finding no sign of him,
he finally cupped his hands around his mouth and
shouted to the men on deck below, "Ahoy there! Man
overboard."

From his vantage point the lookout watched the flurry
of activity his shout created among the crew. Looking
like a many-legged animal, they moved en masse to the
stern. For a long moment they stood staring at the man
waving at them in the ship's wake; finally one resource-
ful sailor began to give orders to start his rescue. In
minutes the *Black Angel*'s captain was once more on
board his vessel, dripping wet and furious with the
woman who had sent him into the drink with her fit of
temper.

"I'll wring her bloody little neck for this," Roarke
ground out as he swiped strands of dripping hair from
his brow. Face dark with fury, he twisted the water from
the tail of the shirt that clung to the contours of his
muscular chest and shoulders like a second skin. No

one spoke as he turned toward the hatch that would lead him to his prey.

He had just reached the portal that separated him from the vixen on the other side when he heard the lookout's cry once more. "Ahoy. British ships to starboard."

Roarke flashed one last seething glance at the door before turning back the way he'd just come. The British navy had saved Brianna's hide for a little while, but once he had dealt with them, she'd find out exactly what happened to anyone who thought to trespass against Roarke O'Connor. His hand itched to tan her rounded little bottom.

Roarke took the spyglass from the man who had taken Nick's place. Jacobs was a good man, willing to follow orders but not quite quick enough mentally to command a vessel should the need arise. He would suit to finish this mission, but Roarke knew he'd have to find a replacement for Nick before another voyage was planned.

"It looks as if it's a convoy, sir," Jacobs said.

"Aye. 'Tis a convoy, but from the looks of it, they're not escorting any merchantman. 'Tis some of King George's finest warships."

Jacob glanced at his captain. "Do you think they've been looking for us?"

Roarke nodded and closed the spyglass. "Aye. But I expected them much sooner. The British spies must be having trouble relaying their information to the Admiralty. Hopefully that's a sign that Beaumarchais's men have been having some effect."

Roarke glanced at his first mate and saw the man's puzzled expression. He'd forgotten he'd not been talking to Nick, who knew the ruse they perpetrated. Ah, how he missed Nick's companionship, especially at times like these. Resigned to his first mate's betrayal, he ordered, "Have the men prepare for battle. I suspect yon warships don't intend to let us pass without a fight."

"Aye, Captain," Jacobs said, giving Roarke a snappy salute before turning to carry out his orders.

Roarke watched him go. It wouldn't be easy with an inexperienced first mate in charge of the men. But there was nothing he could do about it without succumbing to Brianna's demands and breaking all of his own rules. He shook his head and brushed another damp strand of hair from his brow. He had meant what he had said to Brianna. He was captain of the *Black Angel*, and no matter what he felt personally, he couldn't and wouldn't go against his own rules.

Roarke looked down at his soppy clothing and felt another wave of anger warm his insides as the urge to tan Brianna's backside claimed him once more. After he finished with the warships, he intended to settle things between himself and the little vixen below. Roarke glanced toward the enemy ships, which were quickly closing the distance between themselves and the *Black Angel*. His insides seemed to freeze. God! Everything he'd feared was now coming to pass. Brianna was on board the *Black Angel*, and the British navy was going to do everything in their power to send his vessel and all on board to the bottom of the Atlantic. And all that would take would be one cannonball hitting the *Black Angel*'s hold, which was filled with black powder.

For the first time in his life, Roarke now faced an enemy with fear in his heart. He wasn't afraid for himself or his men but for the woman who had only a short while before pushed him overboard. Roarke smiled grimly with realization. The vexatious little beauty below had long ago pushed his heart overboard, and he'd not recovered it before she had claimed it completely for herself.

Roarke's expression darkened. He loved Brianna, but if the British had the day, he feared he'd never get the chance to tell her of his feeling. Roarke called out the order to man battle stations as a British flagship began to maneuver around in an attempt to give the *Black Angel* a broadside hit. The bang of the wooden gunport doors hitting against the hull could be heard throughout the ship as an eerie, waiting stillness settled over the vessel.

For the first time in his life, Roarke raised his eyes heavenward and quietly voiced a prayer for God's protection of those he loved. Acutely aware of his own past sins, he didn't ask God's benevolence for himself. He didn't feel he deserved it.

Still fuming, Brianna sat huddled on the bunk when the first cannon exploded near the *Black Angel* and sent seawater spraying over its stern and through the porthole of her cabin. Shock evaporating her anger instantly, she sprang to her feet and rushed to see what was transpiring even as another cannonball whistled over the *Black Angel* and, with a loud, muffled thump, exploded in the depths beyond. "My God, we're being attacked."

Thinking of only Roarke's safety, Brianna was out of the cabin and running down the passageway before she could consider the danger to herself. She burst out onto the deck as the *Black Angel*'s cannons let loose their first volley, sending cannonballs exploding into the flagship's decks and masts.

Two of the tall timbers trembled, and then, with a squeal of wood torn violently asunder, they fell, taking yards of canvas, ropes, rigging, and crewmen into the ocean. Damaged but not completely crippled, the flagship gave off another volley of cannon toward the *Black Angel*. Experienced in battle, Roarke managed to maneuver the *Black Angel*'s course so she only received a glancing blow from the blast. However, a man-of-war now came in for the kill, tacking around to finish what the flagship had begun. A cannonball exploded on deck, shattering the *Black Angel*'s mainmast. It whimpered and then trembled before surrendering to the forces of nature. Men's screams filled the air as the canvas wrapped about them and then caught fire from the cinders left by the blast. Horrified, Brianna stood frozen as she watched the crew try to put out the flames before they devoured their companions.

"What in the hell are you doing up here?" Roarke growled, fear coiling in his belly at the sight of Brianna on deck. Without waiting for her answer, he thrust her back inside the hatch and gave her a rough shove down the passageway. "Get back to your cabin and stay there. I have enough on my hands without having to worry about you."

Brianna opened her mouth to ask what she could do to help, but the words never left her lips. Jacobs staggered through the hatch and tumbled down the steps to collapse at Roarke's feet. Roarke swore the British to hell as he bent over his first mate and felt for a pulse. His face hardened. Jacobs was dead. Roarke didn't utter another word as he straightened, grim-faced, and left the man who had briefly worked as his first mate. There was no time for grief if he wanted to save the *Black Angel* and the rest of her crew. He tried not to think of the one life that meant far more to him than his own as he stepped once more onto the burning deck.

Brianna looked down at the man lying at her feet and realized that Roarke needed the help of every man on board. With only one thought in mind, she grabbed the lantern from the wall bracket, lit it, and quickly made her way down the three decks to the hold, where Nick had been incarcerated. It took every bit of strength she possessed to pry the lock off the hatch, but she finally succeeded.

"Nick, the British are attacking and Roarke needs you," Brianna said as she flung the door open and held the lantern up to peer into the dark little cubbyhole that had been Nick's cell.

"That's too bad," Nick said, nonchalantly stretching out his long legs. He braced his hands behind his head and squinted up at the young woman who had caused all of his trouble. He smiled grimly up at her.

"Didn't you understand what I said? The British are attacking the *Black Angel*."

Nick's grin never wavered. "I suspected as much when I heard the explosions overhead."

"Nick, Roarke needs you."

Nick's smile faded and his face filled with resentment. "For the past two months that he's kept me locked in his hellhole, he hasn't seemed to need me."

"Damn it, Nick. You and Roarke are just alike. The stubbornest men on earth. You both would rather see us sink to the bottom of the ocean than forget your grievances against one another."

"Did Roarke send you for me?"

"No, but he needs you."

Nick shook his head. "Roarke can handle anything the *Black Angel* has to face."

"But it's not just one warship."

Nick's expression altered visibly. "How many?"

"I saw three."

"Damn," Nick swore as he pushed himself to his feet.

"I can't even be a prisoner without having to rescue Roarke one way or the other."

"Hurry, Nick," Brianna said, holding the lantern to light their way above. As they passed down the last passage, a tremendous blast sent tremors through the *Black Angel*. Having felt the *Merry Widow*'s last throes before she sank, Brianna froze. She grabbed Nick's arms and pulled him to a halt. White-faced, she pleaded, "Protect Roarke, please."

"I'll do my damnedest, *petite*." Grim-faced, he turned and left her.

Feeling it would be far safer in the passageway than in the thin-walled cabin, Brianna folded herself into a terrified ball near her cabin door. She covered her head with her arms to block out the sound of the exploding cannonade. She glanced uneasily at Jacob's body and then staunchly focused her eyes on the wall in front of her, unable to look death in the face while the man she loved still faced it on the deck above. A foreboding chill passed down Brianna's spine, but she shook it off. She wouldn't allow herself to even think that Roarke might be hurt. She had to believe he would be all right or she'd surrender to the hysteria that trembled now at the edges of her consciousness.

The battle seemed to rage for hours. Cries of the wounded and dying filled the smoke-ridden air. The scent of burnt flesh, gunpowder, and tar lay oppressively over the ship as twilight descended to hamper the sea battle that had already claimed one man-of-war and the British flagship as well as their crews.

Hearing the sudden cessation of cannon, Brianna peeked anxiously from beneath her arms. Slowly she unfurled from her cramped crouch like a frozen flower, hesitant and aching from the tension that had held her prisoner during the preceding hours. Her wide, haunted eyes peered into the near darkness as she drew in a shuddering breath. She clamped down on her lower lip to stay its wayward tremble as her eyes came to rest on the opening where the shattered hatch hung haphazardly from one hinge. Early in the battle a blast had rent the portal in two, and now only a few ragged-edged boards were left hanging from its moorings.

Brianna's heart urged her to go above, yet uncertainty and fear of what she would find there made her knees weak as she willed her feet to carry her toward the deck. She stepped out into the encroaching twilight and found herself confronted by a heavy blanket of acrid smoke. She blinked against the stinging smoke that brought tears to her eyes and peered into the gray cloud that obscured the men whose moans she could hear. She could also hear the low, hoarse voices of the men who worked to help their wounded friends.

Though she could see only a few feet ahead, instinct directed Brianna toward the quarterdeck, where she'd last seen Roarke. She stumbled over a splintered spar that had severed several of the steps that led upward. As she fell, she grasped the railing, but not soon enough to keep her from crashing against the broken wood. Intent on finding Roarke, she paid no heed to the rending of material and skin. A tiny trickle of blood moistened the torn fabric of her skirt as she frantically crawled up the remains of the steps. Her desperation mounting, her heart slamming against her ribs, she pushed herself to her feet and searched the gray gloom for the man she loved.

Brianna spied Nick at the helm, and her heart stopped. Shirt ripped, blood matting his dark hair, face pale from the strain, he held the wheel, guiding the crippled ship away from her attackers before they could regroup and launch a final attack on the weakened vessel he now commanded.

Brianna's mouth went dry as she searched the hazy gloom for any sign of Roarke. She found none. Fighting off the panic washing over her, she forced herself to cross the few feet to where the first mate leaned against the wheel.

"Nick, where is Roarke?" Brianna cried as she reached the first mate. He didn't look at her but squinted into the cloud of smoke, focusing all his energy on keeping himself erect. Brianna grabbed his arm and asked again, "Nick, where is Roarke?"

Exhaustion etching deep grooves across his soot- and blood-encrusted features, Nick looked down at Brianna. He blinked against the salty sweat that ran over his brow and threatened to blind him. Preoccupied with trying to keep the *Black Angel* afloat until they could reach the coast, he swiped at his brow before turning his attention back to his duties. "Go below, woman. I don't have the time to coddle you when I'm doing everything within my power to save the few of us who are left."

Hysteria tingled along Brianna's already frayed nerves. She shook her head determinedly. "I'm not going anywhere until I know where Roarke is."

Nick's knuckles whitened on the wheel, and his dark Gallic eyes swung back to rest coldly upon Brianna's face. "You don't want to see him."

Dark shadows danced before Brianna's eyes, but she refused to give way to the faint that threatened. Forcing a calmness into her voice that she didn't feel, she asked, "Where is Roarke, Nick?"

Nick's sooty features hardened as he fought the wave of pain that crossed his heart at the thought of his friend. He glanced toward the dense cloud behind him. "Roarke's dead." Setting his jaw, he turned his attention back to keeping the *Black Angel* on her wobbly course and said, "Now leave me alone and let me do my job. You've cost me enough already. I won't let your interference cost me the lives of the rest of the *Black Angel*'s crew."

Brianna glimpsed Roarke's supine figure through the haze as the wind shifted directions. She was already moving toward him before Nick finished speaking. Cold, dulling pain raced over Brianna as she came to her knees beside the man she loved and looked down at his still, ashen features. Roarke had given his life to help strangers fighting for their freedom, and as a result, she had lost him. A wild burst of anger passed over her as she looked down at his handsome face. "Why did you have to do it? Why couldn't my love have been enough for us? Oh God, Roarke, I need you."

Her anger gone as quickly as it had come, tears of grief streaming down her face, tenderly she reached out to touch his pale lips—lips that had given her so much pleasure, lips that had lit her world with sunshine when they smiled. "Roarke," Brianna whispered, "I love you."

Brianna bent to place one last kiss upon the lips that would never smile at her again. She gasped, her eyes widening with shock, as she felt the faint stirring of his breath. Brianna jerked back and gulped in a shuddering breath, afraid to believe that her prayers had been answered. Swallowing against the sudden burst of hope that he still lived, she laid her cheek against his chest and heard the solid, wonderful sound of his heart.

"God, thank you," Brianna breathed as she pushed herself upright and twisted around to call to Nick. "Roarke is alive."

Tears of joy trembled over her long lashes to trace a glistening trail down her smudged cheeks as she searched for and found the cause of Roarke's condition. A wide, gaping wound in his right side still bled red and angry. Knowing he could not live if he lost too much blood, Brianna jerked up her skirts and tore off her petticoat. After tearing it into strips, she pressed the white linen against the wound and prayed she could stop the bright flow of blood that quickly soaked the material through.

"Nick, Roarke needs a doctor," she cried, changing the compress once more.

Grimly Nick looked over his shoulder. "He'll have it if the *Black Angel* can hold together until we make it to the coast."

"But he needs help now! He'll die if the bleeding doesn't stop," Brianna said, frantic to make Nick realize the situation.

"Woman, we'll all die if we don't make it to shore," Nick said, gripping the wheel in his fight to keep his own feet beneath him. He'd taken a splintered piece of spar in his right leg when the man-of-war had toppled the mizzenmast. He was pooling every bit of strength he had to keep the *Black Angel* on course. Hopefully he'd be able to guide the crippled vessel into the inland waterways and out of sight from the British patrols before he had to give the order to abandon ship. If luck and strength were with him, he could save the *Black Angel*'s cargo and then get Roarke to Whitman Place. There, Elsbeth would know what to do. There, Elsbeth would take care of all of them.

A shadow passed before Nick's eyes and he drew in an unsteady breath as he tightened his hold upon the wheel. If Roarke's earlier calculations were right, they should soon see the coastline and then the mouth of the river.

Nick set his jaw and ground his teeth together as he

braced himself on his left leg. He'd be damned if he'd lose the *Black Angel* or let Roarke die without a fight. If the *Black Angel*'s namesake thought he'd give up his friends so easily, then old man death was sadly mistaken.

Hearing the pain in Nick's voice, Brianna understood his torment. She knew his love for Roarke would make him do everything in his power to save them. She could ask no more of him, for she was helpless herself. God now held all their lives in His hands. Brianna took Roarke's hand and held it. Only prayers and Nick's strength would see them through.

Ghostly, bare-limbed trees sat amid the tall marsh grass that bordered the inlets. Quietly, like a ghost herself, her tall, proud masts shattered and bare, the *Black Angel* limped along the murky waterways that led to the rendezvous point with the rebels. Her tired and battered timbers groaning with despair, at last the *Black Angel* bumped against the mushy black earthen bank of the marsh and then stilled momentarily before giving one last, agonized moan, tipping slowly sideways as she surrendered to the death-rendering cannon wounds that she'd received from the British warships. Water spilled in, drowning her. The *Black Angel* had made her last voyage.

The *Black Angel*'s decimated crew limped or were carried ashore by the men who had come expecting to unload munitions for their troops, not the bloody bodies of the sailors who had risked their lives to bring them the military stores. Brianna stayed close to Roarke's side as two men dressed in buckskins laid him on an improvised stretcher and quietly took him off his beloved ship for the last time. Nick refused to leave the *Black Angel* until all of the men had been taken ashore, then he staggered down the broken steps to the captain's cabin. He crossed to the table where Roarke had spent so many hours working, and rolled up the parchment that contained the plans for the second *Black Angel*. He'd not leave them behind. They would give Roarke a reason to live. Stuffing the plans beneath his arm, he hobbled back up on deck and began to give orders for his men's care. He gave directions to Whitman Place to Roarke's stretcher bearers before he, too, collapsed.

Mordecai nuzzled the soft curve of Elsbeth's neck and murmured, "Uhum, you smell delicious."

Elsbeth brushed her fingers through her husband's thick, salt-and-pepper-colored hair and smiled. "It's nothing but simple springwater and soap. I've been out of perfume for more than a month."

Mordecai raised himself on his elbows at his wife's side. His soft expression faded. "This damned war is taking far too long if it's depriving my wife of perfume."

Tenderly Elsbeth caressed Mordecai's craggy cheek and looked up into his pale eyes. She knew his words were meant only to cover his real feelings. They both had had too many friends die fighting for what they all now termed freedom. They no longer just wanted taxation with representation. They wanted a country of their own, to rule themselves, to be free men without a monarch or noble hierarchy to sit in judgment of those whom they considered less than equal. "Aye. The war has gone on far too long, but it looks as if there is no end."

Unable to remain calm under the surge of emotion his thoughts aroused, Mordecai turned over and sat up. He slid his feet to the cool heart of pine flooring and reached for the nightshirt he'd discarded moments earlier. Tugging it over his head, he stood and crossed to the fireplace, where the flames had begun to die. He tossed another log on the coals before he looked back at the woman sitting in the bed. "Hunter received word that there's a shipment of arms to arrive any day. Hopefully the British didn't also learn of it. The winter will not go easy on our men if they aren't resupplied soon. There has already been word from up north that men are starving and are having to go without boots."

Elsbeth joined her husband by the fire. Her bare toes peeped from beneath her long white flannel night rail. Her white nightcap had come askew, allowing soft curls to frame her plump face. She seemed much like a young girl as she stood looking up at the large man at her side. Yet the large bulge beneath her night rail gave clear evidence that she was soon to be a mother.

Mordecai draped a thick-muscled arm about his wife's shoulders and drew her against him, content within his heart with his life yet perturbed by the events that he could do nothing about, events that could destroy all of his dreams for their future should the British succeed in winning the war. The news of late had been less than encouraging. The thought made Mordecai hug his wife tighter. He laid a hand against the swelling beneath her breasts and felt his child stir. Again he experienced the thrill he'd felt several months earlier when he'd felt his babe kick for the first time. He doubted he'd ever get used to it. Each time, goose bumps tickled up his spine and left him feeling as if he'd come closer to God. Nearly in reverence he spread his fingers over her extended middle. He had created that tiny life growing within his wife's womb, and he'd protect it until his dying breath. That vow in mind, he brushed his lips against Elsbeth's brow. "My lady, 'tis time for you to return to your bed. If you remain standing here in your bare feet, you'll catch your death, and we can't allow that to happen. You must deliver our son in just a few more weeks."

Elsbeth turned in her husband's arms and cuddled against his stalwart body. Her hands barely met around him as she hugged and molded her own rounded form to his sturdy frame. She pressed her cheek against his chest and said softly, "I seriously doubt I'll ever grow chilled in your arms, husband. All I have to do is get near you and my blood heats."

Mordecai rolled his eyes toward the ceiling and felt himself swell with the need to lay his wife back upon the down mattress and bury his throbbing flesh deep within her warmth. But he resisted the urge. The doctor had warned him that it could be dangerous for the mother and child should he give in to his baser needs. Swallowing with difficulty, he held Elsbeth close and brushed his lips against her nightcap. He chuckled at his own dilemma. In truth he found nothing funny about it, but Mordecai knew if he didn't laugh, he'd cry. He set Elsbeth away from him before scooping her up in his arms and carrying her back to the warmth of their bed. He sat her down and tugged up the covers. He smiled at her piqued look. "Love, if you're not careful, you're going to make an orphan of our babe before he's even born, because I'm going to die from the wanting of you."

Elsbeth leaned back against the pillows. She looked up at the man who held her heart, and smiled. "I love you, Mordecai," she said softly, tugging the covers up to ward off the chill that had suddenly settled over the bedchamber.

Mordecai bent and took her soft lips. His kiss said far more than any words man had ever created. He dropped a light kiss on her nose before he straightened. "I think I'll have a brandy before I turn in. Go to sleep, love."

Elsbeth watched her husband close the door behind him. She knew he was worried about the last few messages Hunter had received from General Washington. She also knew that he worried about her and their child's safety. The British had managed to hold on to Savannah and were expected to take Charleston next. At the present time the outcome of the war wasn't looking in favor of the patriots. Elsbeth released a long breath and closed her eyes. She wished she could ease her husband's worries; however, all she could do was to give him her love and support and pray that they would win. She didn't like to even consider the alternative. She had to think positively for her babe's sake as well as her own.

Elsbeth's eyes flew wide at the sound of heavy pounding on the front door. Her mind still dazed with sleep, her heart lodging in her throat at the thought that the British had come to arrest her husband, she quickly reached toward the spot where Mordecai should be. Finding only empty space, Elsbeth bolted upright and moved as quickly as her girth allowed to the side of the bed. Without thinking, she slid her bare feet to the floor and waddled from the room. On the landing below she could hear the voices, several male and, oddly, one female. Elsbeth paused on the stairs and watched as Mordecai bent over a supine figure on a bloody blanket. A woman, her gown in tatters, her dark hair a mass of wild tangles about her shoulders, her features smudged with grime and soot, stood tense and white-knuckled as she watched Mordecai. "What is wrong, Mordecai?" Elsbeth asked, traversing the last few steps to the crowd huddled near the doorway.

Mordecai glanced up at her, his expression grim. "It's Roarke O'Connor and his first mate. They've been wounded."

"Then have them carried upstairs," Elsbeth said, stepping aside to allow the men to haul their unconscious burdens up the stairs.

Mordecai's expression darkened. "They're little more than pirates, Elsbeth. We don't need any more trouble at this time."

Elsbeth looked at her husband, understanding his reaction to Roarke. Hunter and Mordecai had always felt the same way about Roarke O'Connor. They had always judged the man by his actions without truly seeing what caused them. She knew the pain Roarke had endured over the years by being born on the wrong side of the Barclay family blanket. Elsbeth glanced at the young woman who now stood looking at her with eyes that mirrored every nuance of emotion she felt for the unconscious man. She smiled at her reassuringly. Her expression told Elsbeth that she'd found someone else who understood and loved Roarke for Roarke and not for what he'd done in the past.

Elsbeth held out her hand to the young woman. "Come, we'll see that he's comfortable." She glanced back at Mordecai. "Have someone go after the doctor."

Seeing the resolute look on his wife's face, Mordecai shrugged. He'd not argue with Elsbeth over Roarke O'Connor. It'd do no good. His wife could see no wrong in anyone, even a bloody pirate like Hunter's cousin. Mordecai gazed after his wife and the young woman as they followed the stretcher bearers upstairs. He knew Hunter owed Roarke his sister's life, but damn, it was hard to forget the years when the man had been little more than a thorn in his friend's side. Hunter had gone out of his way to try to offer Roarke help, but the man had always thrown it back in Hunter's face. He'd prided himself on taking no charity from a Barclay, no matter how small. The only person Mordecai had ever seen Roarke O'Connor have any tenderness toward was his own wife, Elsbeth.

Mordecai followed the retinue upstairs, and dressed. He'd stop by the small cabin Hunter had built for himself and his wife, Devon, after the British burned Barclay Grove. Mordecai wanted to inform Hunter that his cousin had returned, and if he lived, they could expect trouble. Mordecai glanced toward the closed door of the bedchamber where Roarke now lay. He didn't doubt that Roarke had received his wounds while aiding the British against some of his own countrymen. He'd sell his soul if there was enough money to be made in it.

Chapter 15

Face drawn, dark shadows tinting the soft skin beneath her haunted eyes, Brianna sat next to Roarke's bed, watching the uneasy rise and fall of his chest. She'd not left his side since he'd been brought to Whitman Place. Brianna clutched Roarke's hand, afraid to let go, afraid in that moment that death would take him from her. She glanced toward the dawn creeping over the horizon to banish the last purple hours of night and prayed the new day would also bring an improvement in Roarke's condition. He was steadily growing weaker. The fever that had begun soon after they left the *Black Angel* ate away at his resistance.

Brianna's haggard gaze came to rest once more on Roarke's ashen features. Roarke was a strong man, far stronger than most, but she didn't know how much more his body could take. His wound had begun to heal, yet the fever drained his strength.

"How is he this morning?" Elsbeth asked quietly.

Her attention centered upon the man she loved, Brianna had failed to hear Elsbeth enter the bedchamber. She shook her head resignedly as she came to her feet and looked at the kind woman who had opened her home to them over the protests of her husband. "Nothing has changed."

Her cinnamon gold eyes reflecting her mounting anxiety, Brianna looked back to Roarke. Tenderly she touched his brow, testing it for heat before absently brushing away a dark curl that lay against his pale brow. "His fever still burns." She bent and touched her lips to his before settling once more in the chair beside the bed.

Elsbeth placed a comforting hand on Brianna's shoulder. "You love him very much, don't you?"

Brianna didn't take her eyes off Roarke as she nodded. "Aye. He is my heart. I will die should I lose him."

Elsbeth gave Brianna's shoulder a gentle, reassuring squeeze. "We're not going to let that happen. He'll get better. Just give the doctor's medicine time to work, and don't give up hope."

"I pray that he will, but I'm so afraid."

Again Elsbeth gave Brianna's shoulder a comforting squeeze. "Roarke is lucky to have found someone like you to love."

Brianna drew in a shuddering breath and looked up at the woman she'd come to consider her friend. "How I wish it was so, Elsbeth. But I don't know if Roarke loves me or not. He's never told me that he does."

"Ah," Elsbeth said, understanding Brianna's dilemma. She knew well what it was like to love a man and be uncertain about his feelings in return. "Men such as Roarke often have trouble voicing how they feel, but from what I gather from Nick, Roarke cares for you far more than even he is willing to admit."

Brianna's shoulders slumped and her fingers tightened about Roarke's. "Nick told me the same thing, but I'm afraid he's wrong. Since finding me on board the *Black Angel* after we sailed from France, Roarke has given no indication of even liking me, much less loving me. We've done nothing but argue."

Elsbeth nodded. "That's understandable for the man I

know. Roarke wouldn't tell you how he feels. He's a man who has always kept his emotions to himself. He's lived his life by certain rules and governs his ship in the same manner. He'd not allow himself to let his heart interfere with his duty, no matter what happened or how he felt. It can't be otherwise for a man like Roarke, because there are too many shadows in his past."

Brianna looked up at Elsbeth once more. "You know, don't you? You know what Nick wouldn't tell me about Roarke. You know what makes Roarke the way he is."

"Aye, I know," Elsbeth said, settling herself in the chair beside Brianna's. She glanced at the man lying so still and pale in the bed. His skin was nearly as white as the sheet upon which he lay. She drew in a deep breath. Perhaps what she was going to do would end her friendship with him forever, but she couldn't let Brianna continue to believe Roarke didn't love her. She had to make the young woman understand that it wouldn't be easy to love Roarke, a man whose demons had driven him until he had closed off the heart that had been battered and bruised so often as a child. He'd become a man who wouldn't allow anyone to ever get close enough to hurt him again. He prided himself on that fact. This young woman had managed to break through the barrier he'd erected around his heart, and Elsbeth wanted nothing to come between them to destroy the happiness that they could find together if given the chance to rid themselves of the ghosts from the past. She wanted everyone to experience the same kind of joy she'd found with Mordecai.

Elsbeth took Brianna's free hand and held it. "I guess you deserve to know. I didn't have to ask did you love Roarke. Without you ever saying a word, I could see it in your eyes and every nuance of your expressive face that you love him, and nothing I can tell will alter that fact."

"No. Nothing anyone can say can change the way I feel about Roarke. He is my life."

"I understand Roarke better than most people," Elsbeth began. "I've known him since we were children, and I saw the pain in his face when the other children wouldn't play with him because he wore ragged britches and didn't have the prestige of a family name to give him an entrance to our close-knit society. They made fun of him because of his birth."

Brianna felt Roarke's hand tense beneath her own and quickly looked to see if he had regained consciousness. She released the expectant breath she'd been holding as her gaze moved over his still features. She'd only imagined that he'd moved. Nothing had changed. Sensing that Elsbeth's story would finally make her understand Roarke, she quietly said, "Go on."

Elsbeth began the story of Roarke O'Connor's life, telling Brianna of his years of deprivation and mockery. How he'd stuck out his little jaw and had used his fists against those who slandered him or the woman who had given him life, though she kept food on the table by selling her body. She also told Brianna of the Barclays, his mother's family, who had disowned her when they had learned that she carried Roarke. Elsbeth explained that Roarke's mother had had nowhere to turn for help and had even taken the name O'Connor to keep from adding more disgrace upon her family when she worked the docks for enough money to survive.

Roarke had suffered as much as his mother, but he'd possessed enough of the Barclay pride not to allow anyone to ever know of his feelings. When his cousin, Hunter, had come into his majority and had offered help, Roarke's animosity toward the Barclays had refused to allow him to forgive and forget what his rich and powerful relatives had done to his mother and himself. He had made his own way in the world without name or wealth behind him.

Elsbeth squeezed Brianna's hand as she finished the history of Roarke's earlier years and glanced once more toward his still form. "But I'm afraid that no matter how much he accomplishes or how much wealth he now possesses, he's still that little boy who's afraid of rejection."

She looked back to find Brianna's eyes filling with tears. She gave Brianna's hand a pat and extricated her own. She pushed herself to her feet, her pregnancy encumbering her movements. "Now you see what has driven Roarke. You know that his past has ruled much of his life. He's fought many battles, but he still has one major battle to win if he's to put his past behind him. And that is with himself."

Brianna's lower lip trembled with emotion as she nodded and said, "I will be at his side when the times comes."

Elsbeth smiled warmly down at her young friend. "I knew you would be or I would never have told you. Roarke is a proud man, Brianna. But he is also very vulnerable. Protect his heart with your love."

"I will guard it with my life," Brianna answered as Elsbeth turned and left the room.

Alone with Roarke, the first rays of the morning sun peeping over the window casing to banish the last shadows clinging to the corners of the room, Brianna held Roarke's hand tenderly against her cheek and wept softly for the pain the little boy and the man had endured. Her tears spilled down her cheeks and dropped quietly onto the bed sheet, dampening the fine muslin material. Her words came soft and from her heart as she whispered, "Never again will you suffer, my darling Roarke. No matter what your past, I will always be here for you. And it may take all the days of my life, but I'll do everything within my power to make up for the pain you've suffered because of other people's cruelty. No one has a choice on his birth, and only foolish, heartless people judge a man by it."

Brianna reached out and touched Roarke's beard-stubbled cheek. "I now understand why you were willing to risk everything to help those fighting for freedom here in the colonies. You needed to free yourself of your own past." Brianna drew in a shuddering breath and brushed her lips against Roarke's knuckles. "You are too good a man and I love you too much to let your past destroy the future that we can have together, Roarke. When you're better I'll convince you that we are meant to be together, I promise."

Brianna felt Roarke's fingers tighten about her own. Her head snapped up, her misty gaze coming into contact with deep indigo blue eyes. A wobbly smile briefly touched Roarke's pallid lips, yet the expression in his eyes spoke far more eloquently than any words. Brianna nodded her understanding. He had heard Elsbeth's story. Now there were only three words left to be said between them, and they trembled over her lips. "I love you."

Again she felt a light pressure on her hand before his eyes slowly closed and a look of peace crossed his haggard features. His rough breathing eased and his chest rose and fell evenly. For the first time in days, he didn't have to struggle to breathe.

Brianna knew before she touched his brow that she'd find it cooler. Again her eyes brimmed with moisture and she laid her head down on the side of the bed and wept with relief. Roarke was going to live. Within moments, she, too, was sound asleep.

Brianna stretched her arms over her head, glorying in the beauty of the cold winter's day as well as the fact that today they would be leaving Whitman Place.

She glanced about the room with its woven bed hangings and handmade rugs. Elsbeth had made Whitman Place truly a home. Everything had her loving touch, even the glass jars filled with potpourri that scented the bedchamber with the sweet fragrance of spring on the coldest of winter days.

Brianna smiled. She understood why Roarke considered Elsbeth the closest thing to an angel on earth. In truth, she was one. She'd helped save Roarke's life by giving of herself and her home. Few people would have gone against those they loved to help a man whom others considered unworthy to live. But like herself, Elsbeth knew the true man beneath the hard exterior Roarke presented to a world that had always sought to punish him for things he couldn't control. And Brianna would always be grateful for Elsbeth's friendship.

A light knock at the door interrupted Brianna's musings. She just managed to sit up and draw the covers to her chin before the door swung open to reveal Roarke. Dressed in a fresh white lawn shirt and tight nankeen britches, he filled the doorway. A rakish grin curled his sensuously full lips as his gaze swept down the length of the soft curves hidden beneath the covers. He glanced up and down the hallway and then quietly closed the door and locked it.

"Good morning, Mistress Tarleton. I hope you slept well last eve," he said, crossing the room.

"Very well, thank you, Captain. Did you sleep well? How are you feeling today? How is your side?"

Roarke shrugged as he closed the space between them. He stood looking down at Brianna, his eyes hot with desire. "I would have slept far better had I had company. As for my side, it is healed, as you well know."

The bed dipped with Roarke's weight as he settled himself on the side and reached out to cup Brianna's chin in his palm. His gaze took in her velvety eyes, her slender nose, her high cheekbones, before traveling to her luscious lips, now slightly parted as she drew in a shivery breath.

"You are beautiful," Roarke whispered as he bent and took her lips with his own. His tongue slid into her moist mouth to tease hers until she responded in kind. Roarke felt her tremble as his kiss kindled her desire. A nearly inaudible moan escaped her as she wrapped her arms about his neck and drew him down to her.

Roarke released her lips and looked into her golden brown eyes. The heat of his own passion was reflected in their shimmering depths. He swelled against the tight fabric that covered his loins and shifted his hips so he lay pressed against her soft curves. His voice was husky with emotion as he said, "I want you, Brianna."

Brianna didn't hesitate. She pushed all thoughts from her mind except the man she loved. She'd not allow anything to ever come between them again—not place, event, or person. Roarke belonged to her, and she belonged to him. They loved each other, and she could find nothing wrong or sinful when they made love.

She answered his request by tightening her arms about his neck and drawing him down to her. She took his lips, savoring the taste of him as he pulled away the covers and disrobed. In moments they lay naked in each other's arms. Brianna reveled in the sensation his mouth created on her flesh as his lips traveled down her throat to the soft mounds of her breasts. She arched against him and shivered as he suckled the hard peak. Her skin tingled as his strong, long fingers slowly moved along her flat belly to the dark glen where she already burned to feel him within her. Her honeyed essence moistened the path for his fingers as he enticed her thighs apart and then stroked her tight sheath until he felt her quiver with the need to feel all of him deep within her.

Roarke shuddered. The muscles across his chest and down his scarred back rippled in response to the primitive call. The heat of their bodies emanated the sweet, musky odors of love, tantalizing his senses until his need to taste all of her became unbearable. He laved both nipples until they gleamed in the morning light like dewy jewels and then he began his downward quest, kissing and tasting her flesh until he reached the sweet-fragrant glen that held all the mysteries of the past and future.

Roarke glanced up at Brianna to see her arch her back and open for him, offering all of herself to him. He took the bounty, suckling, tasting, delving, until his own passion-swollen flesh felt ready to explode. He felt a tremor shake Brianna as her flesh caressed his tongue, and he knew in another moment he would be undone. His sinewy flesh gleamed dark against her silken skin as his hard body covered hers. His mouth reclaimed her lips and his tongue slipped inside as he sank his hardened sex deep within the tight warmth of her body. He moaned his satisfaction as she rippled about him, and began to move her hips, beckoning him to fulfill their quest. Roarke's body answered in kind. His thrusts were deep and smooth, sliding easily within the honeyed flesh that held him enthralled.

Together they traversed the physical world where desire and passion burned white-hot. However, as they reached the realm where sun and moon draw their strength, a realm ruled by the God of the Heart, they gave of each other, sharing their union and glorying in the most intimate joining of body to body, heart to heart, and soul to soul. They were one completely for the first time. Shudders shook them and they cried out together in ecstasy as Roarke's seed spilled deep into Brianna's womb.

Their bodies still joined, Roarke and Brianna lay together, savoring their moment of fulfillment. Brianna caressed his dark hair with fingers that still shook from the powerful emotion that she'd just experienced. Quietly she murmured, "I love you, Roarke."

Roarke raised himself on his elbows above her, feeling her breasts still crushed against the wiry mat of hair covering his chest. Her body still held his now-sated member, yet her warmth made him want to remain within that sweet haven forever. He smiled tenderly down at her. "And I love you, Brianna."

Brianna felt tears burn her eyes and quickly blinked to stay them. She had waited so long to hear those words. She moistened her suddenly dry lips but couldn't keep them from quivering as she said, "Tell me again."

Roarke chuckled. "I love you, Brianna. I truly realized how much I cared for you when we faced the British warships. And I vowed should we live, I'd tell you of my feelings even if you decided to toss them back in my face after learning the truth about me."

"I would never do such a thing," Brianna said, looping her arms about his neck. She nuzzled the corded flesh and drew in the heady male scent of him. Her body shook from Roarke's chuckle.

"Aye. I know that now. Nick advised me to tell you the truth, but I feared the consequences of such an action. I know how others have reacted when they learned

I was merely the bastard offspring of the rich Barclay family of Williamsburg."

"Nick advised you to tell me?" Brianna asked, her eyes widening in disbelief.

Another chuckle shook Roarke's lean frame and he moved to Brianna's side. He drew the covers up over them to ward off the morning chill. "I know it's hard to believe, but he was right. I needed to be honest with you. And now that you know the truth about my past, I no longer have any shadows lurking about to destroy our future."

With a wave of a long-fingered hand, he encompassed his whole sinewy length from the tip of his head to the bottom of his bare feet. He grinned. "What you see is what you get."

"And I love every bit of what I see," Brianna said, forcing a lightness into her voice that she didn't feel. She still had secrets in her own past that she couldn't tell Roarke. She swallowed uneasily. What would Roarke do should he learn that the secrets in his past couldn't compare to those in hers?

Roarke pulled her into his arms and lay with her resting against him. A satisfied smile curled his lips as he looked up at the ceiling. He'd never have dreamed that he could feel such contentment. "I was a fool, Brianna. And I nearly lost you. I should have had faith in your love, because you've never given me any reason to believe I couldn't trust you."

Brianna snuggled against Roarke, never wanting to leave the circle of his arms. She pushed the prick of guilt away as she brushed her lips against the hard planes of his chest. She couldn't ruin what she had found by telling him of Lord Montague. It was in the past, and they were far from England and anyone who would know of her sins. "It's over, Roarke," she whispered, for her benefit as well as for Roarke's. "All I want is to go back to Statia and be with you."

"Then you'll have your wish. We sail with the tide tonight. Mordecai has managed to find a ship that will take us through the blockade."

Brianna rose up and looked at Roarke. "Elsbeth seems to have managed to convince her husband that you're not such a bad fellow after all."

Roarke smiled dubiously. "Perhaps. But it's probably the *Black Angel*'s cargo that had any effect upon him. Like Hunter, he's always believed the worst of me. However, he's grateful for the munitions. Like most of us, he has friends who would die without them."

Brianna laid her cheek once more against Roarke's chest. She could hear the steady drum of his heart and wondered how he had survived with all the condemnation. She tightened her arm about Roarke's waist, wanting to wipe out all the hurt. "I love you, Roarke. No matter what happens in the future, my feelings for you will never change."

Roarke turned on his side and looked down at Brianna. "We only have a future, Brianna. The past is dead. I've slayed my dragons and I've won the princess."

Brianna looked up into his dark blue eyes and nodded her agreement. "Yes, Roarke. The past is dead."

A knock on the door interrupted anything more Roarke had been going to say. When they didn't answer immediately, another hard fist banged against the portal, and Nick called out, "Roarke, it's time to stop your dallying and ready yourself to leave. Mordecai says the mounts will be ready shortly."

Roarke dropped a light kiss upon the tip of Brianna's nose and then pushed himself upright. Tenderly he caressed the curve of her cheek. "It's time, love. We'll have to ride down the coast to meet the ship that Mordecai has procured to take us back to Statia. It will take until this evening to reach the point of rendezvous, so you'd best hurry and dress. We'd hate for the ship to sail without us."

"I'll be ready when you are," Brianna said, already climbing from the tall four-poster bed. Her nude body gleamed like sculpted alabaster in the morning sun as she crossed to the armoire and took down the gown Elsbeth had given her. She looked at the soft woolen garment and wondered what would be its destiny. Since leaving England, it seemed she was always wearing other women's gowns. Brianna forced the thought away. She might not have the fabulous wardrobe that she'd left behind at Montvale, but she had something far more precious, Roarke's love. She'd be happy to wear rags the rest of her life as long as she could be with him.

Brianna slipped on the hand-me-down cotton chemise and then slid the gown over her head. Roarke assisted as maid, doing up the laces. However, after kissing each inch of skin before he laced and tied them securely, he and Brianna were both breathing heavily and would have undone all his handiwork had it not been imperative that they leave Whitman Place within the hour. Begrudgingly he left Brianna to finish her toilet.

The farewells were tear-filled. A kinship had developed between Elsbeth and Brianna that both knew would last the rest of their lives. With many hugs and expressions of gratitude as well as promises to visit each other again as soon as the war permitted, Brianna waved her good-byes. She knew she would never be able to repay Elsbeth's kindness. She had saved Roarke's and Nick's lives by opening her home and heart to them. She had befriended Brianna as well as making it possible for her to finally breach the walls surrounding Roarke's heart. For that alone, Brianna would always be in Elsbeth's debt.

The sun sank below the horizon, splashing the sky with gold and magenta. Twilight shadows stretched across the marshes as the riders drew their mounts to a halt along the estuary where the ship awaited, hidden by tall, naked, white-limbed trees and the thick underbrush that made it impassable for all except those who knew the path to the rendezvous point.

The miles the four riders had traveled numbered few, but it had taken since early morning to reach their destination. The patrols the British had scouring the countryside made it nearly impossible to travel without being stopped and questioned. Each time the riders heard or glimpsed anyone, they'd had to leave the road and wait until they felt it was safe to travel again.

Nick was the first to dismount. He grimaced and rubbed his backside and then moved his right leg to ease the soreness his day in the saddle had created in his still tender thigh. The splinter had done little damage to his leg, but he'd suffered from the loss of blood. It had taken him several days at Whitman Place to regain his strength enough to get out of bed. Fortunately, no infection had set in and his wound had healed after the doctor had cleaned and bandaged it. "Damn if I like being land-bound. It's too hard on a man's backside."

Roarke swung a sinewy leg over his horse's back and dismounted. He chuckled at Nick's obvious discomfort as he reached up to lift Brianna from the saddle. "Once you get used to it, Nick, you might come to enjoy riding."

Nick glanced toward the bay Mordecai had given him to ride. His lips curled back in distaste. "I seriously doubt it. There's only one kind of riding I enjoy, and that has nothing to do with a horse and saddle." He gave a wicked grin. "Though on occasion I've been asked to pretend I'm at the races and have to urge my steed to run with my crop. It's strange how some women get excited over the prospect of a riding crop against their round little fannies."

Roarke rolled his eyes and shook his head. Nick and his women were always playing games. He smiled up at Brianna as he slowly let her feet touch the ground. "He'll never change."

"And we'd have it no other way," Brianna said, glancing over Roarke's shoulder at Nick. She saw him stiffen and then glance uneasily at Roarke. Brianna tensed unconsciously, sensing that something was wrong.

"Roarke," Nick said, his tone relaying his angst. He nodded toward the landing.

Roarke glanced in the direction Nick indicated and saw the man standing at the edge of the landing. He tensed.

Brianna glanced from the stranger back to Roarke and watched as his expression altered into the mask she'd come to think of as his pirate guise. She could feel his withdrawal even before he set her away from him. A streak of fear careened through Brianna and her heart began to pound against her ribs. Instinctively she knew the man could hurt Roarke, and she couldn't allow that to happen. He had already suffered enough in his life. She grasped Roarke's arm, drawing his attention back to her. "Roarke, who is he?"

His expression grim, Roarke said, "He's my cousin, Hunter Barclay."

Brianna glanced toward the man Elsbeth had told her about and then back to Roarke. "Roarke, you have to remember the past is in the past. Let us go back to Statia and leave all the bad memories behind."

"I didn't ask him to come here, and I'm certainly not going to run away from him."

"I'm not asking you to run. I'm just asking you to let go of all the bad feelings between the two of you."

Roarke's expression didn't alter. "You ask much of me, love."

"Because I know the man you are. You've overcome so much. You don't need Hunter Barclay's approval, nor anyone's. You are your own man, not a little boy. And I love you."

Tenderly Roarke caressed Brianna's cheek and dropped his head to brush his lips lightly against hers. The guarded look still darkened his eyes, yet he nodded. "And I love you."

"Then that is all that counts."

Roarke straightened and placed Brianna's hand in the curve of his arm. He eyed Hunter coolly as he escorted her to the landing. He paused, assessing his cousin from head to toe, before he said, "I hadn't expected to see you here, cousin."

"We have unfinished business," Hunter said, forcing himself to relax under Roarke's appraisal.

Roarke arched a draw brow. "I didn't know we had any business at all together, finished or otherwise."

"Perhaps I should have said what I had intended to say when I saw you next, but damn it, Roarke. We've always been at odds, and it's still hard for me to even think you might have a decent streak in you when I know that you do."

"How dare you say such a thing," Brianna interrupted, furious with the man whom she'd heard so much about. "Roarke is a decent man. Far more decent than the family that has made his life a living hell."

Roarke stiffened and his voice brooked no argument. "Brianna, that's enough."

Brianna glanced from Roarke's cousin back to the man at her side. She shifted uneasily under the censuring look he gave her. Her cheeks heated. She knew Roarke wanted to fight his own battles, but it was nearly impossible for her not to react when someone attacked the man she loved. "I'm sorry, Roarke."

Roarke draped a comforting arm about her shoulder and gave her a light, forgiving, and understanding squeeze. He felt the same protective instinct toward Brianna.

Hunter smiled. The girl reminded him of his own wife. Devon would fight a bear in defense of those she loved. "I'm sorry. I didn't mean to upset you. It seems that I have a knack for putting my foot in my mouth when it comes to Roarke. I've managed during the past years to eat my entire leg on several occasions, but Roarke always made sure that I enjoyed my meal." Hunter glanced back at his cousin. "The reason I'm here is to say thank you for helping my sister. I can never repay that kindness."

Roarke lifted one shoulder in an offhand shrug. "There is no need to thank me. I was just in the wrong place at the wrong time and couldn't get out of it."

"You may make light of the situation now, but you and I both know the consequences had you not helped Cecilia. The British would have hanged her for stabbing one of their officers."

Roarke couldn't make light of Hunter's statement. He knew his cousin was right. The girl would not have survived. "How is Cecilia?"

"She lives with Devon and myself in the cabin. She's not the same spoiled child she was. She couldn't be after everything she's experienced. But I believe she is going to come out far stronger than she would have if she'd remained at Barclay Grove, pampered and petted. She'll be a woman to be reckoned with someday."

Roarke smiled his relief. He'd wondered if the girl would ever recover from her rape and stabbing her attacker to death. She was fortunate not to have gone completely mad. He had to admire her courage. Few women would have tried to defend themselves as Cecilia had done. "I'm glad to hear it. Give her and your wife my regards."

Hunter pushed the thought of Roarke helping Devon leave him out of his mind. He wanted no more hard feelings between them. They were all fighting for the right to start anew, and he intended everything in his life to follow suit.

Hunter closed the space between them and extended his hand. "I'm afraid I can never make amends for the past, but I hope from this day forward we can try to become friends, to start anew."

Roarke looked down at Hunter's hand and slowly clasped it. "Aye. This is a time for new beginnings for all of us." He glanced down at Brianna and saw her smile. The handshake had finally shoveled the last bit of dirt into the grave of the past. It was buried.

Chapter 16

Brianna lifted her face to the warm breeze that stirred the palm fronds overhead. Life was sweet. Had anyone told her several months ago that she would have found such happiness with Roarke O'Connor, she would not have believed him. It was still hard for her to believe the changes that had taken place between them. Roarke had always been a wonderful lover, yet now he seemed to give of himself completely, holding nothing back.

The only shadow on their horizon was the fact that he had as yet to ask her to marry him. She wanted to become Roarke's wife and begin a family of their own. After having been an only child, she wanted a dozen children to love. She dreamed of their first child, a dark-haired, blue-eyed little boy who was the image of his father. He would be her gift to Roarke, a living symbol of the love they shared.

Brianna leaned back against the palm and closed her eyes, savoring the dream. She could nearly hear the sound of children's laughter as they scampered through the tile-roofed house, playing games and bedeviling one another but always secure in their world because they were loved. Love and laughter would abound in the house overlooking Gallows Bay. Brianna knew she would be content to remain here forever with Roarke and her children at her side.

"I thought I might find you here," Roarke said, sinking down beside Brianna on the bench that had been built to circle the rough boll of the palm.

Brianna's lashes fluttered open and she smiled up at the man who held her heart. "I was just enjoying the day. After the climate in Virginia and France, I've come to appreciate the sultry warmth of the islands."

"Like a rose, you bloom under the warmth of the sun. It kisses your skin with just a touch of gold that makes it look like ivory porcelain." Roarke dropped a kiss on Brianna's shoulder. "I had planned for us to return to the colonies, but I don't know if I want to take you away from the tropics now."

"I will go anywhere you want me to go," Brianna said, taking Roarke's hand and lacing her fingers companionably with his.

Roarke gazed down into her golden brown eyes and knew she did not lie. Her love for him would make her follow him to the ends of the earth should he ask. A tender expression crossed Roarke's face and he drew her hand up to his lips and kissed it. "Would you go down to Fort Oranje with me?"

"Of course I will," Brianna said, puzzled by such a ridiculous question.

"And will you go to the church with me?"

Brianna's heart stilled and then began to beat rapidly within her breast. She looked up at Roarke, her eyes mirroring her hope, but afraid to believe what he was insinuating.

"I will go to the church or anywhere else you want me to go."

"And will you walk down the aisle to become my wife?"

With a squeal of pleasure, Brianna threw herself into Roarke's arms. "Yes, oh, yes, Roarke."

Roarke wrapped his arms about Brianna and held her close. He had never believed himself capable of loving anyone as he loved this one beautiful, enchanting woman.

It had taken him a long time, but he now realized that his resentment toward his mother had prevented him from becoming emotionally involved with any woman before Brianna entered his life. Though he had loved his mother, he had also hated her in many ways. He hadn't consciously been aware of his feeling of bitterness that the years of deprivation had engendered within him until recently. He'd denied ever having such feelings toward the woman who had given him life. However, he'd finally had to face the truth. He'd delved into the deepest, darkest parts of his soul and had recognized the emotions that had fermented over the long years. And he knew until he let go of his resentment, he'd never be able to completely open up his heart to love.

It had taken Brianna's understanding and love for him to finally bury his past and take a long look at his future. And he recognized the fact that without her, he'd have no future. Until that moment he'd never considered marriage as an alternative to the life he'd led. Now he realized that Brianna deserved far more than just being his mistress. She deserved his name and everything that came with it. Their children would never have the stigma of bastardy placed upon them. It was far too heavy a burden for young, defenseless shoulders to carry.

Brianna clasped Roarke's face between her hands and rained kisses all over it until at last, breathing hard, she took his lips aggressively, thrusting her tongue inside his mouth to tease his until she felt his arms tighten about her.

Brianna leaned back and looked at Roarke with eyes

already glazed with passion. She arched a provocative, questioning brow. "Will you take me inside?"

"I could take you right here and now if it were not for the servants," Roarke laughed as he swept her up into his arms and came to his feet. He took the steps two at a time to the balcony and swiftly made his way down the long hallway to his bedchamber. With a kick, he closed the door and strode across the room to the high four-poster bed. Together they fell into the down softness, completely unaware of anything beyond themselves and the passion each stirred in the other.

Several hours later they lay together, sated from their afternoon of lovemaking. Roarke propped himself on one elbow and absently wound a dark curl about his finger as he looked down at the woman he loved. "Will you marry me today?"

Brianna glanced toward the windows, where the afternoon sun had already begun to lower itself behind the horizon. "I will marry you anytime and anyplace, but I'm afraid we've dallied the day away and will have to wait until tomorrow to marry."

Roarke chuckled and pushed himself upright. He grabbed his britches and jerked them on as he stood. "You should know me well enough by now to know that when I want something, I get it. Be ready when I come back, for tonight you will become my bride."

"I'll be ready," Brianna said, straining to hold back the tears of joy that burned the backs of her lids. She raised her lips to accept Roarke's farewell kiss and watched him close the door before she let the tears fall freely. Her dream was going to become a reality within only a few hours.

Brianna's head snapped up as she realized that she had only a short time to prepare for the most important event in her life. She scrambled from the bed and rang for Rhama. She would need a bath, her hair prepared, her gown chosen, and a half dozen other things to be decided within only a couple of hours. She had no time to spare.

The lanterns had as yet to be lit to chase away the twilight that invaded the tavern and cast shadows over the customers enjoying their rum. Ignoring the snores of the drunk who lay slumped with his face buried in his arms at the table next to them, Roselee said, "That's him." She watched Roarke ride past the tavern window before she turned her flashing, angry gaze back to the two men sitting at her table. They, too, were interested in the young woman who had ousted her from Roarke's life. She lifted her tankard of rum and took a long sip before she cocked her head toward the window and said, "That means he's left the bitch at home."

Lord Montague smiled. His quest had nearly come to an end. He had searched all of England and halfway across the world to find Brianna, and now she was only a few miles away. He looked at Tanner. "Take a message to our young friend requesting that she join us on the *Wild Goose* at eight o'clock if she wants to see her friends alive again."

"You think she'll come?" Roselee asked.

"Aye. She'll come. She's too much like her stupid mother to think only of herself. And like that bitch Sabrina, she'll be too noble-hearted to allow anything to happen to her friends."

"Then it'll soon be over?"

"Aye. It'll be completely over after I show Mistress McClure that no one can think to harm me and get away with it," Lord Montague said, completely unaware of the piercing Gallic eyes that narrowed with suspicion even as their owner gave out another loud snore.

Nick kept up the pretense as he listened to the conversation of Roselee and the two men. He frowned and let out another convincing snore. When Roselee and her friends had begun to talk, he'd first thought they were speaking of Brianna. But the man had called the woman he sought Mistress McClure. There was something wrong here that he just couldn't figure out. He'd best take what he'd heard to Roarke and let his sober head sort out the mystery.

Nick remained in his chair until Roselee, Lord Montague, and Tanner left the tavern. Then he quickly set out to find Roarke. He staggered slightly as he made his way out of the tavern and down the twilight-shadowed street. When Roselee and her companions had first entered the tavern, he'd truly been in a stupor from all the rum he'd consumed that afternoon. Since returning to Statia, Nick had made up for all the carousing he'd missed during their voyage with a vengeance. However, he was finding that no amount of rum helped him forget the last hours he'd spent on board the *Black Angel*.

Nick's senses had still been blurred from the rum when their conversation had roused him. He'd pretended sleep and listened as he tried to orient his wits enough to understand what was afoot. Fortunately, the tavern's smoky, shadowed interior had prevented Roselee from recognizing him only a few feet away. Even now as he saw Roarke's mount tied in front of the little tile-roofed church, he didn't fully understand everything he'd overheard. But he knew Roarke would.

Rhama tapped lightly upon the door to Brianna's bedchamber. After hearing her mistress call "enter," she took the small piece of paper to Brianna that the tall, pock-marked man had delivered.

Brianna, intent upon completing the necessary arrangements for her wedding, was giving Rhama further instructions as she opened the folded scrap of paper. The flowers had to be gathered from the garden, and the cook had to prepare the most sumptuous meal of her career. This night was special, and Brianna intended to see that nothing was left undone to mar it. Rhama, caught up in Brianna's excitement, hurried from the room to carry out her mistress's instructions, leaving her mistress to read the message alone.

Brianna, her mind on her wedding, scanned the note once before the import of the hastily scribbled words hit her. The blood slowly drained from her face, leaving her ashen. The fingers she raised to her pallid lips trembled as she again read the message.

Mistress McClure,
    Should you want to see your maid Rachel and her husband alive again, you should meet me at the docks on the ship called the *Wild Goose* at eight o'clock this evening. Tell no one and come alone or their deaths will be on your conscience.
                        Your most humble servant,
                        Branson Tanner.

Brianna crumpled the note in her hand and squeezed her eyes shut. Her heart pounded against her breastbone like a wild bird captured within a cage as her angst rose to terrifying proportions. The man knew her real name and was threatening Rachel and George's lives.

Brianna drew in a shuddering breath and willed herself to stop trembling. There was only one reason the man would know her name. He had been sent to bring her back to England to hang.

Brianna suppressed the urge to scream her anger at

life's unfairness. Here she had found love and within the hour would become Roarke's wife. Now all of that had been destroyed because her past had finally caught up with her.

Brianna rubbed at the pain that shot through her temples. What she had feared had now come to pass. Resignedly she pushed herself to her feet and looked at the haggard face staring back at her from the dressing table mirror. The earth seemed to tremble as the full impact hit her with the force of a fist in the gut. She gasped for breath and clamped a hand over her mouth to stifle her cry of anguish. How Roarke would hate her when he learned of all the lies she'd told. He had opened his soul to her, revealing all the pain of his past. And her foolish belief that her past would never catch up with her had kept her mute. Now that it was too late, she realized the folly of her errant beliefs. Roarke would have understood had she been honest with him, but he'd never forgive her lies.

An agonizing pain ripped through Brianna's heart as she turned away from the wide-eyed visage that reflected the terror and misery consuming her. She crossed to the writing table and sat down. With an unsteady hand she withdrew a sheet of paper and dipped the quill into the inkwell. Slowly, her heart dying with each word she scribbled on the paper, she wrote a farewell note to Roarke.

When she walked out the door of his house, it would be over. It was better for her to sever all ties with Roarke instead of watching his love turn to hate when he learned the truth. It would be far easier on him and herself. She didn't want him to watch her hang for the murder of her stepfather.

Brianna cast one last, lingering glance about the bedchamber where she and Roarke had spent their afternoon loving. She would carry the memory to her grave.

"I'll always love you, Roarke," Brianna whispered, her eyes misting with pain. She closed the door quietly behind her and left the house. She didn't take the donkey cart but walked down the winding road toward Fort Oranje, where she would finally confront the past, which had followed her all the way from England. Brianna paused at the foot of the *Wild Goose*'s gangplank and looked up at the tall masts, standing stark and bare against the darkening sky. Knowing she had no other recourse, she placed her hand on the rope and resignedly made her way on board the vessel. She glanced back toward the mountain where Roarke had built his house, where she had dreamed of their future together. Like her own future, it was dark. Drawing in a steadying breath, she stepped down on the deck. In the distance the church bells pealed eight times. She was on time to meet her fate.

Brianna jumped with a start as Branson Tanner appeared from the shadows like a silent phantom. His large hand closed over her arm before she had time to react.

"This way, Mistress McClure. Your friends are awaiting you," he said. Giving her no time to resist, he drew her toward the hatch opening and down a short flight of stairs to the large cabin that Lord Montague had booked for the journey from England. Tanner thrust her unceremoniously inside and slammed the door behind him.

Brianna had opened her mouth to protest his rough handling of her person when her eyes came to rest on Rachel and George sitting quietly on the window seat in front of the large stern portholes. The words died on her lips as she hurried across the cabin and threw herself into Rachel's arms. "Rachel, can you ever forgive me for all the trouble I've caused you?"

"Mistress, I have to ask your forgiveness. Were it not for me, they would never have found you." Tears of remorse spilled down Rachel's haggard features.

"Rachel, we've been over this before. You had to think of yourself and our babe," George said, putting his arm about his wife's shoulders and pulling her away from Brianna.

Brianna's startled gaze went to Rachel's thickening waistline. "You're going to have a baby?"

Rachel nodded as more tears brimmed in her eyes. A tiny, wobbly smile trembled on her lips as she said, "The safety of my babe was the only reason I would have ever told where you were."

Brianna reached out and took Rachel's hand and gave it a reassuring squeeze. "You did what was right. Never believe otherwise. Your child is far more important."

At Brianna's understanding words, Rachel's last bit of composure crumbled. She turned in her husband's arms and wept out her misery against his comforting chest.

"Such a heart-wrenching sight," Lord Montague said, stepping from the shadows where he'd waited like a great black spider for his prey to fall into his web.

Brianna jerked around at the sound of the voice she'd hated for so many years, a voice that she'd thought she'd stilled with the sharp blade of the paring knife. Eyes wide, she stared up at the man of her nightmares, and for a fleeting moment of unreality, she wondered if she were dreaming all the horror.

"You look surprised to see me, Brianna. Is there no welcome hug and kiss for your dear stepfather? Do you not remember I am the man who raised you, generously sharing everything I had with you and your bitch of a mother?"

Still in a state of shock, Brianna couldn't move as Lord Montague moved toward her. He took her chin and made her look up at him. His smile was deadly as he looked down at her and pressed his fingers into the soft skin. "You little bitch. You thought you could get away with trying to murder me in my own house." He chuckled evilly, drawing Brianna to her feet by the pressure of his fingers on her face. "But I didn't wait six long years to have you deny me. Your bitch of a mother thought her threats would also deter me from having you, but she learned differently."

Brianna's breath stilled at his words. "What do you mean Mother learned differently? She loved you."

Lord Montague thrust Brianna away from him and turned to the table where a long-bladed knife lay gleaming in the lantern light. He picked it up and ran his thumb down the keen edge. His finger beaded red droplets of blood when he drew it away. He smiled grimly as he looked back at Brianna, who stood regarding him warily. "Your mother never loved me. She loved only you. That's why she married me. She wanted what my money could give her. The bitch wanted my wealth for you but wasn't willing to let me have what my money had paid for."

Stunned by Lord Montague's revelation, Brianna could not think of the danger he presented to her. For years she'd condemned the woman who had given her life for being emotionally weak when, in truth, if what Lord Montague said was true, she had been far stronger than even Brianna. She had loved Brianna and had sacrificed her own happiness to ensure Brianna didn't have to suffer.

Lord Montague continued without a flicker of guilt,

"Sabrina really thought I'd bow down to her threats to divorce me because she knew my aversion to scandal. But she soon learned that I don't like threats any more than I do anyone slurring my reputation." He snapped his fingers together and smiled. "Her neck snapped that easily."

"You killed Mother?"

"As I've said before, my dear Brianna. When I want something, I don't allow anything to stand in my way. And Sabrina stood in my way of having you."

Brianna reached out and caught the back of a chair to steady herself against the wave of anger that washed over her. This man had killed her mother. She had known he was capable of many things, but she'd never suspected murder. Blinding, ungovernable rage, so strong that it wiped out all caution, possessed Brianna. Before she could think of the consequences of her actions, she launched herself at the man standing so smugly confident across the cabin. Her claws raked down his thin, malevolent face before he could stop her.

"I'll kill you," she screamed as Lord Montague grappled with her. Tanner, something akin to a smug smile curling his lips, finally moved to draw her away from his employer. His heavy arm came about Brianna, pinning her arms to her side. Her fury unabated, she squirmed to be free of the imprisoning grip. She kicked at his shins and squealed her protest, thrashing about like a wild thing.

"You little bitch," Lord Montague growled, drawing a bloody hand away from his stinging cheeks. He dabbed at his wounds with a white linen handkerchief, staying the bleeding before he turned his attention to the vixen fighting to be free of Tanner's hold.

"You're going to pay far more dearly than I'd first planned for marking me." Lord Montague drew back his fist and slammed it into Brianna's abdomen. The impact jerked her double and she crumpled to the floor as Tanner released her. Stunned and gasping for breath, she lay at Lord Montague's feet. He reached for the knife he'd dropped on the table and slowly bent down to where she lay. He laced his fingers in her dark hair, jerking her head back so that he could smile down into her face. "I wanted to make you mine. I would have given you everything, made you a queen at Montvale, but you thought to defy me." He tightened his fingers in her hair, drawing her head back further. "No one thwarts my wishes, Brianna, as you will soon learn."

Lord Montague laid the keen edge of the blade against the smooth, white column of Brianna's throat. Rachel screamed and jumped to her feet. "No! Don't hurt her. Please."

George made to come to Brianna's aid but stilled as Lord Montague looked up at him and growled, "Make another move and I'll slit her throat like a pig's."

George pulled his wife back into his arms as Tanner withdrew a pistol and aimed it at him. Lord Montague smiled triumphantly. "Take them below. I'll deal with them later."

Tanner followed Lord Montague's order, directing George and Rachel from the cabin with the barrel of the pistol.

"You'll never get away with this," George said, resisting Tanner in the doorway. He couldn't just leave Brianna to die. He had to make an attempt to reason with the madman. It was all he could do without a weapon to defend himself.

Tanner lashed George across the side of the face with the barrel of his pistol, staggering his senses. He sank to his knees and dimly heard his wife's scream over the ringing in his ears.

"Get up," Tanner growled. "Or I'll blow your head off right here."

With Rachel's assistance, George forced his wobbly knees to hold him upright. He leaned against his wife as they slowly made their way down the narrow passageway to the tiny cabin that they'd shared during the voyage from England.

His attention centered upon his victim, Lord Montague paid no heed to the door Tanner had left ajar. He lowered his mouth to the luscious lips he'd craved for nearly six years.

At the touch of his mouth upon hers, Brianna gagged and felt the bile rise in her throat. She attempted to squirm free of his hold, but the burning prick of the knife that accompanied her rash move stilled her. She felt the warmth of her blood trickle down her neck and knew in that instant she'd never leave the *Wild Goose* alive. Lord Montague had killed her mother and now intended to kill her and her friends to satisfy his sick need for revenge.

With a snarl of outrage at her obvious rejection, Lord Montague violently ground his mouth against hers, demanding her surrender. Brianna moaned in pain as her lips were crushed against her teeth and she tasted the sweetness of her own blood. Tears of pain brightened her eyes and ran from the corners of her thick lashes to moisten the soft strands of hair curling about her ashen face.

Lord Montague didn't release his hold upon the knife as he moved to cover her body with his own, imprisoning her with his weight. Freeing her hair, he raised himself to look down at her. He smiled again. "Ah, my sweet Brianna. Like your lips, I will taste your luscious body before I'm done with you."

Brianna knew she would prefer death to the murderer's violation of her body. It and her love belonged to Roarke, and she'd not let this creature defile what she had shared with the man she loved. She spat into his face, daring him to kill her. "You bastard. I'll die before you have me."

The smile altered into a snarl. "If that is your wish, my dear Brianna, I can certainly grant it." His fingers tightened on the hilt of the knife.

Brianna closed her eyes, accepting the fate to come.

"I wouldn't do that if I were you," Roarke said menacingly. "It would mean I'd have to blow your head off."

Lord Montague jerked around to see Roarke filling the doorway, his pistol aimed between Lord Montague's eyes. He relaxed his hold upon the knife and glanced back at the woman beneath him. Brianna's eyes mirrored her heart. Lord Montague ground his teeth together. He'd longed to see that look directed at him. "Who in the hell are you?"

"My name is Roarke O'Connor and I'm the lady's fiancé."

Lord Montague's gaze jerked back to Brianna again. His eyes were full of accusation. "You mean this bitch is your whore?"

Roarke's expression darkened. "I mean I intend to marry this lady. And if you don't move away from her, I won't be responsible for my actions."

Lord Montague grimaced as he eased his weight from Brianna, and she rolled away from him before coming to her feet and running to Roarke. The tall, menacing stranger draped a comforting arm about her shoulders, drawing her protectively against his wide chest.

"Then you have to ask my permission, because I am her guardian and stepfather," Lord Montague said, trying to regain his composure and retain some authority.

He straightened his coat as he came to his feet. However, he couldn't stay the chill of fear that sprinted up his spine at Roarke's chuckle.

"I think not, you bastard."

Seeing the cold, deadly light in Roarke's eyes, Lord Montague took a step back and raised his hands in front of him as if to ward off the Devil. "Tell him, Brianna. Tell him that I am your stepfather."

"You are nothing to me but a vile, evil old man who murdered my mother," Brianna spat from her safe haven at Roarke's side.

Lord Montague's face mottled with a renewed burst of fury. He eyed Roarke through narrowed lashes. "Your bitch calls me murderer, but she stabbed me and left me for dead. I came here to bring her back to face trial for her attempt on my life."

Feeling Brianna stiffen, Roarke glanced down at her. He could see the fear in her eyes as she looked helplessly up at him, and knew in that instant that he'd finally learned all her secrets. He turned his attention back to the man in front of him. The woman he'd come to love could not hurt a fly without dire provocation. As he remembered the other young woman who had stabbed her attacker, his face hardened. "That's too bad."

Misreading Roarke's expression, Lord Montague smirked. "Then, sir, let us desist in further confrontation between us and see that justice is done."

Roarke arched a brow in puzzlement but didn't lower his weapon. "I think you misunderstand, my lord. It is too bad that she didn't succeed in putting an end to your miserable life. It would have saved me the trouble of doing so."

"Surely you can't intend to harm me over a murderous little wench. One day she'll put a blade in your back as well."

Roarke smiled and looked down at the surprised woman at his side. He winked. "I'll take my chances. Now, my lord, if you'll accompany me ashore, I think the port authorities will find your activities very interesting. This is a Dutch island, and we are bound by their laws."

Lord Montague felt like laughing aloud when he saw Tanner come into view behind Roarke. He ordered smugly, "Take him now."

Roarke managed to catch only a glimpse of the man behind him when Lord Montague launched himself. Lord Montague grabbed the hand that held the pistol and tried to wrestle the weapon from Roarke. Brianna sought to intervene on Roarke's behalf, but the force and strength of the two men easily pushed her aside. Tanner made to take Roarke from behind, but a sharp blow from the billy club Nick carried laid him on the floor, unconscious.

The report of the pistol suddenly ended the desperate struggle between the two men. Lord Montague stiffened and stared into Roarke's eyes before slowly looking down at the gaping wound that spread a red stain over his embroidered waistcoat. He looked toward Brianna, reached a shaking hand toward her, and then collapsed at Roarke's feet, dead.

Brianna sank into a chair and buried her face in her hands, unable to look at the man she'd thought for so many months that she'd murdered. He was now truly dead. It was finally over.

Nor could she look at Roarke. He had once again saved her life, yet she feared his rejection since learning the truth about her. She had seen the look on his face when he realized the lies she'd told. Lord Montague

was dead, and she was free to live her life again, but now she feared she had no life to live. Without Roarke, she didn't want to live.

"Look at me, Brianna," Roarke said softly, tipping up her chin and forcing her to look at him. "It's over, completely over. It's time that we go home."

"I can't," Brianna whispered.

Roarke knelt at her side, looking her directly in the eyes. Dark blue met golden brown with understanding and love. "Yes, you can."

"How can you say that after what you've just learned about me?"

"Love, I've known you had secrets since the day we brought you on board the *Black Angel*. But they were yours to keep until you were ready to tell me."

"How can you be so understanding after you've told me about yourself?"

"Because I love you, Brianna. You didn't turn away from me when you learned I was a bastard. You accepted me even when you thought me a pirate. How can I not do the same with you? We've all made mistakes, love." He grinned at her. "But your mistake was believing yourself a murderer. But I would have loved you even if it were true. No man can blame a woman who defends her honor against a man like your stepfather. He was the vilest of them all. He used a position that should garner a child's trust to abuse you. You have nothing to regret, nor do I have any recriminations for what you did, only admiration."

"Do you really mean it?"

Roarke took Brianna into his arms and tenderly kissed her. "Aye. I mean every word. I only pray our children will inherit their mother's courage. But first I think we should get married, don't you?"

Brianna nodded and threw her arms about Roarke's

neck. She wept into the curve of his shoulder, dampening the white lawn of his shirt as he held her close to his heart. Her tears washed away the last shadows that had darkened their future happiness. Tonight they would marry, surrounded by their friends. And though darkness reigned over the small Dutch island of St. Eustatius, their world would be bright and filled with love as they walked down the aisle of the small white plaster church to become man and wife.